PRAISE FOR

Mimi Matthews

The Work of Art

"Matthews (*The Pug Who Bit Napoleon*; *A Victorian Lady's Guide to Fashion and Beauty*) weaves suspense and mystery within an absorbing love story. Readers will be hard put to set this one down before the end."

-Library Journal, starred review

"The author seamlessly combines a suspenseful tale and a soaring romance, the plot by turns sweetly moving and dramatically stirring."

-Kirkus Reviews

"If all Regency Romances were written as well as 'The Work of Art,' I would read them all…[Matthews] has a true gift for storytelling."

-The Herald-Dispatch

The Matrimonial Advertisement

"For this impressive Victorian romance, Matthews (*The Viscount and the Vicar's Daughter*) crafts a tale that sparkles with chemistry and impresses with strong character development... an excellent series launch…"

-Publishers Weekly

"Matthews (*The Viscount and the Vicar's Daughter*) has a knack for creating slow-building chemistry and an intriguing plot with a social history twist."

-Library Journal

"Matthews' (*The Pug Who Bit Napoleon*, 2018, etc.) series opener is a guilty pleasure, brimming with beautiful people, damsels in distress, and an abundance of testosterone…A well-written and engaging story that's more than just a romance."

-Kirkus Reviews

A Holiday By Gaslight

"Matthews (*The Matrimonial Advertisement*) pays homage to Elizabeth Gaskell's *North and South* with her admirable portrayal of the Victorian era's historic advancements…Readers will easily fall for Sophie and Ned in their gaslit surroundings."

-Library Journal, starred review

"Matthews' novella is full of comfort and joy—a sweet treat for romance readers that's just in time for Christmas."

"A graceful love story...and an authentic presentation of the 1860s that reads with the simplicity and visual gusto of a period movie."

The Viscount and the Vicar's Daughter

"Matthews' tale hits all the high notes of a great romance novel...Cue the satisfied sighs of romance readers everywhere."

"Matthews pens a heartfelt romance that culminates into a sweet ending that will leave readers happy. A wonderfully romantic read."

The Lost Letter

"The perfect quick read for fans of Regency romances as well as Victorian happily-ever-afters, with shades of Austen and the Brontës that create an entertaining blend of drama and romance."

-RT Book Reviews

"A fast and emotionally satisfying read, with two characters finding the happily-ever-after they had understandably given up on. A promising debut."

-Library Journal

USA Today Bestselling Author

MIMI MATTHEWS

A Convenient Fiction

PARISH ORPHANS *of* DEVON

A CONVENIENT FICTION
Parish Orphans of Devon, Book 3
Copyright © 2019 by Mimi Matthews

Edited by Deborah Nemeth
Cover Design by James T. Egan of Bookfly Design
Design and Formatting by Ampersand Book Interiors

E-Book: 978-1-7330569-2-2
Paperback: 978-1-7330569-3-9

www.PerfectlyProperPress.com

Dedication

In memory of Ava and John.

Chapter One

Surrey, England
August, 1860

Laura Hayes held her breath until her lungs cried out in protest. The water lapped over her head, leaves and debris floating along the surface in the midmorning sun. She felt something catch in her hair and prayed it wasn't frog spawn. Such indignities were, unfortunately, all too common when submerging oneself in Talbot's Pond.

She'd far rather have sunk beneath the cold waves of the sea, to have felt the tug of the tide, primal and relentless, as it pulled her from the shore. But fashionable seaside resorts were far outside the Hayes family's fortunes at present. And even if they weren't, Margate and Brighton were meant for bathing not swimming.

For now, Talbot's Pond would have to suffice.

It was warmer in Surrey, at least. The sun had shone every day for the past two weeks, a sweltering heat that had prompted her to spend a greater than usual degree of time in the woods. Even now, as the rays filtered through the water, warming her bare limbs, she found herself planning when she could come back again. The day after tomorrow, perhaps. And then again the morning after that.

But she mustn't get distracted. She mustn't lose track of her time.

Only five more seconds to beat yesterday's record. She counted them down in her head, willing her body not to panic for lack of air.

Five.

Four.

Three.

A shadow blocked the sun. It was her only warning before something—or someone—very large splashed into the water beside her. She gasped in surprise, inhaling a lungful of slimy pond water.

And then her body panicked in earnest.

She flailed her arms in a wild attempt to get to the surface, but the very large someone—*yes, definitely a someone*—seized her round the waist in a viselike grip. She was hauled roughly out of the pond and thrown, coughing and sputtering, onto the grassy bank.

"What in blazes are you trying to do?" a man's deep voice thundered out. "Kill yourself?"

Laura could hardly hear him through the pounding in her ears. She pushed herself up on unsteady arms, her chest contracting painfully on another choking cough. "This is" —she wheezed and gasped, her stomach and lungs still recoiling from the unexpected influx of water—"p-private property."

"You're telling me that I'm trespassing?" He gave a hoarse bark of laughter. "I suppose you'd rather I let you drown?"

She drew the back of her hand over her eyes before squinting up at her would-be rescuer. A tremor of unease went through her.

He was a big man. Strapping, Aunt Charlotte would have called him. Tall and broad of shoulder, with dark hair that flopped over his forehead, and a close-trimmed beard and mustache that—upon second glance—might well have been nothing more than a week's worth of heavy stubble.

He was also a stranger. A man she couldn't recall having ever seen before. If she had, she'd surely have remembered. His face and figure were not the sort easily forgotten. Indeed, if she weren't so put out at him for bursting into her private sanctuary and disrupting her peace, Laura might even have admitted to his being handsome.

But handsome or no, strangers weren't welcome in Talbot's Wood, and certainly not during those hours when she was clad in her knickers and availing herself of the pond. There were too many gentlemen who considered a scantily clad female to be fair game.

And he *was* some manner of gentleman. She could tell that much by the cut of his clothes and the quality of his horse—a bay hunter standing at the edge of the clearing with a leather portmanteau strapped to the back of its saddle.

She'd learned to be on her guard where gentlemen were concerned. Not that her rescuer looked as if he intended to ravish her. Far from it. He looked, truth be told, rather angry.

He sat on the bank beside her, one leanly muscled arm thrown over his updrawn knees. His shirt, waistcoat, and Bedford cord breeches were soaked through, his hair half-plastered to his head. Even his leather boots were wet.

A flicker of guilt pricked at her conscience. Had he really believed she was drowning? He must have done. Why else would he jump into the pond with his boots on? Boots that were now damaged beyond all hope of repair.

"I was in no danger," she said.

He glared at her. His heavy-lidded gray eyes were as cold as hoarfrost.

Her stomach fluttered, even as her spine stiffened at his temerity. "And if you're going to sit there staring at me—"

"I'm not staring at you."

"You're scowling at me."

"Because I could bloody well wring your neck."

Her mouth fell open. No man had ever spoken to her thus. Certainly not a stranger. "I *beg* your pardon?"

"How could anyone be so careless—so thoughtless—to even attempt—"

"I wasn't trying to drown myself, you great lummox." If he was speaking plainly, then so would she. "Not that it's any of your business." She sat up on the bank, resting her weight on one hip as she pushed her wet hair back from her face. It had come loose from its plaits. Flower petals, broken twigs, and goodness knew what else clung to the tangled strands. She'd have to wash it this evening if—

The stranger sucked in a sharp breath.

She shot him a narrow glance only to discover him tearing his own gaze away as if he'd just beheld some ungodly horror.

He was now, quite pointedly, looking away from her. He was also turning rather red about the collar.

Her eyes dropped to her chemise and drawers. The faded cotton with its twice-darned seams was wet through, nearly transparent, and clinging to her like a second skin. She inwardly groaned. Could this dreadful encounter possibly get any worse?

"Where the devil are your clothes?" he asked in a choked voice. "Haven't you a gown or a—"

"One doesn't wear a day dress to go swimming."

"You weren't swimming. You were floating beneath the water like some demented Ophelia."

"I was strengthening my lungs." Laura watched as his gaze slid back to her almost against its will. He jerked it away again, his face hardening into a mask of carefully controlled emotion. "And I did not look like a demented Ophelia," she added under her breath. "What an unflattering characterization."

"If you think I ventured into this clearing to flatter your vanity—"

"Why did you venture into this clearing? These woods belong to Squire Talbot. He has signs posted everywhere. You couldn't have failed to notice them. Unless… You *can* read, can't you?"

"Of course I can read—" He broke off. "I was trying to find—" He stopped again. "By God, ma'am, I ask again, *where are your clothes?*"

She folded her arms over her bosom. "There." She motioned with a jerk of her chin. "Beneath the tree."

Her rescuer launched himself to his feet and strode the short distance to where she'd laid out her blanket. A basket of food sat upon it, along with her corset, gown, and boots, all carefully folded into a neat little pile. She'd meant to make a day of it. There was a book and a flask of Aunt Charlotte's freshly made lemonade waiting for her. She'd planned to let her hair and underclothes dry in the sun. But now...

Now she sat shivering on the bank, vulnerable and increasingly embarrassed by her state of undress. Her eyes followed her rescuer as he bent to retrieve her clothes. He walked them back to her, coming only close enough to toss her folded dress and corset onto the grass at her side. He turned away again without meeting her eyes.

Laura swept up her corset. It was old and worn. Quite useless, really. She scarcely had to inhale as she fastened the metal hooks of the busk. When she'd finished, she shook out her skirts and stepped into them. She hadn't worn any petticoats, and she certainly hadn't bothered to wear a crinoline, or even stockings. The resulting ensemble was eminently practical. It was also thoroughly indecent by any standard.

"How did you find me here?" she asked as she buttoned up her bodice. "There's no possible way to see the pond from the road."

"My horse bolted into the woods," he said, still refusing to look at her.

If she had an ounce of sense, she would have bolted, too, leaving her blanket and basket far behind her. But her lungs weren't likely to support such an effort. Not after she'd already taxed them to the limit.

Besides, she didn't run from anything.

In her experience, it was a far more effective strategy to control one's fear. To refrain from escalating a fraught situation by continuing to act as normally as possible.

As normally as one *could* act when one's hair was festooned with frog spawn.

She fluffed out her skirts to no avail. They clung to her wet drawers and legs. "I'm as decent as I can be. If it makes you blush, you'd better leave."

He cast her a cautious glance over his shoulder. "I'm not blushing."

"No?" She walked past him to sink down onto her blanket. Modesty was impossible in such circumstances, but she made a creditable effort. Tilting onto her hip, she drew her knees up alongside her, tucking her bare feet beneath the pooling fabric of her skirts. When she was satisfied that her limbs were well covered, she opened the wicker hamper and, after a moment spent rifling through its contents, withdrew a tortoiseshell comb.

"I'm furious," he said.

Laura concentrated on working the rest of her hair loose from its plaits. It was free in a trice, spilling down past her shoulders in a very wet—and very tangled—ebony veil. She drew a lock between her fingers and began to comb it as she waited for her rescuer to elaborate. He said not a word. "Well?" she prompted.

"Why were you doing that?" he asked abruptly.

"Doing what?"

"Holding your breath under the water."

Her hand stilled on her comb. "I told you. I was strengthening my lungs."

"Why?"

She had to stop herself from telling him. He was a stranger, for heaven's sake, not her friend. "It's no concern of yours, sir."

He huffed. "Of course not." He walked a few steps across the clearing, pausing to rake a hand through his damp hair. "Will you permit me to see you home?"

"Why should you wish to? I'm in perfectly good health."

"You're in no fit state to—"

"To what? Defend myself from strangers? I'm a little wet, that's all." She paused before adding, "Until you, no man has ever accosted me in these woods."

He turned to face her. "I meant no disrespect. I—"

"Yes, I know. You only meant to rescue me. But I need no rescuing, as you see."

"No, indeed." His chest rose and fell on a deep breath. "I overreacted."

Laura lowered her comb. She realized, for the first time, that her rescuer looked more than a little shaken. He was white about the mouth. And his hands were trembling. "There's been no harm done."

"No? I'm glad to hear it." His mouth hitched in a brief, wry smile that didn't reach his eyes. "I'll bid you good day, then, before I compound my crime."

She blinked up at him. But she didn't dare ask what he meant. She was scarcely managing to keep her countenance as it was. "Good day to you, sir."

He bowed. "Ma'am."

And then he was gone.

Alex Archer stifled a groan as he dismounted from his hired horse. He was unaccustomed to riding. In the city he relied on hansom cabs, omnibuses, or—more generally—his own feet. But George Wright's instructions had been clear: Alex was to take the London train to Lower Hawley, and from thence to hire a horse for the remainder of his journey to the vicarage.

"It's not far," George had promised. "Five miles of good road along the edge of Talbot's Wood."

Talbot's Wood, indeed.

Had his horse not thrown him and bolted off into said woods, Alex wouldn't be aching all over, and soaking wet besides.

He wasn't a pauper. Not by any means. But when he thought of the amount of coin he'd expended on his clothing for this confounded venture… And now, to have ruined a new coat and pair of boots—he might as well have set his money alight.

But there was no turning back.

He led his horse down the gravel drive, and after depositing it in the vicarage stables, made his way to the front steps of the house. Sun glinted off the brass knocker on the red front door. It was a cheerful dwelling. The sort of happy home that housed an equally happy family.

The sort of home Alex had never had.

As he approached, his large frame blocked out the sun, casting an ominous shadow over the door. There was no need to ply the knocker. The door swung open on well-oiled hinges, as if the occupant of the house had been waiting for him.

And so he had.

"Archer!" George Wright stood in the doorway, an uneasy smile on his lips. With his tousled blond curls and expressive brown eyes, he looked more like a romantic poet than the son of a humble country parson. "What in blazes happened to you?"

"A minor mishap." Alex returned George's smile with a dry one of his own. "The horse I hired is a menace."

George gave a nervous laugh. He was always nervous in Alex's presence, had been ever since the night they met in Marseilles a year ago, at one of the city's most notorious gaming clubs. Alex had beaten George at cards rather badly that night, collecting what would be the first of his many markers.

"Why do you continue to play with the boy?" one of the club dealers had asked in a private moment. "You must know he'll never make good what he owes."

"He'll pay," Alex had vowed. "One way or another."

It was that very payment which had brought Alex to Surrey.

"Is that old portmanteau all you've brought?" George asked. "Haven't you a trunk? Or a valise?"

Alex followed him into the vicarage. It was a humble dwelling but a clean one, with a freshly swept slate floor and wooden furnishings polished to a high shine. The scent of beeswax and lemon oil lingered in the air. "I left them at the station."

"You don't intend to stay?"

"If you can arrange it so. Otherwise…"

"I *have* arranged it," George said. "I sent a note round to Edgington Park this morning. Miss Talbot responded an hour ago. You can meet her this afternoon, providing she can procure a chaperone."

"A chaperone?" Alex met George's eyes with a flash of irritation. "You never mentioned your visits with Miss Talbot being chaperoned."

"They haven't been. But Henrietta and I practically grew up together. You, on the other hand, are a stranger. An unknown quantity, or so her father says. If she's to go walking with us this afternoon, she must have a chaperone."

"And who is this chaperone to be? A tale-bearing housemaid? A bulldog of an old maiden aunt? What else haven't you told me?"

George backed up a step. "I didn't lie, Archer. I swear to you. Miss Talbot has no female relations. No one who will interfere with your plans. She's only summoning Miss Hayes. A local woman of no account. She lives not three miles from here, at the edge of Talbot's Wood. Miss Talbot often relies on her for companionship."

Alex went still. He was at once assailed by memories of the woman he'd encountered at Talbot's Pond. The feel of her as he'd pulled her scantily clad body from the water. The look of her as she'd sat so demurely on the bank—like a mermaid combing out her hair. His brows lowered. "This local woman... She wouldn't happen to be a raven-haired water nymph, would she?"

"*What?*" George gave a bark of genuine laughter. "Miss Hayes? Hardly. She's a spinster. A regular dogsbody. She won't do anything to cut up your peace, mark my words." He motioned to the stairs. "Come. Our housekeeper, Mrs. Griffiths, has prepared a room for you."

Alex grudgingly followed after him. The stairs creaked under his wet boots. "Where's your father?"

"At the church, drafting his Sunday sermon. He'll be back for supper. You can meet him then—unless we're invited to dine at Edgington Park." George led Alex down a short hall to a snug guest room, complete with a vase of daisies on the washstand. "Mrs. Griffiths looks after us. Has done for ages. If you require anything, just give a tug on the bell pull."

"I need hot water to wash with."

"Ah yes. Stupid of me. I'll have her send some up. Is there anything else?"

"That depends. How soon are we to leave?"

"As soon as Miss Hayes can be summoned. It shouldn't be long. It's not as if the woman has a busy social calendar."

Chapter Two

Aunt Charlotte entered Laura's bedroom, an open letter clasped in her hand. Her normally cheerful face was set into lines of grim resignation. "George Wright has come home."

Laura sat at her dressing table, her head cocked as she dried her freshly washed hair with a piece of rough toweling. At the sound of Aunt Charlotte's voice, she froze. "What?"

"He arrived yesterday morning on the train from London." Aunt Charlotte paced to the window and back again. Her black taffeta skirts rustled along the worn Aubusson carpet that covered the equally worn floorboards.

Laura's black-and-white tomcat, Magpie, watched Aunt Charlotte's progress from his place on the bed, his tail thumping idly against the counterpane.

"He plans to stay the month," Aunt Charlotte said. "Perhaps even longer."

Laura's heartbeat quickened in spite of herself. "Who says so?"

"Miss Talbot." Aunt Charlotte waved the letter. "She's sent you a note."

The damp towel fell from Laura's fingers. She didn't regard it. "You opened it?"

"I should think I did. Henrietta Talbot has no right to summon you. You're not her lady-in-waiting, whatever she might believe."

Laura held out her hand for the letter.

Aunt Charlotte crossed the room to give it to her.

"When did it come?" Laura asked as she opened it.

"Not half an hour ago. You were still in your bath."

Laura's gaze swept over the brief missive. "Mr. Wright has brought a friend with him. Henrietta can't accompany the pair of them without a chaperone. She requests I come directly."

Aunt Charlotte came to stand beside her. She was a woman of magnificent size, and despite a general air of shabby gentility, as regal in her own way as the queen. "I trust you won't oblige her."

"I have no reason not to."

"No reason! My dear girl, you've been half in love with George Wright since you were children. Why must you subject yourself to being in his presence?"

"Calf love," Laura said dismissively. She folded the letter, setting it down on her dressing table between her matching silver-plated hair brushes and the single unopened bottle of scent left over from Papa's last batch of fragrance. "I feel nothing for him now except friendship."

It was the truth, though not the whole of it.

What she felt for George wasn't love—nor friendship, either. What she felt was disappointment. Deep disappointment, not only in him, but in herself for ever having believed him worthy of her affection.

She'd had blinders on when it came to George, ever since she was a girl. Two years ago, those blinders had been unceremoniously ripped off. To see him again now would be uncomfortable, possibly even embarrassing. More so for him than for her, she'd wager. It was he who had inflicted the breach in their friendship. He who had issued the insult.

As for her own conduct, she had nothing to reproach herself with. Nothing save an excess of girlish romanticism and naiveté.

"If he treated you as a friend, I could bear it," Aunt Charlotte said. "But he discounts you. Merely because our family has lately fallen on hard times—"

"It's been three years since Papa died." Laura gave her aunt an affectionate glance. "And times weren't much easier then, if you'll recall."

Aunt Charlotte's lips compressed. "I won't agree with that. You may not have had much money, but when my brother lived, you had standing in this community."

Laura didn't argue with her aunt. What was the point? Aunt Charlotte preferred to live in denial of their present circumstances. In the past, when Laura had tried to discuss the family finances with her, it had only caused her distress. Nowadays, Laura kept such harsh realities to herself. Even Teddy wasn't aware of how bad things really were.

"I'm the head of the family, Laura," he was often wont to say. "It's my burden to bear."

But Teddy couldn't bear it. The fever that had taken Papa three years ago had left Edward Hayes confined to a wheeled chair, a thin wisp of an invalid who—but for the grace of God—would have already slipped away from them.

"I don't suppose Miss Talbot has sent a carriage for me?" Laura asked. Henrietta was unreliable about such things. An heiress herself, it rarely occurred to her that others were not as fortunate as she was. "Or will I have to walk to Edging-ton Park?"

Aunt Charlotte huffed. "She's sent a one-horse gig, driven by one of their tenants of all people. It's meant as an insult, I know it. I came this close to sending him off with a flea in his ear."

"Where is he now?"

"In the kitchen having a glass of lemonade. I knew you would insist on doing Miss Talbot's bidding, if not for her, then to see Mr. Wright again."

"Of course I'll go," Laura said. "Unless you or Teddy truly have need of me this afternoon?"

"Your brother is presently sketching a nest of birds which he's spied from his window. Another day indoors, it seems. The poor boy has no color at all."

At twenty, Teddy wasn't a little boy any longer, though Aunt Charlotte was content to view him so. It didn't help that Teddy had grown petulant of late, refusing to leave his room, and sometimes even refusing his meals.

"I'm henpecked to death here," he would complain. "For the love of God, Laura. Just leave me alone."

Laura was tired of it. Tired of managing her aunt and her brother and the remnants of their household. Tired of trying to stretch their meager income. There was never any progress—

no spark of inspiration as there had been in the beginning. Now, one day was much like another. An endless repetition of stifling obligation. Of needs unmet, and wants which would never ever be fulfilled. Monotonous, that's what it was.

Except for today.

The handsome gentleman at Talbot's Pond had been something new. Something different.

But even that encounter had only lasted a moment. And now here she was again, trussed up by obligation and weighted down with needs, and wants, and monotony.

She pasted on a smile. "Will you help me plait my hair, Aunt?"

Aunt Charlotte gave her a long look. "It's too wet to be seen in public."

"It will finish drying on the drive to Edgington Park. Haven't you been outside today? The sun is fairly blazing."

"And you without a hat or a parasol." Aunt Charlotte moved behind her, and picking up the comb, began to skillfully divide and twist Laura's hair into a plaited roll at the nape of her neck. "You haven't freckled yet, by some miracle."

"Not yet." Laura glanced at herself in the mirror. Her skin was still as pale as porcelain. Perhaps even as pale as alabaster. An enviable complexion, she knew, and one she'd done very little to earn. "Though I daresay I will eventually."

"Can a person freckle when submerged in a pond, I wonder?"

"Anything is possible under the water."

"Hmm." Aunt Charlotte sounded doubtful. "I shall brew up some strawberry water for you. You can apply it to your face when you return home this evening." She met Laura's eyes in the mirror. A shadow of worry clouded her brow. "You'll be home before nightfall, won't you, my dear? You have an early day tomorrow."

As if Laura could forget. She reached up to clasp her aunt's hand. "I'll be home by dinner," she said. "I promise."

Edgington Park was larger than Alex had expected. A sprawling Italianate residence of honey-colored stone, complete with arched windows and three imposing square towers, it stood in the midst of a manicured park, looking for all the world like one of Queen Victoria's lesser palaces. Alex had never seen anything like it.

"It's hideous, I know." George peered out the window of the carriage as the antiquated vehicle came to a shuddering halt at the top of the drive. "The squire has no taste. He believes that the more something costs, the more desirable it is. Anyone could have told him to leave off one of those towers, and half of those windows, too. But would he listen?"

Alex's gaze passed from the garishness of the house to the land that surrounded it. It was lush and verdant—and alive with industry. There were gardeners trimming trees and hedges, and pushing barrow's full of earth. Even more men could be seen in the distance, toiling among the gated fields and various outbuildings, including one that looked to be an orangery.

A burgeoning feeling of satisfaction settled within his breast.

Edgington Park wasn't merely a gentleman's folly, then. It was a proper working farm. One with a vast acreage, if Alex was any judge. Vaster still if it encompassed the eponymous Talbot's Wood.

"Squire Talbot must be a very rich man," he said.

"He's prosperous enough." George opened the carriage door and hopped out. "But it's his daughter who's the wealthy one. She's not only heir to Edgington Park, she's heir to her late mother's fortune as well. It's held in trust for her until her marriage."

Alex followed, shutting the carriage door behind him. George's father, the vicar, was comfortably off, but he didn't employ a footman.

"That he even keeps a carriage is nothing short of miraculous," George had remarked earlier with a derisive snort. "Father prefers to walk. Says it helps him stay close to God."

Alex wondered how much the pious country vicar knew about his son's dissolute lifestyle. Was he aware that George gambled? That he drank, and took opium, and kept company with low women?

It was a wasted existence if Alex had ever seen one. Had he a loving father of his own—a home to come back to in a quaint country village like Lower Hawley—he'd never have squandered his life as George had done.

Then again, if it wasn't for George's vices, Alex wouldn't have been given the opportunity to bend George to his will. That was something to be grateful for, at least.

He straightened his waistcoat as he climbed the front steps. After washing, he'd changed into a fresh suit of clothes—dark trousers, a loose-fitting sack coat, and a white linen shirt with a simply tied cravat. It wasn't too dissimilar from what George was wearing, though perhaps less colorful than his garish plaid.

They'd scarcely ascended halfway up the stone steps when the front doors opened and a young lady emerged. She was garbed in a frothy, striped muslin gown with skirts of a wholly impractical size. The same voluminous skirts that Empress

Eugénie of France had made popular some years before. They floated along behind her as she bounded down the steps, her golden ringlets gleaming in the sun.

"George! I thought I heard a carriage. And here you are at last." She stopped in front of George, a brilliant smile lighting her face. "You've finally come home."

Alex regarded Miss Talbot from a short distance away. Like Edgington Park, she wasn't what he'd been expecting. She was pretty enough, to be sure—if one liked peaches-and-cream English misses with dimpled cheeks and melting brown eyes. Not that he was wholly averse to such wholesome charms. Indeed, if all went according to plan, he'd have to accustom himself to them. Even so, he'd thought to feel something. A flicker of attraction. The merest frisson of warmth in his breast—or in his loins.

But he felt nothing. He was, as always, quite cold to the heart.

"Henrietta." George clasped the young lady's hands. "You look splendid. Do you never age, my dear?"

"By the year, sir. As you'd know if you'd come to my birthday celebration last autumn. Have you no time for your friends anymore?"

"An entire month. And I mean to spend it all in your company." George turned her attention to Alex, his smile a trifle strained. "May I present my good friend Mr. Archer?"

Alex was amazed George could utter the words without choking on them.

"Archer," George continued in the same artificially bright voice, "this is Miss Talbot, the loveliest lady in Surrey."

Miss Talbot looked at Alex, her smile dimming. "Welcome to Edgington Park, Mr. Archer."

Alex bowed. "Miss Talbot."

"My companion should be here any minute," she said. "Shall we walk down the drive to meet her?"

"She's not here yet?" George's lips thinned with annoyance. "When did you summon her?"

"I didn't summon her." Miss Talbot linked her arm through his. "I *asked* her."

Alex clasped his hands at his back as he descended the stairs with George and Miss Talbot.

George hadn't been entirely honest with him.

He'd said Miss Talbot was a neighbor. A childhood friend and nothing more. He'd never once admitted to her having feelings for him.

And, unless Alex was very much mistaken, Miss Talbot *did* have a fondness for George. Whether that fondness was mutual, it was difficult to tell. But if it was…

Good God, had George Wright offered up his own sweetheart to satisfy his debt?

"Is this your first visit to Surrey, Mr. Archer?" Miss Talbot asked, still clinging to George's arm.

"It is, ma'am."

"George said in his note that you'd only recently returned to England. Whereabout are you from originally?"

"London." Alex came to walk at her opposite side. "My parents removed to Paris while I was still in leading strings."

It was the same old lie. One he'd told countless times over the years. He'd almost begun to believe it himself.

"I can't say I blame them," Miss Talbot replied. "I don't know how anyone can bear London. All that smoke and dust and fog. It plays havoc with my father's health. It's why we never go into the city." She gave him a look of polite enquiry. "Do your mother and father still reside in France?"

"Regrettably, no. I lost them during the cholera epidemic of '33."

"Archer was raised by his godfather, Baron Reynard," George said helpfully. "A gentleman of some repute."

"A baron, did you say?" Miss Talbot's eyes flickered with interest. "Are French barons the same as English ones? Or are they—" She stopped short. "Ah! There's Blodgett with the gig. And look, George, there is Miss Hayes, just as I told you she'd be."

A battered one-horse gig rolled up the drive, coming to a halt just ahead of them. The elderly driver was hunched over the box, a tweed cap pulled down over his face. Beside him on the box sat a young lady in a faded gray skirt and caraco jacket, a flat-crowned straw hat atop her head.

Alex stopped with the others.

And then he stared.

Good God, it was his water nymph. The woman he'd rescued from the pond—or failed to rescue, as it were. But she didn't look like a water nymph now. Rather the opposite. Her back was ramrod straight, her gloved hands folded primly in her lap, and her hair—that midnight veil that had been tangled with flower petals and leaves—was bound into a tight roll at her nape.

"What are you waiting for, George," Miss Talbot said under her breath. "Go and help Laura down."

Laura.

There was nothing extraordinary about the name. It nevertheless sent a mild shock through Alex's frame. Not a shock of heat—certainly not the kind of heat he'd anticipated feeling for Miss Talbot. This was something else. Something new and deeply unsettling. It was awareness. Some variety of…recognition.

"Allow me." He didn't wait for Miss Talbot's permission. He reached the gig in a few long strides.

Miss Hayes saw him coming. Her eyes widened almost imperceptibly.

And what eyes she had. Smoke blue, set under a pair of low, and uncompromisingly straight, ebony brows. He'd noted them when he pulled her from the water. That and…other of her attributes.

She looked down at him, a sparkle of accusation in her glare. "*You.*"

"The name is Archer," he said. "And you, I presume, are Miss Hayes."

"I am."

He raised his arms to her. "Will you permit me to assist you down, ma'am?"

She hesitated a fraction of a second. "If you please."

He felt her take an uneven breath as his hands closed around her corseted waist, lifting her from the gig and setting her gently on the ground. She was tall for a lady. A shade over five and a half feet, if he was to venture a guess. Her head came just above his chin. A rarity. He was used to towering over his women.

But Miss Hayes was something different—in height as well as bearing.

She wasn't beautiful, not in the common way. Certainly not in the peaches-and-cream manner of Miss Talbot. But there was an arresting architecture to Laura Hayes's face— an austere sort of balance between her high cheekbones, the straight bridge of her nose, and the firm line of her jaw. Only her mouth betrayed a hint of softness. It was wide and kissable.

And it was frowning.

His hands fell from her waist.

The instant he released her, she stepped away from him to smooth her skirts. "Thank you, Mr. Archer."

"My pleasure, Miss Hayes."

"Laura!" Miss Talbot moved to join them. "I'm so glad you've come. And so grateful your aunt could spare you on my behalf. Can you believe that George has returned to us after all this time? And he's brought his friend, Mr. Archer."

The coachman drove off in the gig, leaving the drive empty. Miss Hayes looked across it to where George remained standing, his hands shoved into the pockets of his plaid trousers. "Welcome home, George."

George inclined his head. His expression was sullen. "Laura."

Alex's eyes narrowed. George had said Miss Hayes was a local woman of no account. A dogsbody, he'd called her. If that was true, why were the pair of them on a first-name basis? And why was George finding it so difficult to look at her?

"How is your aunt keeping?" Miss Talbot asked.

"Very well," Miss Hayes said. "She sends her regards."

"And your brother? How is his health?" Miss Talbot glanced at Alex. "Miss Hayes's younger brother is an invalid, sir. We're lucky he's still with us."

"My brother is well," Miss Hayes said. "We're all thriving, Hen, truly. There's no need to fuss."

"I'm not fussing. It's only that it feels like an age since you were last here. I must know everything you've been up to." Miss Talbot took Miss Hayes by the arm. "Let's go inside and have some tea before our walk, shall we?" She cast a look at

George as the pair of them headed back to the house. "Miss Hayes will not admit to any infirmity, but we must take care to look after her, mustn't we?"

Miss Hayes's face was an impenetrable mask.

As for George, he said not a word.

Alex walked along with him after the ladies. "'A local woman of no account,'" he murmured.

George's face reddened. "It's the truth."

"Is it?"

"She's nothing," he said in a low voice. "No one."

Alex didn't believe it for a moment. "Things aren't as simple here as you would have had me believe."

"They are. Or they would be if Miss Hayes didn't always contrive to make herself the center of attention."

"Is that what she's done?"

"Isn't it obvious? But you need have no apprehension. I shall separate them at the first opportunity. And then you may go about making yourself agreeable to Miss Talbot—or whatever it is you intend to do with her."

"I believe you know what I intend to do with her."

George looked away from him. "Yes," he said tightly. "I know."

Chapter Three

Laura stole another glance at Mr. Archer as she walked beside him down the path that led to the Edgington Park wilderness garden. He looked different than he had before. Not only was he dry—with his suit freshly pressed and his dark hair combed into meticulous order—but he appeared to have shaved, as well.

And the scent of him…

Her stomach performed a queer little somersault.

He smelled of polished leather and lightly starched linen. Of bergamot and spices and clean male skin.

At Talbot's Pond, she'd thought him handsome. Now, she thought him something rather more than that. He was dashing, was what he was. The kind of loose-limbed, devil-may-care hero who graced the pages of penny novels, fighting off evildoers and rescuing damsels in distress.

George Wright looked rather insipid in comparison.

He walked ahead of them with Henrietta on his arm, paying her every solicitude, just as he had in the Edgington Park drawing room during tea.

Laura wondered what Henrietta would think if she knew how improperly her golden-haired lad had behaved on his last visit home? It had certainly come as a shock to Laura. Until then, she'd thought George was her friend. She'd even cherished hopes that he felt something more toward her. That he might, in fact, be on the verge of proposing marriage.

More fool her.

She hadn't told anyone about George's shameful proposition. Not Henrietta, not the vicar, and certainly not Aunt Charlotte. It would only have upset them—and the delicate equilibrium of the village. No one who had known George in his youth would have believed him capable of such behavior. It would have been Laura who was blamed for his rashness. Laura who was ostracized from the small corner of society she'd managed to cultivate in Lower Hawley.

In the end, she'd dealt with the matter all on her own. Just as she dealt with every problem that came her way. She hadn't the luxury of a champion. In the absence of one, she'd learned to champion herself.

"Have you known Miss Talbot and Mr. Wright very long?" Mr. Archer asked.

She resumed looking ahead. George and Henrietta were whispering together, sharing secrets as they often used to do. "Since we were children."

"You grew up together?"

"In a manner of speaking." Laura hesitated before asking, "What about you, sir?" Tea had been a brief affair, dominated by George's tales of his travels. And by Henrietta, who had clucked over Laura more intensely than was usual. There had been little chance to learn anything about Mr. Archer. "How long have you known Mr. Wright?"

"A year, or thereabouts."

"He's never brought a friend home with him before."

"No?"

She shook her head. "I've often suspected that the friends he was making during his travels weren't the sort to merit an introduction to the residents of Lower Hawley. Certainly not to his father."

"You wonder that he's found me worthy of the privilege."

"No, but it is rather curious. It makes me question just what sort of friend you are to him."

He flashed her a wry look. "I might ask you the same, Miss Hayes."

A surge of embarrassment caught her unaware. "You haven't told him, have you?"

The glint of humor in Mr. Archer's gray eyes disappeared. Perhaps it had never been there. "Told him what?"

"About our encounter in Talbot's Wood this morning."

"Ah. That." He paused. "Should I have?"

"Not if you value your freedom." She explained, "It's just the sort of thing that would give rise to gossip. The locals hereabouts love nothing more than spinning harmless interactions into scandals. One word, and they'll have us standing up in front of the vicar."

"Is that all it takes in Lower Hawley?"

"I fear it is."

His mouth curved into a slow smile. "I shall keep that in mind."

The fine hairs on the back of Laura's neck stood up. She cast a discreet glance from Mr. Archer to Henrietta and back again. He wasn't obvious in his admiration for her friend. He didn't stare at her unduly or insinuate himself into her conversation with George. But during tea, Laura had more than once observed Mr. Archer look at Henrietta in a cold and faintly calculating manner.

Was that why such a man as he had come to their village? Not as the hero of the story, but as the villain?

There was certainly something dangerous about him. Something hard and predatory. It was part of what made him so thrillingly handsome. That edge of subtle menace. Rather like a feral wolf.

Was he hunting in Lower Hawley?

Her mouth pressed into a frown. She didn't know Mr. Archer. Even so, she'd thought better of him. He'd seemed different somehow. A rare and mysterious creature in their midst.

But he wasn't different at all. He was—if her instincts were correct—nothing more than a garden-variety fortune hunter.

She'd seen enough of them over the years. Gentlemen in reduced circumstances who came to pay court to Henrietta and her inheritance. They were the impoverished nephews and second cousins of the county gentry. Men who were ill-equipped to snare a wealthy wife on the London marriage mart, and who believed they'd have better odds with a vulnerable country heiress.

Henrietta had always dispatched such predatory gentleman with ruthless efficiency. She was certain to extend the same courtesy to Mr. Archer once she realized what he was up to.

Or so Laura hoped.

"Do you have a profession, Mr. Archer?" she asked.

He was silent for a long moment, the fall of his boots on the hard-packed earth the only sound as they entered the wilderness garden. "Are you asking me if I work for a living?"

The path narrowed, curving through trees that bowed inward into an arch, providing a leafy canopy against the blazing afternoon sunshine. "Do you?"

"I'm not obliged to."

"You're a gentleman of independent means?"

"I'm a gentleman," he said. "A gentleman doesn't soil his hands with labor, Miss Hayes. Independent means or no."

The path grew narrower still, necessitating that she walk even closer to his side. It was entirely by design. Henrietta had once confessed that the landscape artist her father had employed so many years before had dreamed up the wilderness garden at Edgington Park as a trysting place for lovers. Every step through the trees brought one closer to the object of their affection.

Laura wished that Henrietta had chosen somewhere else for their walk. Through the rose garden, perhaps. Or along the drive that led down to the village. Anything other than the intimacy of the wilderness garden path. With every brush of her full linen skirts against Mr. Archer's trouser-clad leg, Laura's heart beat a little more erratically.

"An outdated precept," she replied.

"You believe so?"

"Wholeheartedly. It's been the ruination of many gentlemen who might have otherwise saved themselves, and their families, from ruin."

"You speak with some authority on the subject."

"I do. My father was such a one."

Mr. Archer's expression sobered. "Forgive me. I didn't realize—"

"I'm not ashamed to own it. Had he exerted himself..." Laura couldn't bring herself to finish.

The truth was, if Papa had exerted himself, it wouldn't have changed anything in the end. He'd still have died and left them all. But perhaps there might have been some money to soften the blow of his loss. Some value left in the Hayes's name.

"What I mean to say," she continued, "is that a gentleman shouldn't refuse to work merely because he's a gentleman. The idea is as foolish as a man who can swim refusing to save himself from drowning. What does pride matter if the alternative is death or ruination?"

"Did your father leave you in very straitened circumstances?" Mr. Archer asked. "Or is that too impertinent a question?"

It *was* an impertinent question. As a rule, one's personal finances were never discussed in polite company. It simply wasn't done.

But she'd been the one to broach the subject.

She supposed it was a consequence of how they'd met. Much like the darkening wilderness walk, it gave the illusion of intimacy to their conversation. As if the two of them were acquaintances of long standing.

"We're not in straitened circumstances," she said. Her conscience gave a sharp pang of protest at the falsehood. "That is, not entirely."

There was no point dissembling. He'd seen her in her twice-mended underthings, for pity's sake. She nevertheless couldn't shake the last remnants of her pride.

"For a time, my family was quite well known in the world of fragrance. Perhaps you've heard of Hayes's Lavender Soap? Or Hayes's Lavender-Scented Powder?"

Mr. Archer gazed down at her, the whole of his attention fixed on her face. "I can't say that I have."

"What about Hayes's Lavender Water? It was in all the shops four years ago. A purely respectable fragrance. You might have given some to your mother once—or to a sweetheart."

"The sweethearts I had four years ago weren't the sort to wear respectable fragrances. As for my mother…"

"Let me guess. You've never given her such a frivolous gift."

"I might if I'd ever known her."

She inwardly flinched. Good heavens. His mother was dead. Long dead, if Laura inferred correctly. She met his eyes, thoroughly chastened. "Now it is I who must beg *your* forgiveness."

Mr. Archer returned her gaze without animosity. "Freely given."

"I lost my mother at a young age, too," she said.

"Did you?"

"She succumbed to a wasting disease when I was but six years old. I don't remember much about her, except…I know that she loved the water. She was the one who taught me to swim."

"A pleasant memory."

"You must have some of your own."

"Not a solitary one." They walked several steps in silence before he spoke again. "Was your father a perfumer, then?"

"He didn't call himself such. He considered it only a hobby. But we had a factory in London, and a distillery in France. They're shuttered now, but once…"

"What happened?"

"He grew bored with lavender products. He was set on trying something new. Fashionable perfumes, made with exotic spices and animal oils—musk and so forth. He sank all of his capital into the venture. Regrettably, it didn't have the same mass appeal as lavender water."

"And that was enough to ruin him?"

"Not on its own. Had he lived, he might have rallied. But a year later, an outbreak of scarlet fever came to Lower Hawley. Papa was gone within a day. I nearly lost my brother, as well."

"I'm sorry to hear it."

"Yes, it was a very dark time. I still think of it often, wishing things had transpired differently. A futile exercise."

"It's a miracle you didn't contract the fever yourself."

"Oh, but I did, Mr. Archer. Indeed, it tried very hard to take me, too." Her mouth lifted in a fleeting smile. "I was simply too stubborn to let it."

Alex returned Miss Hayes's brief smile with a faint one of his own. Farther down the path, George and Miss Talbot walked arm in arm. When they'd set out, Alex had fully intended to accompany Miss Talbot himself. George had seemed agreeable to the idea. But as they'd descended the steps from the house, Miss Talbot had caught George's arm. After that, George had made no effort to extricate himself.

In any other circumstances, Alex would have been angry. He had only a month, after all. Not nearly enough time to achieve his ends. Every minute counted. Every second.

But he wasn't angry.

He was—much to his astonishment—scarcely thinking of George Wright or Henrietta Talbot at all.

"Is that why you were strengthening your lungs in Talbot's Pond?" he asked, gazing down at Miss Hayes's face.

A blush tinted her cheeks.

No doubt she was thinking of how he'd pulled her scantily clad form from the water. He couldn't help but think of it, too. Not only for the pleasurable memories it conjured, but for those that were decidedly less so.

He hadn't been in the water—physically in the water—in ages. He'd been on boats, of course. The steamers to France, and the rowboats that paddled him to and from the shore. But he hadn't held his breath and dived beneath the waves. Not since that unfortunate day in North Devon so many years ago.

Granted, Talbot's Pond wasn't the raging sea. It wasn't even very impressive in terms of woodland ponds. But as he'd crashed below the surface, a host of images had flooded his brain. He hadn't been prepared for them. Hadn't wanted them.

It was the past.

A past he preferred to forget.

"Partly," Miss Hayes said. "My lungs *were* a little weak after the fever."

"And now?"

"I'm much stronger. Strong enough that I hope, one day soon—" She broke off, her ebony brows knitting.

He gave a short laugh. "Oh no, you can't stop there."

"Can't I?"

"And leave me in suspense?"

"It's foolish, really." Her expression turned rueful. "What I hope—what I dream of—is that one day I shall be able to swim in the sea."

The good humor Alex had felt only seconds before evaporated into the ether. "That's your dream? To go swimming?"

"In the sea, yes." She folded her arms, seeming to rest them on the swell of her skirts. "You don't care for the water, I take it."

He focused his attention on the narrow path as it meandered through the wood. "How do you come by that conclusion?"

"After you pulled me out of the pond, you were distraught."

"Hardly."

"You were," she insisted. "Don't deny it."

He inhaled an unsteady breath. It was dark and cool in the wilderness garden, the sun through the branches creating a mosaic of shifting shadows that played on the boulders that lined the path—and on the face of the lady at his side. It was the closest thing to intimacy, this brief moment of darkness in the middle of the blazing afternoon.

"When I was a boy," he said in a gruff voice, "I rescued a friend from drowning. It was a very near thing—for the both of us. It's not the sort of experience one easily forgets."

Miss Hayes's expression softened. "Was your friend in a pond, as I was?"

"He was in the sea. Deep beneath the waves."

She searched his face. "And ever since you've gone about rescuing people, have you?"

He removed his tall beaver hat to run a hand over his hair. "Not in a long while."

Rather the opposite, in fact.

During his years on the continent, it had been his business to lure unsuspecting gamblers like George out into deep water. It was how Alex made his living. Thousands of pounds wagered on the turn of a card. He had an innate skill for gaming. A cool-headedness that served him well under the most strenuous circumstances. It enabled him to win far more than he lost. And win he did—often substantially.

But no more. Not if his plans for Miss Talbot came to fruition.

He was done with cards. Done with a life of rootless wandering. At long last, it was time to settle down. He couldn't permit himself to be distracted.

And Miss Hayes *was* distracting.

So much so that, in the seconds before he'd taken his leave of her at the pond, he'd felt the unholy urge to take her in his arms and kiss her. An emotional aftereffect of diving into the pond, no doubt. A brief desire for warmth. For human connection.

Fortunately, good sense had prevailed.

If there was any warmth to be enjoyed, he must find it with Henrietta Talbot. And he would. On that he was determined.

"Not until today," Miss Hayes said. "When you attempted to rescue me."

He cast her a humorless glance. "*Attempted* being the operative word."

"I told you I was in no danger. And even if I had been—" She gave a dismissive shrug. "I can take care of myself."

"So I observed." From the little he'd seen of her thus far, Miss Hayes seemed a capable sort of female. One who might well disrupt his plans if given half the chance. "Does Miss Talbot often employ you as her chaperone?"

She looked up at him, frowning. "Why do you ask?"

Before Alex could form an answer, Miss Talbot called to them over her shoulder. "Don't dawdle! My wishing bridge is just up ahead."

George flashed him an apologetic glance. He and Miss Talbot had outpaced Alex and Miss Hayes by several yards. A few yards more and they would leave the canopy of branches behind and step out into the sunlight.

"We're right behind you!" Miss Hayes called back. As the others continued ahead, she lowered her voice. "Squire Talbot is complacent about many things, but his daughter's reputation isn't one of them."

Alex settled his hat back on his head. "Why is it that I get the distinct impression that you're warning me off?"

"Perhaps I am."

The sun filtered through the leaves, hotter and brighter, as the branches opened once more to the blue summer sky. Ahead of them, a small wooden bridge crossed a man-made waterway, its shallow bed littered with smooth river stones and the odd glint of coins.

The wishing bridge, as Miss Talbot had described it during tea. *Her* wishing bridge.

Alex had thought it childish then, and even more so now. He preferred the darkness of the woods to the unforgiving light of day. And as for wishes—

Well.

They'd never done him much good, had they?

Miss Hayes looked up at him from beneath the brim of her straw hat. "You're a stranger here, Mr. Archer. Surely you didn't expect to be left alone with Miss Talbot unsupervised?"

He had, actually. George had promised him unfettered access. It was one of the benefits of Miss Talbot being his childhood friend. There would be no chaperones. No strictly surveilled visits. "I understood the rules to be more lenient in the country."

"As compared to where?"

"London, during the season."

"I can't speak to that," she said. "I've never had a season. But I can assure you, sir, in Lower Hawley, a lady of Miss Talbot's standing is never left unprotected. She may not have a mother, or a female relation in residence at the Park, but there are plenty of others who keep a watchful eye."

"Such as yourself."

Her chin lifted a fraction. "Such as myself."

Alex was torn between warring feelings of admiration and annoyance. Miss Hayes was throwing down the gauntlet. And not to protect her own honor, but to protect that of her friend. A friend who had treated her with grating condescension since the moment of her arrival. A friend who hadn't even bothered to send a proper carriage to collect her.

"Ah. I see," he said. "You've appointed yourself her guardian as well as her chaperone."

"Nothing of the sort. I don't like to see any lady taken advantage of by a—"

"By a what?" He looked down at her, a flare of anger taking him unaware.

She gazed steadily back at him. "You know what you are better than I do, Mr. Archer."

His chest tightened. He had the sudden sense that she could see straight through his fine clothes—straight through his gentlemanly accents and bearing—to the yawning hole of emptiness that lay beneath. For an instant, he felt stripped bare. Utterly defenseless. Just as he had as a boy.

It wasn't a pleasant sensation.

"Indeed, Miss Hayes. And knowing that, may I tender you a piece of advice?"

Her brows lifted in question.

"Stay out of my way, ma'am," he said.

Her smoke-blue eyes kindled at his words. "Or what, sir?"

He bent his head close to hers, sinking his voice to a mocking undertone. "Or the next time I encounter you, alone in a secluded wood, I won't treat you with as much gentlemanly forbearance as I exercised this morning."

Chapter Four

Laura stood beside Henrietta on the wishing bridge, her arms folded on the wooden rail. She was glad to rejoin the others. She hadn't the patience for any more of Mr. Archer's warnings. Gentlemanly forbearance, indeed. She supposed he was threatening to kiss her, or some such nonsense.

Then again, who could say?

There was a perpetual edge of sardonic humor to his voice. As if he were teasing her. Laughing at her.

Or at himself.

It made his sincerity difficult to gauge.

And as for kissing her…

Well. She was no green girl to be provoked thus by a man. Especially one who couldn't take the matter seriously. As if the very idea of kissing her was nothing more than a joke.

An inconsequential event he could reference as casually as he might comment on the weather.

There was nothing casual about kissing. Not to her.

She knew that because she'd been kissed before. Only once, it was true, but that had been quite enough. The experience had been a thoroughly unpleasant one. Devastating, really. For a time, she'd believed it was her fault. That she'd done something—said something—to engender such clumsy handling. Such casual mistreatment.

"But I thought—" George had stammered, seconds after she'd slapped his face. "Haven't you always *wanted* me?"

In the intervening years, Laura had come to view the incident as a valuable lesson. To some gentlemen, it wasn't the content of a lady's character that mattered, but only the content of her bank account. If her fortune exceeded a certain amount, she was worthy of respect—and of an offer of marriage. If not…

She could expect to receive another sort of offer.

Henrietta leaned over the rail, her voluminous sleeves pillowing against Laura's. "We have a tradition at Edgington Park," she was explaining to Mr. Archer. "Every year, when we celebrate my birthday, all the guests at my party come to this exact spot and make a wish. I insist upon it."

Mr. Archer stood on Henrietta's opposite side. On arriving at the bridge, he'd smoothly taken George's place, leaving George to stand next to Laura. "Do these wishes come true?"

Henrietta tittered. "What a question! No one knows except the person making them. Your wish is meant to be a secret."

George stared down into the rippling water. "There must be fifty pounds or more down there."

"Probably," Henrietta said with the same careless laugh.

Laura followed George's gaze to the glinting coins below. Fifty pounds would be a blessing to the Hayes family at the moment. A blessing to any poor family, really.

"Are these wishes confined to your birthday, Miss Talbot?" Mr. Archer asked.

"Lord, no. You may make a wish today, if you like. Providing you have brought a coin." Henrietta looked to Laura, a shadow of compassion moving over her face. "Will you make a wish, Laura?"

Laura hadn't brought any money with her to Edgington Park. The only coin she possessed was safely in her reticule at home, waiting to purchase the railway ticket that would take her to London in the morning. She forced a smile. "Not today, Hen. I shall wait for your next birthday."

"I'll make a wish." George thrust his hand into the pocket of his garish plaid trousers and withdrew a halfpenny. "I could do with some luck."

Henrietta produced a coin of her own from a hidden pocket in the froth of her India muslin skirts. "I'll make a wish, too." She looked to Mr. Archer. "Will you, sir?"

"I will." From his place beside Henrietta, Mr. Archer briefly caught Laura's eye. "I have an extra shilling, Miss Hayes, if you'd—"

"She can't make a wish on a borrowed coin," Henrietta interrupted sharply. "It's the rule."

Laura returned Mr. Archer's glance. "I'm obliged to you for the offer, but Miss Talbot is right."

And so she was. That didn't prevent a disconcerting swell of gratitude from building in Laura's breast. Mr. Archer owed her no such courtesy. They'd been at daggers drawn not five minutes before. He had no reason to be civil to her, let alone solicitous. And yet…

She stole another glance at him from beneath her lashes as he leaned over the rail with Henrietta and George. What a strange gentleman he was! Both hero and villain, by turns.

If the offer of a shilling could be termed heroic.

"Do you have your coins at the ready?" Henrietta asked the two men. "Splendid. Now, all you must do is close your eyes, make a wish, and throw it in."

"Throw in the coin and *then* make a wish," George said. "Isn't that the way?"

Henrietta shot him a look. "The order doesn't matter, only the intent."

While the others made their wishes, Laura wandered down from the bridge to the grass-covered bank beyond. It had been months since she'd last visited Edgington Park. Months since Henrietta had issued an invitation to tea or to dine. Their lives had become too different. As children, it hadn't mattered as much. Now, however, two weeks shy of her twenty-fifth birthday, Laura felt keenly how little the pair of them had in common.

"You've changed," Henrietta had accused during one of Laura's last visits. "Sometimes I think I don't know you at all."

"Sometimes I don't know myself," Laura had replied.

Nowadays, she preferred Talbot's Pond to the company of her former friend. Any free time she had was spent there. The water was her sanctuary. Her private domain.

Or it had been until Mr. Archer made his appearance.

He was still on the bridge, making himself agreeable to Henrietta. Laura would have to put her on her guard. Not that Henrietta couldn't discover the man's motives for herself.

Despite her pettishness and well-developed sense of frivolity, Henrietta was quite canny when it came to detecting fortune hunters.

"Laura." George stepped down onto the grass to join her, leaving Henrietta and Mr. Archer to talk alone on the bridge. "It's been a long while."

"Two years," Laura said.

"Longer than that." George rubbed his cheek, as if in recollection of how their last meeting had ended. "It was Christmas, don't you remember? The year you came out of mourning for your father."

"I remember everything."

His gaze slid guiltily away from hers. "Looking back on it…I may have had too much of Squire Talbot's punch."

Laura sighed. "Let's not pretend, George. Do me that courtesy, at least."

His lips thinned. "You could have refused to come today."

"I came for Henrietta, not you."

"As her chaperone. What a lark." He paced a few steps before coming to a halt in front of her. His golden hair curled along the edge of his collar and brow, a sharp contrast to the darkness of his hat and the bright fabric of his plaid suit. "I trust you won't interfere."

"Interfere with what?"

"You know very well what I'm talking about."

Laura regarded George with a vague sense of contempt. She wondered how she could have ever thought him pleasing. How she could have ever believed him her friend. He was—she realized now—a fundamentally weak man. "Where did you meet him?"

"At a gaming club in Marseilles." George smirked. "You look surprised."

"I'm surprised that you answered me honestly."

"Why shouldn't I? You're nothing if not a good little secret keeper. You might have tattled on me at any point these past years, but you—"

"Perhaps I'm merely biding my time."

He scowled.

"What do you know of him, George?" she pressed. "Where is he from? Who are his people?"

"Does it matter?"

"Of course it matters. You've brought him here—introduced him to your friends, and to your father, I presume."

"Not yet. Father hasn't been home all day."

"You've provided an introduction to Henrietta."

"Why shouldn't I have? It's only an introduction. She's quite at liberty to snub him."

Only an introduction? As if it were some minor thing.

An introduction from a lifelong friend—a gentleman who had lived his entire life in the village, and whose father was the vicar for heaven's sake—was very different from the sort of introductions made by casual acquaintances. It was a voucher. A personal bond. A promise that the man being introduced was worthy of intimate friendship. Of sacred trust.

George introducing Mr. Archer was tantamount to his stamping the man with a golden seal of approval.

"And now you mean to remain here with him for an entire month?" She was incredulous. "Doing what, pray?"

"Doing nothing," George said. "It's to be a holiday for us. An August idyll."

Laura didn't like the sound of it. "If you're fond of Henrietta at all—"

"You don't understand these kinds of things, Laura. You've never seen anything of the world. Never lived anywhere outside of Lower Hawley." Perspiration dotted George's brow. "If you had, you'd realize that Henrietta could do a great deal worse than a fellow like Archer."

Her gaze drifted over George's face. What she found there startled her. "You're afraid of him."

George swiftly turned away. "Don't be stupid."

"It's dreadfully hot." Henrietta made her way over the bridge on Mr. Archer's arm, joining them on the bank. "Shall we walk back to the house? I have a sheaf of new music since last you came to visit, Laura. Some marvelous duets. If you'll play the piano for us, perhaps George and I might attempt them?"

"It sounds a grand idea to me," George said.

"Do you sing, Mr. Archer?" Henrietta asked.

He smiled. "Not very well."

Henrietta wrinkled her nose. "How unfortunate. But not to worry. There's plenty to occupy us until the dinner hour. And then you may meet my father."

Laura walked along at Henrietta's side as they returned to the house. A footman in immaculate livery opened the front door of Edgington Park for them. He waited in the marble-tiled hall as they divested themselves of their hats, gloves, and bonnets.

"We'll have some refreshment in the music room," Henrietta informed him. "And tell Cook we shall have three additional places at dinner." She looked to Laura. "You *are* staying, aren't you?"

Laura shook her head. The hour was growing late. There was still much to be done at home. "I promised Aunt Charlotte I'd be back before nightfall."

Henrietta's mouth pursed. "Really, Laura."

"Really, Hen. I have time enough to play a song or two for you, but then I must set out. I'm traveling to London in the morning."

Henrietta's pout softened. "Are you? To see that odious solicitor of yours? I can't begin to fathom why he won't attend you here."

Laura felt the weight of Mr. Archer's gaze upon her. She ignored it. "Mr. Weatherwax is a very busy man. He hasn't the time to come to Lower Hawley."

"When will you return? Not until the following morning, I daresay. Which means I shall have no one to chaperone me all day."

Laura refrained from pointing out the many other ladies in Lower Hawley who might be willing to play chaperone. "I shall be home by Wednesday afternoon. You may send someone for me then. Or come to Bramble Cottage yourself if you'd like to call on my aunt."

"I may at that," Henrietta said. "Perhaps we all shall."

Two hours later, as dusk settled over the Surrey countryside, Laura was conveyed home in a one-horse gig driven by an aged groom from Squire Talbot's stables.

It was but a short distance by carriage—past the boundary of Edgington Park, along the border of Talbot's Wood, and to the gate of the ramshackle cottage which housed the remaining members of the Hayes family.

After climbing down from the gig and bidding the groom safe journey, Laura stood at the gate for a moment. The garden was woefully overgrown, the warm evening air heavy with the perfume of summer roses. They were everywhere. An explosion of fragrant yellow and orange blooms ran wild along the walls, framing the windows and arching over the front door.

She inhaled deeply.

Perfume was in her blood. The redolence of roses. The exotic sweetness of jasmine. And the clean, wholesome bouquet of lavender.

She wasn't her father. She couldn't create new fragrances—and didn't aspire to. But she knew the importance of scent. It was love, and loss, and memory. A single sniff was all it took to bring the past alive.

But there was no future in it. Not for her, and not for Teddy. Not so long as Mr. Weatherwax held the reins.

A candle flickered from Teddy's third-floor window. He was still awake—and still drawing, no doubt.

She made her way inside and up the creaking stairs. A short rap at his bedroom door was enough to announce her presence.

"I saw the gig from the window," Teddy said as she entered. He was hunched over his desk, the candle sputtering beside him. "Good thing Aunt Charlotte didn't."

Magpie was stretched out on Teddy's bed. Laura gave him a scratch on the head as she passed. "Where is she?"

"Gone down the lane to look in on Mrs. Pole's baby. She said she'd be back in a quarter of an hour."

Laura leaned down to brush a kiss against her brother's temple. With his inky black hair and gray-blue eyes, he might have been her copy. But there was no fire in him. No vibrancy. As a boy, he'd had more strength of will. Now, however, on the cusp of reaching his majority, Teddy seemed to have given up. In the past month alone, his face had grown thinner, his shoulders narrow.

"What have you been working on today?" she asked.

"Preliminary sketches of the birds." His face was pale in the candlelight, his complexion sickly for lack of sunshine. "I'll begin painting tomorrow."

"Outside?"

He didn't answer.

She pulled up a chair beside the desk and sat down. "This won't do, you know."

"I'm not in any mood for a lecture. I've already had enough of them from Aunt Charlotte."

"I'm not lecturing."

He cast her a baleful look. "I don't see why I shouldn't do what makes me happy. You're always running away to the pond. No one stops you from going."

"I wish you'd come with me."

"In this?" He made an impatient gesture at his wheeled chair. "No, thank you."

"Yardley can carry you down, and then we—"

"Don't be daft. Yardley can barely carry himself up and down the stairs. He's pushing seventy."

"He's not a day over sixty," Laura said. "But I take your meaning."

John Yardley had worked for the Hayes family for as long as Laura could remember. He was butler, footman, and man-servant. Capable enough for most things, but not as able to perform his physical duties as once he had.

"It's the rheumatism, Miss Laura," he'd confided to her only last week. "It does give me a twinge on occasion."

Laura leaned back in her chair, regarding her brother with a thoughtful frown. "There's no use dithering about it any longer. We must simply hire another footman. Someone younger and stronger who can be more of a help to you."

"How do you propose we pay him?"

"Let me worry about that."

Teddy gathered his sketches into a pile, shuffling them straight before thrusting them into a drawer and slamming it closed. "I wish you would confide in me."

"I do confide in you."

He snorted. "You don't."

"Would it set your mind at ease to know every misera-ble detail?"

Teddy bent his head, his mouth pressed tight. "Our cir-cumstances *are* miserable, then."

"I have it all in hand."

"Do you?"

"As near as can be." She reached to smooth a lock of Teddy's hair from his brow. "You need only concern your-self with getting well."

Teddy drew back from her touch. "You'll speak with Weatherwax tomorrow?"

Laura's hand fell to her lap. "I will."

"And if he—"

"He won't. He can't. The law is on our side."

"The law is an ass," Teddy muttered. "That's what Shake-speare says."

"I daresay he's right," Laura replied. "But it's all we have at present."

Alex didn't drink to excess. Didn't do anything to excess, really. When one had only one's wits to rely on, one couldn't afford to have one's senses addled. Fortunately, Squire Talbot wasn't the sort of gentleman to press food and drink on his guests.

Indeed, as dinner progressed in the cavernous dining room at Edgington Park, the squire seemed to cede the whole of his duties as host to his daughter.

It led Alex to wonder whether Miss Hayes might not have been exaggerating when she'd told him that the squire fiercely guarded Miss Talbot's reputation. As one course led to the next, Alex began to get the impression that Squire Talbot wasn't in the habit of doing anything fiercely. He was, it seemed, little more than a country farmer. A man more interested in the workings of his estate than in his daughter's matrimonial prospects.

"You must come back tomorrow afternoon," he said. "I'll take you round the home farm. We have the finest pigs in Surrey."

"Really, Papa," Miss Talbot protested. "Mr. Archer isn't interested in *pigs*, of all things."

"But I am," Alex replied. "Keenly interested. I should be grateful for a tour."

Squire Talbot looked down the table at George. "And you, Wright?"

George held out his wineglass for a footman to refill it. It was his fourth refill thus far, and he was starting to show the effects of it. His cheeks were ruddy, his manner less formal. "Can't say I've ever been interested in farming. I prefer city life to a country village. Far more civilized, to my mind."

"Rubbish," the squire said. "There's nothing more civilized than orderly crops, healthy livestock, and modern machinery. Prosperous farms like Edgington Park are the backbone of England. Your father understands that well enough. He's often complimented my methods of—"

"I beg you, Papa," Miss Talbot interrupted. "No more talk of farming. Not when our guests have only lately returned from the continent. I'd far rather hear about Paris than pigs."

Squire Talbot gave his daughter an indulgent glance. "Quite right, my dear. Plenty of time to talk about farming tomorrow, when I take Mr. Archer out on the estate."

Miss Talbot was true to her word. She kept the conversation to fashionable topics, presiding over the remainder of their meal with all the aplomb of a society doyenne. And when they'd finished the final course, drunk their after-dinner coffee, and indulged in another round of soulful duets in the music room, it was she, and not her father, who walked them out to the drive and bid them adieu.

"Call on me again soon," she said as Alex and George climbed into the vicar's carriage. "When Miss Hayes is back from London."

The carriage rolled away, the coachman clucking to the horses.

Alex settled back into the shadowy corner of his seat, arms folded.

"My father will be home," George said with a hiccup. "Shouldn't have drunk so much wine."

"Does your father disapprove of drinking?"

"He disapproves of anything that brings a man pleasure." Another hiccup. "Must be why he wants me to marry. Knows I'll be miserable. Even if…"

"Even if what?"

George scrubbed at his face. "I wouldn't marry her. Couldn't."

"Miss Talbot?"

"Miss Hayes," George said, slurring his speech. "Laura."

Alex's gaze sharpened in the darkened interior of the coach. "What about Miss Hayes?"

"Made her an offer, last time I was home. Not at all the thing." George's mouth spread into a stupid grin. "She slapped my face. Hard. I fancy I can still feel it."

Alex's jaw hardened at George's admission. The mere idea of it…George and Laura Hayes.

Not but that he hadn't suspected something of the sort.

He'd have had to be blind not to recognize the dark undercurrents that ran between the pair of them. He would have liked to question George on the subject—to find out more about what had happened between him and the mysterious Miss Hayes. But mere seconds later, George was snoring contentedly, his head lolled against the seat.

It didn't matter, in any case.

Alex hadn't come to Lower Hawley to ensnare himself with a penniless water nymph. He'd come to ensure his future.

He'd acquired some degree of wealth in the years since he'd left North Devon. Substantial winnings in nefarious London gaming clubs, and at the tables in private gaming establishments all over France. It had been sufficient to assure his comfort in a suite of luxurious rented rooms, and to procure first-class passage on railways and steamships. But it wasn't enough. It would never be enough without property.

Property was the thing.

And for a man of his pedigree, the only way to attain such property was to marry an heiress.

Fabricating his antecedents had been simple enough. He'd spent decades on the continent. Who was to say his parents hadn't died during the cholera epidemic? As for Baron Reynard, should anyone go looking, they would find the old sharper alive and well in Biarritz—and more than willing to claim Alex as his godson.

All that had remained was to garner a proper introduction. An entrée into the world of some country squire's daughter. A wealthy young woman Archer could woo and win.

When George had first described Henrietta Talbot, she'd sounded like just the sort of young lady Alex was looking for.

She was beautiful, and accomplished, to a degree. But she wasn't as canny as she thought she was. Alex was confident he could catch her, by fair means or foul. Catch her, marry her, and secure his future.

The prospect should have been appealing. It certainly had been when he'd first conceived the idea. Now, however, a growing sense of unease had invaded his peace. Things weren't as they seemed in Lower Hawley. He had the distinct feeling that he was rushing toward a destination that was spinning rapidly out of his control.

And he didn't like to be out of control.

The carriage came to a rattling halt in front of the vicarage. He opened the door and jumped out before turning to assist George.

It wasn't the first time he'd hauled George Wright's drunken carcass out of a coach. At one time or another, Alex had delivered George back to his rooms reeking of alcohol, smoky with opium, or stinking of the cheap scent of a third-rate whorehouse. It all depended on the night of the week—and on how much ready coin George had in his pocket when that night began.

Alex had come to view it as the price of doing business with the man.

As he hoisted George up, the front door of the vicarage swung open. A small, gray-haired gentleman in dark trousers and a well-worn frock coat emerged. Had Alex any doubt as to his identity, the leather-bound Bible clutched in the gentleman's hand would have confirmed it.

"Oh dear, he's been at Squire Talbot's port, I see." The vicar urged Alex into the house. "You must be Mr. Archer. I'm sorry I wasn't here to receive you. But you've had a good meal at the Park, I trust."

"Very good, sir."

"Squire Talbot's cellars are rumored to contain some of the finest vintages in Surrey. My son seems determined to prove it. Put him in the parlor, if you please. He can sleep there tonight. No one will disturb him."

Alex did as the vicar bid him, half dragging George into the vicarage parlor and dropping him onto an overstuffed sofa near the hearth.

George yawned mightily, one booted foot stretched out on the cushions and one set on the floor.

"Oh, dear," the vicar said again as he looked at him. And then he raised his gaze to Alex. There were crinkles around his eyes. Evidence of a man who smiled more than he frowned. "Leopold Wright, at your service." He extended his hand.

Alex shook it. "Alex Archer. Thank you for having me to stay."

"You're very welcome, sir. I was just reading my scripture for the evening. The parable of the prodigal son. It seems rather apt at the moment. If you'd care to join me?"

It had been a long time since Alex had opened a Bible, let alone read a scripture. But when the vicar gestured toward the pair of winged chairs near the cold fireplace, he sat down without a word.

The vicar lowered himself into the remaining chair and opened his Bible on his lap, his finger holding his place in the text. "Many view the parable as one of repentance and forgiveness. Of a man brought low after riotous living. But the scripture is much more than that. It's a story of homecoming. Of reconciliation. 'For this thy brother was dead, and is alive again; and was lost, and is found.'"

Alex felt something deep within him give way as the vicar recited the scripture. He didn't want to think about homecomings. About brothers resurrected from the dead.

"My son hasn't been home for a long while," the vicar said when he'd finished reading the parable. "I believe he's come back due to your influence. For that, I can only thank you." He looked at Alex over the rim of his wire-framed spectacles. "Do you have a family, sir?"

Alex returned the vicar's gently enquiring gaze. "I did. A lifetime ago."

"Are they still living?"

Were they? Alex had done his best not to find out. Nevertheless, there had been no avoiding the news that Justin Thornhill had wed the daughter of a wealthy nobleman last September. An earl's daughter, if one could believe it. The announcement had been in the London papers for all to see. It had been the very incident that had sparked Alex's own interest in finding a wealthy wife.

As for Tom Finchley and Neville Cross…

Alex didn't know. He didn't *want* to know.

The orphanage at Abbot's Holcombe was a part of his past. The ache of hunger. The ice-cold dormitories. The ever-present fear of punishment. Of death. It had been a lifetime ago. So long ago that he could almost fancy it had happened to another person.

"Some of them," he said. "I don't know about the others. It's been many years. Decades."

The vicar nodded. "Then I shall pray that you will be reunited with them, as my son has been with me."

Chapter Five

Laura stepped out of the crowded railway carriage onto the busy platform at London's Waterloo Station, her valise clutched in her hand. Porters shouted over the blare of the whistle, and travelers hurried past her, striding every which way through the smoke and steam. They scarcely spared her a glance. It was a relief, really. She never felt entirely at ease venturing into the city, especially when unaccompanied.

She could think of only three occasions she'd done so in the past three years—once right after Papa's death, and then twice more when Teddy's health had necessitated that she appeal to Mr. Weatherwax for a larger allowance.

Harold P. Weatherwax was a distinguished solicitor in his middle forties. Their father had employed him to write contracts and other documents for the family business, as well as to draft his will. Weatherwax had been a young man then, with precious little legal experience. His services had come at a bargain. Now, however, he was a canny practitioner with a stable of clients far more important than the Hayes family—or so he claimed. It was the chief reason he was never at liberty to call on her in Lower Hawley.

She smoothed a hand over her dark blue traveling gown as she walked to the nearby cabstand. There, she hired a hansom to take her to Fleet Street. Mr. Weatherwax was expecting her at half past two. She had no time to spare.

Next month was Teddy's birthday. He would be one and twenty. A man grown, as far as the law was concerned. Which meant that their time under Mr. Weatherwax's power was almost at an end.

It was quite clear to her under the terms of Papa's will. Teddy would now be responsible for what little remained of the Hayes family's business. All that was needed was for Mr. Weatherwax to cooperate. And why shouldn't he? After all, it was he who had set out the very rules by which they were all bound.

As she bounced along the streets of London in the ill-sprung hansom cab, Laura felt rather optimistic about the whole thing. It was Teddy who remained doubtful. He'd never cared for Mr. Weatherwax. Never trusted him.

"The law is the law," Laura often said in response to Teddy's predictions of doom and gloom. "Even if he is a villain, he must abide by it."

She firmly believed that, even now.

A short time later, the cab came to a halt in front of Mr. Weatherwax's office. It was a narrow white building with a polished brass nameplate and freshly swept steps. "Shall I wait, ma'am?" the jarvey asked.

Laura climbed out, giving her skirts a shake to dislodge the straw and other debris her hem had picked up on the floor of the cab. "That won't be necessary." She paid the man from the few coins in her reticule. "Thank you, sir."

He tipped his hat to her before clucking to his horse and driving on. The rattle of the cab, and the clip-clop of the horse's hooves, echoed behind her as she climbed the steps to the door and firmly applied the knocker.

A young maidservant answered the summons, opening the door just a crack and peering out with wary eyes. She wore a mob cap atop her mousy hair, and an apron over a home-spun gown.

"Miss Hayes to see Mr. Weatherwax," Laura said. "I have an appointment."

The maidservant drew back. "Best come in, then, miss. I'll take you to him."

Laura followed the maidservant through a narrow hall and up the stairs to Mr. Weatherwax's office. He was just visible through his half-open door, sitting at his desk in his shirtsleeves, scowling over a document of some sort. When he saw Laura, he cast it away and stood, swiftly buttoning his waistcoat over the paunch of his stomach and shrugging on his frock coat.

"Miss Hayes." He came to greet her. "Punctual as always."

He extended his hand and she took it, ignoring the flicker of distaste that went through her when he pressed her palm a fraction of a second longer than was necessary.

"Mr. Weatherwax," she said, withdrawing her hand. "Good morning."

"It certainly is now." He turned to address the maidser-vant who remained lingering by the door. His countenance darkened. "Fetch the tea tray, Patience. And don't dally." And then, more sharply, "Off with you, now!"

Patience—if that was truly her name—shot out of the office with the speed of a startled hare.

"A workhouse indigent," he said by way of explanation. "I've taken her on as a maid-of-all-work. Just on trial, mind. But it isn't ideal. Not by any means. The stupid creature can scarcely brew a proper pot of tea."

Laura felt a pang of sympathy for the frightened girl. Mr. Weatherwax could unsettle anyone. One always had the impression that he was a hair's breadth from losing his temper. "I have no need of refreshment," she said.

"Naturally you do. You've come all the way from Surrey. You must be parched as well as fatigued." He ushered her to a chair across from his desk, standing over it as she sat down. She glanced up at him in question.

"Forgive my impudent stares, Miss Hayes. It's been two years since last we met. I'd quite forgotten what you looked like."

Laura folded her hands primly in her lap. She hadn't forgotten him. He was sporting the same sparse, oily beard and mustache that he had on her previous visits. The only difference was that now the hair on his head was thinning to match. To compensate, he'd combed it across his scalp, anchoring the brown strands with a thorough application of pomade. "Yes, it's been a very long while, sir. And I haven't a great deal of time to spare—"

His gaze flicked to her valise. "You're staying overnight?"

"At Mrs. Swan's Hotel for Ladies. I'm catching the train back to Lower Hawley first thing in the morning."

"Have you plans for dinner this evening? I expect Mrs. Swan serves an adequate meal, but it will be nothing to dining at Claridge's. If you would join me—"

"Oh no, I couldn't possibly," Laura said quickly. Dine with Mr. Weatherwax? Good gracious. The mere idea of it was enough to send a tremor of revulsion through her. But she didn't dare offend the man's pride. "That is, perhaps some other time? The rail journey has been rather taxing."

He frowned down at her a moment before his features softened with masculine condescension. "I forget how fragile you are."

Her spine went rigid. Fragile, indeed! "Mr. Weatherwax, you are very civil, but if we could please address ourselves to the matter at hand—"

"Yes, yes." He went to the great leather chair behind his desk and took a seat. The upholstery creaked beneath his weight. "You wish to discuss your father's will."

Laura saw no need to beat about the bush. "My brother comes of age next month. He'll be one and twenty on the seventeenth."

Mr. Weatherwax steepled his fingers in front of him. "And how is your brother faring? Is his health much improved?"

"It's improving steadily."

"But not enough for him to come here today."

A vague sense of foreboding made her hesitate. "As to that…"

"It's a fair question, Miss Hayes. Much as I enjoy your charming presence, by rights it should be your brother I'm dealing with, not you. Your father's will states in no uncertain terms that if, by the age of five and twenty, you remain unmarried, the whole of the family business—interests, property, and so forth—goes to Edward Hayes on his twenty-first birthday." Mr. Weatherwax's mouth curled into a patronizing smile. "And you *are* unmarried, are you not?"

Her hands tightened in her lap. "I am."

"And have you any intention of marrying before your twenty-fifth birthday?"

Anger rose in Laura's breast. It took an effort to keep it from infiltrating her words. "My twenty-fifth birthday is in two weeks, sir. That's hardly enough time—"

"Am I to take that as a no?"

"No," she ground out. "I have no immediate plans to marry."

He smiled again. "Then we're at an impasse. With your brother too ill to fulfill his responsibilities—"

"He's not too ill. Really, Mr. Weatherwax, if my brother—"

"If your brother were competent in mind and body, Miss Hayes, he would have come to meet with me himself—to settle matters and to receive an accounting of where things stand. As it is, I remain convinced that he is *not* competent. He's ill, and far too frail for me to hand over control to him. Given the circumstances, I cannot believe that your father would have wished me to do so."

She opened her mouth to object, but Mr. Weatherwax held up his hand, silencing her.

"It would be a gross dereliction of my duty," he said. "An act verging perilously close to malpractice."

"But my father's will—" Laura began, a note of desperation creeping into her voice. "It couldn't be clearer."

"His will can be challenged. Indeed, it *shall be* challenged if you insist on your brother taking control. There is no judge who would remove me from my role. Not when they see how truly unfit your brother is. It's frankly a mercy for me to remain in charge of your affairs, my dear." He looked up at the door. "Ah. And here is Patience with our tea."

The maidservant entered the room, the teapot and teacups rattling on the tray in her arms.

"Set it down," Mr. Weatherwax ordered. "Here on my desk. Don't make a to-do out of it."

No sooner had the maidservant set down the tray than Laura stood, prompting Mr. Weatherwax to rise from his chair. "I beg your pardon," she said, "but I must wash my hands."

Mr. Weatherwax's mouth tightened. "Yes, of course. Rail travel is appallingly dusty. Patience! Show Miss Hayes to the washroom. Be quick about it."

The maidservant led Laura out of the office. "The necessary is just down the hall, miss."

Laura's heart beat heavily in her chest. She felt, rather suddenly, as if her corset had been laced several inches too tight. At the door to the washroom, she stopped and pressed a hand to her midriff.

"Are you ill, miss?" the maidservant asked softly. "You've gone all pale-like."

"I just need a moment to catch my breath," Laura said.

The maidservant's face creased with sympathy. "He's upset you, has he?"

Laura was too out of sorts to mind the impertinence. "He has, rather. He must be a dreadful gentleman to work for."

"Oh, I don't work for him. Not like he thinks."

Laura glanced up. "Don't you?" She didn't know whether the girl was speaking the truth or not. She hardly cared. "I thought I was going to be rid of him today."

"There are other solicitors, miss. Better ones. My own master is the best of the lot."

Laura entered the washroom to stand in front of the porcelain basin. She needed to splash her face and wrists with cold water. And then she needed to go home. Nothing was making any sense anymore.

The maidservant came in after her. "Here, miss." She reached into the bodice of her dress and pulled out a scrap of paper. Her voice sank to a whisper. "I have his card." She offered it to Laura.

Laura took it without looking at it. "I'm obliged to you," she said as she placed it in her reticule. "Truly."

And she was.

But the very thought of hiring another solicitor made her feel even worse. They hadn't any money to spare for the expense of it. And even if they had, what use would it be? It was Mr. Weatherwax her father had put in charge of things. He couldn't simply be replaced on a whim, no matter how insufferable and overbearing he was.

"He saved me mum from being sent away," the maidservant went on. "He's the best solicitor in London."

Laura managed a faint smile. She felt rather like weeping. "Well, perhaps one day I shall call upon him for help. Until then, I fear I'm quite on my own."

Alex was just finishing breakfast when the vicar's housekeeper, Mrs. Griffiths, ducked her head in the door of the vicarage dining room. She was a plump, older woman with a kindly face and a brutally efficient manner. The sort of female servant accustomed to ruling over a bachelor household in much the same way an unmarried sister might do.

"Miss Talbot from up at the Park is calling for young Mr. Wright, sir," she said. "Shall I wake him? Or shall I tell her—"

"No need to wake George." Alex downed the last of his coffee, wiped his mouth with his napkin, and stood. "I'll see Miss Talbot. If you'll show her into the parlor?"

"Yes, sir." Mrs. Griffiths bobbed a curtsy before disappearing back through the door.

The vicar had departed for his office at the church well before breakfast. And George was still abed, having developed an acute case of nausea after his night of heavy drinking. The slightest movement provoked another episode of retching.

For all intents and purposes, Alex was on his own.

Miss Talbot couldn't have called at a more opportune time. Despite his misgivings about her suitability—and about her relationship with George—Alex was still resolved to have her. Country-bred heiresses were thin on the ground. He didn't have the luxury of being picky.

Besides, Edgington Park would make up for a wealth of minor deficits on the part of its mistress. Even if Miss Talbot was besotted with George, and even if she was a bit spoiled and frivolous, it was but a small price to pay for gaining control of such an estate—and such a fortune.

When he entered the parlor, she sprang to her feet in a rustle of ruffled Indian muslin. "Mr. Archer, is it true? Is George unwell?"

"A minor stomach complaint. Nothing a day in bed won't cure." Alex bowed over Miss Talbot's outstretched hand. "You look very well today, ma'am."

"In this old gown? It's nothing very fine, though I did have it made in Paris." She glanced impatiently about the room. "Is George's father not at home? Has he not summoned the doctor?"

"The vicar's gone to the church to work on his Sunday sermon."

"He didn't see fit to stay with George?" Miss Talbot's bee-stung lips pursed with disapproval as she resumed her seat. "How very unfeeling."

"He left at dawn. George was still asleep."

"At least you're here. That has to be some comfort to poor George in his time of need."

Alex doubted whether George registered his presence at all. When last he'd ventured upstairs to George's room, he'd found George heaving into a chamber pot, his countenance a distinctly yellowish hue.

"Do you expect he'll be recovered by Thursday?" she asked. "I'd hoped we might have a picnic on the grounds of Edgington Park. I've already instructed Cook on what to make. But if George won't be well enough to join us—"

"He'll be well enough." Alex debated whether to join Miss Talbot on the sofa or to take the chair across from her. He chose the latter. There would be time enough to press his suit during the next month.

"Things aren't going at all as I planned them," Miss Talbot said. "First Laura must away to London, and now George is ill. It isn't very much of a homecoming for him."

"Miss Hayes is coming back tomorrow, is she not?"

"On the three o'clock train, or so she said." Miss Talbot sighed heavily. "Oh, but it will be too late then to do anything worthwhile. And Laura will insist on reporting to her family afterward. Heaven knows how long that will take. I don't expect we'll be able to lure her away until Thursday."

"Hence your picnic."

"Precisely. It will be a treat for her—and for George."

"For me as well," Alex said.

Miss Talbot gave him a dimpled smile. "I shall endeavor not to bore you, Mr. Archer."

"There's no danger of that, ma'am."

"Isn't there? You strike me as being altogether more sophisticated than the rest of us. You've been living on the continent for such a long while. Lower Hawley must seem rather dull when compared to Paris and Marseilles."

Alex wondered how much George had told her. Not too much, he'd wager. "Not at all. One grows tired of French casinos and supper parties with displaced aristocrats. The English countryside is a welcome change."

"One can enjoy the countryside without learning the inner workings of a farm," she said. "You needn't feel obliged to accept my father's offer of a tour. He won't be offended if you beg off this afternoon."

"On the contrary. I'm quite looking forward to learning more about Edgington Park. Farming is a particular interest of mine."

"Indeed?" Her brows lifted. "Do you intend to settle in the country, sir?"

"I hope I might," he said. "If I meet a suitable lady."

"I can't say I didn't wonder. You spent a great deal of time talking with Laura yesterday." Her smile turned brittle. "She hasn't a bean, you know. And her brother and aunt are dependent upon her. No gentleman could ever persuade her to give them up."

Alex regarded Miss Talbot with interest. Was she jealous of Miss Hayes? Or merely the type of lady who bristled at any perceived competition? "I haven't any designs on Miss Hayes."

It was the truth.

Miss Talbot looked somewhat mollified. "I daresay I shouldn't have said anything. Laura is a childhood friend, and very dear to me. But a gentleman should be made aware of such matters before he risks his heart."

"I assure you, ma'am, my heart is in no danger."

"I'm glad to hear it. I wouldn't like anything to disrupt my arrangements for George's homecoming. I have so many things planned for us." Her brown eyes lit with excitement. "On Thursday we'll picnic, and Friday we'll drive into the village in Papa's barouche, and then…next week…" She leaned forward on the sofa. "I'm planning a grand excursion for us all."

"That sounds promising," he said. "Where will this grand excursion take us?"

Miss Talbot beamed. "Just you wait and see, Mr. Archer. Just you wait and see."

Chapter Six

Laura disembarked from the train at the Lower Hawley station, her valise clutched in her hand. It was only a humble platform halt with a ticket office. Nothing like the railway stations in London. Indeed, at half past three in the afternoon it was all but empty.

She crossed the platform, one foot in front of the other, never knowing from one moment to the next how she was managing to hold herself upright. Her chest was tight with emotion, her traveling dress dusty and rumpled from the journey. She needed a bit of privacy. Someplace she could indulge in a brief spate of tears before returning home to share the grim news with Teddy and Aunt Charlotte.

Empty as it was, there was no such privacy to be found on the platform. She descended the wooden steps to the dirt road. A farmer was nearby, loading up his cart with goods.

She didn't notice the smaller gig on the opposite side of him until its driver called out to her.

"Miss Hayes."

Her head jerked up at the familiar deep voice, even as her spirits sank down to her boots. She was in no mood to spar. "Mr. Archer. Good afternoon."

He stood beside the gig, securing a trunk onto the back of it with a length of rope. A heavy-boned chestnut gelding dozed in the traces. "Have you just returned from London?"

"As you see." Her fingers tightened on the handle of her valise. "What are you doing here?"

"Retrieving my trunk from the station agent's office."

She hadn't thought her spirits could get any lower. "You're staying, then?"

"For the month, at least. Miss Talbot has a great many activities planned."

"Well…" She could think of nothing more to say to him. Her thoughts were too much occupied with her own troubles at present. "I shall leave you to it." She turned to go, only to stop short when he called after her again.

"Where are you headed?" he asked.

"Home," she said. "To Bramble Cottage."

"May I drive you?"

"No thank you."

His mouth tilted up at one corner. He had a disconcerting way of half smiling. As if he were amused by some private joke. "Come, Miss Hayes. It's hot as Hades this afternoon. I'm certain you'd rather ride than walk."

"I can't. Not with you."

"Why not? There's nothing objectionable about a gentleman driving a lady in an open carriage." He held out a hand to her. "Come. I insist upon it."

Laura gave in with a defeated sigh, her shoulders sagging under the weight of it all. What difference did it make in the end whether she walked or rode? She'd have to go home eventually. She grudgingly put her gloved hand in his and allowed him to help her up onto the seat. "Whose carriage is this?" she asked as she placed her valise at her feet.

"It belongs to the vicar." Mr. Archer vaulted onto the seat beside her and gathered up the reins. The dozing chestnut sprang to life. "He couldn't spare a manservant to come to the station."

"The vicar keeps on very few servants." The gig started forward with a lurch. Her hand clenched around the padded seat. "You've met him, I assume."

"Monday night when George and I returned from dining at the Park." Mr. Archer's mouth hitched again. "He read me the parable of the prodigal son."

"How appropriate."

"Indeed." The horse plodded along at a leisurely pace. Mr. Archer seemed little inclined to urge him on.

"George can't have liked being sermonized at." He never had in the past. It was one of the reasons he'd left Lower Hawley.

"He wasn't in any fit state to object."

"Oh." Laura felt a flicker of disappointment. It shouldn't have come as any surprise to her. George had always had a propensity for heavy drinking. Two years away would have only worsened the habit.

She wished, all at once, that he'd never returned home. That he'd never brought Mr. Archer with him. It was a distraction she didn't need—couldn't cope with.

"Haven't you anyone to come and fetch you?" Mr. Archer asked. "A groom or a manservant or someone?"

Laura looked out at the passing scenery. Trees, shrubs, and stray patches of wildflowers lined the deserted road. The railway station was closer to Edgington Park than to Bramble Cottage. In the distance, she could just make out the dense overgrowth of Talbot's Wood. She longed to be there. To submerge herself beneath the cool surface of the pond. There was nothing of the world underwater. No unmet expectations. No burdens too heavy to carry. Nothing save herself and the sound of her own beating heart.

"Miss Hayes?" Mr. Archer said.

She cast him a distracted glance. "I'm sorry. What did you say?"

"I asked why no one was here to collect you."

"We don't keep a carriage any longer," she said. "Nor a coachman to drive one."

"How did you arrive at the station yesterday?"

"I walked."

"And you intended to walk back today? Alone?"

"It's perfectly safe."

"I don't doubt it. All the same, it seems rather ramshackle for a young lady to be traipsing about unaccompanied."

"It's unexceptionable in the country." She paused before adding, "And I'm not a *young* lady, Mr. Archer. I shall be five and twenty soon."

"And therefore, at your last prayer."

Her lips compressed. "Some people hereabouts might say so."

"Then some people hereabouts would be foolish beyond permission. You're a long way from an aged spinster, Miss Hayes. And an even longer way from being able to wander about unremarked—either here or in London. You should have taken someone with you."

"It's no concern of yours, sir."

"No, it isn't. And yet…" He fell silent a moment, his expression thoughtful. "I suppose I feel responsible for you."

"I can't think why."

"I did all but save you from drowning on Monday."

"You did no such—"

"The both of us wet to our skin and you in your knickers. It leaves an impression on a fellow."

Heat rose in her face. "A gentleman wouldn't mention such things."

"But I'm not a gentleman, as you pointed out at Edgington Park." His tone was dry. "Indeed, I believe you came perilously close to labeling me a fortune hunter."

"And I have no fortune. So you can have no interest in me, sir." She rose from her seat, even as the carriage rolled on. "You may set me down here."

"God's sake, Laura!" He hauled on the reins. The chestnut gelding came to a stumbling halt, the gig jolting behind it.

Her heart hammered as she moved to jump out. The skirts of her traveling gown wound precariously round her legs. "I'm obliged to you for bringing me this far, but I—"

"What in blazes is the matter with you?" Mr. Archer leapt down from his seat. He was in front of her in an instant, reaching to grasp her round the waist a fraction of a second before she tumbled down in a tangle of skirts. "Are you trying to break your neck?"

She permitted him to assist her down and then backed swiftly out of his arms. Her eyes stung with the threat of tears. "I would prefer to walk the rest of the way. If you would—"

"Laura," he said again. His voice was husky with concern.

Her temper flared. "And I don't recall giving you permission to use my Christian name! That's the second time you've—"

"This is the second time I've come to your rescue. If that's not a basis for some familiarity, I don't know what is."

"You haven't rescued me from *anything*." The words came out harsher than she'd intended. Tears quickly followed, spilling hot onto her cheeks. She dashed them away. "No one can." She spun on her heel to leave.

Mr. Archer caught her firmly by the elbow, preventing her escape. He loomed over her. "What is it? What's happened?"

"I want to be left alone."

"This isn't about my teasing you, is it? There's something else going on."

"Let go of me," she said. "Or I shall scream."

His hand fell from her elbow. "I'm not trying to plague you. But if I've upset you—"

"Really, Mr. Archer. Your appearance in Lower Hawley isn't as earth-shattering as you seem to believe. My present state has nothing at all to do with you. I simply need a moment to compose myself. I'm in no fit state to see my family—and I have no inclination to cross swords with you." She dropped an abrupt curtsy. "I bid you good day, sir."

With that, she turned and strode blindly into the woods.

It wasn't far to Talbot's Pond. Her secret place. Her sanctuary. At least, it had been until Mr. Archer had unceremoniously shown up there yesterday morning.

But he didn't matter now.

Nothing mattered except her disastrous meeting with Mr. Weatherwax. She'd had a whole night to reflect on the subject, and she still couldn't quite believe it. Couldn't quite accept that all of her careful plans had come to naught.

What was she going to tell Teddy and Aunt Charlotte?

More to the point, what in the world was she going to do?

As she made her way deeper through the trees, her full skirts caught on the leaves and underbrush that surrounded Talbot's Pond. Once there, she sank down on the grassy banks in a spill of petticoats and wrinkled silk. Tears leaked from her eyes. This time, she didn't bother to dash them away.

She wasn't a great one for weeping. It was a pointless exercise. Her emotions were better spent in solving problems and making plans. Easy enough when one had a surfeit of ideas. There was always something else to try. Another method by which to trim the Hayes family's budget. To keep them all clothed, shod, and fed.

It had occurred to her yesterday, as she'd left Mr. Weatherwax's offices in London, that she hadn't adequately prepared for failure. And now, having to face it was a shade more than she could bear.

She covered her face with her hands and wept.

Once started, the tears were impossible to quell. She wept until they'd fully run their course. It might have been a quarter of an hour. Perhaps even longer. She had no sense of time. It had been ages since she'd cried her heart out so thoroughly, scarcely able to draw breath between sobs.

It was better this way, she thought as she rummaged in her reticule for a handkerchief. The cottage was no place for tears or expressions of hopelessness. There was enough of that from Teddy and Aunt Charlotte. If they knew—if they even suspected—that she was despairing, it would send the rest of the household into an uproar.

She dried her tears with her handkerchief, blew her nose, and raised her head.

And then she froze.

Mr. Archer sat on a boulder nearby, her valise on the ground at his side. His head was bare and his coat unbuttoned. He looked as though he'd been there for a long while.

A crashing wave of embarrassment rendered her speechless. She could think of nothing to say. Nothing to excuse her appalling lack of self-control. And that he should witness it! No one had ever seen her weep to such a degree before. No one in her family, nor of her acquaintance, would have believed her capable of doing so.

But now…

She could only look at Mr. Archer through swollen eyes, mortified at the thought of how thoroughly wretched she must appear.

As for Mr. Archer, he uttered not a word as he rose and went to the edge of the pond. He extracted a folded white linen handkerchief from the pocket of his waistcoat, and crouching down, dipped it into the water and wrung it out. When he'd finished, he came back to where she knelt in the grass, and sank down on his haunches in front of her.

Laura's heart hammered as he took her chin in his fingers and tipped her face up to his.

He held the wet handkerchief at the ready. "If I may?"

She didn't answer. Couldn't answer.

Mr. Archer didn't wait for her permission. He didn't seem to require it.

Her eyes fell closed as he blotted her face. His touch was soft and careful. Almost tender. She couldn't fathom how such a big man could be so gentle. But she had no will to ponder it. She was too tired. Too weary in heart and soul.

The cool water was a relief on her hot eyes and cheeks. A breath shuddered out of her. She didn't know how long she'd been holding it.

"There," Mr. Archer murmured. "That's better."

As if she were a small child and not a woman grown! But she couldn't find it in herself to be offended. Rather the reverse. The husky, soothing tone of his deep voice worked its way into the center of her being. Like the vibration of a finely made cello, striking a pleasant, echoing hum through her veins.

She raised a hand to her face to take charge of the handkerchief. Her fingers brushed his. "Let me—"

"Of course." He relinquished his hold of it.

Laura finished mopping her face, holding the wet handkerchief over her eyes for another long while. She felt Mr. Archer draw back. Heard him get to his feet and move away from her. When she at last let the handkerchief drop, he was seated once again on the boulder, his back resting against the curving tree trunk behind him.

"The vicar's horse—" she began, her voice the veriest croak.

"Grazing happily near the road."

"You can't leave him there."

"He's quite safe, Miss Hayes."

She inhaled a steadying breath, forcing herself to meet his eyes. "Mr. Archer, I—"

"We needn't speak of it."

"But surely you—" She broke off. The last thing she wanted was to start another onslaught of tears. "You shouldn't have followed me here."

Mr. Archer regarded her from beneath lowered brows. His mouth was set in a pensive frown. "No. I most definitely shouldn't have."

Truer words Alex had never spoken. Indeed, he had the unsettling premonition that he would come to regret having gone into the woods after Laura Hayes. That doing so had been one of those impulsive decisions that would cast a shadow over the whole of his life.

But what else could he have done?

As she'd plunged into the woods, her smoke-blue eyes brimming with tears, he'd seen no other choice but to go after her. It had, in that moment, seemed a gentlemanly imperative. Not only because she'd forgotten her valise—though that had certainly provided a rational excuse. Not because she was beautiful and fascinating and vexing as all hell. Not because he *cared*. He didn't care. He couldn't. Not about her.

"I have no fortune," she'd said before attempting to leap from the carriage. "So you can have no interest in me, sir."

And she was right.

He *knew* that. It was a fact. One that couldn't be altered. Laura Hayes wasn't for him. What he needed was a quiet, uncomplicated heiress. A young lady who would permit him to go on as he had before—cold, unmoved, untouchable. A female who wouldn't rattle the very framework of his carefully crafted existence.

"You may leave now," Miss Hayes said. "I'm quite all right. Very much myself again. There's no need—"

"When you've composed yourself, I shall drive you home. And I'll hear no argument on the subject."

Her mouth tightened. He expected her to challenge him. But though she plainly bristled at his high-handed tone, she said nothing at all. Seconds later, she moved to rise on unsteady legs.

Alex went to her at once, catching both of her hands in his and helping her to her feet.

She stood in front of him for a long moment, head bent, hands clasped intimately in his. She didn't say anything. Neither did he. But something passed between them as surely as speech. He felt it resonating within him. An unseen chord—unplayed, unheard, these many years. It brought a lump to his throat, and a burning prickle to the backs of his eyes.

Her hands squeezed his once. In gratitude, he thought. And then she let him go.

"I'm ready," she said.

He inclined his head before retrieving her valise and turning back in the direction he'd left the gig. The vicar's horse was still there, loosely tethered to a tree, munching contentedly on the overgrown grass and weeds at the edge of the woods.

Miss Hayes was quiet as Alex helped her up onto the seat and then vaulted up himself. When he took up the reins, the horse reluctantly moved into action, a clump of weeds still dangling from its mouth.

"It's not far," she said, her gaze fixed on the slow-passing countryside. "Less than two miles."

It was the last she spoke to him until they reached the gates of Bramble Cottage.

Alex had never seen such a profusion of blooms. The afternoon heat was heavy with the scent of them.

He'd expected a smallish manor house, rather like the brightly polished vicarage with its cheerful red door. But there was nothing particularly cheerful about the Hayeses' home, or the delirious perfume that surrounded it. With its chipped plaster, sagging shutters, and overgrown gardens, it looked for all the world like something out of a children's fairy story. A wild, lonely place that might have been cursed or enchanted in equal measure.

"We haven't a proper gardener anymore," Miss Hayes said.

"Don't apologize." His gazed drifted from the climbing roses to the clusters of sweet peas, stock, and lavender that surrounded the gate. "It actually rather reminds me of you."

She made a sound low in her throat. "Thoroughly abandoned."

His mouth curved in a reluctant smile. "Bewitching, I was going to say."

"That's only the fragrance of the flowers. It plays havoc with everyone's senses."

Alex wasn't so sure. He would have said so, but at that instant the front door of the cottage creaked open. A portly blond lady emerged onto the path. She was garbed in acres of black silk, her chin trembling as she looked out to the drive.

"Laura?" she called. "My dearest, where have you been? We expected you an hour ago."

"My aunt Charlotte," Miss Hayes said under her breath. "I shall have to introduce you."

"By all means." He tied off the reins and set the brake before jumping from the gig to assist her down. He'd scarcely set her on the ground before she was opening the gate and dispensing with the introductions.

"Aunt Charlotte, this is Mr. Archer, a friend of Mr. Wright's from London. Mr. Archer, my aunt, Mrs. Bainbridge."

Mrs. Bainbridge looked at him, frowning. "Mr. Archer. I thank you for bringing my niece home."

"It was my pleasure, ma'am."

"She'll no doubt have told you that it was unnecessary. We make shift for ourselves in Lower Hawley." Her gaze fell on Miss Hayes's face. "Laura, what in heaven—"

"It's fine, Aunt," Miss Hayes said. "I'm fine." She shifted her valise to one hand, setting her other hand on her aunt's back. "Shall we go inside? We mustn't keep Mr. Archer. Not in this heat."

Alex stood at the end of the path, watching them go. He hadn't expected to be invited in. But as Miss Hayes and her aunt disappeared inside, the door shutting firmly behind them, he admitted to a certain curiosity—if not outright concern.

What had happened today to make Miss Hayes weep as she had? He'd never before seen a lady so desolate. So utterly undone. Certainly not a lady as self-contained and dignified as Laura Hayes.

It was something to do with her visit to London and the meeting she'd had with her solicitor. Mr. Weatherwax, wasn't that his name? It would be the work of a moment to discover more. Perhaps he could help her? Perhaps he could—

But he shouldn't.

And wouldn't.

He had no reason to do so, and every reason not to.

Alex climbed back into the gig and set the horse in motion with a slap of the reins. Bramble Cottage grew smaller behind him as he drove away from it, down the road that led past Talbot's Wood and onto Edgington Park, and thereby, his future.

He didn't look back.

Nothing in his life had ever been achieved by succumbing to sentiment. He had to think of himself. Only of himself, and his interests. For if he didn't, who else on earth would?

Chapter Seven

"I've never heard anything so preposterous!" Aunt Charlotte paced the confines of Teddy's bedroom, her silk skirts and starched petticoats swishing with every step. "The nerve of the man—the absolute, unmitigated nerve."

Laura sat in a low-backed chair beside Teddy's bed, trying not to look and sound as bleak as she felt. "It's early days yet. We still have time—"

"One month." Teddy was in his nightshirt, tucked under a quilt, his back propped up against a mountain of pillows. Magpie was curled up beside him. "And then he'll take control of everything for good and all."

Aunt Charlotte twisted her lace-trimmed handkerchief in her hands. "If my brother were alive—"

"Don't speak to me about Papa," Laura said. "The whole of this is of his devising."

"An old will. It surely doesn't reflect the reality of what was in his mind—"

"His *only* will. That's all that matters. And Mr. Weatherwax is the executor. The decisions are his to make."

Teddy's eyes met hers. "Until I come of age. That's what you've always said."

"That's what I understood to be the case." Laura gave her brother an apologetic look. "I never considered that he would argue against it. I didn't think he *could* do. But now—"

"We must simply hire another solicitor," Aunt Charlotte said. "We must challenge Mr. Weatherwax's authority."

"We can't afford another solicitor. We can scarcely afford—" Laura stopped herself from saying anything more. Indeed, she'd already said far too much.

"How bad is it, Laura?" Teddy asked.

"It isn't good," she admitted at length. "But we're not in debt. That's something, at least. And we haven't yet been forced to go hungry, or to wear rags. I have my health, and so does Aunt Charlotte. We can surely find a way to—"

"If Weatherwax won't allow us to seek a loan so that we can reopen the distilleries, what is it he means for us to do?" Teddy's expression tightened with anger. "Let me guess. He proposed that we sell them."

"He did," Laura said. "He advises that we sell all of the properties." Weatherwax had been pressing them to sell ever since Papa died. He seemed intent upon it. It was the safest course, or so he claimed.

"And if we don't, what then?" Teddy asked. "Are we to languish here, waiting on his charity?"

"It's not charity. It's our very own money. Yours, anyway, once you come of age."

"But he says that won't matter. That my coming of age doesn't matter. Because I'm crippled. Because I—"

Laura reached to briefly clasp Teddy's hand, silencing him. "He didn't say that. He merely fears that your ill health will be an impediment to your taking charge of our property. He thinks he's doing us a courtesy."

"He's threatening to take us to court to maintain his power, Laura. He's going to claim I'm incompetent. You said yourself—"

"I said too much. Perhaps I misstated his intentions."

"You didn't."

"Teddy…does it mean so very much to you to gain control of things?"

"You know it doesn't. I was going to drop it all in your lap. But this is different. Weatherwax isn't family. He's an encroaching buzzard. God knows what state our finances are truly in."

"If my brother were alive…" Aunt Charlotte wrung her hands. "He can't have meant for any of this to happen."

Laura ignored her. "It seems to me that we have three options, none of them very good."

Teddy and Aunt Charlotte both fell quiet, their gazes settling on Laura in silent expectation.

Laura took a steadying breath. "First, we can permit Mr. Weatherwax to maintain control of our finances and our property."

Teddy exploded with anger. "How can you even suggest—"

Aunt Charlotte's voice rose to match his. "That man can't be trusted an inch—"

"Yes, yes." Laura held up a hand. "But we must consider, if Mr. Weatherwax maintains control, we shall go on—I assume—much in the same way we have been since Papa died. Things will be tight, but we shall rub along well enough as long as no catastrophe befalls us. If circumstances become too grim, we can always consider selling one of the properties."

Aunt Charlotte's lips thinned. "I cannot like it, Laura."

"Nor I." Teddy folded his arms. "What's our second option?"

Magpie chose that moment to uncurl himself, stand up, and perform a languorous stretch. When he'd finished, he jumped from the bed, landing on the wood floor with a thump. The door creaked on its hinges as he let himself out of the room.

Laura rubbed her forehead. She could feel the beginnings of a megrim. "We can hire another solicitor to challenge Mr. Weatherwax. We'd have to borrow the money to pay him somehow. Perhaps from Henrietta? She's never been tight-fisted. And then...we'd just have to hope that the new solic-itor would prevail. For if he didn't..."

"If he didn't," Aunt Charlotte said grimly, "then we'd have made an enemy of Weatherwax to no good purpose."

Laura nodded. "Exactly. And I don't like to say so, but...I sense a vindictiveness in Mr. Weatherwax. If we fought him and lost, I suspect he would show us no mercy."

Teddy's narrow face had gone a shade paler, the blue shadows under his eyes becoming more pronounced. "And our third option?"

Laura's stomach clenched into a knot. "That's a bit trick-ier." She hesitated, her mouth suddenly dry. "By rights, a half interest in Hayes's Perfumes should be mine."

"Only if you marry before your twenty-fifth birthday, my dear," Aunt Charlotte said. "And even then, the half interest would belong to your husband, not to you. My brother didn't believe in ladies involving themselves in the family business. Foolish man."

"I daresay Papa thought he was being fair and equitable. He didn't allow for the fact that I'd be a spinster, and Teddy would be an invalid."

"It hardly matters now," Aunt Charlotte replied. "With you unmarried, the whole of it goes to Teddy. And since Weatherwax is going to claim Teddy is too frail to take control—"

"But if you marry—" Teddy looked at Laura, his gaze burning with a new intensity. "You would have a half share."

Laura gave her brother a rueful grimace. "My husband would, anyway."

"Husband?" Aunt Charlotte looked between the two of them in confusion. "What husband?"

"And therein lies the difficulty." Laura leaned back in her seat. "Who would I marry? Or—more to the point—who in the world could be prevailed upon to marry *me*?"

Aunt Charlotte stopped pacing and turned to face them. "Why, it must be George Wright, of course! Heaven's above, I don't know why I didn't see it straightaway. You've always worn the willow for him. And now he's returned—"

"Not George," Laura said, a touch sharply. "Even if he did wish to marry me—which he doesn't—"

"How do you know—?"

"I know. I also know that I'd never marry him. Not if he were the last gentleman on earth."

Aunt Charlotte's face fell. "But then…what other choice is there? Single gentlemen aren't in abundance in Lower Hawley. Certainly none who would be willing to marry into a family such as ours."

"No," Laura said. "We haven't much to recommend us, have we? And we've very little time before my birthday arrives. Not even enough time to call the banns." She moistened her lips. "Which is why…I think we're going to have to settle for option two. We'll consult with another solicitor."

"How?" Teddy wondered. "You've already said we haven't the money for it."

"I'll ask Henrietta to lend it to us. Just the consulting fee, mind. We don't even know yet if we have a case against Mr. Weatherwax. I don't want us pressing forward with no hope of success. There are unscrupulous solicitors who would happily wring every last penny out of us in pursuing fruitless claims. We must proceed with caution."

"Perhaps we should speak with a local solicitor?" Aunt Charlotte suggested. "Someone in Guildford or—"

"No, it must be London. We need a solicitor who's canny, as well as capable." Laura reached for her reticule. "A maid-servant at Mr. Weatherwax's office recommended someone."

"A maidservant!" Aunt Charlotte's brows shot up. "What would a maidservant know?"

"I haven't any idea. But she gave me a solicitor's card." Laura withdrew it from her reticule and handed it to her brother. "Someone in Fleet Street."

Teddy looked it over with a frown. "Thomas Finchley, Esquire."

Laura nodded. "The best solicitor in London, apparently. I shall write him a letter this very afternoon. Then, in the morning, I shall call on Henrietta and broach the subject of a loan."

Aunt Charlotte's face creased with worry. "And if Mr. Weatherwax finds out?"

Laura rose from her chair. "We shall simply have to pray that he doesn't."

Alex leaned back against the trunk of the oak tree under which Miss Talbot had spread out their picnic blanket. Or rather, one of her footmen had. The liveried servants had followed along behind them from the house, carrying plates, cutlery, and provisions, as they traipsed the grounds of Edgington Park looking for the perfect picnic spot.

Henrietta Talbot was in her element. Kneeling in a heap of fine muslin skirts and ruffled petticoats, she doled out cold roast chicken and other comestibles from a hamper. "For you, George." She handed him a plate heaped with food.

George took it, barely succeeding in hiding a flinch. At the vicarage, he hadn't been able to keep down his breakfast. "What I need," he'd said earlier that morning, "is the hair of the dog that bit me."

"What you need," Alex had returned, "is to attend to your debts."

It had been enough to sober George. And when Miss Talbot's invitation had arrived from Edgington Park, summoning the pair of them to a picnic on the grounds, he hadn't dared to refuse.

Alex's gaze drifted over him before settling, once again, on Miss Hayes. She was resting on her hip not far from Miss Talbot, her more modest spill of linen skirts bunched up about her ankles, revealing a glimpse of well-worn leather half boots. Since her arrival, only minutes before they'd departed the house, she'd been assiduously avoiding meeting his eyes.

While he couldn't seem to stop himself from looking at her.

It was aggravating at best. Infuriating at worst. When it came to Laura Hayes, he appeared incapable of exercising control.

By rights, he should have been angry at himself. Instead, he was irritated with her.

The plaguing female.

There were faint shadows under her smoke-blue eyes, and a general air of distraction to her manner. She'd hardly strung five words together since they'd sat down.

"You're peaky, Laura." Miss Talbot passed her a plate of food. "You must eat something."

George picked at the chicken on his own plate with a grimace. "No one could eat the amount you've given us, Hen. You've been too generous, as always."

"I suppose you'd rather I brought something from Papa's cellar," Miss Talbot said. "But you can't drink your meals, George. You'll make yourself ill."

"By the by, what *have* you brought to drink?" George asked. "Lemonade, I suppose."

"Naturally. And a bottle of elderberry wine—"

"Aha!"

"—of which you may have *one* glass. Really, I don't know what sort of dissipated life you've been leading in London, but you're home now, and you can't make such a spectacle of yourself as you did when you came to dine at the Park."

"Every fellow drinks to excess on occasion," George grumbled. "Even your father, I daresay."

Miss Talbot glanced at Alex. "Even you, Mr. Archer?"

George laughed. "Archer doesn't do anything to excess."

Alex accepted a plate of food from Miss Talbot. "A man mustn't be a slave to his vices."

"A commendable philosophy," she said. "Don't you agree, Laura?"

Miss Hayes looked up from peeling an orange. For a fraction of a second her eyes locked with his. "Indeed."

Alex's fingers tightened on his plate. He felt the unwelcome urge to draw her away somewhere private. To *talk* with her. To find out if she was safe and well—and to ask if there was anything he could do to alleviate her burdens.

The last was perhaps the most disturbing impulse of all.

He turned his attention to Miss Talbot. She was cutting her chicken into dainty, ladylike bites. She was beautiful. And surprisingly astute, as well. He hadn't expected her to reprimand George for his drinking, however gently. "Do you often picnic on the grounds?"

"If I can get a party of friends together. Everything is better in company, don't you find? But it must be a select company, else it fast grows tedious." Miss Talbot popped a piece of chicken into her mouth. "You look skeptical, sir, but there is good society to be had in Lower Hawley."

"I don't doubt it," Alex said. "Country villages hide all manner of treasures." Miss Talbot blushed prettily, but it was Miss Hayes's face to which his gaze gravitated, quite against his will. "The housekeeper at the vicarage mentioned a Roman ruin."

George reclined back on his elbows, his plate of food abandoned beside him. "An old heap of moldering stones. It used to bring in all sorts of cranks to the village."

Miss Talbot made a face. "It still does on occasion. And Papa still permits them onto the grounds."

"They were a ramshackle lot." George looked at Miss Hayes with a sudden grin. "Do you remember that German fellow? The one who kept asking you to translate for him?"

Miss Hayes continued to section her orange. "He was a harmless tourist."

"He was impertinent," Miss Talbot retorted.

"Do you speak German, Miss Hayes?" Alex asked.

She briefly met his eyes again. "A very little. Not enough to mention."

George laughed. "She said hello to his party of travelers *auf deutsch* and the fellow was smitten."

"Hardly." Miss Hayes ate a section of her orange, pausing to wipe the juice from her mouth with her napkin. "They were friendly people, that's all. And happy to meet anyone here who spoke their language." She glanced at Alex. "My father was accustomed to traveling to France for his business. He sometimes ventured into Germany, as well. And even into Spain, on occasion. He could greet everyone in their own language."

Alex smiled slightly. "And taught you to do the same?"

She sectioned another wedge from her orange. "He didn't plan on my brother and me remaining all of our lives in Lower Hawley."

"I'd have invited your brother today if I thought he'd come," Miss Talbot said. "It's been ages since I've seen him. He was always such a dear, trailing after me wherever I went. Why, he must be practically a man grown by now."

"He'll be one and twenty next month," Miss Hayes replied.

Miss Talbot looked aghast. "One and twenty? Good lord. It makes me feel positively aged."

George snorted.

"How in the world does he occupy himself?" Miss Talbot asked.

"Sketching and painting, mostly," Miss Hayes said. "He's become a competent landscape artist, and he's quite skilled at sketching wildlife. I've encouraged him to submit some of his drawings to a natural science journal in Edinburgh."

"Have you? Perhaps I shall hire him to paint my portrait one day." She gave Miss Hayes a beneficent smile. "You may tell him so. It will give him something to aspire to."

Alex wondered if Miss Talbot's condescension rankled. Miss Hayes hadn't yet shown any impatience with her friend. And there was no sharp edge to her tone when she addressed Miss Talbot. But Alex couldn't imagine anyone not feeling some degree of resentment. He knew all too well what it was like to be of unequal status. A veneer of respectability—of wealth and reputation—had done nothing to quell decades of feeling inadequate.

He'd been only a stripling lad when he'd left North Devon, angry and desperate—willing to do anything to get away. He'd even been willing to betray his friends. What use were they when the rest of his life was a misery? Better to save himself. To find a way to forge ahead on his own.

He hadn't reckoned on what his life would be like without them.

There was no one now who truly knew him. No one he could confide in. No one he could trust. His life on the continent had been that of a well-heeled vagabond. Alone in both good times and bad. A man with no purpose, except to survive.

Which is why he'd come home to England. If there was purpose to be found, it was here, in the land. Money couldn't buy true belonging. For that, one needed property. A tie to the soil. Plenty of men had married country-bred heiresses to obtain it. Why shouldn't he?

When Squire Talbot had taken him out to inspect the home farm, he'd regaled him with information about crop rotation, fertilization, and the various benefits of livestock feed. Edgington Park was a well-run enterprise. The workers seemed capable, and the tenants happy. Alex was certain that he could find happiness there, too.

He didn't feel it now. He didn't feel anything for the estate, truth be told. Nothing save the overwhelming determination to have it. As for happiness and contentment—that sense of connection, of being made whole—he trusted that would follow when at last the Park was his.

It had to.

They finished their luncheon, Miss Talbot presiding over their conversation like a queen amongst her loyal subjects. Nothing of importance was discussed. They spoke of trifling things: Squire Talbot's new barouche, the sweetness of this year's summer fruit, and the shipment of sprigged muslin that had just arrived at the village draper.

"I've ordered a new dress to be made from it. The same style Empress Eugénie is known to favor." Miss Talbot smoothed her skirts. "Not too dissimilar from this one."

Alex was no expert on women's clothing, but he knew the power the Empress of France wielded when it came to the shape of a lady's hat or the size of her crinoline. "You're an admirer of hers, I take it."

"Every lady is. The empress sets the fashion for the civilized world. Isn't that right, Laura?"

Miss Hayes didn't disagree. "She inspired a perfume some years ago. Empress Eugénie's Nosegay. I watched my father make it once. It had extract of musk in it, and geraniums, roses, and vanilla. It was quite a distinctive scent."

Alex looked at her, wishing to God he didn't find her so fascinating. "Do you know how to make perfume, Miss Hayes?"

"Not very well. But my father sometimes permitted me to accompany him to the distillery. I made it my habit to watch everything he did there. To teach myself a little of the business." A faint smile edged her mouth. "The power of observation."

His gaze held hers. "I know it well."

And so he did. Nearly everything he'd learned about being a gentleman had been learned through observing others. He'd had no teacher. No mentor. Only his own wits to guide him.

It had helped that the gaming clubs where he plied his trade attracted men of every class. There were ample opportunities to practice his skill at aping the manners, speech, and bearing of titled lords and well-to-do businessmen. Plenty of chances to learn how to comport himself.

And how not to comport himself.

George tipped his hat down over his face. "By God, it's hot."

"Don't you dare fall asleep," Miss Talbot warned. "We're going to walk to the Roman ruin after lunch."

"The devil we are."

"Mr. Archer hasn't seen it yet."

"Then take him there," George said, "by all means."

Alex said not a word. For once, George was doing what he was supposed to do. He was arranging for Alex to be alone with Miss Talbot. Alex should have been glad of it. It was all part of the plan. And yet…

The end result left him uneasy. Not only would *he* be alone with Miss Talbot, *George* would be alone with Miss Hayes.

She'd slapped his face once, George had said.

He'd also said that he couldn't marry her. Which meant that he'd *considered* marrying her. Which meant that he was attracted to her, damn him. And that he couldn't be trusted.

"We should all go," Alex said abruptly. "Or none of us."

Miss Talbot dropped her plate down on the blanket. "On second thought, you can show Mr. Archer the ruins, Laura. It will give me the opportunity to speak with George alone."

George peered at her from beneath his hat. "Don't be daft, Hen. It's you who's hostess, not Laura."

"I don't mind it." Alex rose from his place under the tree. He dusted off his trousers. "I could do with a bit of exercise."

It was a strategic mistake. He needed to remain with Miss Talbot. It was she who held the key to his future, not Laura Hayes. Indeed, the more time he spent in Miss Hayes's company, the more risk he ran of doing something foolish. Something that would endanger his entire scheme.

Miss Hayes's eyes found his. "It's more than a bit of exercise. It's three hills away. Three *steep* hills. We'd be well advised to skip it in this weather."

"A Roman ruin? Nonsense. I'd be glad to have a look at it." He held out his hand to her. "Shall we?"

Laura walked along at Mr. Archer's side over the grassy, tree-scattered grounds of Edgington Park. She didn't know how she'd ended up escorting him to the Roman ruin. She should have made some greater objection. It wouldn't have taken much. The whole point of her being here was to act as chaperone. In setting off with Mr. Archer, she wasn't only abdicating her duties to Henrietta and Squire Talbot, she was failing in her duties to her family.

She had to get Henrietta alone so that she could ask her for the money to hire a new solicitor. She'd meant to call on her this morning, but moments before she'd set out, an invitation had arrived from Edgington Park.

"A picnic," Aunt Charlotte had said in disbelief. "In this heat?"

And it *was* hot. Dreadfully so. Perspiration dotted Laura's forehead and pooled in the hollow of her bosom. She was thankful for the broad brim of her straw hat shielding her face. As for the rest of her—a linen day dress wasn't very cool when combined with stockings, petticoats, corset, and horsehair crinoline.

Mr. Archer couldn't be feeling much more comfortable. His sack coat was unbuttoned, his cravat loose at his neck.

"You'll never win Miss Talbot this way," she said as they crested the final hill.

He shot her a sharp look. "What way?"

"By going off alone with me. You'd have done better to have stayed with her."

"I did try."

"Not very hard."

He shrugged. "She obviously wished to speak with Mr. Wright about something."

"Scold him, more like."

A grim smile edged Mr. Archer's mouth. "I'm certain he deserves it."

"Probably, but it's not likely to have much effect. Lectures and scolds have never achieved anything with George, except to hasten his departure from Lower Hawley."

"The vicar doesn't strike me as a particularly stern parent."

"He wields his authority gently, but he does wield it. I suppose that over time it must have begun to pall."

"Death by a million cuts?"

"Something like that."

He fell silent a moment. And then: "You and Mr. Wright have a history." It wasn't a question.

Laura glanced at him. "Has he said so?"

Mr. Archer met her eyes. "He says that two years ago you slapped his face."

She inwardly flinched. What had the pair of them been discussing for *that* to have come up? She shuddered to think. "I'm surprised he admitted it."

"He was half-seas."

She huffed a short laugh. "Naturally."

"Did you?"

"Did I what?"

"Slap him across the face?"

She held Mr. Archer's gaze. "With all of my strength."

He looked steadily back at her, his expression completely unreadable. "He doesn't have anything to do with what happened yesterday, does he?"

"George?" She stopped short at the top of the hill, under the wide branches of a magnificent yew tree with a split trunk. A stretch of grass spread out before them, the stones of the Roman ruin in the distance. "No. Why would he?"

Mr. Archer stopped as well. The tree cast his face in shadow. "I haven't any idea. I don't know what upset you." He paused. "I'd like to know."

"Why?"

"Perhaps…" He looked away from her, the lines of his firm jaw set as immoveable as granite. "Perhaps I could help you."

Her stomach trembled. It was nerves. Either that or the threat of butterflies. One was as bad as the other. "You can't."

"Try me."

His deep voice sent another tremor through her core. "The ruin," she said. "We should—"

"It's thousands of years old. It can wait another hour."

An hour? Did he mean for them to linger here together— to talk—for as long as that?

Under other circumstances, Laura might have resisted. But she was hot and tired, and overwhelmed by her responsibilities. A good night's sleep had done little to remedy her poor spirits. "Very well. But I shouldn't like anything I tell you to go further."

Mr. Archer turned back to her, a glint of wry humor in his eyes. "I can keep a secret, Miss Hayes."

"I expect you can. But these aren't just *my* secrets. They're my family's secrets."

"I'll guard them as if they were my own."

Laura didn't know why, but she believed him. And she wanted to unburden herself. Needed to most desperately. "I've told you about my father's perfume business."

His mouth hitched at the corner in that wolfish way of his. "Hayes's Lavender Water, suitable for mothers and sweethearts alike."

"Yes, well…since my father's death, the business—what remains of it—has been under the control of his solicitor."

"The fellow you visited in London?"

"An odious gentleman who won't permit us to do as we like with the property that was left to us." She walked deeper beneath the branches, arms folded at her waist. "It's meant to come to my brother at his majority, but yesterday…I learned that Mr. Weatherwax is refusing to cede control."

Mr. Archer followed after her into the deep shadow of the yew tree. He removed his hat. "Can he?"

"He says that my brother is unfit, purely because he's an invalid. He says that he'll happily take us to court to prove it. Unless I can find a way to challenge him, my family must resign themselves to living on the quarterly allowance he provides us. It isn't enough. Not nearly."

"I suppose it's out of the question to simply ask the man for more money?"

"There isn't any more. But there could be. There *could* be. If only the business were in the hands of someone who wasn't afraid to take a few risks."

"Your brother?"

She nearly laughed. "Not my brother. *Me*."

"Ah, I see."

"You don't." She could read as much in his face. "You think I'm just a silly impetuous female. But sometimes, Mr. Archer, in life as well as business, we must be bold. We must risk everything to gain even more. And so I would have done if my brother gained control."

His brows lowered. "I don't think you're silly, Miss Hayes."

"No?"

"I think you're…"

"What?" she asked.

But he didn't answer.

She bit her lip. Despite the intimacy of their previous meetings, he was still practically a stranger. His approval shouldn't mean anything to her one way or the other. But it did. For whatever reason, it meant a great deal.

"What recourse do you have against your solicitor?" he asked.

Laura exhaled. "Very little, as far as I can tell."

She refused to mention the possibility of her marriage. It was less than two weeks until her twenty-fifth birthday. So... not even a possibility anymore. Not unless some noble, heroic figure were to gallop up on a white horse and carry her away to Gretna Green.

"The only thing I can think of is for us to hire another solicitor to challenge Mr. Weatherwax's authority. But—" She blushed. "We can't afford it."

Mr. Archer's gaze seemed to soften. "You needn't be embarrassed."

She turned her face from his. She couldn't bear to see him looking at her with compassion—or, even worse, pity. "I'm not embarrassed. There are others far worse off than we are. But when I think of Teddy, and all the things we could be doing to help him get well, if only..." A bitter laugh emerged from her throat. "*If only*. The two most useless words in existence."

"And two of the most oft uttered."

She leaned her back against the tree trunk, forcing herself to once again meet his eyes. "I've written to a solicitor in London. I hope to hear from him by the end of the week."

Mr. Archer rested his hand on the trunk. It was inches from her shoulder. "How much do you require to hire him?"

"I don't know yet. Whatever it is, I intend to ask Miss Talbot to lend it to me." She gave him a humorless smile. "Perhaps you and I aren't so very different after all. Each of us hoping to gain a little of her fortune."

He arched a brow. "Only a little?"

"All of it, in your case. Unless you've changed your mind about pursuing her?"

"Is there any reason I should?"

Laura didn't answer. She could think of several reasons. But she didn't want to talk to him about Henrietta.

"Miss Hayes," he said. "If you need money for a solicitor, it would be my privilege to give it to you."

His offer was as surprising as it was unseemly. Any lady would be properly offended. And Laura was, to a certain degree. At the same time, an unsettling surge of gratitude clogged her throat, just as when he'd offered her coins at the wishing bridge. "I'm obliged to you, but...I could never accept it. You must know that."

"Why not?"

"For the obvious reasons. Because you're a single gentleman, and I'm an unmarried lady. It would be scandalous to accept money from you."

"I don't see why. No one would ever have to know about it. It could be our secret."

She frowned at the thought. "And then I'd be indebted to you."

"A gift, I said. Not a loan."

"It would still put me under an obligation."

"Would that be so bad? To be obligated to me in some way?"

"I believe it would. Besides, if the solicitor fails to wrest control from Mr. Weatherwax, I'd have no way to repay you."

"I think you might," he said. And then, before she had a moment's inkling of his intention, he bent his head to hers and kissed her, very gently, on the lips.

A flush of unexpected warmth infused Laura's veins. For the barest instant, her mouth softened under his. And then—

Common sense returned with all of the force of a steam-powered locomotive.

She jerked back from him with a start, nearly conking her head against the tree trunk. "I *beg* your pardon!"

Mr. Archer stared down at her. He appeared as stunned as she felt. Indeed, to judge from his slack-jawed look of astonishment, one might think she'd transformed into some variety of mythical creature at the merest touch of his lips. A mermaid, perhaps.

Or a two-headed monster.

It was a lowering thought.

His hand fell from the tree. "Miss Hayes—" He broke off. "Laura—"

"Don't," she warned him. "Don't dare presume some greater intimacy—"

"Forgive me." He took a step back from her. "I don't know what I was thinking." An incredulous laugh. "Nothing, apparently. I think I must have run mad."

More lowering still.

Laura was glad of the set down, however unintentional. She'd rather be angry and insulted than hurt—or tempted. "Do you often go about kissing ladies in such a hurly-burly fashion?"

"Never." He raked his fingers through his hair. "Truly, Miss Hayes. I'm sorry for having offended you. I daresay it was all of this talk of boldness and taking risks. I lost my head for a moment. It won't happen again."

His apology should have mollified her. He meant it— anyone could see that. And she *did* believe him. He wouldn't kiss her again.

She should have been relieved. Instead, she felt vaguely disappointed.

Brief though it was, Mr. Archer's kiss had been nothing like George's. Her heart was still thumping rapidly from the wonder of it. So soft and tender—and so very surprising to them both.

"Why did you do it?" Her voice was almost a whisper. "Is it because I'm in reduced circumstances? Because I haven't a father or a brother to defend me from—"

"No." His denial was quick and fierce. "It has nothing to do with your station in life. My God. If you only knew—"

"Then why?"

"Because…there's something between us. Some thread of connection. I feel it every time I look at you."

"I feel it, too," she admitted.

He gave her a tormented look. "Do you?"

She nodded. There was no point in denying it. "I wish I didn't feel it."

"I wish the same. But now we've acknowledged it…perhaps we've robbed it of its power. We can move on. Forget any of this ever happened."

"*Can* you forget?" she asked.

Mr. Archer settled his hat back on his head. "I'm sure as hell going to try."

Chapter Eight

Over the next three days, Laura saw Mr. Archer often, but never again did she confide in him as she had on the way to the Roman ruin. And never again did he attempt to kiss her. He scarcely looked at her, truth be told. All of his energies were directed toward Henrietta—walking with her, talking with her, and generally making himself agreeable.

When they went to the village shops, Mr. Archer sat next to Henrietta in the barouche. When she played the pianoforte in the Edgington Park music room, he was at her side, turning the pages of her music. And when they strolled in the Edgington Park rose garden, he bent his head to Henrietta's, sharing private words with her that provoked her blushes and laughter.

Laura wasn't jealous. How could she be? She had no claim on Mr. Archer, and wasn't likely to ever have one. She had no fortune to lure him. Nothing but her poor self and whatever meager attraction he felt toward her.

Not that it really mattered.

She had too much on her mind to care what Mr. Archer was up to with Henrietta.

Even so…after three days in company with him, his single-minded attention to her friend began to grate. How changeable he was! How utterly adept at playing the doting suitor. Was there nothing real about the man? Nothing meaningful or true?

He seemed a sinister chameleon, capable of changing his personality to suit his company. There was nothing of the honest gruffness she'd experienced in him when he'd hauled her out of the pond, nor of the gentleness he'd shown her when he'd dried her tears. He cast her no brooding glances, and showed no signs of the frustration he'd exhibited when he'd backed away from her under the yew tree. Indeed, there appeared to be nothing authentic about Alex Archer at all.

On Sunday, Laura saw him in church. He was seated in a pew at the front, along with George, Henrietta, and Squire Talbot. It was the pew reserved for the squire and his family, a seat of honor many rows away from where Laura humbly sat with her Aunt Charlotte.

After the service, Mr. Archer lingered behind to be introduced to some of the villagers.

Henrietta glanced back at him with a smug smile as she and Laura walked out of the church together. "He's not as handsome as George," she said, "but he *is* handsome."

Laura didn't know how her friend could say so. With his dark good looks and commanding height, Mr. Archer fairly put George in the shade. To Laura's mind, there was no comparison at all. "Are you considering marrying him?"

Henrietta's voice dropped to a whisper. "Marriage? My goodness, Laura. The things you say."

"Well?"

Squire Talbot's barouche was waiting ahead, the coachman seated on the box, and a footman poised to open the door for his mistress.

"He hasn't asked me," Henrietta said. "I've only known him a week."

"A week in which you've been in his company every single day."

"As have you," Henrietta returned. "And you're not in expectation of a proposal."

"I've seen more of George, of late, than I have of Mr. Archer."

It was the truth. Since Mr. Archer had turned his attentions to Henrietta, Laura had been thrust into George's company far more than she cared to be. Granted, things between them were a little easier. But she didn't trust George. There was a furtive sort of restlessness about him. As if he were counting the seconds until he could get away from Lower Hawley and back to the depraved life he'd been living in town.

"Poor George," Henrietta said with sigh. "He's not the best company, is he? I expect he finds all the fresh air and outdoor activity a tedious ordeal."

"It's good for him," Laura said. "Whether he likes it or not."

"My feelings exactly." Henrietta stopped not far from her father's barouche. "I'm pleased that Mr. Archer enjoys the country. He's very well suited to Lower Hawley, don't you think?"

What Laura thought was that Mr. Archer would be well suited anywhere. She wondered how he really felt about their little village. How appealing would ruralizing be if there wasn't the promise of a fortune at the end of it? Not very appealing at all, she suspected. "He's certainly been game enough for all of the activities you've planned."

"Yes, he's very indulgent of my whims. And Papa approves of him, too. The two of them get on so well together." Henrietta gave Laura a narrow glance. "Do you know, I thought he looked at you rather too much in the beginning. Now he looks at you not at all."

"Mr. Archer?"

"I daresay he found you interesting at first. Even pretty."

Laura recognized the sharp hint of jealousy in Henrietta's tone. It instantly put her on her guard. She couldn't afford to make an enemy of Henrietta Talbot. Especially not when she'd only just borrowed twenty pounds from her.

It was too much, but Henrietta had insisted.

"You will pay it back, of course," she'd said. "Within a twelve-month, shall we say? At six percent interest?"

Laura's stomach clenched just to think of it. She hadn't expected that Henrietta would make her a gift of the money. She'd fully intended to pay it back, whatever the sum. But her friend's businesslike attitude toward the request—speaking of payment terms and interest, and even requiring Laura to sign a note—had made Laura distinctly uneasy.

"Nonsense," she said. "Mr. Archer is completely smitten with you."

"Do you really think so?" Henrietta asked.

"I know it." Laura felt like a liar and a fraud. Even worse, she felt like a poor friend. She should be warning Henrietta, not encouraging her. "But, Hen…"

"If you're going to tell me that I know nothing about him, and that he may very well be a fortune hunter, you may save your breath to cool your porridge." Henrietta resumed walking to the barouche. The footman opened the door for her and assisted her up into her seat. "I have it all well in hand, Laura."

Laura stood at the arched iron gate at the edge of the church's small graveyard. Carriages and smaller gigs of every type jockeyed for position on the road—some coachmen waiting to retrieve their masters and mistresses, and some attempting to leave with their occupants in tow.

Parishioners were still spilling out of the church. Sunday services with Mr. Wright were generally well attended, but this Sunday it seemed the entire village had turned out to celebrate George's return—and to get a glimpse of the mysterious friend he'd brought back with him from London.

When Squire Talbot finally arrived at his barouche, ready to depart, he wasn't alone. Mr. Archer was with him, smiling at whatever it was the squire was telling him.

Laura's fingers tightened on her prayer book. She felt a flicker of self-consciousness. Even more so when Mr. Archer's gray gaze briefly fell to hers. He immediately looked away, but not before she'd seen that his smile of a moment before had disappeared.

"Miss Hayes," Squire Talbot said. "Good day to you."

"Good day, sir." She doubted whether anyone heard her. Henrietta was immediately occupied with addressing Mr. Archer, and the squire was busy climbing up into the seat of his barouche and issuing instructions to the coachman.

Laura turned and went back into the church to collect her aunt. She found her slumped in the front pew, the vicar standing over her with a look of concern. "What is it?" Laura hurried up the aisle. "What's happened?"

Aunt Charlotte waved her away. "Only a dizzy spell." Her face was flushed, twin spots of color standing out on her cheeks. "I'm quite recovered now."

"It's the heat," the vicar said.

"Is that all?" Laura sat down beside her. "Are you certain it's not your heart, Aunt?"

"No. I don't believe so. Though it is racing a trifle." Aunt Charlotte gave her an apologetic look. "Perhaps we should summon Dr. Taylor?"

Laura rubbed a reassuring hand up and down Aunt Charlotte's silk-clad arm. "Yes, I daresay we should." It would be another expense, but Laura didn't begrudge it. Some things were too important. "Where is your fan?"

"In my reticule."

Laura retrieved it. It was a painted paper confection, more decorative than useful. She nevertheless snapped it open and waved it briskly in the vicinity of Aunt Charlotte's face.

"Best take her home, Miss Hayes," the vicar said, "and see that she has something cool to drink."

"Are you able to walk back to the cottage?" Laura asked.

The vicar's brows shot up over the rims of his spectacles. "You walked here? Oh dear. I didn't consider." He looked about him. "I can't think where my son has got to, but— Ah! Here is Mr. Archer."

Laura looked up with a start. Mr. Archer was coming up the aisle toward them, his tall beaver hat in his hand.

"Mrs. Bainbridge has taken a turn, I fear," the vicar told him. "Can I trouble you to drive them home in the gig?"

"Oh no," Aunt Charlotte objected. "I wouldn't dream of imposing—"

"I'll hear no objections." The vicar smiled. "Mr. Archer would be only too happy to oblige, wouldn't you, sir?"

Mr. Archer inclined his head. "Of course. I'll fetch the gig from the stable."

Laura sat with Aunt Charlotte until he returned. He didn't send someone to tell them he and the gig were ready. Instead, he came back into the church himself and offered Aunt Charlotte his arm.

"Mrs. Bainbridge? If you'd care to lean on me?"

Aunt Charlotte took hold of his arm gratefully. "Thank you, Mr. Archer. I confess, I feel quite undone."

Laura walked along with them, eyeing her aunt with worry. The gig was waiting at the gates, the padded seat only big enough for two. She took a step backward. "If you'll drive my aunt back to the cottage, I'll join her there presently."

Mr. Archer's gaze jerked to hers. "You mean to walk back?"

"Yes, I— *Oh!*" She emitted an unladylike squeak as he caught her round the waist and tossed her up onto the seat. Her skirts billowed about her. "There isn't room," she protested. "I don't mind walking—"

"We'll fit," he said grimly.

And they did.

Though it meant that Laura was pressed shoulder to knees against Mr. Archer's side the entire way home. She scarcely drew breath until he stopped the gig in front of the cottage and jumped down. When next she looked at him, he was vaguely red about the collar. Perhaps he'd felt the discomfort of it, too? The peculiar sensation of being so close to a person of the opposite sex. A person that one was strangely attracted to. That one had kissed.

Then again, perhaps it was only the heat?

He helped Aunt Charlotte down from the gig.

Laura didn't wait for him to help her, too. She caught her skirts up to one side and leapt down herself. Mr. Archer shot her a dark look. "I'll run ahead and get one of the servants," she said.

By the time she ran through the gates and up the path, John Yardley was already at the door. She quickly explained what had happened, and with his assistance, she and Mr. Archer got Aunt Charlotte into the house and up the stairs to her bedroom.

"Laura?" Teddy called out from his room across the hall. "What's going on?"

"In a moment, my dear," she called back. "Yardley? Fetch Mrs. Crabtree with my aunt's tonic." And then to Mr. Archer: "If you could just help me get her onto the bed?"

"Allow me," he said. "If I may, Mrs. Bainbridge?"

"I fear I'm too heavy," Aunt Charlotte protested.

"Nonsense." Mr. Archer settled Aunt Charlotte effortlessly onto the mattress, pausing to adjust a pile of goose-down pillows behind her back.

In that moment, Laura's heart swelled with an emotion that was almost painful. It was something more than gratitude. Something more than anything she'd ever felt for a gentleman before.

She turned abruptly away.

"What is it, my dear?" Aunt Charlotte's voice was tremulous. "You've not taken ill, too, have you?"

Laura gave a huff of laughter. "Wouldn't that be a marvelous end to our day." She turned back to face her aunt. "I'm fine, you know that. I'm *always* fine."

"Miss Laura?" Mrs. Crabtree came to the door, a brown medicine bottle in her hand. She'd been their cook since Laura was a child, and after Papa's death had taken on the additional role of housekeeper. Any other servant would have left them by now, but Mary Crabtree was loyal to the bone. "I've brought Mrs. Bainbridge's tonic."

"At last." Aunt Charlotte extended her hand to Mrs. Crabtree. "You go on now, Laura, and tend to your brother. Mrs. Crabtree is all I need."

"Tonic first," Laura said. She waited while Mrs. Crabtree administered it.

Aunt Charlotte swallowed a spoonful and leaned back with a sigh. "My heart is calming already. Don't send for the doctor, Laura. Let me rest awhile first. The tonic may be all I need."

"Are you certain?"

"Yes, yes. Give me an hour and we shall see. No need to have Dr. Taylor ride out for nothing." Aunt Charlotte smiled weakly at Mr. Archer. "Thank you for coming to my aid, sir. So very kind of you."

"I'm at your service, ma'am," Mr. Archer said.

"Laura!" Teddy called out again.

Laura left her aunt's room, Mr. Archer close behind her. "My brother," she said. "If you'll give me a moment."

"I should like to meet him."

"Would you?" Laura looked up at him. Her pulse skipped. He was unnervingly close. "I'll have to ask him. He may not be well enough for visitors today."

"I'll wait."

She rapped once on Teddy's door before entering. He was at his desk, sitting up straight in his wheeled chair, a pile of half-finished drawings strewn before him.

"What the devil is going on?" he demanded. "Is someone here?"

She told him about Aunt Charlotte—and about Mr. Archer's assistance. "He'd like to be introduced to you, if you feel equal to it."

Teddy made an impatient gesture in the direction of the door. "Send him in."

Alex wandered down the upstairs hall of the cottage while Miss Hayes talked with her brother. It was lined with wood-paneled doors, the floor covered with a worn floral carpet. Not all of the doors were shut. A few hung half-open on their hinges, giving glimpses of what lie within. In one, he saw a heavy four-poster bed with faded blue hangings. It had a needlework quilt spread across the bottom of it, and a walnut table at its side, adorned with an oil lamp and a pewter jug of freshly cut flowers.

Miss Hayes's room, he'd wager.

There was a faint fragrance to it. Roses and lavender, and freshly starched petticoats. Something sweet and clean and unmistakably *her*.

He gave the door a gentle push. It swung wide, revealing a marble fireplace, an imposing mahogany wardrobe, and a silk-draped dressing table littered with feminine bric-a-brac. His gaze drifted over the crystal perfume bottles, enameled containers, and set of silver-plated hairbrushes.

How easy it was to imagine her sitting there, arranging her ebony hair. His chest tightened with unwelcome emotion at the thought of it.

Helpless frustration followed.

What the devil was he doing? Lurking about outside Miss Hayes's bedroom like some starving stray dog outside of a butcher's shop?

But the room called to him, just as its owner did. *Home*, it seemed to say. A place of respite, and peace. Of crisp sheets and soft pillows.

The orphanage had had none of those things. There, he'd slept in a cold dormitory with dozens of other boys, housed two to a bed. He and Tom Finchley had shared a mattress of perpetually damp, insect-ridden straw. It had never been clean enough. Warm enough.

It had never been a home.

Not like Bramble Cottage. And not like Miss Hayes's room, the intimacy of it beckoning to him so sweetly. It took an effort to withdraw from her door and return back the way he'd come.

He'd spent the past three days avoiding her. As much as she *could* be avoided when she was acting as companion to Henrietta Talbot.

And now, here he was, in her house—practically in her room—not avoiding her at all.

If he had any sense he'd return to the vicarage. There was no reason to remain now that Mrs. Bainbridge was settled. No reason save a flicker of curiosity about Miss Hayes's brother—and a nearly overpowering concern for Miss Hayes herself.

"Mr. Archer?" She emerged from her brother's room, holding the door open. "If you'd like to come in?"

It was a large room, not unlike her own, except for a general sense of masculine clutter. An enormous black-and-white cat sat on the bed. It regarded Alex with large, unblinking eyes.

Miss Hayes gave it a scratch beneath its chin. "This is Magpie."

Alex stopped briefly to pet the cat. The smug beast permitted his touch, much in the way a god might permit obeisance from a worshipper.

Miss Hayes advanced into the room. "And this is my brother, Edward Hayes."

Near the window Miss Hayes's brother was seated in front of a desk in a wheeled chair. He was in his shirt sleeves, a conspicuous ink stain on his right cuff. "You may call me Teddy," he said, extending his hand. "Everyone does."

Alex shook it firmly, surprised at the young man's strength. "Then you must call me Alex."

"Are you staying long in Lower Hawley?"

"If things go well."

And they *were* going well. Squire Talbot seemed to genuinely like him. He'd taken Alex out on the estate more than once. Had shared brandy and cigars with him in his study. Had even solicited Alex's opinion on installing a private gasworks.

Things with Henrietta Talbot were advancing at equal speed.

Not only had they progressed to addressing each other by their given names, only yesterday he'd come very close to kissing her. She'd been flirting with him all afternoon in that haughty way of hers. And he'd been flirting right back, inclining his head to hers to make some teasing remark. She'd swiftly turned her face up, bringing her pouting lips a fraction of an inch from his.

Her intention had been unmistakable—and very much in accordance with his plans. And yet…

And yet, he'd drawn back from her, as sharply as Miss Hayes had drawn back from him that day under the yew tree.

It had annoyed Henrietta. And it had left Alex angry and confused—and more resolved than ever to avoid Laura Hayes.

She stood at the tall window near her brother's desk, her slim hands clasped loosely in front of her. Her dress was clearly her Sunday best. It was dark blue silk, with unflounced skirts, wide sleeves, and a delicate velvet ribbon belt. A dated fashion, but it flattered her figure, brought out the blue of her eyes, and gave her fair skin a luminous glow. "Mr. Archer has come to Lower Hawley to court Henrietta Talbot," she said.

Alex stiffened. More than anyone else in the village, Miss Hayes saw him for exactly what he was. A fortune hunter. A villain. Even so, something about her blunt statement rankled.

"Miss Laura?" the housekeeper's voice sounded from the threshold. "Your aunt is asking for you."

"Yes, Mrs. Crabtree. In a moment." Miss Hayes looked to her brother. "Will you—"

"I'll be fine."

"Very well." She cast Alex a brief glance as she passed. "If you'll excuse me."

He inclined his head. "Miss Hayes."

No sooner had she gone than Teddy met Alex's eyes, his brows lifted in enquiry. "Henrietta Talbot? Not my sister, then?"

Alex went still. He'd thought no one else could discern his burgeoning attraction, but—Good lord. How obvious was it? "Are you asking me if I'm courting your sister?"

"Are you?"

"I don't have that honor, no."

Teddy frowned. He had a sharp face, thinner than his sister's but no less striking. "She's not without protection, you know."

"You?" Alex felt an unexpected pang of sympathy for the boy.

"And my Aunt Charlotte."

"I see I shall have to watch my step."

Teddy reached for some of the papers on his desk. They appeared to be half-finished sketches made with pen and ink. "I must thank you for looking after my aunt."

"Not at all."

"She has a dodgy heart. The doctor makes her take syrup of digitalis. It's sufficient for now, but one day…" He shuffled his papers. "My sister doesn't think I realize."

"Your sister is the one who manages the household? Not your aunt?"

"Aunt Charlotte?" Teddy gave a short laugh. "No. It's Laura who looks after us."

Alex wasn't entirely surprised. Of course Miss Hayes was the one shouldering all of the family burdens. Doubtless she'd been doing so since her father's death. No wonder she was searching for a way to salvage the remnants of the family business. To recover her brother's paltry inheritance from the clutches of their unscrupulous solicitor.

"You haven't rescued me from *anything*," she'd told him that day alongside the road. "No one can."

A knot of helpless frustration settled in his midsection. There was nothing he could do to save Miss Hayes. Nothing that wouldn't jeopardize his own plans. He was risking enough just being here. Henrietta Talbot was a jealous creature. When she learned that he'd driven Miss Hayes home, that he'd remained to visit her family, she'd suspect the worst. And then, God only knew how much it would set back his progress with her.

He should leave at once. Bid Miss Hayes and her brother good afternoon and return to the vicarage. It was the wisest course. The one best designed to keep him out of Miss Talbot's black books.

But he didn't leave.

Instead, he moved closer to Teddy's desk. "Are those finches?"

"They nest outside my window. It's difficult to capture them from this angle. I can't seem to get it right."

"You might see them better from outside."

Teddy's expression tightened. "I don't go outside anymore."

"Why not?"

"Isn't it obvious? I'm confined to my chair."

"Permanently?"

Teddy exhaled a frustrated breath. "If you're asking whether or not I can move my legs, the answer is yes. They're not without feeling. But they're too weak to be of any use to me. I can't climb the stairs, or leap in and out of a carriage. Up until this spring, our manservant was obliged to carry me up and down the stairs like a babe."

"What happened?"

"His rheumatism became worse, that's what happened. He doesn't have the strength anymore."

Alex picked up a sheet of paper, examining the delicate lines of the sketch. Teddy Hayes was talented. Gifted, even. He shouldn't be shut up in his room, looking at birds through a poorly washed window. "Your aunt was very weak when we brought her back from the church," he said casually. "I had to lift her onto her bed."

Teddy's gaze jerked up. "Did you?"

"Quite easily." Alex paused. "I'll help you down to the parlor, if you like."

Teddy stared at him. "*Now?*" His Adam's apple bobbed on a swallow. "But you're leaving directly, aren't you? How would I get back upstairs?"

Alex returned the sheet of paper to the desk. "I suppose I shall just have to stay awhile longer."

Chapter Nine

"At the age of thirteen? Alone in Paris?" Teddy stared at Mr. Archer, the plate of mutton and potatoes in front of him quite forgotten. "How did you survive?"

"In great style," Mr. Archer said.

Teddy and Aunt Charlotte burst into peals of laughter.

Laura managed a smile of her own as she sipped her glass of wine.

Mr. Archer had stayed for Sunday dinner.

She still couldn't quite believe it. Even as she watched him banter with Teddy, it felt like a dream. An impossible one, at that.

Not only had he helped her brother downstairs, he'd promised to stay long enough to help him back to his room at the evening's end.

It was an unexpected kindness. One for which Laura should have been grateful. And she *was* grateful. Just as grateful as she'd been when he helped Aunt Charlotte.

She was also vaguely suspicious.

After so many days of avoiding her, why had Mr. Archer decided to linger? To help Teddy, and to dine with them, entertaining them with stories from his life on the continent?

Was this more of him playing the chameleon? Or was this Mr. Archer at last being himself?

"But how?" Teddy asked.

"I'd been on holiday with my godfather in Alexandria," Mr. Archer said. "He was detained on business, and sent me back to Marseilles ahead of him on the steamer. During the journey, I had the good fortune to meet a well-to-do traveler. He took me about France with him for a time. Told people I was his son."

Teddy went off into another gale of laughter.

Aunt Charlotte, by contrast, was aghast. "Why in heaven would he tell people that? He wasn't some sort of villain, was he?"

"The worst sort, Mrs. Bainbridge. Monsieur Giraud was a sharper."

Aunt Charlotte's wineglass froze halfway to her lips. "A *what*?"

"A professional gambler," Laura said.

Mr. Archer looked at her—really looked at her—for the first time since they'd sat down to eat. There was a roguish glint in his gray eyes. It provoked a rather disconcerting frisson of warmth in her belly. "Precisely. He'd been driven out of France five years before, when the police shut down the public gaming houses in '37."

"Let me guess," Teddy said. "He took on a new identity so that he could return. A well-to-do traveler—"

"With a son," Mr. Archer finished for him. "That's right."

"But why?" Laura couldn't help asking. "For what purpose? If the gaming houses were closed—"

"Only the public gaming establishments were shut down, Miss Hayes. There were still plenty of private ones in operation. They did a steady business. A fellow like Giraud could make a great deal of money before the proprietors caught on."

"Weren't you afraid you'd be arrested?" Teddy asked.

Mr. Archer finished the remainder of his wine in one swallow. "I was thirteen. Evading the Sûreté was part of the fun."

"My word," Aunt Charlotte breathed. "What a thrilling life you've led, sir. It's like something out of one of Mr. Dickens's novels. I wonder that Baron Reynard permitted you to set out so young."

"There are boys younger than thirteen in Her Majesty's Navy," Mr. Archer said.

"Not gentlemen's sons, surely."

Mr. Archer's smile tightened. "No, indeed, ma'am."

Teddy chose that moment to discreetly drop a scrap of meat under the table. There was a rustling sound as Magpie retrieved the morsel.

Laura shot her brother a warning glance.

"What?" he mouthed, all innocence.

Mr. Archer gave no indication that he noticed the exchange, or the cat begging under the table, but when Laura next looked in his direction, she could have sworn she saw a flash of laughter in his eyes.

"Your godfather must be a singular fellow," Aunt Charlotte said. "I daresay he was relieved when you returned home unscathed. A boy of thirteen hasn't the judgment to be traveling alone on the continent."

"He wasn't entirely alone, Aunt," Teddy said. "He was with a notorious gambler. That's rather like"—he waved his fork—"traveling about Greece and Italy with one's classics tutor."

Aunt Charlotte protested the characterization, but Teddy only laughed.

The clink of cutlery punctuated their conversation. Dinners at Bramble Cottage were informal affairs. The dining room was small, with exposed beams running lengthwise across the low ceiling, and no gas lighting to illuminate their meal. Instead, the room was lit with tallow candles, and in the absence of a footman, the hot serving dishes, and the carafe of watered wine, were left out for them to serve themselves.

Laura refilled Mr. Archer's glass. "You must know all manner of card tricks."

"Indeed not. Giraud guarded his secrets with his life. When we parted, I was none the wiser."

She gave him a doubtful look. "But you *do* play, don't you?"

"I do," he said.

There was a wealth of meaning in those two words. Laura sensed it as surely as if he'd confessed to being a sharper himself.

"Then you must play with us after dinner, sir," Aunt Charlotte pronounced. "We used to enjoy a lively game of whist before my brother passed away. The four of us played on every occasion I came to visit, didn't we, Teddy?"

Teddy grimaced. "Aunt Charlotte could never be prevailed upon to play anything else."

"My husband was a keen whist player," Aunt Charlotte said. "God rest his soul. We often had card parties at our little house in Leicester." She cut off a slice of her mutton. "He'd been gone less than a year when the wire came from Mrs.

Crabtree telling me of the fever. By the time I arrived in Surrey, my poor brother was gone, and Teddy and Laura were as near to death as they could be."

Teddy speared a piece of potato on his fork. "Aunt Charlotte stayed on to nurse us. She's been here ever since."

"Oh, we played a great many card games while you recovered, didn't we, Teddy? We'll see how much you remember of what I taught you."

Laura eyed her aunt with concern. Her cheeks were flushed, just as they'd been at church. "You mustn't overtax yourself."

"There's no question of that my dear. Not now I've had my tonic and a little rest."

"Even so," Laura said, "it's better to err on the safe side, don't you agree? We don't want to end the evening by summoning Dr. Taylor." She paused, adding, "And we mustn't monopolize Mr. Archer. He's a guest at the vicarage. They'll be expecting him back by now."

Mr. Archer didn't dispute the fact. "Perhaps another time?"

Aunt Charlotte heaved a sigh. "Indeed."

"You *will* come back, won't you?" Teddy asked.

"I will," Mr. Archer promised. "You have my word on it."

Later, after he'd helped Teddy back upstairs and bid goodbye to her aunt, Laura walked Mr. Archer out. Yardley had fetched the vicar's gig from the stable, and was waiting with it at the gate.

"You should put your brother on the ground floor," Mr. Archer said. "It would be easier for him."

Laura's full skirts brushed against his leg. The path through their overgrown garden was almost as intimate as the wilderness walk at Edgington Park. "We've tried to move him countless times since Papa's death. He's always refused. He insists on keeping the view from his window."

"Ask him again. He may feel differently now that your manservant isn't able to assist him."

"I will." She stopped at the gate. The vicar's gig was waiting on the other side of it, Yardley holding the horse's head. It stamped its hooves with impatience. "Mr. Archer—"

"Alex." He stood, gazing down at her. "Your brother and I are already on a first name basis. Surely the two of us needn't stand on ceremony."

She made no reply. Not because she couldn't think of the words, but because there were too many of them. Too many things she wanted to tell him, too many things she wished to say.

His expression softened. "I'd like to call you Laura, if I may."

Butterflies fluttered their wings in her stomach. She moistened her lips. "Very well."

His mouth curved up at one corner. As if he were teasing her. But there was a warmth in his gaze that hadn't been there before. "Thank you for dinner."

"Thank *you*. You were awfully good with Teddy. I haven't seen him talk so much in years."

"He's easy to talk with."

"There aren't many who find him so. I think you must have younger brothers."

Something flickered at the back of his eyes, dark and troubled. "Not a one. But I remember what it was like to be his age."

"He should be away at school," she said. "My father attended Cambridge. I'd hoped that, one day, Teddy might be strong enough to do the same."

"You could arrange for private tuition."

"We can't. Not at present. But if things go as planned with our new solicitor—"

His brows lifted. "You managed to borrow the money from Miss Talbot?"

"I did. She was very generous." Laura didn't mention the note she'd signed. And she certainly didn't mention Henrietta's strictures on the perils of borrowing money from friends: *Neither a borrower, nor a lender be.* It would all be worth it if Papa's will could be resolved in Teddy's favor. "Now we need only wait to hear if we have a case."

"You must tell me if there's anything I can do."

"There isn't. But I'm obliged to you for the offer. Your kindness is—"

He shook his head, frowning. "Not kindness."

"Whatever it is—whatever prompted your consideration for my aunt and my brother—"

"I thought only of you."

She stared up at him. Her heart thumped heavily. "You shouldn't say such things."

He looked steadily back at her. "Why not, if I mean them?"

Why not, indeed? It only set her pulse to racing and encouraged her to dream impossible dreams. Dreams were dangerous things. They made one dissatisfied with reality.

"It's getting late." Mr. Archer cast a glance at the gig. The horse tossed its head and gave another stamp of its hooves. "I should go. The vicar will be thinking the worst."

"Yes, of course." She held out her hand to him. She wasn't wearing her gloves. Neither was he. "I expect I'll see you tomorrow afternoon at Edgington Park."

"I expect you will." He took her bare hand gently in his, but he didn't shake it. He turned it palm down, and then, before she could comprehend what he was about, he drew it to his lips and pressed a kiss to her knuckles.

It was a courtly gesture. Not at all the sort of thing a modern gentleman might do. But it made her heartbeat quicken and the butterflies in her stomach soar to life.

"Good night, Laura," he said.

She drew her hand away as soon as he released it, conscious of Yardley's presence on the other side of the gate. "Good night."

Monday morning, Alex and George arrived at Edgington Park on horseback in answer to a summons from Henrietta, only to find their young hostess in a temper fit. She stormed about the fashionable drawing room in a flurry of French silk, a crumpled note held in her hand.

"I sent for Laura to join us over an hour ago," she said, "and have just received this message from her aunt. She says Laura is out *all* morning. That she won't return until the afternoon. Out *where*, I ask you? What could possibly take all morning?"

"Maybe she's gone to the village?" George suggested. "Or back to London to visit that solicitor of hers?"

Henrietta fumed. "I begin to regret lending her that money. If I knew the result would be her ruining my plans—"

George gave Henrietta a sharp look. "What money?"

"I don't believe she's gone to London," Alex said before Henrietta could answer.

"Where is she, then?" Henrietta demanded.

"Does it matter?" George asked. "You'll see her later, won't you?"

"But I need her here *now*. I wanted to tell all of you about the excursion I have planned. I've put so much effort into arranging it." Henrietta flounced down on the sofa. She looked very near tears.

Alex felt a flicker of annoyance. She was spoiled and pettish. A young lady used to getting her own way. It shouldn't irritate him. He'd recognized what she was from the first day they'd met. Recognized it and accepted it. If he wanted Edgington Park, he was going to have to continue to accept it.

He schooled his features into a mask of polite concern. "Why don't you tell us about it?"

"Yes, do tell us, Hen." George went to sit beside her. "You can tell Laura later. She won't mind if we hear it first."

"Oh, very well." Henrietta gave a dramatic sniffle. "I've arranged for all of us to go to Margate. Papa is coming, too, and I'm to invite Laura's aunt and her brother. I've already booked rooms at the York Hotel."

"Margate?" George looked dubious. "By rail?"

"We'll leave Friday morning and have a whole two days ahead of us at the seaside. Papa says we must return on Sunday. That's when all the rabble come down from London on their weekly excursions. But still, we shall have two nights there in a beach hotel, and there will be music and dancing and all manner of fun." She turned to Alex. "Doesn't it sound a treat? The weather is perfect for bathing."

"It sounds…" Alex was at a loss. He had no desire to go to Margate. The sea brought nothing but bad memories.

Then again, Laura would likely be overjoyed at the news. He was sure he could muster some degree of enthusiasm for her sake. Margate was, after all, a long way from the beaches of North Devon.

"It sounds splendid," George finished for him. "Especially in this heat. Don't you agree, Archer?"

"Wholeheartedly," Alex said.

Henrietta brightened. "I knew you would both approve."

For the better part of the next hour, she chattered happily about their impending excursion as she served them tea and chocolate-covered biscuits. There was little else for them to do in Laura's absence, and Henrietta seemed reluctant to enlist anyone else as her chaperone.

When at last Alex and George rode away from Edgington Park, it was with the promise to return later that afternoon. It was already half past eleven, the sun blazing in the sky.

"Lord, but I need a drink," George muttered. "I've had enough tea and lemonade this past week to float a steamer ship."

"I'd have thought you'd drunk your fill last night."

"At the Park? God, no. Henrietta's taken to being as ruthless as the village barman. She cut me off after the first glass. Probably for the best, now I think of it. I had to keep all my wits about me making excuses for why you weren't available to join us."

Alex sighed. This whole affair was becoming a tedious ordeal. "I trust she believed them."

"Who knows? Can't say it'll make much difference in the end. It's only a matter of time before she discovers you were dining with Laura Hayes—and then the claws will come out." George chuckled. "You should have seen the look on her face when she learned that you drove Laura and her aunt home after church."

"On your father's direction."

"So I told her. *And* that Mrs. Bainbridge was ill. But Henrietta isn't the most reasonable female when she's in a temper."

A spark of anger threatened to ignite Alex's own temper. He compressed his lips into a hard line. "You never mentioned any flaws in her temperament when we were in France."

"I don't consider jealousy a flaw. Not of a permanent kind. A sensible husband could easily break her of the habit." George shot him a cautious look. "I say, you do still want all of this, don't you? You haven't changed your mind about our agreement?"

"I haven't changed my mind."

"Good. Because I've been talking you up a storm. If she doesn't think you a veritable Lancelot by the time you propose, it won't be my fault."

Alex looked ahead of them down the road. The edge of Talbot's Wood was just visible in the distance. He felt the same damnable urge—the same magnetic pull—that had drawn him to Laura Hayes the previous evening. That same unfathomable longing that had prompted him to stay for dinner. To kiss her hand.

It was becoming harder and harder to resist it. To turn his back on the attraction he had for her.

At the moment, it was downright impossible.

"Go back to the vicarage," he said. "I'll join you there later."

"Where are you off to?" George asked.

"A brief errand." Alex didn't linger to explain. He kicked his horse into a canter, leaving George far behind him.

It was only a short distance to Talbot's Wood. He slowed his horse to a walk as he rode into them, down a narrow tree-lined dirt path, going as far as he could on horseback before he was obliged to dismount. He led his horse the rest of the way, tying him loosely to a tree not far from the pond.

The green-hued water glistened in the sunlight, the surface littered with flower petals and fallen leaves.

Laura wasn't in the water, but it didn't take long to find her.

She was asleep on a blanket beneath the same oak tree where he'd sat last week. Her ebony hair was unbound, half-dried from the sun, and her muslin dress was damp about the bodice and skirts. One arm was draped across her midsection, the other beside her face—a face that looked younger, and far more vulnerable, in sleep than it did during her waking hours.

Alex's heart clenched as he looked at her.

He wasn't a romantic. It nevertheless struck him that she rather resembled an enchanted princess from one of the fairy stories of his youth. The sort of beautiful maiden who could only be awakened by true love's kiss.

It was sentimental rubbish.

He wasn't a boy any longer. He was three and thirty. And Laura Hayes was no enchanted princess. She was all too real.

Breathtakingly real.

He sank down beside her. It would be easy to steal a kiss. God knew he wanted to. But there were limits, even to his villainy. "Laura," he said gently. "Wake up."

Her lashes fluttered.

"Wake up," he said again.

"Mmm." She turned her head, her eyes opening slowly. "What time is it?"

"Almost noon."

Her smoke-blue gaze came to rest on his face with uncharacteristic languor. His stomach tightened. She was still half asleep.

Until, suddenly, she wasn't.

Her gaze sharpened, and all at once, she struggled to a sitting position. "What are you doing here?"

"I came to find you."

"How did you know—?"

"Common sense. Henrietta summoned you, and when you didn't respond…" He shrugged. "I assumed you'd be here. Either that or gone to London to speak with that new solicitor of yours."

"He hasn't replied to my letter yet."

"No?"

"I'm going to write him again when I get home." She pushed her hair back from her face. "I thought Henrietta wouldn't expect me until this afternoon. Was she very upset?"

"In a bit of a state. She's made plans for an outing and was anxious to tell you about it."

"What sort of an outing?"

Alex saw no reason to keep it secret. "A trip to Margate."

Laura's eyes widened. She sat up straighter, fully awake now. "The seaside? Are you joking?"

"It's no joke. She's planned two days at the beach. And she means to invite your brother and aunt, as well. You'll be guests of her and her father at the York Hotel."

"When?"

"They leave on Friday and return on Sunday."

"*This* Friday? My goodness."

"Will you go?"

Laura's expression turned wistful. "I'd like to. So very much. Though I shall have to speak with my aunt—and with Teddy. The beach won't be compatible with his chair."

"Let me worry about your brother."

She looked at him with a start. "You're going, too?"

"I think I must."

"Because of Henrietta." She studied his face. "But you don't even like the sea."

"No, indeed. But there's nothing to say I must go into the water."

"You'll be there, around it. Will that not be upsetting to you?"

"The mere sight of it? I've seen the sea before, you know. Crossed it during the journey from France, rowed over it a time or two as well. As long as I'm not obliged to go into it, I'll be fine."

"I wonder…" She reached into her basket, withdrawing her tortoiseshell comb and a handful of hairpins. "Does the friend you rescued as a boy have the same fear of the sea that you do?"

Alex had a sudden image of Neville Cross. He'd been a handsome, fair-haired lad. Always kind, despite the cruelty all around him. His head had been bleeding when Alex pulled him from the water. He'd been unconscious. Had looked as if he were dead.

"Do something!" Alex had cried, coughing and sputtering as he collapsed on the beach. "He's still alive!"

Tom Finchley had stood there, white-faced. So had Justin Thornhill, his clothing soaked through. It was Justin who'd gone in after Neville first. Always the hero. Always doing the exact right thing.

It had made no difference in the end.

"I don't know," Alex said. "I haven't seen him in twenty years or more."

Laura gave her hair a cursory comb before twisting it into a thick roll at her nape and securing it with several pins. It was the practiced, no-nonsense action of a lady who was used to looking after herself. "Why not?"

Another shrug. "One grows up."

She flashed him one of her all-too-perceptive looks as she anchored the final pin into her hair.

"And I'm not *afraid* of the sea," he added. "I merely prefer to stay out of it."

"There's nothing wrong with being afraid."

He gave her a wry smile. "Awake less than ten minutes and you already presume to lecture me?"

"I'm not lecturing you. If I was, it certainly wouldn't be on the topic of sea bathing."

His brows lifted in enquiry.

A faint flush of color rose in Laura's cheeks. "Why do you wish to marry Henrietta? Is it purely because of her fortune?"

The question took him off his guard. He endeavored not to show it. "Do you think her entirely devoid of charm?"

"No. I think she's beautiful. Probably the most beautiful lady in Surrey."

He almost laughed. She could say that, when she was sitting in front of him, looking like an enchanted princess come to life? His water nymph. The lady who haunted his dreams—who was, even now, threatening to upend all of his carefully laid plans. "Not the *most* beautiful, surely."

She didn't react to the compliment. No doubt she thought it was as false as all the rest of him. "I also know her to be generous," she said. "And quite accomplished. Far more so than I am."

"In other words, she can play and sing and embroider the requisite number of seat cushions."

"Don't mock."

"I'm not mocking. Only acknowledging that I recognize her personal attributes—"

"Her *many* personal attributes."

"Recognize them and discount them. For my purposes, they mean nothing." He hesitated before admitting, "It's the estate I'm after."

"Edgington Park?" Laura's brow furrowed. "It *is* grand, but nothing very special, I shouldn't think. Does it hold a particular attraction for you?"

"It's not the park itself—not the architecture of the house, nor the design of the gardens. It's the property. The land."

"The farm, do you mean? The crops, and the livestock?"

"Not only that. It's the history of the place. The way it links people together. Anchors them to something tangible and real."

She paused, seeming to consider. "I expect some people do feel anchored to the land. Especially if it's been passed down from one generation to the next—and if it forms the bulk of their livelihood."

"It's not the wealth it generates. Not entirely. It's something more than that." He tried to explain, however poorly. "Land is the only thing that gives a man a sense of connection. Of meaning. Unless he has it, he never truly belongs anywhere."

"Is that what you're searching for? A sense of belonging?"

A lump formed in his throat. She made it sound so simple. As if he might have found it anywhere. "I suppose I am."

Something in her expression softened. "You don't want land, Alex. What you're looking for is a family."

Her words pierced him to his soul. He recoiled when she uttered them, his gaze jerking away from hers. He felt, for one stark instant, as if she'd knocked the breath out of him. As if she'd opened all of the shades in a darkened room, exposing him to the brutal light of day.

"Don't you have a family?" she asked. "I know your parents died of the cholera—"

"They didn't die," he said.

Only three short words, but he felt the power of them as surely as he'd felt the power of hers. It was a mistake. He knew it as soon as he confessed it. An error in judgment that could put all of his plans at risk.

She fell quiet for the space of a heartbeat. "Didn't they?"

He turned back to her, expecting he knew not what. But there was no censure in Laura's eyes. No anger that he'd lied to her, and to her family. There was only compassion. Concern. A desire to help. To understand.

And he knew then that she cared for him. Not the fiction he'd created, but *him*. The man.

The realization struck his resolve a mortal blow.

Just like that, the carefully constructed façade he'd hidden behind since arriving in Lower Hawley cracked and splintered, shattering at his feet like so much broken glass. In that brief moment, there was nothing between them. No more lies. No more artifice. There was only him. Alex Archer. Vulnerable, exposed.

"I never had a mother. I never had a father, either. I never had any relations—not even a godfather." His chest constricted with long-suppressed bitterness and regret. And shame. So much shame he thought he would choke on it. "I grew up in a parish orphanage. A miserable place, far from here. A place I've spent all of my life trying to forget."

She stared at him, her bosom rising and falling on an uneven breath. The silence stretched taut between them.

And he knew he'd said too much. That he'd confided too much. That he'd probably ruined everything.

"Haven't you anything to say?" he asked at last. "Anything at all?"

Laura opened her mouth to reply. The words that tumbled out appeared to shock her as much as they did him. "I have a family," she said. "You should marry me."

Chapter Ten

Alex couldn't have looked any more stunned if Laura had slapped him just as she'd once slapped George Wright. Indeed, he looked *more* surprised than George had. Surprised, and strangely, uncharacteristically, vulnerable.

"What?" The single word was so soft she barely heard it.

"I have a brother and an aunt. And I have myself." She felt flushed and breathless. Unable to stop the words from coming. "We're not a large family. Quite small, really. But we all belong to each other, whatever comes. Wherever we are is our home. That's what you're searching for, not land. Not riches."

His throat convulsed on a swallow. "Laura…"

"If you married me, you would have a family, too. But not wealth and property. Not a grand estate like you'd have if you married Henrietta."

A fleeting expression of longing shone in his eyes. Bitter longing. He wanted her. She knew it. Why else had he kissed her? Why else did he continue to seek her out? And yet when given the chance to have her—to have her honestly, legally, before the eyes of God and man—he was reluctant. No, not reluctant. Unwilling.

"I can't marry you," he said.

Something inside of her—some small, bright bloom of hope—withered and died. Gone, as if it had never been there at all. In its place, she expected to feel embarrassment. To be ashamed that she'd ever given voice to such a foolish notion. But it wasn't her pride that hurt at his refusal.

At least, not only her pride.

She affected a look of unconcern. "Of course you can't. I have no fortune."

"No, you don't. But…it's not just a matter of money." He rubbed his hand over the back of his neck. "There's no place in my life for unfettered emotion. If I care about anyone too deeply, things always go wrong. I begin to make mistakes. What I need is predictability. Quiet, dispassionate routine." His gaze cut to hers. "Marrying you would be like marrying the storm. And I've had enough of the storm in my life."

"You're looking for calmer seas."

"I'd as soon have no sea at all."

"Pity." Laura stood and dusted off her skirts. They were still damp, half-sticking to her bare legs. "I'd taken you for a gentleman with more mettle."

He rose to his feet. The sunlight cast a shadow over his face. "A wise man knows his limitations."

"I don't think you're wise. I think you're a coward."

His jaw hardened. "Laura—"

"You believe you can have a full life without feeling anything? As if you're a spectator, standing by the side of the road, watching the parade go by? Never risking anything—never getting hurt?" She made a scoffing sound. "That's not living."

"I'm afraid I've hurt you."

"You couldn't. You don't have the power."

"I believe I do." A frown marred his brow. "I should never have kissed you."

She bent to collect her blanket. Her hands were trembling. "What has that to do with anything?"

"It may have given you a false expectation—"

"You must think me a very green girl." She gave the blanket a brisk shake before thrusting it into her basket. "That wasn't my first kiss, you know."

His frown deepened. It was very nearly a scowl. "Nor mine."

"Well, there we are." She looped her basket over her arm. "In any event, I'd hardly call it a kiss. It lasted all of two seconds. Scarcely worth remembering."

"Is that so?"

Her stomach was trembling, as out of control as her hands. She was baiting a wolf, and she knew it. It was childish and stupid. But part of her wanted to hurt him, just as he'd hurt her. "I consider it no more memorable than a buss on the cheek from an aged uncle. Not half as memorable as the kiss I shared with George."

His mouth curled into a slow, sardonic smile. "Remind me to teach you not to overplay your hand."

She gave him an uncertain look.

"George?" His smile broadened. "Really, Laura?"

"He did kiss me."

"And you slapped him across the face. 'With all of your strength,' isn't that what you told me?"

It was her turn to frown. "You're very smug."

"A lady like you isn't likely to fancy a fellow like George Wright."

"What do you know of ladies like me?"

"Enough to recognize that you'd never lose your heart to a wastrel."

"Is he a wastrel?" She walked past him. "When I was a girl, he seemed a perfect gentleman. I thought myself in love with him. Had he proposed marriage, I would have accepted him without hesitation."

"When you were a girl," Alex repeated. "In your salad days."

She shot him a glare over her shoulder. "Oh, do go away! I don't know why you came here if you're only going to tease and devil me."

"I'm not entirely certain myself." He followed after her. His horse was tethered ahead.

"You'd do better to avoid me completely," she said. "Indeed, I wish you would."

His smile faded. "Do you mean that?"

She turned back to him. There was nothing sardonic about his expression now. If she was disposed to girlish daydreams, she might almost fancy that he cared for her. "I don't know. Meeting as we did...it's given us a false sense of familiarity. But we aren't friends, are we? We aren't really anything to each other at all."

"I should like to be a friend to you," he said.

Her gaze briefly fell from his. It took an effort to keep her countenance. "I don't think we *can* be friends."

His voice lowered to match hers. "Don't say that."

"Why not, if it's true? Friends should be honest with each other. They should show each other who they really are. How is such a thing even possible with a man like you?"

"A man like me." His large frame loomed over her, as motionless as if her words had turned him to stone. "And just what sort of man is that?"

"A chameleon," she replied without hesitation. "You change yourself to suit your company. I've seen it with my own eyes. One moment you're one way, the next another. As if you're a completely different man. I can't even be certain that half of the things you say aren't elaborate fictions created to aid your deception."

"You think I've lied to you?"

"Haven't you?" Her gaze drifted over his face. He was so ruthlessly handsome. So pleasing in physical form and outward manner. But there was always something else there—something lurking behind his eyes. A secret self, hidden from the world.

It was as if he wore a very lifelike mask.

She'd only seen him without it on two occasions. The first day they'd met when he'd pulled her from Talbot's Pond. That had been the real Alex Archer. That man, wet and shaken, standing over her on the bank.

And then again, today, when he'd confessed to being an orphan.

There had been a rawness to his countenance. A heart-breaking vulnerability.

"That story you told us at dinner," she said, "about the sharper you traveled with as a boy. Was there really such a man?"

He fell silent for a long moment. "There was," he admitted at last. "But his name wasn't Giraud."

"It's all a version of the truth, then. Not the whole truth."

His mouth quirked. "Does anyone ever tell the whole truth at a dinner party?"

She refused to let him make a joke of it. "What about the things you've told Henrietta? You said that your parents died in Paris. That you were raised by your godfather, Baron Reynard. And now you tell me that you're an orphan. That you have no family at all. I don't know what to believe."

"What does it matter? You and I—"

"The truth *always* matters." A frustrated huff of breath escaped her lungs. "But as for the rest of it—" She shook her head. "You're right. It makes no difference. After you marry Henrietta—"

"Henrietta Talbot has nothing to do with it. I haven't even proposed to her yet. Besides," he added, "she may well refuse me."

A flicker of curiosity compelled Laura to meet his eyes. "What would you do if she did? Leave Lower Hawley, I presume."

"Probably."

"And then?"

He gave an eloquent grimace. "Find another heiress."

"And a gentleman like George to provide the introduction?"

"I don't know about that. Gentlemen like George aren't easy to come by." He paused before explaining, "Wastrels who have more than a passing acquaintance with a marriageable young heiress. Meeting George in Marseilles was something of a godsend."

"I'm sure God had nothing at all to do with it," Laura said.

When Alex stopped to untie his horse, she continued down the path without him. The hurt and embarrassment she'd felt at his refusal were fading, but her pride still stung.

Her momentary lapse of good sense stung even more.

She had every reason to want to be married before her twenty-fifth birthday, but what in heaven had she been thinking to propose marriage to *him*? She hardly knew the man! Granted, he was handsome. And he *had* shown extraordinary kindness to Teddy and Aunt Charlotte. But was that all it took to win her heart? She wouldn't have thought so.

And yet, she'd asked him to marry her. Stupidly. Impulsively. Without a thought for reality.

The words had just seemed to bubble up from an untapped well of feeling deep inside her. An emotional response to the way he'd described what he hoped to gain from Edgington Park.

As if an estate—a soulless piece of property—could ever provide a true sense of belonging.

Love and acceptance could only come from people. From family. Those nearest and dearest to one's heart.

But Alex didn't have anyone near to his heart. He was alone. Entirely alone.

And she'd ached to draw him into her life.

But he didn't want her, or her family. He'd rather have Henrietta and Edgington Park.

Well, he was welcome to both, with her good wishes. As for herself, she needed more than kindness to her family. More than wolfish good looks. She needed a gentleman who would love her. Sacrifice for her. Give up his schemes, and choose her and her alone.

It was never going to happen. Not with him.

Alex Archer simply wasn't that kind of man.

"A letter came while you were out!" Aunt Charlotte called out as Laura entered the cottage.

Laura stripped off her hat and gloves, and stepped out of her muddy half boots. She made her way into the parlor in her bare feet. "Something from Henrietta?"

Aunt Charlotte was seated on the sofa, a paper fan in her hand. "No. That is, you did receive a note from Miss Talbot, but the letter I speak of is from London. I've put it on the mantelpiece for you."

All Laura's anxiety over her ill-thought-out proposal to Alex Archer slipped away. She hurried to the fireplace and retrieved the letter from the mantel. The return address was written in heavy black ink, the name of the sender not the one she was expecting. At least, not entirely.

The Law Offices of Finchley and Fothergill

She looked up at her aunt. "Finchley and Fothergill?"

Aunt Charlotte wafted her fan. "I know nothing more than you do, my dear."

Laura opened the letter, devouring the contents where she stood.

Dear Miss Hayes,

I have your letter of the 15th inst.

In reply thereto, I beg to inform you that Mr. Finchley, being currently engaged in a matter involving Mr. Weatherwax, is unable to represent you. He will, however, make himself available for consultation and referral on the 31st of August at the hour of half past eleven of the clock in the forenoon.

Please respond to confirm your appointment.
Sincerely,
J. Poole, clerk

Laura read the letter again before handing it to her aunt. "What do you suppose he means 'engaged in a matter involving Mr. Weatherwax'?"

Aunt Charlotte's face clouded with worry. "Perhaps the two of them are working together?"

"Or against each other," Laura suggested.

Her aunt didn't seem to hear her. "He may have already told Mr. Weatherwax that you've written, seeking another opinion. And if Mr. Weatherwax knows—"

"Surely that would breach some ethical rule or other? Communication with one's solicitor is meant to be sacred, isn't it? Like a priest and penitent, that's what Papa used to say."

"But Laura, my love, Mr. Finchley isn't your solicitor. Not yet."

Laura bit her lip. Had she already bungled everything before she'd even met the man? "If Mr. Weatherwax and Mr. Finchley are indeed working on a case together, I doubt Mr. Finchley would have offered to consult on the matter—or to refer me to another solicitor."

"I really couldn't say, dear. I know nothing of solicitors and their ways. If your father were here…"

"Don't fret, Aunt Charlotte." Laura pressed a swift kiss to her aunt's cheek as she bent to retrieve the letter. "I'm going to tell Teddy."

Aunt Charlotte gave her an affectionate pat. "Order a bath as well. You smell of pond water."

Laura grimaced. She did, rather. "I'll have Yardley bring in the tub."

Since Papa's death, baths were taken behind a screen in the kitchen. Yardley carried in the tub and Mrs. Crabtree filled it with hot water from the fire. It wasn't conducive to a leisurely soak, but it was efficient enough for washing. Even so…

As she bounded up the stairs to her brother's room, her skirts clutched in her hands, Laura imagined the additional staff they could hire if everything turned out the way she planned it.

There would be a footman to assist Teddy, and to help Yardley haul the tub up the stairs. A housemaid to relieve Mrs. Crabtree of doing the laundry, dusting, and scrubbing the floors. And to relieve Laura, too, from all those hours spent in the kitchen each week clear-starching their muslins and lace.

Perhaps, if the Hayes family's finances were restored to some of their former glory, they might even afford a small open carriage, and a pair of horses, to take Teddy out for a daily airing.

"Laura?" Teddy called as her footsteps sounded in the hall. "Aunt Charlotte said a letter came from the solicitor?"

She entered his room smiling, determined to put as positive a light on the situation as possible. "It did. I've brought it for you to read."

He was at his desk, as always, garbed in an ink-stained linen shirt and dark woolen trousers. His black hair stood half on end.

She ran her fingers through it as she came to sit down beside him. "It's past time I cut this."

"Don't fuss." He took the letter from her and then waved her away.

She watched his face as he read it. His reaction wasn't very different from Aunt Charlotte's.

"I don't know how you can smile," he said when he'd finished. "For all we know, Weatherwax is about to cut our household allowance in half."

"I won't believe that. Solicitors are bound by oaths of confidentiality."

"Like doctors?" Teddy snorted. "Someone should inform Dr. Taylor. He's never hesitated to share the business of our family's health with the entire village."

"Our family's health isn't exactly a secret."

Teddy gave her back the letter. "You'll go to London?"

"I will. At the very least, Mr. Finchley can provide us with the name of another solicitor."

"The 31st is the day before your birthday. You haven't forgotten, have you?"

"I'm not likely to forget *that*," she replied with a laugh.

Teddy didn't join in her laughter. "Laura…" He contemplated her for a long moment. "Do you wish you'd married?"

"What a question!"

"Do you?" he pressed.

She looked at him, her smile fading. "What's brought this on?"

"Mr. Archer—Alex—seems a good sort of fellow. I did wonder—"

"You may cease your wondering. Alex Archer hasn't a grain of interest in me. Not in that regard."

"He does. The way he looked at you at dinner… I think he must be half in love with you."

Laura stared at her brother. The very idea of Alex being in love with her—half or otherwise—was enough to make her heart turn over.

She wondered what Teddy would say if she told him that she'd proposed to the man. Proposed, and been unceremoniously rejected. No doubt her brother would expire from mortification—just as Laura had felt like doing the entire walk home from the pond.

"He most certainly isn't," she said. "Of that, I can positively assure you."

"Why else would he help Aunt Charlotte? Why else would he help *me*?"

"Because he likes you. And who wouldn't? You're the most intelligent, talented person I know. Anyone would be lucky to make your acquaintance."

Teddy turned red about the collar. "I don't know about that. But I do like him, Laura. And so does Magpie. He doesn't allow just anyone to pet him."

Laura glanced at her brother's bed. Magpie was in his usual spot, stretched out asleep after a night of hunting. "How well I know it."

"He never liked George."

"No indeed." She hadn't thought much of it at the time. Now, however, it struck her that cats could be uncanny judges of character. "It seems Mr. Archer has a way of getting around animals, as well as people."

"Is he coming back to visit?"

"I believe he is. And not only that…" She told Teddy all about the proposed trip to Margate, unable to keep the excitement out of her voice. "Won't it be marvelous?"

"And he's going to spend the entire two days helping me?" Teddy looked doubtful. "Surely he'll want to bathe."

"Oh no. He doesn't care for the sea. He says he'll be quite content to stay with you—if you can tolerate his company, that is. Besides, you'll have Yardley to look after you. It isn't as if Alex will have to do everything."

"Still…it sounds a big to-do. I don't know if I…"

"What?" she asked softly.

"I don't know if I have the strength. I haven't done anything—gone anywhere—since the fever. What if—"

"All you need do is say the word, and we'll stay home. No one will think the worse of you." She gave him an encouraging smile. "But if you choose to go, you may make some sketches of the sea and the seabirds. And if you become weary, you can doze in the sunshine, with the salty air on your face, and the sound of the water lapping on the shore to lull you to sleep."

He laughed. "That's your dream, not mine. All but the sketching. I *would* like to draw something new. If Alex is certain to be there—"

"He will be," Laura said. "He promised me."

Chapter Eleven

Alex nearly broke his promise to Laura Hayes.

The night before their trip to Margate, George drank all the sherry in the vicarage. And not just the kind the vicar was accustomed to offering his guests. George drank the cooking sherry, too.

And then he dosed himself with laudanum.

It had been prescribed to the housekeeper for an injury some years before. There was naught but a few spoonfuls left in the bottle. Not nearly enough for George's purposes.

Alex found him ransacking the housekeeper's cupboard for more, and hauled him upstairs to his room.

George paced the floor like a caged animal. "I must return to London. To St. James's Street. I've two bottles of whiskey in my rooms. I need to get them. I need—"

Alex leaned against the closed door, arms folded. "You need to get control of yourself, before I begin to lose my temper."

George flashed him a hunted look. "You have your blasted introduction. What more do you want from me?"

"I want everything you promised me."

"Henrietta's fortune? It could take weeks longer for you to win her. Months before you're wed. Do you mean to hold those markers over my head until Judgment Day?"

"When I've married Miss Talbot, I'll burn your markers. Until then—"

"You've made me your hostage."

"Hardly. This is your home, not a prison."

"A home I left two years ago! You can't keep me here." George picked up a teacup from atop a chest of drawers and flung it against the wall. It shattered with a crash, shards of porcelain exploding in every direction. "Tea! I'm sick to death of tea. Sick to death of this place."

Alex observed George's display, unmoved. "If you're quite finished…"

"You don't understand, Archer. These drips and drabs of wine and sherry won't suffice. I must have something proper to drink. And in large enough quantities to settle my spirits. I need oblivion—or excitement." His expression turned sly. "A woman would do. Perhaps I'll have another run at Laura Hayes? She may be more amenable now she's older."

Alex was across the room in two strides, his hand twisted in George's cravat. He lifted him nearly off his feet. "If you go near her—if you even think of it—"

"You'll what?" George choked out. "Kill me?" His mouth twisted. "Go ahead."

Alex released him, stepping back as George fell to the floor, coughing. Rage surged through his veins, raw and primitive. He could have easily torn George apart. Part of him still wanted to. And for what? For merely mentioning Laura's name?

What in blazes was wrong with him?

He didn't lose control. Not ever. And certainly not over a woman.

"I'm not going to kill you," he said. "And I'm not going to permit you to kill yourself."

George's face crumpled. He put his head in his hands and began to cry.

Alex had met drunkards before. The kind of men who couldn't go a day without a bottle of whiskey or gin. He hadn't thought George was as far gone as that. In France, George had often been foxed, but he'd loved gambling as much as drinking. As for the opium he'd begun taking…

Oblivion or excitement, wasn't that what he'd said?

As if he was trying to blot out reality. To erase all traces of natural thought or emotion.

Laura had accused Alex of doing the same. Of suppressing his feelings. Of never risking anything for fear of being hurt.

But he wasn't the same as George, surely.

"It was a mistake to allow you to drink, even in small amounts. From now on, you'll take no wine with dinner. No spirits of any kind."

George looked up at him bleakly. "You're a monster."

"Rather the opposite," Alex said. "This is me at my least monstrous. This is me trying to save your life."

Two hours later, when the vicar finally returned from visiting sick parishioners in the village, George was in bed asleep.

"Something's happened, hasn't it?" The vicar asked. "I can sense when the household's been in an uproar, even if my servants don't see fit to inform me of it. The expression on Mrs.

Griffiths's face… It can only be because of George." He looked at Alex with weary eyes. "Will you join me in the parlor?"

Alex sat down with him in the same chairs they'd occupied the night of Alex's arrival in Lower Hawley. Beeswax candles were lit on the mantel, casting the room in flickering shadows.

"Is it drink?" the vicar enquired. "Or something stronger this time?"

"Three bottles of sherry," Alex said. "And a dose of laudanum."

The vicar glanced to his drinks table, where the decanter that usually held his sherry now stood empty. "Is this how he comports himself when he's away from home? Or is it worse?"

Alex didn't answer.

"Worse, then." The vicar sighed. "I've suspected for some time, but I did pray that my suspicions were unfounded. People are capable of change, Mr. Archer, with the Lord's help."

"I doubt that God has much to do with George's proclivities."

"How wrong you are, sir. God has everything to do with it. From the day George reached his majority, he's been determined to throw all of the Lord's teachings back in my face. It's my fault. I've been a poor messenger. Too strict and unforgiving. A failure as both a vicar and a father."

Alex didn't know quite what to say. "I believe all children rebel against their parents at some time or another," he managed at last. "Young men, especially."

"Do they? I suppose I must take comfort from the fact." The vicar removed his spectacles to massage the bridge of his nose. "Did you rebel against your godfather when you were a young man?"

Alex hesitated. He wasn't deeply religious. Nevertheless, he couldn't bring himself to lie outright to a man of God. He'd already lied so much, merely by omission. "My godfather and I have a unique relationship. More akin to business acquaintances than father and son."

"Unlike George and I. I've been every inch the father to him. Too much so, he'd say. Always meddling in his affairs." The vicar settled his spectacles back on his face. "You'll watch over him, won't you? He's destructive, my boy. Bound to hurt himself, or some other person. I feel responsible—"

"I'm keeping a close eye on George, sir. You need have no concerns on that score."

"I'm obliged to you, Mr. Archer. Don't think I don't realize the sacrifice you make. It's a thankless task, looking after my son. One that will require you to postpone your pleasure on occasion. With George in his present condition…he won't be in any fit state to accompany you to the seaside, I fear."

The hell he wouldn't.

Alex intended George to be up and ready to depart at half past seven, even if he had to dress him, drag him out of the house, and bodily throw him into the carriage.

"I trust his absence won't upset all of Miss Talbot's plans," the vicar said. "Nor yours."

"George will be fit enough to accompany us," Alex assured him. "You may rely on it."

Sure enough, George sauntered into the breakfast room in the morning, looking only a little worse for wear. He made no mention of his drunken episode the night before. And when Miss Talbot and her father arrived in their barouche, he bounded down the steps and greeted them with genuine enthusiasm.

"There's a second carriage for Laura's family," Henrietta said. She was seated across from Alex, looking as stylish as a fashion plate in her white linen seaside ensemble. "We've only room for one more in the barouche."

"A great deal of fuss," Squire Talbot muttered.

"There's nothing wrong with fuss, Papa," she replied. "Not if the end result is pleasure."

George grinned. "Hear, hear!"

The barouche rolled along the now familiar country road that led past Talbot's Wood to Bramble Cottage. Alex's stomach tensed with anticipation as they approached.

Since parting from Laura at the pond, he'd tried very hard not to think of her proposal. And even harder not to think of the words that had preceded it.

You don't want land. What you're looking for is a family.

A family.

She'd never know the seismic jolt those words had delivered. Would never know how much he'd been tempted.

He couldn't marry her. Couldn't love her. But he could be a friend to her. A friend to her brother, and her aunt. There was nothing dangerous in that, surely.

Unless one could call a rapid pulse and a swiftly beating heart a danger.

He experienced both the moment he set eyes on her.

She came down the garden path to meet them as the carriage pulled up to the cottage gate. Like Henrietta, she was garbed in linen—a cream-colored skirt and loose-fitting jacket trimmed in black braiding. There was a wide-brimmed straw hat in her hand. "Good morning," she said, smiling.

As they all exchanged greetings, a footman opened the door of the barouche to hand down Henrietta. "You'll be wanting Alex to help with your brother," she said, "but I may as well come, too, in case your aunt requires any assistance."

Alex jumped down from the barouche to follow the two ladies into the cottage. He wondered who Henrietta thought she was fooling. Her penchant for petty jealousies was plain for all to see.

She linked her arm through Laura's as they entered the hall. "I've brought you one of my bathing dresses. Pray it fits."

Laura laughed. "I shall swim, even if I must leap into the sea with all of my clothes on."

"Ladies don't swim, Laura," Henrietta retorted. "They *bathe*."

Mrs. Bainbridge came down the stairs to meet them, her plump face aglow with pleasure. "Oh, Miss Talbot! How good of you to come and fetch us. So generous. And Mr. Archer! So very obliging of you to help with my nephew."

Laura met Alex's eyes. The conversation between Henrietta and Mrs. Bainbridge seemed to fade into the background. He was certain he could hear his heart pounding.

At that moment, he'd have given anything for a private word with her. Just a brief second or two alone so he could put her at her ease.

Not that Laura appeared particularly uncomfortable in his presence.

Indeed, one would never know by looking at her that she'd proposed marriage to him only a few days before.

As for Alex, he could think of little else.

Good God, he'd told her about the orphanage. He'd laid himself bare. And in response she'd offered him her family. She'd offered him herself.

It would be the ruination of him. To reach out and take what he wanted, absent the cold calculation that had guided his life since leaving North Devon. He couldn't do it. A lifetime of gambling, and he simply couldn't bring himself to take the risk.

A life with Laura would be too honest. Too real. She had the uncanny ability to strip away his defenses. To see right through him. He was bound to disappoint her in the end. To hurt her, or to be hurt in turn.

And he'd been hurt enough in his life.

"My brother is waiting upstairs," she said. "If you wouldn't mind helping him to the carriage? Yardley will carry out his chair."

Alex gazed down at her. Was that a faint blush in her cheeks? Or merely a product of the excessive heat? The former, he suspected.

Which meant that she was thinking of him just as he was thinking of her.

The realization should have pleased him. He didn't want to be easily dismissed or forgotten. Not by her. But he didn't want her to suffer, either. To be uncomfortable or embarrassed because of something he'd done.

"Of course," he said.

He left the ladies talking in the hall. Upstairs, Teddy was seated by the window in his wheeled chair. John Yardley, the Hayeses' grizzled old manservant, stood nearby

"You're here," Teddy remarked as Alex entered his room. "I wondered if you'd keep your word."

"That's not a very flattering admission."

"Why? Do you always keep your promises?"

"No," Alex said. "But I mean to keep this one." He looked about Teddy's room. "Is there anything else you require? Paint pots? Brushes? An easel and canvas? A cat?"

"Magpie is in the kitchen with Mrs. Crabtree. She's going to look after him while we're gone. As for the rest, it's already packed." Teddy gestured in the direction of his bed. Two large bundles lay atop it. "Yardley is going to carry them down."

Alex's mouth quirked. "I wasn't serious."

"I am. Laura said I may sit on the shore and paint. She said you promised to stay with me in case I needed help, which I won't. But if the tide should come in and my chair gets stuck—"

"I'll remain beside you, whatever happens. Unless," Alex added gravely, "you begin to bore me."

"I'm only going for Laura's sake."

"As am I. If you're quite ready?" Alex bent down to him.

Teddy put his arm around Alex's neck, his hand gripping tight to Alex's shoulder. "Go ahead."

Alex lifted him easily out of his chair, and with one arm around his waist, helped him down the stairs and out to the closed carriage that waited behind the barouche.

Mrs. Bainbridge was already inside. Alex assisted Teddy into the velvet-cushioned seat across from her. "Put this over your legs, my dear," she said, draping him with a carriage blanket.

"It's baking hot," Teddy protested.

Laura came up behind Alex. She held out her gloved hand. "Would you mind very much?"

"Not at all." He helped her into the carriage, trying not to inhale the intoxicating scent of her. Roses, and lavender, and freshly pressed linen. Trying not to think of how wonderfully her hand fit into his, or to feel the feminine swirl of her skirts against his legs.

She was halfway inside before Henrietta cried out in objection.

"You're riding in the barouche with us, Laura!"

Laura glanced back. "I'm riding with my family, Hen. It's only to the rail station."

Henrietta's face tightened, but she didn't argue. Only when she and Alex had resumed their seats in the barouche did she voice her irritation. "It was a mistake to invite Laura's family."

"Rubbish," Squire Talbot said. "It will do the boy good."

"Much that I care," Henrietta retorted under her breath. "Laura is supposed to be keeping company with me. Now she'll give all her spare time to her brother and her aunt. It's excessively tedious, and much of the reason we don't socialize any longer."

George caught Alex's eye. And then he laughed. "What an entertaining holiday this promises to be."

Henrietta glared at him. "I don't know what you find so funny." She turned her glittering gaze on Alex. "And you, sir. I can't believe you've resigned yourself to sitting on the sand with Laura's brother. What's the point of visiting the seaside if you won't go into the water?" Her voice took on a wheedling note. "Perhaps if my father were to sit with Teddy—"

"I'd refrain from swimming whether Teddy was present or not," Alex said. "It's no reflection on you."

"But if I were to insist—"

Alex smiled at her efforts, even as he felt a faint twinge of regret. She would never truly know him. Never understand what it was that had made him the man he was today. "You may save yourself the trouble, Miss Talbot. There's nothing on this earth that could compel me to go into the sea. Not even you."

Chapter Twelve

Margate, England
August, 1860

With the inevitable train delays, and various confusion regarding the changing of platforms as they traveled through London, they didn't arrive in Margate until Friday evening. By then it was far too late to venture out onto the beach.

After checking them into the York Hotel on Margate's Marine Parade, Squire Talbot recommended dinner, and then bed—a suggestion seconded by Aunt Charlotte.

Laura didn't argue. She was dusty and tired, and desperately in need of a bath. She and Aunt Charlotte withdrew to their shared room, where Henrietta's lady's maid assisted in making them both fit for the public dining room.

Dinner was a subdued affair, concluded rapidly. Following that, a good night's sleep was all that stood between Laura and the sea.

That, and the growing multitudes of tourists that greeted them when they emerged from their hotel on Saturday morning.

Margate was one of the most popular seaside resorts in England. A relatively easy distance from the hustle and bustle of London, it drew crowds of people every summer—even more so now that it was accessible by railway.

"It's cheapened the place." Aunt Charlotte walked out along the jetty with Laura. "Just look at them. You'd never see such vulgar behavior at Brighton."

Laura didn't know what behavior her aunt was speaking of. As she looked out at the crowded beach, bookended with its imposing white cliffs, she didn't feel scandalized. She felt giddy. Euphoric.

It was beautiful.

The dark turquoise sea was calm as glass near the shore, rolling up on the clean, even sand in frothy waves. Circling seabirds squawked in the sky above, while men garbed in striped waistcoats and trousers and women in fashionable cotton and linen seaside costumes adorned the beaches below. It was a chaos of top hats, straw bonnets, and ruffled parasols.

And in the distance stood the bathing machines—the women's at one end of the beach and the men's at the other. They were nothing more than wheeled, wooden dressing rooms, really, with doors at each end. Some were still up on the shore. Others had been drawn out into the water by horses. A tentlike canvas covering was attached to the exit door of the machine, allowing bathers to descend into the sea without exposing themselves.

"Telescopes," Aunt Charlotte said with a huff. "And promiscuous bathing. I never thought I'd see the day."

"Where, Aunt?" Laura craned her neck.

Several older ladies, both on the public promenade and seated on the beach, were employing telescopes and other magnifying mediums to look out at the water. Laura supposed they might be ogling the bathers, but it was difficult to tell. As for promiscuous bathing…

There *did* appear to be one gentleman splashing about with a group of ladies not far from the shore. Mixed—or promiscuous—bathing wasn't permitted at Margate, or any respectable watering place, but no one seemed to be objecting to the breach.

No one, save Aunt Charlotte.

"Unseemly," she said under her breath.

Henrietta came to join them, her hand pressed to the floppy straw hat on her head to prevent the wind from taking it. "Is he even wearing a costume?"

"*What?*" Aunt Charlotte's head jerked back. "Do you mean to suggest—?"

"I read about it in Papa's newspaper," Henrietta said. "Gentlemen visiting Margate often go into the water in a primitive state. The authorities haven't had any luck forcing them to wear bathing costumes." She looked to Laura with a grin. "Shall we go down?"

Laura touched her aunt's arm. "Why don't you join Squire Talbot?"

"Oh, but Laura—if one of these *primitive* fellows should approach you in the water—"

"I shall laugh at him," Laura promised.

It was what the ladies in the water were currently doing with the gentleman in their midst—laughing at him, and *with* him, as they splashed him with water.

"I don't mind a gentleman bathing with us," Henrietta confided as she and Laura walked off together to the bathing machines. "It's silly for the town council to forbid it. Why, what if the gentleman was your brother? Or your husband?"

"True enough," Laura said absently.

She gazed out past the sand and to the rolling waves beyond. Farther from the shore, fewer people were in the water. The sea wasn't as calm there. It was vast and wild. Limitless.

"Laura? Did you hear me?"

Laura turned back to Henrietta. "I'm sorry. Did you say something?"

"I said that I wish Alex and George could bathe with us. Wouldn't that be enjoyable? But there's no chance of that, is there? Not with Alex looking after your brother." Henrietta shot a narrow glance back down the beach where Teddy was seated behind his easel. Alex stood nearby, his back to the sea.

Laura had had precious little contact with him since he'd handed her up into the carriage outside Bramble Cottage. From the time they had boarded the train in Lower Hawley, to their arrival at the York Hotel, Henrietta had commanded all of his attention. Laura hadn't particularly minded. She'd been too much in awe of her surroundings—and too much occupied with settling her aunt and brother. But now…

She looked at him, a little wistful.

Like most of the fashionable gentlemen at the seaside, he was wearing a sack coat and matching trousers in a neutral shade of tan. Unlike the rest of the men, however, Alex managed to make the staid ensemble look dashing.

His coat was unbuttoned, pushed back by his hands on his hips to reveal the tan waistcoat, white linen shirt, and loosened necktie beneath. And his head was uncovered, his dark hair disheveled from running his fingers through it.

He looked like precisely what he was: a rogue. A feral wolf in sheep's clothing.

Only a fool would fail to recognize the danger he represented.

"I'm going to marry him," Henrietta announced.

Laura's gaze jolted back to her friend's face. "*What?*"

"I know he wants to marry me."

"Has he asked you?"

"Not yet, but he's implied his intentions in dozens of ways. I expect that soon he'll broach the subject properly. And when he does, I mean to accept him."

The bottom seemed to fall out of Laura's stomach. "But Hen…you don't know him. It's been less than two weeks—"

"Papa was of the same view. Until I pointed out to him that two weeks of daily meetings—of seeing the object of one's affection every day for hours on end—is the equivalent of months of courtship. Why, during a London season a lady meets a gentleman once in a ballroom, and then again for ices at Gunter's, or a visit to the botanical gardens. An outing or two later, the fellow's proposing. And no one objects to that, do they?"

The cry of the seabirds and the shouts and laughter of the children on the beach softened to a hum in the background. Laura's head was spinning. She stared at Henrietta, her mind latching onto a single sentence. "*Is* he the object of your affection?"

"I believe so. And I'm the object of *his* affection—of that I'm certain." Henrietta smiled. "Do you know, Laura…he almost kissed me last week. He stopped at the final moment, his lips over mine. He's a decent sort of gentleman, for all he pretends to be a worldly sophisticate. But I have a mind to tempt him." Dimples popped in her cheeks. "If he doesn't kiss me by Sunday, it will not be my fault."

Laura opened her mouth to say something. An objection. A warning. She didn't know what. But Henrietta forestalled her.

"Yes, I know, he may well be a fortune hunter," she said, "but what gentleman of my acquaintance isn't? They all want Edgington Park, and they all covet my inheritance. It's to be expected when one is situated as I am." She linked her arm through Laura's. "A man who cared nothing for what I can bring to a match would be a simpleton. And I've no intention of marrying a simpleton, no matter how noble he might be. Indeed, such a worthy suitor would likely bore me out of my wits."

Laura allowed Henrietta to steer her down the sand. The sparkle of wonder she'd felt on arriving at the seaside faded to a dull shine.

Alex Archer didn't belong to her. He never had.

"I should like to be a friend to you," he'd said.

Not her sweetheart. Not her husband. And certainly not her love. Just her friend. And very soon, the husband of Henrietta Talbot.

Laura's heart twisted. For a moment, she didn't know how she could bear it.

But she'd borne it before. With George. In the weeks after he'd made his insulting proposition, she'd wanted to hide in her room, weeping tears of heartbreak and anger by turns. Such girlish dramatics would have been a luxury then, just as they were now. A luxury she couldn't afford. Not when there was a household to run, a brother and aunt to look after, and clear-starching to finish in the kitchen.

"Are you all right?" Henrietta asked.

Laura pasted on a smile, refusing to betray the pain that Henrietta's happiness caused her. "I'm always all right."

She had to be. What other choice was there?

The York Hotel was an elegant establishment situated directly opposite the harbor, its three stories of windows facing out to the sea. Alex crossed the crowded lobby, his head bent and his hands thrust into his pockets. After an afternoon spent on the beach, he was more than ready to retire to his rooms to wash and change for dinner.

It wasn't that Teddy hadn't been good company. Indeed, with his caustic remarks and dictatorial demands, Laura's brother was surprisingly amusing. He was rather talented, too. Alex had enjoyed watching the progress of his preliminary sketches, and the resulting effect when he'd transferred his ideas to paint and canvas.

George had even joined them for a time, long enough for Alex to observe the decided tension between him and Teddy.

"You don't like him?" Alex had asked when George left them for the bathing machines.

"He's a scoundrel," Teddy had said, squinting at his canvas as he applied another dab of blue. "He treated my sister abominably two years ago. I don't know why he ever came home."

Alex hadn't been able to get any more information out of Teddy, except to learn that Teddy himself was partially in the dark regarding George and Laura's infamous falling out.

It didn't matter, in any event. Laura had no need for Alex's protection. She'd dealt with George once before, all on her own, and seemed more than capable of dealing with him again should the need arise.

There was no point in fretting over her. In worrying about her safety. Her comfort. Her happiness.

It was time to get his head on straight. To remember why it was he'd come back to England.

And it hadn't been to lose his heart to an impoverished perfumer's daughter.

He glanced out the front windows of the hotel as he passed them on the way to the staircase. The calm, untroubled waters of Margate were nothing like the wild and raging seas of North Devon. There, he'd been out of control. A victim of the storm.

Here, he was master of his own destiny. Whatever happened, it would be his choice.

He entered his hotel room on the third floor. George stood in front of the looking glass in his shirtsleeves, frowning as he tied his cravat.

"Squire Talbot expects us downstairs in half an hour for a preprandial drink," he said. "You'd better hurry and change."

Alex stripped off his coat. "If you think you're drinking tonight, I advise you to think again."

"You can't be serious. I know I rather lost control of my urges that night at the vicarage, but I've been dry as a bone ever since." George met his eyes in the mirror. "Come, Archer. We're on holiday. A glass of wine with dinner can do no harm."

"One glass leads to another, which leads to a bottle, and then God knows what else. I've no intention of dragging your drunken carcass out of a gin shop at four in the morning— or worse."

"Worse? In Margate? Drunken sailors, maybe, but I doubt there are gin shops and opium dens along the promenade." George fastened his cufflinks. "You're becoming an old woman."

Alex ignored the barb. He didn't care what George thought of him. All he needed was for George to stay sober and clear-headed until this affair was brought to a close. Alex hadn't come this far in the game to end it playing nursemaid.

"A drop of wine—or whiskey, come to that—never harmed anyone," George said. "If you had any notion of what I suffer—"

"Is it too much to ask that you hold up your end of the bargain?"

"What about *your* end?" George heaved an impatient breath. "Do it tonight, will you? There's dancing at the assembly rooms. Henrietta was nattering on about it earlier. You can propose to her during the waltz. It's what I would do, if I were you."

Alex paused in the act of unbuttoning his waistcoat. He couldn't stop himself from asking: "Is that how you proposed to Laura? At a dance?"

George bent his head, resuming his toilette with increased focus. "That was another sort of proposal."

"What sort, exactly? You've never made it clear."

"If this is a preface to you mauling me about as you did at the vicarage—"

"It's simple a question. One with a simple answer, I trust."

George's lips compressed. And then: "I asked her to be my mistress."

Alex's hand froze on his cravat.

"She'd just come out of mourning, and there I was, half-seas over on Squire Talbot's Christmas punch. I knew she'd always fancied me. Ever since we were children. So I kissed her, and I mumbled some rot about setting her up in a townhouse, after which she slapped me." George slipped his waist-coat on over his arms. "And then I went to London, found a chorus girl to warm my bed, and congratulated myself on a lucky escape."

"And now you're back."

"Not of my own volition."

"I trust you have no intention of repeating your offer."

"Do *you* want her? Is that it?" George turned from the glass. "Forgive me if I get confused. I thought it was an heiress you required. A lady with a substantial property. Henrietta Talbot, in fact."

Alex didn't reply. How could he when he didn't know the answer himself?

"She is in the palm of your hand. If you don't take her…" George huffed. "Well, it doesn't seem fair, does it? That you should keep my markers when I've all but delivered Henrietta to you on a silver platter."

Alex went to the washstand and filled the basin with water. "No, it isn't fair. But life seldom is, is it?"

They dined in the hotel's public dining room, all of them dressed in their evening finery. Squire Talbot presided over their party at the head of table. Alex was seated between Henrietta and Mrs. Bainbridge. Laura sat opposite him, between George and Teddy. There was no opportunity to speak to her. It would have been unseemly to talk across the table. Besides which, she was thoroughly engaged with her brother, discussing his progress at painting, by the sound of it.

She was also extraordinarily beautiful, garbed in a silk evening dress with a ribbon belt and a low, lace-trimmed neckline that revealed the curve of her porcelain shoulders and hinted at the swell of her bosom.

After a few brooding stares in her direction, Alex made a point of directing his attentions to Henrietta. She was equally lovely in a gown of printed pink, her golden ringlets pinned atop her head in a profusion of rosette-studded curls.

"I'd no notion it would be so crowded," she said. "But it seems every London clerk and his wife has come to stay. And we must endure their company, both on the beach and here at the hotel."

"You can blame the railway," Alex said. "It's democratized Margate."

Henrietta raised a spoonful of soup to her lips. "To think this hotel was once patronized by royalty!"

Alex wondered what Henrietta would make of his own pedigree—or lack of one. He had no illustrious antecedents. No grand familial connections. Indeed, if he were to wager on his bloodlines, he'd bet everything he had on his mother having been a scullery maid, or a common prostitute. As for his father...

He'd long suspected that, like Justin Thornhill, he'd been sired by the notorious Sir Oswald Bannister, baronet. Sir Oswald had owned Greyfriar's Abbey, a ramshackle estate in North Devon, situated high on a cliff overlooking the sea. Renowned for his drunkenness and lechery, he'd been one of the orphanage's foremost patrons—which was no surprise when one considered that the place was populated with several of his bastards.

Justin had been one of those bastards. As a lad, he'd been tall, dark, and leanly muscled, just as Sir Oswald had been. He'd also possessed Sir Oswald's distinctive gray eyes—as stormy as the fog over the Devon sea.

Alex had been blessed with many of the same features. Unlike Justin, however, Alex had never seen a scrap of proof that Sir Oswald was his father. He had only his instincts to guide him. Instincts that had told him, from a young age, that Justin must be his brother.

Since coming to Lower Hawley, Alex had been thinking of Justin more frequently. He'd been thinking of Tom, too. Of how he'd looked when last Alex had seen him; beaten, bloody, and betrayed. And of Neville, lying on his sickbed in the orphanage, unable to formulate even the simplest words without a struggle.

"I'm sorry," Alex had whispered to him. "But I have to go. I have to get away from here."

He'd been consumed by an almost feverish sense of urgency. There had been no time to wait on wiser counsel. No time to work things out with Justin or Tom. Alex had known how the story ended for boys like him. They were disposable— and he was more disposable than most. There was nothing special about him. He hadn't Justin's nobility, or Tom's razor-sharp mind. He had only his good looks. A handsome face and figure that had ended up doing him far more harm than good.

He'd known then that, if he wanted saving, he would have to save himself. Even if that meant burning all of his bridges behind him. At the time, he'd believed he had no choice. All he'd been able to think of was getting away from there.

And he had got away. As far away as a boy could get with one hundred pounds in stolen gold coins.

It had turned out to be very far away indeed. So far that Alex had almost been able to erase the past. But the past was never really gone. Not when one had done what he had. The memories clung to him like ghosts. The specters of Justin, Tom, and Neville.

Laura had said he was looking for a family. But he'd had a family once. Had them, and thrown them away. Sacrificed them. All to save himself.

In his darkest moments, he'd begun to wonder if it had been worth it.

Shortly after eight o'clock, Squire Talbot and the rest of their party made their way to Cecil Square and the imposing stone-faced building which housed Margate's public Assembly Rooms. The entrance was flanked with Doric columns through which ladies and gentlemen of every class poured into the ballroom.

Mirrors and stuccoed decorations adorned the walls, and in the corner a small but enthusiastic orchestra played reels, quadrilles, and waltzes.

Alex danced twice with Henrietta, and twice with Mrs. Bainbridge before he finally approached Laura. To have refrained would have been unforgivably rude—tantamount to a snub.

"It's a waltz," Laura said, as he led her out onto the floor. "Perhaps the next dance—"

"Henrietta can't object, if that's what you're afraid of."

Her chin lifted a notch. The gaslight from the chandeliers flickered in the glass-studded combs she wore in her hair. "I'm not afraid."

"Good." He curved his hand around her waist, drawing her close as the music started. His heart thumped heavily. He'd only taken her in his arms on one prior occasion. It had been the day they'd met, when he'd hoisted her out of the pond. At the time, he'd been in no mood to appreciate the way she fit so perfectly against him. But now…

Well.

Her hand tightened on his shoulder as he spun her into a swooping turn.

"Gracious," she breathed. "It makes one rather dizzy."

Alex wondered how often Laura had been called upon to dance the waltz in Lower Hawley. Not very often, he'd guess. He gathered her closer. "Focus on my eyes."

Her smoke-blue gaze met his. A flush of color crept up her throat and into her face. He felt a little warm himself, but he didn't look away from her. Their eyes remained locked together as he moved her about the floor in rhythm to the swaying chords of the orchestra—first slowly, and then with increasing speed.

"Better?" he asked.

"Yes."

"We can go slower if you like."

"No. It's just that—" Her blush deepened. "I've only ever danced the waltz with Teddy. And that was years ago. Long before he became ill."

Alex raised his brows. "Are there no assemblies in Lower Hawley?"

"None I've attended since my father died. I'm woefully out of practice. Any second, I expect to trip over my own legs—or yours."

"I'll take care of you," he promised.

Her mouth lifted into a smile.

And they danced, staring into each other's eyes, saying nothing for an endless, suspended moment. Until…

Until it was all simply too much for him. Too much intimacy. Too much silence fraught with unexpressed emotion.

"I didn't see you on the beach today," he said after the next swooping turn.

"I saw you."

He gave her an alert look. "Did you?"

"With Teddy. You must have left the hotel very early."

"Ah. That." He flashed a sudden grin. "Your brother wanted to be out with the morning light. He thinks he's Mr. Turner, painting the seascapes of Margate."

She laughed. "I daresay he does."

Alex gazed down at her with what he knew must be a stupid, besotted smile. Her laughter did odd things to him. It seemed to unmake him, and then put him back together in a strange, new way. "What about you? Did you enjoy bathing in the sea?"

"It wasn't at all what I was expecting." Her full skirts swung against his legs as he waltzed her around the crowded floor. "Did you know there's a large woman at the exit to the bathing machines who grabs hold of you, thrusts you straight down under the water, and pulls you back up again? They call her 'the Dipper.'"

"Good God."

"She dipped Henrietta, and then she dipped me. Apparently, it's all part of the fun of sea bathing, but I confess I could find no enjoyment in it."

"I should think not. It sounds appalling."

"And that wasn't even the worst of it. Once she dipped us, we were stuck under a canvas awning. Six of us ladies, with no view of the sky, and scarcely any room between us, paddling in place in our woolen bathing costumes like a pack of wet dogs."

"I can't imagine you ever looking like a wet dog."

She laughed again. "Is that meant to be a compliment? If so, I shudder to think what sorts of praises you've been heaping on Henrietta's head."

His chest constricted. "Laura…"

She looked up at him, smiling.

And he wanted to tell her that she was extraordinary. That she was beautiful and brave. That it made his heart ache to look at her.

But he couldn't say any of those things. He didn't dare. Not when it couldn't lead anywhere.

His voice went gruff. "I'm not known for my fulsome compliments."

"Pity. Henrietta likes a pretty compliment now and then."

"And you don't?"

She lifted one bare shoulder in a shrug. "I've no experience with them. Not from anyone I care about. Those are the only compliments that matter."

The music swelled, the chords gathering to a close.

His hand tightened at her waist. "Then what I say wouldn't mean anything anyway. Not to you."

Her smile dimmed. "I expect not."

"Because you don't care for me."

"How can I care for you? You are not mine."

It was the last thing she said to him. Seconds later, when the music ended, he let her go. She went back to her aunt and her brother—and to George and Henrietta, who had just finished dancing themselves. But Alex didn't follow. As the orchestra struck up a polka, he shouldered his way through the crowd and out the front doors through the colonnade.

Once on the street, he inhaled a ragged breath of cold night air. It was sea air, salty and damp. It burned in his lungs, and in his memory.

He'd walked away from the people he cared about before. Left them without a backward glance. This time was no different, surely.

But perhaps *he* was.

Chapter Thirteen

*L*aura settled the strap of her waterproof mackintosh bag more firmly over her shoulder as she crossed the beach with Henrietta. It was—along with the woolen bathing costume within—yet another item she'd borrowed from her friend. Though Henrietta could be pettish, she was really quite generous most of the time. Generous, kindhearted, and worthy of every happiness.

Or so Laura had been telling herself since last evening.

She was determined to be happy for her friend. There would be no more pining after Alex Archer. Instead, Laura was going to refocus her attention back where it belonged.

"Don't do anything foolish," Henrietta said. "The sea is too dangerous for ladies to be mucking about in it."

"It isn't dangerous. Only look." Laura nodded at the water. The morning sun was shining brightly, reflecting down upon a sea that was as smooth as a sheet of glass. "There's not a wave in sight."

"It *is* rather calm this morning," Henrietta conceded. "Though why you should want to swim in it, I don't know. I'd never expose myself to those old biddies with their telescopes. And they weren't the only ones ogling bathers yesterday. I saw a fellow or two with a telescope as well. Horrible creatures. I'll not call them gentlemen."

"I don't know what they imagine they can see," Laura said. In truth, she didn't really care. Her borrowed bathing costume covered her from shoulders to knees in acres of dark blue wool. It was modest enough by anyone's standards. Besides, she hadn't come this close to fulfilling her dream only to forgo it because of a few beach-faring busybodies with spyglasses.

"It's a shame we can't stay another day," Henrietta said. "How divine it would be to go dancing again this evening! But Papa is anxious to get home. He can't be away more than three days without fretting about the estate. If it were up to him, we'd have already left this morning."

Laura was glad they were taking a later train. It gave her one last chance to go into the water. And this time, she was determined not to abide by the silly rules.

"Perhaps I'll have a dance at Edgington Park when we return?" Henrietta suggested. "Or a ball?" Her eyes brightened. "I know! I shall plan a betrothal ball. Something grand. An event the villagers will talk about for years to come."

Laura gave her a sharp look. "He didn't propose last night, did he?"

"Gracious, no. There wasn't any privacy. But when he danced with me, and when he gazed into my eyes... Oh,

Laura. I pray that one day you shall know what it is to be admired by such a man."

"We *are* speaking of Mr. Archer, aren't we?"

"Who else?"

"You danced with George, as well."

"Oh, George is a dear. I won't argue *that*. But if I were to marry him, I'd spend my entire life managing his little weaknesses. Monitoring his drink, and seeing that he didn't wager too much at cards."

Laura smiled. "If anyone could manage him, you could."

"There's no question of that. But I'd far rather have a tall, dark-haired stranger sweep me off my feet. Someone with a little bit of mystery about him." She glanced at Laura. "What about you? You've always admired George."

"I haven't. Not for a long while."

"What? But I thought—"

"And he's never cared for me," Laura said. "Not like that. It's you George has been holding a candle for, ever since we were children. We asked him once, do you remember? Whether he favored guinea gold or raven black?"

Henrietta gave a sudden tinkling laugh. "Oh, I'd quite forgotten. He said guinea gold, didn't he? George has never had any tact."

"No, he hasn't."

"But it didn't hurt you, did it, Laura? Being second to me?"

"It might have once, when we were children. Not anymore."

Two open bathing machines stood ahead, their large wooden wheels parked in the wet sand. One was already hitched to a horse, waiting to be hauled out into the sea.

"What luck," Henrietta said. "We'll be right beside each other."

"Good," Laura said. "We can—"

"Laura!" Teddy's voice called out to her.

She looked back over her shoulder to see her brother waving in her direction. He was seated on the beach in his wheeled chair, nearer to the jetty than the water.

Alex was with him. He raised a hand in greeting.

She lifted her hand in return, even as her stomach performed a disconcerting somersault.

"You are not mine," she'd told him last night.

And he never would be.

The sooner she accustomed herself to that fact, the better it would be for all of them.

"Really, Laura," Henrietta scolded as the pair of them walked on. "You should say something to your brother."

"About what?"

"About shouting your name out across the beach as if you were a common doxy." Her lips pursed. "And what are the pair of them doing so close to the women's bathing machines? They should be farther away from us."

"They're not that close. No more so than anyone else this morning. It's the machines that move from day to day. Can't you tell? Yesterday they were closer to the cliffs."

"Going in the water today, ma'am?" one of the gentlemen driving the horses asked. He was a weathered fellow of indeterminate age, sitting sideways on the horse's back, with a straw hat pulled down over his brow.

"We are," Laura said. "You go ahead, Hen. I'll use the other machine."

A heavy-set woman assisted Laura up the steps, closing the door behind her. The bathing machine was windowless, equipped with benches on either side, and wooden pegs on the walls. Laura quickly removed her skirts, petticoats, and bodice, and unhooked her corset. She was in the process of opening her bag to retrieve her bathing costume when the machine lurched forward.

Yesterday, she hadn't expected the jolting motion, and had been tossed from side to side, nearly losing her balance. Today, however, she was ready for it. As the horse pulled the machine out into the water, she braced her body against the wall, and slipped into her bathing costume.

Composed of a knee-length tunic, Turkish trousers, and a belt, the cumbersome ensemble wasn't ideal for swimming. Nor were the canvas slippers she was obliged to wear, secured with ribbons that laced up her legs.

How much easier it would be to wear only her chemise and drawers! Or to leap into the water in a primitive state as the male swimmers were rumored to do.

But this wasn't Talbot's Pond. And she was no man.

She tugged an oilskin cap over her plaited hair and tied it beneath her chin. When the attendant opened the exit door, Laura was ready. "You needn't dunk me. I know how to swim."

"As you please, ma'am." The woman assisted her down, squeezing tight to her arm until Laura was submerged in the water. "Off you go, now."

Laura waded out from beneath the canvas awning that shielded the steps of her bathing machine from public view. Henrietta was already there, along with several other ladies, paddling in the surf.

"Fine weather today!" an older lady bellowed in Laura's ear.

"Your first time at Margate?" a younger lady enquired. "Did you arrive on the steamer?"

Laura made polite replies, conversing in what she supposed was the way many genteel strangers conversed when on holiday at one of England's watering places. "I'm going a little farther out," she said at length.

"Be careful, Laura," Henrietta warned.

Another of the older ladies watched Laura with concern. "Are you a strong swimmer, my dear?"

"I am," Laura said. "My mother taught me."

And she *was* a strong swimmer. Though the sleeves of her tunic impeded her arms, and though her Turkish trousers weighted down her legs, she managed to cut through the water with a sure stroke.

Several yards from the other ladies, she dived beneath the surface. All those hours spent strengthening her lungs in Talbot's Pond hadn't been for nothing. She was able to dive deep, before turning in the water and kicking her way back to the surface.

"Are you nearly finished?" Henrietta asked after a quarter of an hour had passed. "I'm ready to get out."

"Go ahead," Laura said. "I'm going to swim awhile longer."

"Laura—"

"It's all right. I'll meet you on the beach."

Henrietta pursed her lips, but she didn't argue.

Laura wouldn't have heard her if she had. She dived again and kicked away from the bathing machines. She swam until she was no longer surrounded by curious travelers. Until the noise of the beach was drowned out by the sound of the surf. Until she had no thought for romance, or money, or London solicitors.

It was freedom. Glorious freedom. Everything she could have imagined, and more.

It was also exhausting.

The sea was still smooth as glass, but beneath the surface, there was an unmistakable undertow. She hadn't noticed it at first. It was subtle closer to the shore. Only when she'd swum out far past the bathing machines, did she begin to feel the relentless power of it.

It caught her in its grasp before she recognized the danger. When she did, she tried to swim against it, kicking as hard as she could—so hard that one of her canvas slippers came loose.

How had she managed to drift so far from the shore? Had the current been pulling her out the entire time?

She stroked her arms through the water with renewed effort. They were beginning to feel heavy. So were her legs. Had she pushed herself too far? The shore seemed a very long way away now. And her lungs were burning.

A flare of panic set in.

Perhaps she wasn't as strong as she'd thought she was.

Alex stepped back to view Teddy's painting from a different angle. It was the seashore—that much he recognized. As for the rest...

"There's something compelling about it," he said. "A feeling of movement. Of emotion, rather than accuracy. But I'm no expert."

"It's an experimentation with light. The way it hits the water." Teddy cocked his head, squinting as he laid down another swipe of color with his brush. "If it comes out well, I'll give it to Laura for her birthday next week."

Alex went still. "I'd no idea it was her birthday."

"She doesn't like anyone making a fuss over it. Especially not this year."

"What's so special about this year?"

"She'll be five and twenty." Teddy raised his head, looking out past Alex's shoulder. "There's Henrietta. I wonder where Laura is?"

Sure enough, Henrietta Talbot walked toward them from across the sand. Her dress was a little wrinkled, and her golden hair somewhat flattened—from a bathing cap, Alex suspected.

"Good morning," she said brightly. "Have you seen Laura?"

A frisson of tension tightened Alex's muscles. "What do you mean?"

"She's not been by, has she?"

"Wasn't she with you?"

"Yes, but…she wanted to swim away from the others. She said she'd meet me on the beach. It didn't occur to either of us to specify the place. Do you suppose she's gone back to the hotel?"

"We'd have seen her walk by," Teddy said.

"Perhaps you didn't notice?"

Teddy gave Henrietta a vaguely contemptuous look. "Don't be ridiculous. Even if we didn't see her, she would have seen us. It makes no sense for her to have passed by without saying anything."

Alex stared out at the sea, past the women's bathing machines. It was too far away to make anything out. He flashed a look at Henrietta. "Stay with Teddy."

"But where are *you* going?" Henrietta demanded.

"Just wait a moment!" Teddy objected at the same time.

Alex scarcely heard them. He was already striding down the sand to the women's bathing machines. It was early in the morning. The beach wasn't yet as crowded as it had been the previous day. There were a few fashionable couples having their morning promenade on the jetty. And the cadre of elderly ladies with their telescopes were seated near the bathing machines.

"I beg your pardon, ma'am," he said to one of them as he plucked her telescope from her fingers. "If I may?"

"I say, young man!" she cried out. "Look here! That isn't a plaything!"

"Heavens," a second elderly lady gasped. "Is he looking at the bathers?"

Alex ignored them. The telescope wasn't very powerful, but it was strong enough to permit him to see out past the machines. Unfortunately, the sun was shining too brightly for him to get a clear view. There was a glare on the water.

"May I borrow this?" He didn't wait for permission. As he set off, he heard the ladies' voices behind him rise to a crescendo.

"Get back here, sir! Get back here, I say!"

"He's stolen it, Mildred! Summon a policeman!"

He didn't stop until he reached the shore. The water was calm, lapping up onto the sand in a gentle froth of sea foam. It wet his shoes and the hem of his trousers as he took another step forward and raised the telescope to his eye.

Some of the female bathers were visible, wading just beyond the canvas awning of their bathing machines. It was difficult to tell one from the other. Their hair was covered in matching oilskin caps, their torsos nearly indistinguishable in drooping wet wool.

"Alex!" Henrietta ran toward him across the sand. "What in the world are you doing?"

He looked back at her sharply. "I told you to wait with Teddy."

"That manservant of his... Yardley, or whatever his name is, is with him now. Papa and Mrs. Bainbridge are up on the promenade as well."

"What color was Laura's bathing dress?" he asked.

"It's *my* bathing costume, actually. She borrowed it from me—" She stopped short at the look on his face. "It's dark blue, with a white trim."

Alex looked through the telescope. Laura wasn't with the other bathers. He couldn't see her anywhere.

A visceral fear rose within him, squeezing at his heart and lungs. He was vividly reminded of that day on the cliffs at Abbot's Holcombe so long ago. The sea hadn't been smooth then. It had been wild. A roiling stew.

He'd been climbing down the cliff face with Justin, Tom, and Neville, just as they'd done dozens of times. Clinging to the familiar outcroppings. No one had noticed the rocks skittering beneath Neville until it was too late.

Neville had tried to move away from the crumbling stones, and in the process, had lost his foothold. He'd slipped sharply to the right, his hands scrabbling on the rocks. And then he'd fallen. He'd struck his head and gone down into the sea, where he disappeared. As if he'd never been there in the first place.

Justin hadn't hesitated. He'd dived in after him, straight from the cliff face, heedless of the danger.

Alex and Tom had descended the rest of the way to the beach. And they'd waited, and waited, Alex pacing the water's edge like a caged lion. But when Justin, at last, came out of the sea, Neville wasn't with him.

"I couldn't find him," he'd said as he struggled for breath. "He's gone."

"No." Alex had shaken his head. "No."

And then, amid Justin and Tom's shouts of protest, he'd gone into the sea himself.

Fear hadn't mattered. Reason hadn't mattered. He'd been too desperate. Too unwilling to accept that Neville had been taken from them.

Margate wasn't Devon. And Laura Hayes wasn't Neville Cross. But as Alex stood on the beach, he felt that same stifling sense of desperation.

"You're making a spectacle of yourself," Henrietta said. "Laura *can* swim, you know."

"Not in the sea, she can't." He scanned the water. There was a glint across a low swell of waves in the distance. A shadow of dark blue on the surface. It was probably nothing. But—

Dear God, it looked remarkably like a person.

"I don't see how you would know that. It isn't as if—" Henrietta broke off with a cry. "What are you doing? Come back here!"

Alex scarcely heard her as he ran out into the surf. The part of his brain still functioning registered the fact that there were no small boats about—no sailors who could be applied to for assistance. There were only bathers with indeterminate swimming skills, paddling in the shallows.

There was no one else to help her. No one else who could possibly get to her in time.

It was the last rational thought he had before he kicked off his shoes, tore off his coat, and dived into the sea.

The cold water swallowed him whole, seeping straight through his trousers and shirt to chill him to the bone. It surged all around him, a living, breathing thing with a power and a will of its own.

He'd always been a strong swimmer. A burst of adrenaline made him even more so. He struck out for where he'd seen her. Where he'd *thought* he had seen her. Far past the women's bathing machines, and out to where the sea began to churn and pull, a dangerous, primitive force that could easily kill a man.

Or a woman.

But Laura wasn't there. The silhouette Alex had seen on the water was gone.

Which meant that he'd been mistaken. Or…

That her lungs had filled with water. That she'd sunk beneath the waves and drowned.

He dived deep, the water closing over his head. A flash of memory—Neville's body sinking into icy darkness—nearly caused him to recoil. But he pressed on, down, down into the murky depths.

It was silent as death under the water, the only sound the rapid pounding of his heart. He swam until his pulse roared in his ears. Until his chest burned for want of air. He needed to breathe. But if *he* needed air, then so did she. And she must be here somewhere. She *must* be here.

He felt about with his hands, moving blindly in the water. This is what it had been like to go into the sea after Neville. This feeling of burgeoning panic. Of lungs struggling for breath, and a sob building in his throat, as again and again he dived into watery darkness.

Laura had called him a coward. A spectator standing alongside the road of life. Never risking anything. Never *feeling* anything.

But he felt something now. It gave him a strength he didn't have. He prayed it was enough.

He dived deep one last time.

As he reached out, a drooping swathe of wool connected with his hand. And miraculously…there she was. Laura. Suspended in the depths of the water.

For a fraction of a second, he thought he must be hallucinating.

And then he gathered her in his arms and kicked with all of his might toward the sunlight.

They broke the surface together, Alex gasping for air. But unlike the day he'd pulled her from Talbot's Pond, there was no indignant sputtering from Laura. No calling him a lummox and telling him he was trespassing.

She was lifeless, her face as white as bleached bone.

Cold fear surged through his veins. He made for the shore, swimming halfway on his back, pulling her along with him.

A small crowd of onlookers had gathered to watch. As Alex dragged Laura up onto the sand, he vaguely registered the presence of Henrietta and George. Teddy was there as well. Yardley must have helped him down from the jetty.

"Laura!" Teddy cried.

"Is she dead?" Henrietta asked.

"She's not breathing," George said.

A stranger shouted for an attendant to fetch someone from the coast-guard station at the summit of the cliffs.

"It's too late," a woman exclaimed. "She's been drowned."

The sound of Teddy's voice cut through the roar of chatter: "Do something!"

Do something.

The same words Alex had uttered on the beach so many years before.

But there was no Justin Thornhill to save the day this time. No Tom Finchley to assist him. It was up to Alex alone. And this time, *this time*, he couldn't afford to make any mistakes.

He rose up on his knees. "Get back!"

Some in the crowd obeyed him. Others remained where they were.

Alex leaned down over Laura. He put his hands on her wool-clad midsection and pushed upward to force the water out of her lungs. Once, twice, and then again, to little effect.

Desperation made him reckless—heedless of the crowd. He might even have cursed a time or two, commanding Laura to *wake up*. All the while, his mind raced over his limited options for reviving her.

In Marseilles, he'd once seen a sailor resuscitate a man with a pair of bellows. But Alex didn't have any bellows, nor was there time to have someone fetch a pair. In place of them, he did the only thing he could think of. He bent his head and covered Laura's half-open mouth with his own.

The gasps from the crowd reached a fever pitch.

Laura's lips were cold as ice. He exhaled into her mouth, giving her as much breath as she might have received from one pump of the bellows.

"This is outrageous!" a woman said shrilly.

"Unhand her, sir!" an elderly man joined in.

"Leave him be!" Teddy shouted. "That's my sister."

Alex breathed into her mouth again. It was surely nothing like he'd seen done in France. And it was probably too late anyway. She'd been too long in the water. He hadn't been fast enough. Strong enough.

He drew back from her face, setting his hands on her midriff once more, and pressing with all of his might—so forcefully he feared he might crack her ribs.

Laura gave a choking cough.

Relief tore through him. He swiftly turned her over, holding her in his arms above the sand as she expelled the water from her lungs in great heaving retches.

The crowd closed in.

He had only moments before they took her away from him. Any second, she'd be wrapped in towels and conveyed back to the hotel.

He leaned down to her one last time. Her lashes fluttered, black as soot against her pale cheeks, as he whispered in her ear.

When he drew back, her smoke-blue eyes met his.

"Do you understand?" he asked.

She gave a weak nod.

And then the coast-guardsman was there, along with Mrs. Bainbridge and the squire. Alex sank back onto the sand, exhausted, as they bundled Laura up and carried her away.

Chapter Fourteen

Surrey, England
August, 1860

Laura sat in the window embrasure, her stocking feet curled up beneath the skirts of her worn muslin day dress, and stared out at the overgrown cottage garden below. Beside her, Magpie gave a lazy yawn. He'd been her only companion in her misery—a silent companion, at that. Something to be grateful for. She had no stomach for judgmental lectures, nor even for well-meant commiseration.

Since arriving back in Lower Hawley, her spirits had sunk to heretofore unimaginable depths. She hadn't wept, and she hadn't yet flown into a temper at the unfairness of it all. She was too numb to do anything, really.

Dr. Taylor had recommended rest and quiet. "Another week and you'll be back to yourself," he'd promised.

Laura didn't know how she could be. Not in one week. Not ever.

Alex Archer was gone.

She'd last seen him on the beach Sunday morning when he'd rescued her. In the ensuing hours, as Aunt Charlotte and one of the maids had stripped her out of her wet bathing costume and put her into a steaming hot bath, there had been no word of him. Only her aunt's grim expression, and the weighted looks of the hotel staff, signaled that anything significant had happened.

When Laura and the rest of their party had boarded the train home later that afternoon, Alex wasn't on it.

"Mr. Archer has disappeared," Aunt Charlotte had whispered, her face creased in distress. "Squire Talbot says he called for his luggage, hired a cab, and simply…left."

"To where?" Laura had asked.

"Does it matter?"

Laura supposed that it didn't. Nothing seemed to matter at the moment.

They'd been back home for nearly two whole days, and there had been no callers. No sign of Henrietta or George, and no visits from the villagers, either—though they were certainly buzzing with gossip by now.

Laura was being properly shunned.

Which made it even more surprising when, later that morning, Aunt Charlotte came to her bedroom and informed her that Henrietta was downstairs.

A flicker of surprise prompted Laura to turn her head from the window. "Is she? Why?"

"She'd like to see you." Aunt Charlotte wrung her hands. "Oh, I realize it's long overdue. But you know how she is. And who can blame her in this instance? Mr. Archer was practically her betrothed."

"He wasn't."

"Near enough, as far as she's concerned. It's only natural that there should be some ill feeling on her part. I mean to say…the man made a spectacle of himself kissing you on a public beach. You! A female too weak to resist. He's compromised you beyond recovery. How could Miss Talbot ever marry him now?"

"He wasn't kissing me, Aunt. I've told you a half dozen times. He was sharing his breath. If you don't believe me, you must at least believe Teddy. He was on the beach when it happened."

Aunt Charlotte gave an eloquent snort. "Sharing his breath, indeed. A likely excuse."

"You weren't there. Not until after he'd revived me."

"I thank God every day that I wasn't. But I've had the events of that morning described to me by more people than I care to count. I don't know how I shall ever hold my head up in the village again. And I can't begin to imagine how *you* ever will. Not without allies. Being civil to Henrietta Talbot would go a long way toward repairing your reputation. If you'll only come down to the parlor and greet her."

Laura turned back to the window. She drew her silk shawl more firmly about her shoulders. "I'm not well enough to come downstairs today."

"Oh, Laura, can you not make the effort—"

"She may come and see me up here if she likes. We are old friends, after all." Laura couldn't keep the edge of bitterness from her voice. Henrietta had been as cold as ice toward her on the train home from Margate. As if it had been Laura's fault that she'd nearly drowned.

And perhaps it was.

Had she been exercising adequate care for her reputation, she'd never have swum off alone. She'd have abided by the rules set out for genteel young ladies. Resisted the temptation of the open sea, and stayed safely near the shore.

Now, as a result of her actions, it wasn't only her own life that was affected. Aunt Charlotte, Teddy, and even Alex were all suffering from the upheaval caused by Laura's reckless decision.

Aunt Charlotte gave Laura's shoulder a gentle squeeze. "My darling. We haven't been the luckiest of families, I know, but we shall rally again, just as we've always done. You mustn't take it too much to heart."

Laura covered her aunt's hand with her own. "Do send up Henrietta."

A short time later, preceded by the creaking of the stairs and the squeak of the loose floorboard in the hall, Henrietta entered Laura's bedroom. She might have stepped straight out of the pages of the *Englishwomen's Domestic Magazine*. Her striped afternoon dress was the height of summer fashion, her flounced skirts standing wide over a wire crinoline.

Laura made no move to rise from the window embrasure, nor did Magpie. He watched Henrietta's approach with a sapient eye.

"Laura." Her voice was frosty. "Your aunt says you've been ill."

"Indeed," Laura replied in equally cool tones. "I nearly drowned two days ago, in case you've forgotten."

"As if I could!" Henrietta crossed the room, her skirts brushing against the heavy furniture. "It was your own fault, you know. If you hadn't insisted on swimming away from the bathing machines, none of this would have happened."

Laura didn't dispute the fact. She knew only too well who was to blame for the situation she found herself in. And it wasn't Alex Archer.

"Why couldn't you have stayed with the rest of us in the shallows?" Henrietta asked. "Why must you always make yourself the center of attention?"

"Is that what you think I was doing?"

"It doesn't matter what I think. I haven't come to quarrel with you." Henrietta walked to the mantel. There was an old carriage clock there, and a red-and-white porcelain spaniel with a chip in its ear. "George came to dine at the Park last night. He told me some very interesting things about Mr. Archer after Papa retired."

"*Mr.* Archer?"

"I won't be familiar with a man of his reputation," Henrietta said primly. "I regret that I ever was."

Laura sighed. "Go on then, what did George have to say?"

Henrietta touched the porcelain figurine with one gloved finger. "He told me that he owes Mr. Archer money. Ten thousand pounds in gaming debts, to be precise."

"Ten thousand pounds!" Laura sat up straighter. "How on earth…?"

"Mr. Archer is a notorious gambler, apparently. One of the most dangerous on the continent. George was well in his clutches before he realized the sort of villain he'd become involved with." Henrietta picked up the figurine. "He has no way to pay his debts. Not even if he were to seek employment. He could never hope to earn such a sum. It's a dastardly situation Mr. Archer has put him in."

Laura doubted very much that George would ever stoop to seeking employment, no matter how much money he owed. "I should think the vastness of the sum speaks more to George's weakness than Alex's villainy."

"You didn't see George as I did last night. He wept when he confessed the whole of it. You see, it was *me* Mr. Archer wanted. In exchange for George introducing us, and helping to assure a match, Mr. Archer promised to forgive all of his debts."

Laura had wondered what hold Alex had over George. What it was that had made George seem so afraid of him. The truth behind their relationship was diabolical, though not wholly surprising. "He didn't want you," she said. "He wanted Edgington Park."

Henrietta gave her a sharp look. "You don't mean to say that you *knew*?"

Laura shrugged one shoulder. "Not of their bargain, or that George owed him money. But I knew he was after your estate."

"How did you know? Who told you?"

"Does it matter?"

Henrietta's lips thinned. "I daresay it doesn't. With Mr. Archer gone for good—"

"You assume he isn't coming back."

"Of course he isn't. Why would he?"

Why indeed.

Laura twined her fingers tight in the folds of her shawl. "For his ten thousand pounds, if for nothing else."

"George doesn't have it. And after Mr. Archer's public display at Margate—"

"He saved my life, Hen," Laura said quietly.

"Nonsense. There was a coast-guardsman on the cliffs. There were men with rowboats just near the shore. Mr. Archer had no call to play the hero." She returned the porcelain dog to its place on the mantel. "And to think that he pretended to dislike the sea! As if he were afraid of it."

"He *was* afraid." Laura knew that much to a certainty. He'd been afraid, and he'd gone into the water anyway. For her.

"He certainly wasn't. You should have seen the way he dived beneath the waves, without a moment's hesitation. And then—when he kissed you—"

"It wasn't a kiss."

"It looked like one, and that's all that matters."

Henrietta was right. The fact that Alex had pressed his mouth to Laura's on a public beach, in front of a crowd of onlookers, was damning. No one seemed to care *why* he'd done it. Not even if the act had saved her life.

"I begin to suspect that you'd far rather he let me die."

Henrietta turned to her with a scowl. "You're twisting my words. I only—"

"You only wanted him for yourself, and now he's entangled with me, and you can't bear it. Well, you are just going to have to learn to bear it. Just as I did when George chose you again and again."

Henrietta's mouth fell open. "Are you jealous of me?"

"I'm not jealous of anyone. I merely think it hypocritical—"

"I'm no hypocrite. I simply speak as I find."

"Yes. Hypocritically."

"What's wrong with you?" Henrietta burst out. "You're being an absolute shrew to me. Heaven knows I don't deserve it."

"Forgive me for being blunt. In case you hadn't noticed, I have a great deal on my mind at present."

"Which is why I've come. To tell you that I realize what happened wasn't wholly your fault. Aside from that, I don't know what else I can do."

"You can be my friend," Laura said. "If you ever were to begin with."

"Of course I'm your friend!"

"When we were children, perhaps, but for many years I think you've preferred to look on yourself as my patroness. You seem to congratulate yourself on your charity in visiting me, or including me in one of your outings."

"I never—"

"And then, at the first sign of scandal, you abandon me. As if our friendship were no more important to you than—"

"Because I didn't call on you yesterday?" Henrietta's eyes flashed. "If you must know, I was rather busy, first comforting George, and then placating my father about having welcomed an international villain into our home."

"If I recall, you were equally busy when my father died. And busier still when my family's fortunes took a turn."

Henrietta's hands balled into fists at her sides. "That's unfair! I condoled with your family on more than one occasion. If I haven't seen you as often since, it isn't for the reasons you're intimating. The world doesn't revolve around you—"

"Why did you want me to be your companion?" Laura asked abruptly. "We hadn't seen each other in months. You might have asked anyone."

Henrietta didn't answer.

"What was it about George's return that prompted you to summon me?"

"Whatever you're implying—"

"All I know," Laura said, "is that George was never so attractive to you as when I fancied him. Just like the dolls we used to play with as children. You only ever wanted the toys that other girls did. That was part of your fun, wasn't it? Having something that everyone else wanted? That *I* wanted?"

Henrietta's face was ashen.

Laura felt a little ashen herself. She didn't know if she was destroying their friendship, or salvaging it. "But I don't want George anymore. I haven't for a very long time. It was Alex I preferred. Which meant that you must prefer him, too."

"You're painting me out to be a horrible person."

"That's the difficulty of it. You aren't horrible. You're a good person. Generous. Kind. But when it comes to suitors—to possessions—you're not very nice, Hen. Not to me."

"And what of you?" Henrietta returned. "Did it never occur to you how *I* feel? George may claim to admire me, but he was forever looking at you. Mr. Archer was, too. You always contrive to make yourself more interesting—more appealing in spite of your lack of fortune. Is it any wonder I sometimes like to put you in your place?"

"We're not in competition."

Henrietta folded her arms. "It often feels as though we are." She came to the window, and plumped down beside Laura.

Her arrival displaced Magpie. He leapt from the window embrasure, his tail twitching with irritation as he trotted from the room.

"It could never have worked between Mr. Archer and me anyway," Henrietta said at last. "He would have been far too difficult for me to manage."

It was the closest thing to an olive branch Laura was likely to get. She didn't have the heart to reject it. "No more difficult than George."

"Oh, George is easy. If you can limit his drinking, and give him a purpose to which he can turn his attention." Henrietta frowned. "Though I will have to address his gambling habits."

"Does this mean—?"

"That I'll marry him? I expect I will. Someone must take George in hand. I suppose it was always going to be me."

"I wish you luck."

"I'd wish you the same if Mr. Archer hadn't disappeared without a trace." She cast Laura a curious glance. "Did you really like him, Laura?"

"I still do," Laura said. "Very much."

"Enough to have him as a husband?" Henrietta laughed. "Well, if you can manage it, I'll see that the church is decked out in ribbons and roses myself—*and* I'll loan you Papa's carriage."

Laura smiled. "Generous to a fault, just as I said."

Henrietta's cheeks dimpled. "Naturally. You're my oldest friend. And we *are* still friends, aren't we? Despite our quarrels?"

"I hope we are," Laura said.

"I meant it about your wedding, you know. Though I don't expect Mr. Archer will be your groom. George said he's likely gone back to France. I daresay we'll never see him again."

Laura didn't believe it. She couldn't. Alex was coming back to Lower Hawley. He had to be. She needed him to redeem her reputation. To put things right with her family, and with the villagers. Without him, she was ruined. Everything was ruined. All of her hopes for the future. Her plans for the perfumery. Her very standing and credibility as a lady.

It was she who'd put it all at risk. And now it was up to him to make it right. To play the hero once more.

She prayed he wouldn't let her down.

Chapter Fifteen

Wednesday morning, Laura ventured outside of the cottage for the first time since their return home. It was still hot as the dickens. Even the heads of the roses were drooping. She nevertheless twined her fringed silk shawl through her arms before stepping out the back door. The chill she'd received from her ill-fated swim hadn't yet left her. She could still feel it all the way to her bones.

The back of the cottage was even more overgrown than the front. It sloped down in a wild tangle of fragrant blooms to a crumbling stone boundary wall at the bottom of the garden. Within its limits were dirt paths that wound their way beneath arbors sagging with the weight of climbing roses, and alongside iron benches that were nearly swallowed whole by untamed bushes of flowers and clusters of colorful weeds.

She looped a basket over her arm. It held a pair of gardening shears and the tattered old gloves she sometimes wore when cutting back the thorny branches of the rosebushes. But she didn't feel much like gardening this morning. Her spirits were mired in the same despondency that had plagued her ever since they'd returned home from Margate.

It was only two days until her Friday appointment with Mr. Finchley. She had to find her way out of the doldrums before then. There was no question of forgoing the journey to London, and no one she could send in her place. She must go herself and see what Mr. Finchley advised them to do. It was their only hope for besting Mr. Weatherwax.

As for the possibility of her marriage…

It no longer merited thought. Her birthday was on Saturday. Even if she had a groom at the ready, there was no time left to journey to Gretna Green.

She wandered down the garden path, stopping next to a bush of red roses. They were as fragrant as the bottle of rose perfume on her dressing table. Full bodied and sweet, without being cloying. She broke one off at the stem and lifted it to her nose.

"Your aunt said I might find you here."

Laura turned sharply.

Alex Archer stood inside the back gate. He was clad in riding clothes—dusty cord breeches, leather top boots, and a rumpled coat. His hair was windswept, his jaw darkened with several days' worth of heavy stubble. He looked travel-worn and exhausted—and far more wolfish than usual.

Her basket slid from her nerveless arm.

He strode forward to catch it before it could hit the ground. "You look as though you've seen a ghost."

She pressed a hand to her corseted midriff. "I feel as if I have."

His mouth tugged into a rueful smile. "That shocking a sight, am I?"

Her heart thumped wildly. "You are, rather." She sounded breathless, as if she'd just walked a brisk half mile. "When did you—?"

"I arrived at the front door not five minutes ago. Your aunt gave me a chilly reception. No doubt I deserve it. I hadn't intended to be away so long. One night, at the most. But that's London for you, especially when dealing with the clerks at Doctors' Commons."

Laura had no idea what he was talking about. Her head was spinning.

"Come." He took hold of her elbow and directed her to a bench beneath the nearest rose arbor. "Sit down before you swoon."

"I've never swooned in my life."

"Humor me."

She sank down on the bench, folding her trembling hands in her lap. "I didn't know when you'd come back. Or *if* you'd come back. I was beginning to think—"

"What? That I'd fled? Never to be seen again?"

She bit her lip.

Alex sat down beside her. He wasn't smiling any longer. "Didn't you hear what I said to you on the beach?"

"Y-yes." Her mouth went dry at the memory of it. "You said that I was yours now. And that you were mine."

"I meant it."

"You don't have to—"

"I *meant* it." His voice was as sure and strong as forged steel. "I wouldn't have said it otherwise."

On the beach, Laura had heard his whispered words as if in a dream. She'd wanted so desperately to believe them. Three long days later, however, foolish romantic notions had been eclipsed by hard common sense. "You only said it because you were concerned about my reputation. You must have known you'd ruined it."

"I suspected I might have done," he said frankly. "But in the moment, I confess, your reputation wasn't at the forefront of my mind."

She felt the same deep urge to believe him. To believe that she was his. That he wanted her. Cared for her. It was a primitive, feminine impulse, void of all logic. Laura endeavored to ignore it. "It doesn't matter now. The damage is done. There's no undoing it."

"It matters to me. A great deal." He studied her face, frowning. "You look ill."

A surge of self-consciousness caught her unaware. She was in an old day dress with a faded stain on the bodice, her hair twisted back in a haphazard roll at her nape. He seemed to have a knack for catching her at her worst. It was irritating, really. "What an unflattering observation."

"There are marks under your eyes. As though you haven't been sleeping."

"I haven't been. Not very well. After what happened at Margate—"

"Which is exactly why I was in such a rush to get everything in order. It's the only way to counter the harm to your reputation."

"I don't care about my reputation!"

He went still.

Laura briefly looked away from him. "That is…I do care, but only in so much as the damage to it harms my family." She forced her gaze back to his. "If I'm upset, it's not because you've ruined me. It's because I've realized that I'm not as strong as I thought I was. That I'll never be strong enough, no matter how hard I try."

"Because you couldn't make it back to shore on your own?"

"Because of everything! Being weak. Unable to manage things. The family's finances, and Teddy's inheritance. My plans for the future of the perfumery, which will likely come to nothing. And now I've put the entire family in the most dreadful predicament."

"You don't always have to be strong, Laura. Your family doesn't expect you to be."

"They do. They're depending on me." She was mortified to feel the hot sting of tears in her eyes. "And I've let them down in every way." Her voice quavered. "I can't save them from anything. When it came to the point, I couldn't even save myself."

"Lucky I was there."

She gave a huff of laughter. It sounded more like a sob. "Yes. Very lucky. Now I've ruined your life as well."

"My dear girl, you couldn't ruin me if you tried. My reputation is already as black as the devil."

My dear girl.

The casual endearment was a soothing balm to her frayed nerves. Whether he meant it in earnest, Laura didn't like to guess. It was enough that he was here. It *had* to be enough.

She dashed a tear from her cheek with the back of her hand. "Don't I know it. George has been telling Henrietta all of your secrets."

Alex's expression betrayed only a mild interest in the subject. "I wasn't aware he knew any."

"He says you're the most dangerous gambler on the continent."

"Is that all?"

"Do you deny it?"

"Being dangerous?" He shrugged a shoulder. "Gamblers are only dangerous to the people who owe them money."

"George claims that he owes you ten thousand pounds."

"Ah."

"Is it really so much as that?"

"It makes little difference now. Given the circumstances, I expect I'll have to forgive George his debts. There's no hope of him repaying them. I knew that well enough when I played against him."

"What about Henrietta?"

"What about her?"

"You were going to marry her. To live at Edgington Park with her and her father. To learn about farming. That's why you came here, isn't it? Why you forced an introduction out of George? You wanted an estate of your own."

"That's all over."

Laura gave him a searching look. "How do you know? Have you spoken to Henrietta?"

One corner of his mouth hitched up. "Are you asking me if I went to Edgington Park? If I called on Henrietta before coming here?"

"Did you?"

"Of course I didn't. I came straight from the railway depot. Just look at the state of me." He paused before adding, "I didn't have to talk to Henrietta. I knew I was finished with her the night you and I waltzed together. I realized then…"

"What?"

He gave a short, husky laugh. "I won't bore you with sentiment."

Butterflies unfurled their wings in her stomach. "It wouldn't bore me. Indeed, I'd very much like to hear it."

"There's little point. I've thought about our situation a good deal, and it seems to me that, going forward, we'd do better to leave sentiment well out of it."

The butterflies vanished. In their place, she felt a vague tremor of foreboding. "I don't understand."

"I've compromised you, quite publicly. There's nothing we can do to mitigate the damage—except to marry."

"Each other?"

He scowled. "Well I'm certainly not suggesting that you marry George."

Under other circumstances, Laura might have smiled at his reaction, or even laughed. But there was nothing humorous in his proposition. He was talking of a marriage void of sentiment. A cold and formal union, entered into for no other reason but to save her reputation.

He didn't love her. Didn't care for her.

"It needn't be anything more than what it is," he said. "A means of redeeming your honor. I won't make demands of you. I won't expect you to—"

Her eyes searched his. She saw something there. A flicker of sadness. Of grim resignation. "Expect me to what?"

"To pretend to feelings that you don't have. I know what I am. And I know what I deserve." His jaw hardened with resolve. "You'll have my name, that's all. In every other respect, you may go on as you always have. If that's…If that's what you wish."

"What you're describing—"

"Call it a marriage of convenience."

Laura's brows knit. "It doesn't sound like a marriage of any kind. It sounds like a lie. A fiction."

"A convenient fiction, then. But one based in law. The marriage itself will be real enough. I have the license to prove it."

Her heart skipped a beat. "You've obtained a marriage license?"

"Why do you think I went to London?" He reached into an interior pocket of his coat and withdrew a folded paper. "It's a special license."

Her eyes widened. She'd only ever heard of such a thing in novels. It permitted a couple to marry wherever and whenever they pleased—without the burden of calling the banns. She took it from Alex, her pulse accelerating as she read it over. "We could marry tomorrow if we wished."

"We could." He regarded her steadily. "Does this mean you agree? That the arrangement meets your approval?"

Arrangement.

She swallowed. "If this is a proposal, it's a very poor one."

"I hadn't thought one necessary. Doesn't the proposal you made me at Talbot's Pond still stand?"

"You refused me at Talbot's Pond."

"Stupid of me." He reached out and took her hand, engulfing it in the strong clasp of his fingers. "Laura…"

Her heart was somewhere in her throat. "Yes?"

"That day at the pond…I meant what I said about there being no place in my life for unfettered emotion. I can't care about anything too deeply. Every time I have—" He broke off. "Let's just say that things haven't ended particularly well."

"Was there another lady you cared for?" she asked. "A relationship that went wrong?"

"What? No. There's never been another woman. Not one who's tempted me the way you have." A fleeting smile touched his lips. "You're a siren."

Heat crept up her throat and into her cheeks. "I'm certainly not."

"You are. I don't think I've had a rational thought since the day I first encountered you. You've disrupted all of my plans. Thrown my entire life out of balance. Good God, you lured me back into the sea. No one else in the world could have done that."

"You make it sound as though whatever you feel for me is against your will. As if I've cast a malevolent spell on you."

"A spell, yes, but not a malevolent one. I daresay the effects of it will pass once we part."

His words chilled her. "You intend to marry me, and then… leave Lower Hawley?"

"Not immediately, no. We're trying to quell an existing scandal, not ignite a new one. We must live together for a time. A month or two, at least. And then—at some point in the future—if you wish it, we can quietly go our separate ways."

If she wished it, he kept saying. If she *wished* to have a marriage of convenience. If she *wished* to part from him. As if he was reluctant to inflict himself on her. As if living with him— being his wife—were some awful punishment he hoped to spare her from.

"Would you have done Henrietta the same courtesy?" she asked.

"Henrietta was different."

She stiffened. "I see."

"No, you don't." His hand tightened around hers when she tried to withdraw it. "I didn't care for Henrietta."

"Oh." Her voice was a mere thread of sound.

He did care for her after all. Cared for her so much that he was willing to leave her. It was some sort of logic. The ridiculous masculine kind, no doubt.

"Whatever you choose to do," he went on, "you'll have my name, and any financial support you require. Having a husband may even carry some weight with that London solicitor of yours."

"More than you know," she said. "But surely you needn't contemplate leaving. Just because things have gone wrong in the past—"

"Things don't go wrong, Laura. *I* go wrong. I'm not a good man. It's been many years since I aspired to be one."

"Nonsense. You may not be a good man, but…you're not a bad one, either."

"Faint praise," he said. "Though more than I deserve."

"I mean it." She pressed his hand. "A black-hearted villain would never have gone into the sea to rescue me. Not if it meant destroying all of his plans with a marriageable young heiress."

He looked down at her hand, curled safely in his. "Yes, well… This particular black-hearted villain wasn't thinking entirely clearly at the time."

"And now you mean to marry me, though you must know that you could easily find another wealthy lady to wed."

His gaze lifted to hers. "I daresay I could. There's only one problem."

"Which is?"

"She wouldn't be you."

Her heart turned over.

"Will you marry me, Laura?" he asked. "Will you consent to be my wife?"

A humid breeze stirred the roses on the arbor. Their sweet perfume drifted in the morning air. A fragrant promise for the future, or so Laura thought. A promise not just for her, but for Teddy and Aunt Charlotte, too. They were going to be all right. *Everything* was going to be all right. All she had to do was say yes.

And so, she did.

"Yes," she said. "I will."

A spasm of emotion crossed over Alex's face. It was gone as quickly as it had appeared—a tiny crack in the mask he always wore. He raised her hand to his lips and pressed a kiss to it. "You honor me."

Laura could think of no reply. Speech seemed wholly inadequate—unnecessary too. After only an instant, he released her hand. The moment had passed.

"Here, I have something for you." He once again reached into his pocket. "Another reason I traveled to London. I keep one or two valuables in care of a bank there." He produced a small cylindrical box bound in red morocco leather. "This is one of them."

Laura hadn't much experience with fashionable jewel cases, but she recognized one when she saw it. She took it from him with trembling fingers and very slowly opened the hinged lid.

Her breath stopped in her chest.

Inside the box, settled on a bed of velvet, was a single flawless ruby set in a band of antique gold.

Her eyes flew to his. "Is this—?"

"A betrothal ring. A wedding band. Whatever you wish to call it." He removed it from the box. "I believe it will fit you. If not, I can send it out to a jeweler." He took her hand again, and slipped the ring onto her third finger. It caught briefly on her knuckle before sliding firmly home. "There. Perfect."

She stared down at her hand. The ruby smoldered with liquid fire, as red as a drop of blood against her pale skin. It seemed significant somehow. Far too significant a ring for a mere marriage of convenience. "It looks very old."

"You don't like it?"

"I do. Very much. But…where did you get it? Is it a family heirloom of some kind?"

"I told you," he said, "I was born an orphan. I haven't any family."

She looked up at him. This mysterious, fascinating, complicated man that would soon be her husband. Her heart thumped hard. "You do now."

Chapter Sixteen

Alex stood in front of the rickety wooden wash-stand in Teddy's bedroom, lathering his jaw with lemon verbena-scented shaving soap. After accepting his proposal, Laura had insisted he come inside and refresh himself from his journey.

There was little alternative.

He had no accommodations in the village yet. And the vicar wasn't likely to welcome him back at the vicarage—not now that he knew the shameless way Alex had exploited George.

"A marriage of convenience." Teddy sat across the room in his wheeled chair, watching Alex shave with a doubtful expression. "And Laura's agreed to it?"

"She has." Alex's chest tightened to recall it.

He hadn't known what to expect when he'd approached Laura in the garden. And when she'd consented to marry him—when he'd slipped the ruby ring on her finger—there was a part of him that couldn't quite take it in.

She'd been right to accuse him of being a chameleon. His life since he'd left North Devon was one of artifice and illusion. But his proposal to Laura had been all too real.

Had she refused him, it would have been a devastating blow.

"When?" Teddy asked.

Alex wiped his hands on the wet cloth that hung beside the basin. "We haven't set a day yet." He picked up his shaving razor. "But soon."

"Tomorrow," Teddy said.

"If that's what your sister wants."

The door creaked open a crack. It was the cat, poking its head through. When it saw Teddy, it trotted the rest of the way into the room and jumped onto his desk.

Teddy gave the beast a cursory stroke. "She will. Her birthday is on Saturday. She'll want to be married before then."

"You're very certain."

"I know my sister. She'll do what she thinks is best for everyone—even if it makes her unhappy in the end."

Alex's hand stilled on his razor, midway through a downward stroke along the edge of his jaw. He met Teddy's gaze in the mirror. "You don't sound as if you approve of our marrying."

"I don't disapprove. If not for you, she'd have drowned at Margate. I know that. So does my aunt, though she won't admit it. You saved Laura's life. But that doesn't give you the right to make what's left of it a misery."

"I don't intend to. Which is why I'll likely be leaving at some point in future."

"Huh." Teddy appeared unimpressed by this revelation. "Where will you go?"

"France, probably." Alex resumed shaving. His beard came off in a series of practiced flicks of the razor. "It would be better for all involved."

"Better for you, you mean." Teddy picked up the cat from his desk and dropped it gently onto the floor. "Is the idea of living here with her so unappealing?"

"It's not about her."

"In other words—"

"In other words, it's between your sister and me." Alex rinsed his razor in the basin. "Some things, my lad, are none of your business."

"I'm Laura's brother. She'll always be my business. If you harm her—"

"I'm not going to harm her."

"You'll break her heart."

"I doubt that," Alex said.

He didn't have Laura's heart. She was fond of him, certainly. Fond enough to accept his proposal. But love was something else entirely. He hadn't experienced it yet in his life, and he didn't expect to.

"You don't know much about women," Teddy observed.

Alex chuckled as he finished shaving. "And you do?"

"I've been in love before."

"Have you now?" Alex cast Teddy an interested glance. "With whom, may I ask?"

Teddy gave him a wry look. "Henrietta Talbot."

Alex's brows shot up. "*Henrietta*? I thought you despised her."

"I don't *despise* her. I merely recognize her for what she is. A small-minded, provincial petty tyrant. One doesn't notice so much at first, but in time it's all too clear."

Alex wiped the remaining soap from his jaw. "What happened?"

Teddy shrugged. "I grew out of it. Every man does."

"You make it sound as though falling in love with Henrietta Talbot was a rite of passage for the gentlemen of Surrey."

"I daresay it is. She's very beautiful."

"Not as beautiful as your sister."

"Oh, Laura's all right. She doesn't bore a chap, at least." Teddy rolled his chair back from his desk. "I don't expect she'll bore you."

Alex dried his face with the cloth. "Chances are, I won't be around long enough to find out."

Teddy said nothing in response. The look of disapproval on his face was reply enough.

When Alex finished washing and changing, he assisted Teddy down the stairs to the parlor and helped him get settled on the sofa. Mrs. Bainbridge was already there, seated in a winged chair near the fireplace. She'd been decidedly cool to Alex since his arrival.

"Where's Laura?" he asked.

"She's gone to the kitchen to see about tea. We're very informal here, Mr. Archer. Had you sent us word that you intended to arrive today, we might have been better prepared."

"For that, I must beg your pardon," Alex said. "And for causing you any distress. I've been too much on my own these past years. One forgets the common courtesies."

She pursed her lips. "I think you might have at least mentioned you were going to London to procure a special license. Had we known, it would have alleviated much of our worrying."

Alex apologized once more before withdrawing from the room to find Laura.

He didn't like making excuses for his behavior. Didn't feel he owed them to anyone. Apologizing was simply a matter of form. A means of smoothing over ruffled feathers, so one could get on with the business of the day.

In this case, however, Alex had to own that Mrs. Bainbridge was right.

Perhaps he should have sent word of his whereabouts to Laura and her family. On arriving in London, it had certainly crossed his mind. But when it came to the point, he hadn't been equal to sending a telegram. Not because he hadn't had the time, and not because he lacked the courtesy, but because—in all truth—a part of him had wanted, quite badly, to simply disappear.

He hadn't been lying to Laura about the dangers of his caring for people. There would always be a part of him that couldn't be trusted or relied upon. The more he cared for someone, the greater his betrayal would be in the end. His past provided ample proof of that fact. He'd loved Justin, Tom, and Neville like brothers. They were the closest thing he'd ever had to a family, and he'd betrayed them worst of all.

On boarding the train from Margate, Alex had felt the urge to betray Laura, too. To leave her behind before he hurt her even worse than he'd hurt them. It would be a noble action, he'd told himself. A sacrifice which would, ultimately, spare her from being bound forever to an unscrupulous villain.

In the end, such sentiments were no match for his own selfishness. As he waited for the clerk to fill out the special license in Doctor's Commons, he came to accept the simple truth: He wanted Laura too much to let her go.

"You're mine now," he'd whispered to her on the beach. "And I'm yours."

It had been a foolish, impulsive thing to say. A sentiment brought on by her words to him as they'd waltzed together. But he'd meant it, God help him.

There had been no turning back from that moment. No running away. He might be a villain. A selfish, heartless, rogue. But Laura was his. Bound to him as surely as if they'd already been joined in matrimony.

All that remained was to make their connection legal.

Alex found her in the pantry cupboard off the kitchen. She'd changed into a clean morning dress, her hair freshly arranged in a plaited coil at her neck, secured with a pair of combs.

She stood up on the toes of her slippers, stretching her arm to reach the top shelf. When she saw him, her face brightened. "Just the fellow I need. Can you reach that tin?"

He stepped past her, briefly resting his hand on the small of her back. "What is it?"

"Sugared biscuits. Mrs. Crabtree made them for our tea yesterday."

He retrieved the tin with ease. "Here you are."

"Thank you." As she took it from him, their bare fingers brushed.

A frisson of heat flickered low in his belly. She smelled of summer roses, lavender water, and starched linens. Clean and fresh and sweet. "Laura…"

She looked up at him. "What is it?"

"After tea, I have to pay a visit to the vicarage."

"To see George?"

"To speak with the vicar. I owe him some kind of explanation."

"He may not be in any mood to hear one. With everything George has been saying, he's predisposed to think ill of you."

"With good reason."

A cloud of worry darkened her brow. "It's not going to be a pleasant visit, I fear."

"No. Which is why it's better to get it over with. Especially if we want the vicar to marry us." He paused, suddenly uncertain. "You do wish to marry in a church?"

"Of course."

Mrs. Crabtree chose that moment to poke her head around the corner. Though she saw them both standing together, plain as day, she addressed her remarks to Laura as if Alex wasn't there. "Did you find those biscuits, miss?"

"Yes, indeed. Here they are." Laura handed her the tin. "Do you need my help with anything else, Mrs. Crabtree?"

Mrs. Crabtree's mouth tightened a fraction. "You attend to your guest, Miss Laura. I'll bring the tray in soon as it's ready."

"I often help," Laura confided after the housekeeper had gone. "I suppose she doesn't care for me to admit it in company."

"You cook?" Alex was unable to keep the note of surprise out of his voice. Ladies weren't supposed to assist in the kitchen, no matter how straitened their circumstances. Cooking was servants' work.

"A little," she admitted. "Why? Do you think it beneath me? I assure you it isn't. After my father died, we couldn't afford to keep on the kitchen maid or the parlor maid. It was up to me to help Mrs. Crabtree with some of the chores—and the meals, as well." A faint flush of color rose in her cheeks. "I'm not ashamed of it."

"Nor should you be." He knew very well how Laura felt about work. She'd informed him the first day they'd met that being a gentleman—or a lady, for that matter—was no excuse not to do what one needed to survive. "All the same," he said, choosing his words with care, "I'd rather you didn't spend your days toiling in the kitchen. After we're married, you must employ more help. A maid or two, and a footman."

"Alex—"

"Don't quibble. I may not be landed gentry, but I'm no pauper. Fifty or sixty pounds per annum in servants' wages isn't likely to bankrupt me."

"It's not that. Indeed, if things go according to plan with Hayes's Perfumes, you won't have to lay out any money on my account at all." Her ebony brows drew together. "Would you like me to go with you to the vicarage?"

"Riding pillion on my horse?" He half smiled. "That would be charming—though unadvisable, I think."

"Yes, I suppose you're right. Will you be coming back directly?"

He shook his head. "I need to find accommodations in the village. A room at the inn. Something. Best to keep this looking as aboveboard as possible."

"It's a little late for that. The whole village is already brimful of gossip about you being a villain, and my being your unwitting victim. It can hardly get any worse."

"Let's not tempt fate, shall we? You and your family have to live in Lower Hawley. You'll be here long after I'm gone. It won't hurt to try to right the ship before I leave."

"Ah yes. Your plan to marry me and then quietly disappear." She smoothed her hand over his waistcoat. "I have more to say on that subject."

His breath hitched. These little proprietary touches of hers would be the end of him. "Say it, by all means."

"Not now. It requires a longer conversation than can be had in a pantry cupboard." She hesitated, her fingers toying absently with one of his buttons. "I can't ride behind you on your horse, but there's nothing to say we can't walk together to the vicarage."

"In this heat?"

"It would give us time to talk."

He covered her restless fingers with his hand. "Is it that important?"

Laura gave him an odd, measuring look. "Yes. I believe it is."

Laura kept pace with Alex as they made their way along the curving path that led through Talbot's Wood. It ran parallel to the road and had the benefit of being partially shaded by the branches of the trees. The heat was still oppressive, but less so than it might otherwise have been.

She wondered if he regretted agreeing to walk the distance to the vicarage with her rather than ride. He'd been quiet since they left the cottage.

Not that she could blame him.

Tea with Aunt Charlotte and Teddy had been a tense affair, punctuated by thinly veiled statements of censure, and outright disbelief. Aunt Charlotte clearly didn't think that Alex would keep his word to marry Laura. While Teddy seemed to be more concerned that he would.

"It's not worth it," he'd told her in a private moment. "Not for our sakes."

"I haven't agreed to marry him for the sake of the family," Laura had replied. "Not entirely."

It was the truth.

She'd said yes to Alex's proposal because she was fond of him. More than fond, if she was honest with herself. She actually *liked* him.

There were practical considerations, too, of course. Marrying him would help to smother some of the gossip that now surrounded the Hayes family. It would also ensure that at least fifty percent of the family business was out of Mr. Weatherwax's control.

It was the latter which weighed most heavily on Laura's conscience.

"Alex?"

He glanced down at her.

"Do you remember what I told you about my family's perfume business? About how Teddy is meant to inherit the whole of it upon his majority?"

"Yes," he said. "What about it?"

She slowed her pace. "There's something else. Something I didn't mention before. It hardly seemed relevant at the time. Indeed, until today, it had no bearing upon our relationship at all. But now…I can't possibly marry you without you knowing."

A wry smile flickered in his eyes. "A dark secret? You intrigue me."

"Don't tease. I'm trying to be forthright about all of this. It's something that affects you, just as much as it will affect the rest of my family."

His expression sobered. "Go on."

She took a steadying breath. "There's another element to my father's will. A provision for me, in a roundabout way.

It states that, if I marry before the age of five and twenty, I inherit half of the business."

Alex stopped on the path to look at her.

She came to a halt, forcing herself to meet his gaze. "More to the point, my husband inherits half of the business."

"Your husband," he repeated.

"Papa didn't believe that women should involve themselves in affairs of business. Not in a formal capacity."

"What are you saying?"

"Only that, if you and I marry before Saturday, half of Hayes's Perfumes will legally belong to you."

Alex's face was impossible to read.

She pressed on in spite of it. "I'd thought—or, rather, hoped—that once it did, you would permit me to manage it. I have plans, you see. Have had for the last three years. Teddy and I have been waiting for him to come of age so I can set those plans in motion. We never seriously considered my marrying. I hadn't any desire to do so. But now—"

"Is this why you said yes to my proposal?"

She blinked up at him. "What? No. That is…I'm sure it carried some weight in my decision, but—"

"How much weight?" His voice was strange. Deeper than usual, with an underlying hint of…something.

"I don't know. Does it matter?"

He said nothing for a long moment. And then: "No, I suppose not. This isn't a love match, after all."

Laura felt the sharp edge of his words all the way to her heart. Had he insulted her—rejected, or humiliated her—it couldn't have hurt any worse. She looked ahead down the path, focusing on the trees and the shrubs, their leaves shimmering in the sunlight. "No," she agreed at last. "It's a marriage of convenience, that's all. And one that will see you much better off than you anticipated."

He folded his arms, staring down at her with that same unreadable expression. "How much better off?"

"Let me see." She smoothed her skirts, vaguely registering that her palms were damp. "There's the flower farm in Dorset—about two hundred acres, with an attached distillery. A factory in London. And a property in France—another flower farm with a distillery nearby."

"Your family owns all of the land?" He sounded incredulous.

"Well…yes. How else do you think we earn enough to live on? Mr. Weatherwax leases out the land in Dorset to the farmer who owns the adjoining property. As for the London factory, and the distillery in France, they've been shuttered since my father died. Mr. Weatherwax has often tried to convince us to sell them, but Teddy and I have held firm."

"What do you plan to do with them?"

"Open them back up, of course. And not for perfume production. We won't make my father's mistake. We'll return to making lavender water. Only this time, we'll have other fragrances available as well. Rose, orange blossom, and the like. All we need do is borrow the funds to get production started."

Alex walked to the edge of the path and stopped. His back was to her, his shoulders taut beneath the lines of his coat. "And what's to prevent me from selling my half share as soon as we marry?"

Her heart leapt into her throat. "You would never!"

He turned back to face her. A warm breeze ruffled his hair. The section he wore combed back from his brow, fell down over his forehead. "You don't know that."

She looked at him, speechless.

"You don't know anything about me, Laura. Except that I'm a gambler and a fortune hunter. A man with no family, no friends, and no fixed address. Not the best credentials for a business partner."

"No, but…you wouldn't just be a business partner. You'd be my husband."

A muscle twitched in his cheek. "Worse and worse. Husbands routinely squander their wives' fortunes."

"I don't have a fortune. Nowhere near it."

"You have the potential for one. Much more than I knew."

"Only if we work for it. Only if we take the risk. To simply sell the land and the distilleries would be a poor decision. One that would garner but a fraction of the income we could earn if we put them to use."

"We," he echoed. "You and Teddy?"

"You and I." She took an uncertain step toward him. "Teddy wants no part in managing the business. He trusts me to do what's right for us all."

"And, in turn, you must trust me?" His lip curled in a sardonic smile. "I wouldn't advise it."

She closed the remaining distance between them, coming to stand in front of him, so close that her full skirts billowed against his legs. "Why are you being so disagreeable?" She laid her hand on his arm. "Is it because I didn't tell you about all of this before?"

His gaze fell to her hand, lingering on the ruby ring he'd put on her finger. "I'm not being disagreeable. I'm being realistic."

"You're being perfectly churlish. Saying that you'll sell my half of the business. That's not realistic. That's cruel. Whatever else you are, you're not that."

"You think not?"

"I know you aren't. I've seen how you are with Teddy, and with Aunt Charlotte. Not to mention the fact that you risked your life to save mine. You're no unfeeling brute. Not by a long chalk." When he would have looked away from her, she lifted her hand to his cheek, gently compelling him to meet her eyes. "What is it you're afraid of?" she asked softly. "Is it so unthinkable that you might have a life here?"

"Not unthinkable, no." His voice went gruff. "It's bloody terrifying."

"Because you care for me?"

"If I didn't, I'd have nothing to lose."

Her heart twisted with sympathy for him. "I see." She smoothed his hair from his brow. "In that case, you're simply going to have to trust me."

He bent his head to hers. "What about you? How can you trust me? How do you know I won't squander your share of the business, and leave you no better off than you were before?" His gaze was troubled. "I don't want to hurt you, Laura."

"Then don't." She leaned against him. "I have faith in you."

"You haven't any reason to."

"That's what faith is, isn't it?" She stroked his cheek. "Besides, you couldn't be any worse than Mr. Weatherwax."

Alex huffed a laugh. "If that's the bar by which I'm being measured—"

"You've already surpassed it with miles to spare."

"The man must be beyond all hope."

"He's insufferable and overbearing, is what he is. I've hated dealing with him these past years." She couldn't suppress a self-satisfied smile. "I can hardly wait to see the look on his face when he learns that I've managed to marry before my birthday."

"Will you have to see him again?"

"I'm afraid I must. Not only to sort out the legalities for my half of the business, but to make another argument for Teddy's half. I'll have to go to London on Friday. I already have an appointment with another solicitor." She frowned. "I wonder if I should keep it?"

"Is it purely to force Weatherwax's hand?"

"That was the original idea. Unfortunately, Mr. Finchley isn't able to represent me. He's only agreed to see me in order to refer me to another solicitor. Still, I…" She trailed off. "What is it?"

Alex took a step back from her. "*What* did you say?"

Her hand fell from his cheek. She looked at him in bewilderment. "Which part? Was it about Mr. Finchley?"

He visibly flinched. "Is that his name?"

"Thomas Finchley, Esquire. That's what his card says." She searched Alex's face. It was slowly draining of color. "Have you had dealings with the man?"

"Have *you*?" he returned.

"No. I haven't even communicated with him. Not directly. The letter I received was signed by his clerk. It was he who set the appointment."

"Cancel it."

"But why—"

"It's unnecessary." He turned his back to her for a moment. Laura heard him take a ragged breath. She had the impression he was exercising brutal control over his emotions. "Whereabouts in London was this solicitor located?"

"On Fleet Street. Not far from Mr. Weatherwax's office." She touched his sleeve. "Alex…who is he?"

He ran a hand over the back of his neck. "I don't know. He might be no one. Or…"

"Or?"

"He might be a boy I knew once in the orphanage. A former friend."

"You don't wish to find out?"

"No." He gave her a wry look. "We didn't part on the best of terms."

She frowned up at him. "Why do I have the feeling there's more to this story?"

"That chapter of my life has been closed for a very long time. I'd rather not revisit it."

She nodded slowly. "Very well. We don't have to speak of it if you don't wish to."

"I don't," he said. "Not now. Not ever."

Chapter Seventeen

Tom Finchley was alive.

Not only alive, but alive and well, and apparently thriving—in Fleet Street, of all places. Only a short railway journey and a hansom cab's drive away.

As Alex stood at the window of the vicarage parlor, waiting for the housekeeper to summon the vicar, the reality of it ran over and over again in his mind. He worried at it like a child picking at a slowly healing wound. Drawn to the pain of it. Unable to leave it alone long enough to heal.

What were the chances that returning to England—to Lower Hawley, of all places—would have thrown him so swiftly into Tom's path? Surrey was a long way away from London, and an even longer way from North Devon. It had seemed a safe destination. An inoffensive place in which to marry and set down roots.

It had been a miscalculation of epic proportions.

Better he had stayed in France. Better he had never come back to England at all. But then…

Then he'd never have met Laura.

He cast her a brooding glance. She was seated on the sofa, hands folded neatly in her lap. The ruby ring glinted against her skin.

It was bad enough that she'd insisted on coming with him to the vicarage. Now she knew something of his past as well. The part of his past he was most ashamed of. His betrayal of Tom Finchley.

A former friend, he'd told her.

He could have more accurately described Tom as a brother.

There was a part of Alex that thanked God Tom was alive. In the days before Alex had left North Devon, Tom had been articled to a London solicitor. Of all of the orphans, his future has seemed the brightest. It was only fair. Tom had always been smarter than the rest of them.

"Just compensation for being small," he'd told Alex once. "You, Justin, and Neville can carve out your futures with brute strength. I shall have to use my wits."

Alex vaguely remembered being jealous of his friend's good fortune. Unlike Tom, Alex had been apprenticed to old Mr. Crenshaw, the cantankerous apothecarist in Abbot's Holcombe. Crenshaw had been poorly suited to train up a willful boy of twelve, choosing to communicate more with a crack of his walking stick across his apprentice's back than with his words.

And then there were Crenshaw's friends.

One fellow in particular who had patronized the apothecary shop. Gilbert Morley. A man who had been all too interested in Crenshaw's young apprentice.

Alex had spent years erasing the events from his memory, but it was the work of seconds to call them back again. The leering looks. The sly innuendo. The feelings of powerlessness, and revulsion.

"What a strapping lad you are," Morley had said the first time he'd seen him. He'd come into the shop when Alex was alone. Had backed him into a corner. "Anyone ever told you that?"

Alex's gaze had darted to the door, willing Crenshaw to return.

"And such a handsome face." Morley's eyes had raked over him from head to toe. "I like a comely boy, meself. A healthy young lad like you."

It had never gone any further than a single, encroaching touch. Alex had run away before it could. But if he'd stayed…

The reality of what might have happened to him turned his stomach.

Had Mr. Fothergill, the grim-looking solicitor who took Tom from the orphanage, been as unforgiving as Crenshaw? As despicable as Morley? Or had Tom been brought along in his profession with patience and kindness?

It seemed that some of their little brotherhood were destined to do well in life. Tom was a successful solicitor, apparently. And Justin was now married to an earl's daughter. An heiress, in fact. He'd even gained ownership of Greyfriar's Abbey.

And what of Neville?

Was he alive and well? Or had his fall from the cliffs at Abbot's Holcombe ultimately killed him, or damaged him in some permanent way?

For over two decades, Alex had resigned himself to not knowing. But now…

"You're very quiet," Laura said.

He forced a half smile. "The calm before the storm."

No sooner had he spoken than the parlor door swung open, and the vicar entered the room. He looked as he always did—his gray hair rumpled, his frock coat slightly worn, and his spectacles perched halfway down his nose. "Mr. Archer. Miss Hayes. This is a surprise."

"Mr. Wright," Alex said.

George trailed in after his father. His hands were thrust into his pockets.

The vicar motioned both men to sit. "There were many who thought we'd seen the back of you, sir." He flicked a reproving glance at Laura. "Your aunt was among them."

Laura didn't appear surprised. "Aunt Charlotte's predisposed to worry."

"With good reason, it seems." The vicar settled himself in a chair before once again addressing Alex. "My son has been telling me all sorts of things about you, Mr. Archer. Am I to assume that's why you've come?"

Alex took a seat next to Laura on the sofa. "It is."

"It's none of your business, father." George leaned against the mantel. His expression was sullen. "I shouldn't have said anything. Don't know why I did."

"Because you thought I wasn't coming back," Alex said. "But here I am, as you see."

George scowled. "Where the devil did you get to? Had I known you'd return—"

"To London. To purchase a special license." Alex took Laura's hand in his. It was silky warm, her slim fingers threading through his. "Miss Hayes has consented to be my wife."

Understanding registered in George's eyes. Anger quickly followed. "What about Henrietta? You and I had a bargain—"

"George." The vicar raised a hand to silence him. "Let us speak about this in a civilized manner. We are not savages." He turned to Alex. "About this bargain…am I to understand that my son owes you money? A sum he lost to you at the gambling tables in France?"

"He does, sir."

"And that the sum exceeds ten thousand pounds?"

Alex inclined his head.

The vicar's eyes were suddenly weary. "You and I must come to terms then. We honor our debts in this household."

"I told you, it's nothing to do with you," George said to his father. "I already negotiated a way to pay it back."

"I know all about the way you arranged to pay your debt," the vicar returned with uncharacteristic venom. "By sacrificing the life of an honorable young woman."

"It was only an introduction. Henrietta wasn't obliged to marry him."

"That poor girl deserved better from you."

George snorted. "That *poor* girl is three times as devious as I am, and twice as devious as Archer. If you can't see that—"

"Enough, George. I won't hear you justify your sin. All I require from you—"

"All you require is perfection. That I meet your unmeetable standards."

"Not that you meet them, only that you aspire to them. The same thing I would ask of any of my congregation."

"I'm not your congregation," George said. "I'm your *son*."

"Enough," the vicar said again. "I won't have us repeat this old argument in company." He removed his spectacles. "Mr.

Archer, I'm in no position to scold you when my own son is the architect of your transgression, but I must say that—"

"There's nothing George has done that I didn't intend him to do," Alex said. "When I met him in Marseilles, I saw that he was a man with no head for cards—or for liquor. I took advantage of both in order to achieve my ends. It was badly done of me. I've come today to beg your pardon for it."

"To beg my pardon?" The vicar blinked.

"And to forgive the debt." Alex felt Laura squeeze his hand. No doubt she thought it was a heroic gesture. To give up ten thousand pounds—a king's ransom.

Alex knew better.

There had never been any chance that George would actually pay the sum. Alex had only continued to play against him because he knew there was another sort of compensation to be had. A chance to meet and marry an heiress. To win for himself what Justin Thornhill had somehow managed to gain—a wife of fortune and property.

But that was all over now.

"You don't owe me anything," he said. "Neither of you do."

"You're forgiving the whole ten thousand pounds?" George's hand gripped the mantel until his knuckles turned white. "Are you in earnest?"

"Dead earnest."

George seemed to sag in his boots. "Good lord, but I need a drink."

The vicar looked as relieved as his son. "Mr. Archer…I don't know what to say."

"You needn't say anything," Alex replied. "I can only hope, in time, we might put this whole unfortunate episode behind us. Not just for my sake, but for Miss Hayes's sake, as well."

Laura's mouth tilted into a cautious smile. "We'd like you to marry us, sir."

"Indeed?" The vicar settled his spectacles back on his nose. "I daresay it's necessary. People have been talking a great deal, and none of it to the good. It's the way of things in a small village. I've tried to dispel the worst of it. And I intend to go further. This Sunday, my sermon will be on the scripture from Second Kings, when Elijah put his mouth upon the mouth of a dead boy and revived him with his breath. Not all such behavior is the stuff of scandal."

"Mr. Archer saved my life," Laura said. "If not for him…"

Alex's throat tightened. He didn't want to think about what might have happened if his rescue attempts had failed. If Laura had died there on the beach at Margate. The very idea of it was too painful to contemplate.

"Quite right," the vicar agreed. "Would that an understanding of that would be enough to quell the gossip."

"Will marriage be enough to stop it?" Alex asked.

"I believe it will. Nevertheless…" The vicar paused, frowning. "I should hate to think that was your only motivation to wed. The bonds of matrimony are sacred. They shouldn't be entered into lightly."

"We aren't entering into it lightly," Laura said. "Marriage was in our thoughts well before the incident at Margate."

"It's true. We spoke of it only last Monday." Alex's thumb moved over the curve of Laura's finger. "Didn't we, Miss Hayes?"

The most delicate of blushes rose in her cheeks. "We did," she agreed. "So you see, it's not merely because of the scandal."

"In that case," the vicar said, "it would be my profound pleasure. Have you a date in mind?"

"We do. Tomorrow morning at the church." Laura cast Alex a questioning look. "Is that all right?"

Alex gazed steadily back at her. Tomorrow she would be his. Not just for an hour, or a day, but for all time. His wife—even if he left her. "It's perfect."

The vicar himself conveyed the pair of them back to Bramble Cottage in his carriage. From there, Alex retrieved his horse from the stable and made ready to depart for a hotel in the village.

"While I'm there, I'll send a wire to Weatherwax," he said as he and Laura stood alone outside the garden gate. "I'll tell him we expect him here without delay."

"He'll never come."

"He will," Alex assured her. He gathered up the reins and mounted his horse.

"Are you're returning for dinner?" she asked.

He smiled. "I wouldn't miss it."

Laura stood at the gate as he rode away. When she returned to the house, she found the vicar seated alone in the parlor. Magpie was curled up on a sofa cushion, watching him.

"Your aunt has gone to fetch a book for me from her room. But do sit, Miss Hayes. This gives us an opportunity to talk."

Laura had a sinking feeling that she was in for a lecture. She perched on the edge of the sofa next to Magpie.

The vicar wasted no time in getting to the point. "Your aunt tells me this is to be a marriage of convenience."

Her spirits sank further. Why on earth had Aunt Charlotte felt the need to tell him *that*?

"You'll forgive me mentioning it," he went on. "I was under the impression that it was by way of being a love match."

She stroked Magpie's head. Her words, when she spoke, were far calmer than she felt. "Whatever gave you that idea?"

"You have no fortune, Miss Hayes. It's common knowledge in Lower Hawley. Yet Mr. Archer—a man who is best described as a fortune hunter—has betrothed himself to you. What reason could he have other than love?"

"My reputation was at risk. After what happened at Margate—"

"A fact which would be of no concern to a fortune hunter. Certainly not a man unscrupulous enough to take advantage of a drink-addled boy like George."

"I beg your pardon, sir, but...George isn't a boy any longer."

The vicar waved his hand. "Oh, I know very well my son isn't blameless in this. At the same time, I have to wonder what sort of man would be so lost to finer feeling as to exploit a weaker creature to his benefit? To lure that creature into deep play, and deeper drink, only to hold it over his head for months on end? To torment him and make his life a misery?"

Laura stared at him, stunned. He made Alex sound like a monster. A true villain, incapable of kindness or compassion. "That isn't quite what happened. Not in the way I understand it."

"Then I thank God you don't know the worst of it. Nor should you, a young lady such as yourself." His brow creased with concern. "I fear you have a tiger by the tail, my dear. Such a creature isn't capable of being tamed."

"I don't wish to tame him."

"But you think to keep him here with you after you marry? To make a house pet of him, as you have of this one?"

Laura's hand stilled on Magpie's back. "No, I—" She broke off. "I believe Mr. Archer can be happy here."

"Ah well." The vicar sighed. "Who am I, of all people, to disbelieve in miracles?"

Chapter Eighteen

The vicar's words stayed with Laura long after he'd gone. She thought of them all through dinner, even as Alex bantered with Teddy, and Aunt Charlotte commented on Laura's impending nuptials. She had to force herself to eat and drink at regular intervals, lest anyone notice.

Several times Alex caught her eye across the table. His gaze was questioning. Laura always returned it with a smile. There was nothing to worry about. Nothing to fear.

She didn't have a tiger by the tail, nor a wolf. Alex Archer might still be a mystery—an enigmatic figure with no family, no friends, and no fixed address—but when it came down to it, he was just a man.

A man she fully intended to marry.

When she arrived at the church in the morning, she found it decorated with fresh flowers and greenery, and filled with the familiar faces of friends and acquaintances from the village.

Word traveled fast in Lower Hawley.

It was Henrietta's doing. Not only had she sent the squire's carriage to Bramble Cottage to collect Laura and her family for the ceremony, she'd seen to the decoration of the church, too. She sat in the front row between her father and George—the latter of whom appeared to be there on sufferance. Aunt Charlotte and Teddy sat in the front, as well.

As Laura walked down the aisle in her white muslin day dress, sprigs of lavender woven through her hair, she felt a distinct pang of sadness. For the first time in a very long while, she wished that her parents were alive. Her father to walk her down the aisle, and her mother to send her off.

But such sadness didn't last.

How could it when Alex was waiting at the front of the church, looking at her so intently? He took her hand in his as he repeated the vicar's words in a deep, strong voice, giving every indication that he meant them.

Laura almost believed he did. And yet…

She couldn't escape the feeling that it was all for show. The way he looked at her. The way he recited his vows. It was for the benefit of those in attendance. The friends and neighbors she'd be left with if he departed for France—or wherever it was he proposed to disappear to.

He wasn't pledging his life to hers. He was saving her reputation. Quelling the gossip for good and all. He didn't mean any of it.

Laura wished she could say the same.

To her the vows were a sacred contract. She knew she would honor them, that she'd remain faithful to Alex Archer for the whole of her life.

A melancholy thought.

He might leave her in three months. And then where would she be? A wife in name only. Nothing but her ring, and her wedding lines, to prove she had a husband.

The ceremony was over before she knew it. She faced the wedding guests on Alex's arm, feeling flushed and breathless, and very married indeed.

"Mrs. Archer," Yardley said, pumping her hand. "I wanted to be the first to say it."

Aunt Charlotte sniffled into her handkerchief. "Oh, Laura. If only my brother were here to see you! How like Her Majesty you look when she wed our dear Prince Albert. The same white dress and flower crown. So elegant. So beautiful."

"She looks nothing like the Queen," Teddy said. "Except for her dress being white, and even that doesn't bear any resemblance."

"It's a compliment of the first order," Aunt Charlotte said.

"No," Teddy replied firmly. "It isn't."

When they left the church, Squire Talbot's carriage was waiting. It was draped with the same blooms and greenery as had been used to adorn the church.

"It will convey you both back to Bramble Cottage." Henrietta embraced Laura, her voice dropping to a whisper. "By the by, I've torn up the note you signed. You may consider that twenty pounds my wedding gift to you."

"Thank you, Hen." Laura hugged her back. "And for the flowers in the church. You made everything so lovely."

"Good luck, Laura." Henrietta extended her hand to Alex, her manner suddenly formal. "And to you, Mr. Archer. I trust you will take care of her."

"I intend to, Miss Talbot."

Seconds later, Alex assisted Laura up into the carriage. He climbed in after her, taking a seat at her side. The wedding guests who had come outside to see them off gave a little cheer.

Laura waved to her aunt and brother. They would follow in the vicar's carriage, along with Yardley, back to Bramble Cottage where Mrs. Crabtree had prepared a wedding breakfast.

"You do look beautiful," Alex said as the horses sprang into motion. "Beautiful, and happy." He studied her face. "*Are* you happy?"

She smiled. "Shouldn't I be?"

"I don't know," he said. "Given the circumstances…"

"The circumstances aren't as grim as you imagine." Laura had been reminding herself of that fact all morning. "First you saved my life, and now you've saved my reputation. I have no cause to be anything but grateful to you."

His mouth quirked. "Gratitude isn't the precise emotion I was hoping to inspire from you on our wedding day."

She slipped her hand into his. "It's more than gratitude."

He made no reply, but his fingers closed around hers with a possessive strength.

"I had a thought this morning," she said after a long moment. "A somewhat revolutionary one."

"Did you?"

"What if, from now on, we were honest with each other? What if there were no more half-truths? No more convenient fictions?"

"A dismal prospect."

"Why do you say so?"

"What you're proposing is absolute candor. Laying all of our cards on the table, so to speak. Even those cards we've been dealt that are…less than ideal."

"Yes, I believe I am. Whatever brought us to this juncture, we're husband and wife now. We should begin as we mean to go on."

"With honesty." He sounded skeptical.

"With honesty. Even if we eventually part forever."

His brows lowered. "Laura…"

"You said it would be my decision. That, if I wished it, one day we would quietly go our separate ways." She tried to keep her voice light. "Is that what you want? To return to your old life in a month or two?"

He stared down at their joined hands for a moment, an expression on his face that was difficult to read. "The truth?" His mouth twisted into a grimace. "I don't know anymore."

Laura absorbed his words in silence. She wasn't surprised by them. She'd sensed his growing uncertainty when they'd walked in Talbot's Wood yesterday. "Shall I tell you what I'd like?"

His gaze lifted back to hers.

"I'd like this to be a real marriage, not a marriage of convenience," she said. "I'd like you to stay with me."

"For how long?"

"The usual length of time." She managed a faint smile. "Until death, I believe the vicar said."

Alex didn't smile in return. "Forever, in other words."

"Or…for as long as you're able."

"With you, at Bramble Cottage. As man and wife."

She moistened her lips. "Yes."

"In every way."

Heat rose in her cheeks. "Would that be so terrible?"

He gave a short, humorless laugh. "No. It wouldn't be terrible at all. Not for me. For you, on the other hand—"

"It wouldn't be terrible for me either," she said swiftly.

His eyes searched hers. She'd never seen him looking so serious. "And what if I leave you with child?"

Her face was positively burning now. Such things weren't discussed. Not even by married couples. It took all of her wherewithal to hold his gaze. "Would you leave? If I fell pregnant?"

"I don't know what I'd do, or how I'd manage to ruin things. I'm not a good man, Laura."

"So you keep saying. But except for your nefarious arrangement with George, I've seen no evidence of the fact. Rather the opposite. Since the day we met, you've been every inch a hero."

He gave her an odd look. "How wrong you are."

She would have questioned him further, but there was no time. The carriage slowed as it rolled up to the gate in front of Bramble Cottage. As the horses came to a halt, they whickered. Another team of horses answered back.

Laura looked out the window. A hired carriage was parked just ahead on the road. "I wonder who that is?"

She didn't have to wonder long.

The words had hardly left her mouth when the door of the carriage opened, and Mr. Weatherwax stepped out.

Alex hadn't given much thought to the Hayes family's solicitor, except insofar as the man was a nuisance—a nuisance that would likely be eliminated by Alex and Laura's marriage. When he'd sent the wire to London yesterday, he'd expected Weatherwax to respond in some form or another. An angry letter, perhaps. Or a grudging visit on Friday. But to see the man standing in front of Bramble Cottage less than twenty-four hours after being informed of his client's intent to marry was…interesting.

Laura's reaction, however, wasn't quite so academic. Indeed, at the sight of Weatherwax, her entire demeanor changed. Gone was the glow in her cheeks she'd had since she'd walked down the aisle—and the even brighter glow she'd possessed while broaching the subject of consummating their marriage. She'd gone pale, and grave, her body fairly vibrating with tension as Alex assisted her down from the carriage.

"What on earth is he doing here?" she asked under her breath.

"Miss Hayes! I must speak with you immediately!" Weatherwax hurried toward them, only to stop short. His gaze flicked over Laura's white dress and flower crown. He staggered back a step. "Dear God, ma'am. Don't say I'm too late?"

"Too late for what, sir?" Laura asked.

"To stop this travesty. What can you have been thinking, Miss Hayes?"

"It's Mrs. Archer now," Alex said. "We've just come from the church."

The solicitor's face fell. "You *are* married, then." He withdrew a handkerchief from his pocket and blotted the perspiration from his brow. "This complicates matters."

Alex felt Laura's hand tighten on his arm. He covered it with his own. "Let's go inside, shall we? There's no need to discuss family business in the street."

She nodded. "Yes. Do come in, Mr. Weatherwax. You'll want some refreshment after your journey."

Mrs. Crabtree met them at the door. She looked as surprised to see the solicitor as they were.

"Mr. Weatherwax has come down from London to speak with me," Laura explained.

"But your guests," the housekeeper protested. "I've a wedding breakfast to serve."

"This won't take long," Laura said. "We'll go into Papa's bookroom. If you would be so good as to bring some tea?"

Alex hadn't yet seen the bookroom at Bramble Cottage. Far smaller than the parlor, it was located under the stairs and looked to be the place where Laura balanced the accounts. A desk was angled in the corner, heaped with leather-bound ledgers, ink pots and quills, and a tallow candle burnt almost to its nub. An old settee and chair graced the middle of the room, the fabric upholstery on the seats worn through from years of use.

Laura motioned for Weatherwax to sit before going to the desk and closing one of the ledgers. She straightened the others, tucking away a few scraps of paper within their pages. "I apologize for the clutter."

"Don't apologize," Alex said. "It isn't as if you were expecting anyone."

"Not in the bookroom, certainly." She took a seat on the settee, arranging her skirts as Alex came to stand behind her. "Why have you come, sir? We didn't anticipate you until tomorrow at the earliest."

Weatherwax availed himself of the chair. He tucked his handkerchief back into his pocket. "When last we met at my office, ma'am, you said, quite emphatically, that you had no intention to marry."

"Nor did she," Alex said. "Until I proposed to her."

The solicitor's gaze shot to his. "With respect, sir, it's my sworn duty to look after the interests of Miss Hayes and her brother. It would be preferable if she and I spoke privately."

Alex rested his hand on Laura's shoulder. It was as possessive a gesture as his standing behind her. "I think not."

"You may speak freely," Laura said. "Mr. Archer is my husband now. We haven't any secrets."

Weatherwax's face went a shade paler.

Alex recognized a guilty conscience when he saw one. He wondered what crime the man had committed. Had he stolen from Laura and her brother? Fudged the books or pocketed a portion of the rents? "Out with it, man. Best to confess your sins before we bring in another solicitor to discover the extent of them."

"Another solicitor?" Weatherwax gave Laura a look of alarm. "Have you consulted with someone?"

"I've made enquiries," Laura admitted. "After your unwillingness to relinquish control—"

"Your brother is an invalid. I had every reason to be reluctant. And as to you consulting with some other solicitor…a regrettable action, to be sure. Deeply regrettable in every respect. London is populated with unscrupulous solicitors. Men who haven't the faintest notion of legal nuance."

"I didn't consult with one of those," Laura said. "I wouldn't have done. You must give me some credit, sir. I dealt with Mr. Finchley in Fleet Street. He came highly recommended."

"*Thomas* Finchley?" Weatherwax echoed in a strangled voice. "Of Finchley and Fothergill?"

Laura nodded. "Yes. That's right."

Alex wouldn't have thought the man could get any paler. Good God, was the mere name of Tom Finchley enough to provoke such a reaction? His erstwhile friend had been a slim, bespectacled boy. Not the sort of fellow to strike fear into the hearts of those he encountered.

What had the intervening years done to him?

"A villain," Weatherwax said. "He bends the law to his purpose. I wouldn't advise—"

"We're past that, surely," Laura said. "I'm married now, before my birthday, and my brother will reach his majority next month. We haven't any more need of you, sir. All that remains is for you to hand over the relevant documents, the deeds of ownership and so forth, so that we—"

"Miss Hayes…" Weatherwax cleared his throat. His pallor had degenerated from bleach white to pea green. "Regarding your father's estate—"

"Mrs. Archer," Alex corrected again. He regarded the solicitor with interest. "You don't have the documents, do you?"

Weatherwax tugged at his cravat. "As to that—"

"What do you mean, you don't have them?" Laura asked. "Are they back at your office? Have you mislaid them somewhere?"

"He hasn't mislaid anything," Alex said. "He's taken it."

"No, no," Weatherwax objected. "I took nothing from you, ma'am. Everything I've done has been engineered to increase your wealth, not to diminish it. These are the perils of investing, you must understand. There's nothing criminal in suffering losses."

Laura's shoulder stiffened under Alex's hand. "What losses? What have you done, sir?"

"You may as well make a clean breast of it," Alex advised the solicitor. "We'll find out one way or another."

Weatherwax darted him a narrow glance before returning his attention to Laura. "After your father's death, there was marked interest in the properties in London and Dorset. A buyer came forward. Another perfumer. He offered a healthy sum. I'd have been a fool not to take it."

"You *sold* them? Both of them?" Laura's hand pressed to her midriff. "Oh, how could you?"

"It was in the best interest of you and your brother—"

"You had no right!"

Alex's squeezed her shoulder. "Easy. Let him speak." Let him bury himself, Alex wanted to say. The devious swine.

Weatherwax drew himself up in righteous indignation. "Indeed, ma'am. By the terms of your father's will, I had every right. There is nothing that requires me to inform you of my actions, only that I act with your best interests in mind— which I did, most assuredly."

"Then where is the money from the sale of the properties?" Laura asked. "Why is it that my brother and I have been obliged to live like paupers these three years? The flower farm in Dorset alone—"

"As to that…" He cleared his throat. "A series of bad investments. All of them made with the best of intentions—"

"All of the money is gone," Laura said. "Is that what you mean?"

"I'm afraid it is. A fact for which, you must believe, I feel a deep regret."

"Then what have we been living on?" she asked. "How have you been paying our quarterly allowance?"

"The remainder of the estate still earns a small sum. On occasion, I've been obliged to supplement it from my own income—an action which I've undertaken purely out of my deep regard for you and your family."

"How dared you." Laura's soft voice was thick with fury. "To steal from us, and then to presume to make us the objects of your charity—"

"You have it wrong, ma'am. The actions I took—"

"I want proof," she said. "I want to see it in writing. All of the transactions you undertook on our behalf. All of the money you paid to us from your own accounts. I want every last penny accounted for."

"Miss Hayes—"

"*Mrs. Archer.* And I *will* see it in writing, sir. I have no reason to believe anything you say to me." Laura stood abruptly. "I need a moment to compose myself before the guests arrive. Pray excuse me."

Alex followed her from the bookroom, but not before shooting a warning glance at Weatherwax who was hovering above his chair. "Stay."

Weatherwax slumped back down.

Laura walked quickly through the hall, making her way to the stairs. Alex caught her by the arm at the bottom of the steps and turned her to face him.

"Look at me," he said.

She was biting her lip, her eyes shimmering with unshed tears as they met his.

"It's going to be all right," he said gruffly. "Do you understand me? Everything is going to be all right."

Her mouth trembled. "All of my plans—"

"Hush. Just…trust me. God knows I'm no saint, Laura, but I'm asking you to—"

"I do trust you."

His heart clenched. "Good." He brought his hands up to cup her face. "I'm going to have words with the fellow, and then I'm going to pitch him out into the street. Do you object to that plan, Mrs. Archer?"

"Alex—"

"Do you?"

Her throat rippled on a swallow. "No. I don't suppose I do."

Alex waited until she was safely up the stairs before returning to the bookroom. Weatherwax was still in his chair, the mantle of aggrieved solicitor firmly about his shoulders.

"Mr. Archer," he said briskly, "I don't know who you are or where you've come from, but I warn you, sir, I fully intend to find out. And if anything should strike me amiss—the slightest whiff of fraud or deceit—I'll see that this marriage is annulled."

Alex came to stand in front of Laura's deck. "You're welcome to try." He leaned back against its edge, folding his arms. "But I wouldn't advise it. Not when you're guilty of fraud and deceit yourself."

Weatherwax puffed his chest. "A slanderous charge. I could bring suit against you for that, sir. My reputation as a solicitor—"

"I wonder what another solicitor would have to say about your conduct?" Alex paused. It was a stab in the dark. "Tom Finchley, perhaps?"

The effect was instantaneous.

Weatherwax's face changed color, and he sputtered his words. "A villain of the first order! And he'll have no room to accuse me of anything unethical. The man put a spy in my office. The shameless guttersnipe stole a file from me, and then disappeared. It's a dark game Finchley and Fothergill play. Everyone knows it. The very notion of Miss Hayes consulting with the man—"

"Mrs. Archer," Alex corrected automatically.

The idea of Tom having grown up to be a villain both fascinated and disturbed him. Alex hadn't parted from his former friend on the best of terms. He'd hurt and betrayed him. How much of that betrayal had shaped the man Tom was today?

It was a troubling thought.

"Mrs. Archer, then," Weatherwax amended, as if the name left a bad taste in his mouth. "You'll forgive my skepticism. She said nothing of you at our last appointment. The very idea that there was time for the two of you to meet and marry—"

"A whirlwind courtship."

"And now you summon me here to lay claim to half of the Hayes business. You don't waste any time on pretense, do you, sir?"

"Which brings us to the crux of the matter," Alex said. "How much of the business is left?"

The solicitor seemed to crumple. "The property in France is all that remains."

"And the profit you made selling the other properties?"

"I invested the proceeds from both the sale of the Dorset and the London properties into a canal scheme. It was guaranteed to be a success. I had it on good authority." Weatherwax withdrew his handkerchief again and blotted the perspiration from his brow. "Unfortunately, the project ultimately failed, absorbing all of the stakeholders' money. There is some residual litigation over the matter, but it appears unlikely that any of the investors will recoup their losses. Not to a significant degree. These are the risks of doing business—"

"My wife wants to see the relevant documents. Bills of sale, bank records, and the like. You will have them here by tomorrow morning. Send them by messenger. My wife is in no mood to see your face again."

Weatherwax gaped. "But Mr. Archer—"

"Shall we say nine o'clock at the latest? That's not too unreasonable." Alex straightened to his full height. "And now, I require you to write a letter confessing everything you've done."

Weatherwax leapt to his feet. "A confession!"

"It will save time later should you choose to deny your actions." Alex collected blank paper, quill, and ink from Laura's desk. He thrust them into the solicitor's hands and ushered him out of the bookroom. "You may perform the task in the kitchen."

The last thing Alex was going to do was leave the man alone with the household ledgers. God only knew what sort of underhand business he might get up to.

"Mr. Archer!" Mrs. Crabtree appeared in the hall, the tea tray in her hands. "The wedding guests are arriving!"

"I'll fetch my wife." Alex shoved Weatherwax forward. "In the meanwhile, if you would be so good as to show this fellow to the kitchens? He has some work to do."

The housekeeper scowled at Weatherwax, but she asked no questions. In the Hayeses' household, it seemed that the solicitor was universally known—and disliked.

Alex could muster no sympathy for the man. He'd crushed Laura's dreams. Stolen the future she'd planned right out from under her. Alex was half tempted to thrash the fellow.

A fine sight that would be for Laura. Her new husband engaged in fisticuffs with the family solicitor on their wedding day.

He sighed heavily.

"What's going on?" Teddy appeared in the hall in his wheeled chair. "And why the devil is Weatherwax here? I haven't seen him since my father's funeral."

Alex looked at his new brother-in-law. "He brought news about your father's will."

"Bad news?"

"It isn't good." Alex frowned. Laura was accustomed to keeping things from her brother. Alex wasn't so circumspect. He could see no reason for it. "You and I need to have a talk."

Teddy's face grew solemn. "Very well." And then: "It's about time."

Chapter Nineteen

*L*ater that evening Laura readied herself for bed with some trepidation. Alex was downstairs speaking with her brother. He'd said he'd join her in half an hour. Not to bed her, she didn't think. It was their wedding night, true, but neither of them were in any mood for romance.

She'd stumbled through their wedding breakfast as if in a dream. Greeted their guests with a brittle smile pasted on her face, and partaken of Mrs. Crabtree's carefully prepared dainties, never tasting a morsel. It had been so much sawdust in her mouth.

Alex had done better than she had. Every time she'd glanced in his direction, he was smiling or laughing. Ever the chameleon.

They'd had no time alone in which to talk. Even when the last guest had gone, there was still Teddy and Aunt Charlotte to contend with. It was an awkward business being a newlywed couple without a home of their own, or a place to depart to for their honeymoon. Instead, they were obliged to remain at Bramble Cottage, very much at loose ends.

Alex had occupied the time by assisting with moving Teddy's things to a bedroom downstairs—a long overdue project that absorbed the remainder of the day.

Laura was grateful for her new husband's consideration toward her family, but she owned to a certain sense of frustration.

What had happened with Mr. Weatherwax?

And what was Alex going to do now that there was no wealth or property to keep him here?

"It's going to be all right," he'd promised her.

Lord above, but she'd believed him.

It was a strange sensation to let someone else shoulder a burden. She felt both lighter in spirit, and a little queasy. How could she relinquish control over something so important? Not just her future, but Teddy's?

She brushed out her hair and slipped into a nightgown. It was the farthest thing from bridal finery. There was no French silk or broderie lace. Only unrelieved white cotton, covering her from her neck to her toes. Its one concession to femininity was a thin—slightly frayed—white ribbon woven at the wrists, neckline, and hem.

Alex had lived abroad for decades. He must have encountered all manner of sophisticated women in seductive negligees. She felt countrified and childish by comparison. Even worse, she felt poor. Far poorer than she had this morning.

She'd told him he would have half of the perfume business, and now there was nothing left of it. No wealth. No property, save a dilapidated distillery in France.

He had no reason to stay now.

She climbed into her bed and pulled the quilted counterpane up to her chin.

Not five minutes later a knock sounded at the door.

"Come in," she called out.

Alex entered, shutting the door behind him. He stood there, his back against the closed door, gazing at her in the candlelight. After a long moment, he cleared his throat. "In bed already?"

Laura wished she could see his face. Not that it ever revealed much. "It's been a long day."

He advanced into the room. He was in his shirtsleeves, his cravat loose at his neck. "It has. And an eventful one."

"I've been waiting for you to tell me how you managed to resolve things with Mr. Weatherwax."

"There's been no opportunity." Alex removed his cufflinks and set them down on her dressing table with a soft clink. "We can talk now, if you like."

Laura struggled to a sitting position amongst the pillows and blankets. The counterpane fell to her waist. She resisted the urge to pull it up again. Alex had seen her in far less than a cotton nightgown. Besides, he was her husband now. There was no reason to indulge in false modesty. "I would. If you're equal to it."

He continued undressing, as casually as if it were an everyday occurrence to be inside her bedroom after dark. "You might rather hear it in the morning. It will disrupt your sleep otherwise."

She watched him remove his cravat and unfasten the top buttons of his shirt collar. Her pulse skipped. "My sleep is already going to be disrupted."

He shrugged out of his waistcoat, draping it across the back of a chair in the corner, before bending to remove his boots.

"I've never shared a bed with anyone before," she said. "Not even with a friend or relation."

He glanced up at her. His mouth hitched in a smile. "Nervous?"

"A little," she admitted.

"Don't be."

Laura smoothed her blanket over her lap with unsteady hands. It was easy for him to say. No doubt he'd shared his bed with dozens of women.

He straightened to untuck his shirt from his trousers. Reaching a hand behind his neck, he stripped the loose-fitting linen garment off over his head.

She sucked in a sharp breath. His bare torso was all lean muscle and bronzed skin. Strong, and powerful, and rather thrilling to look at. She couldn't seem to tear her gaze away.

He cast her another look. A flush of color darkened his neck. "You're staring."

She brought her hands to cover her face, squeezing her eyes tight as she stifled a mortified groan. "I'm sorry. I can't help it."

He didn't reply. Not in words. But she heard the sound of fabric rustling, of feet padding across the carpet to the bed.

A flash of panic constricted her chest. Dear lord, had he removed his trousers? She wasn't ready for such intimacy.

The mattress depressed beside her, the ancient four-poster bed creaking as he sat down. "Open your eyes," he said gently.

She did as he asked, darting a wary glance downward. He was still wearing his trousers. Not only that, he'd put his shirt back on. Her gaze lifted to his, confused. "What—?"

"Let's not complicate things. Not until we've talked."

Her bosom rose and fell with equal parts relief and disappointment. She didn't know what she wanted him to do—or not to do. Her emotions were in a tangle. "You must think me an absolute ninny."

"I think you charming." He reached out and very softly brushed her cheek with his knuckles. "Charming. Beautiful. Brave beyond measure."

"Not brave. I'm quivering with nerves. And my face must be as red as a tomato."

His fingers traced the edge of her jaw. "Your blushes enthrall me."

She trembled at his touch. "I can't imagine why."

"I suppose because there's not much that can inspire them."

"You inspire them. And with some regularity, as I'm sure you're well aware."

His half smile briefly spread into a full one. "Is that it? No wonder I'm so fond of them."

"Alex—"

"Right, no more teasing." His hand dropped from her face. "You want to know about Weatherwax."

The solicitor's name was as effective as a douse of cold water. Laura sobered instantly. "Yes, though I've been trying not to dwell on it. On losing so much of what I promised Teddy—and what I promised you."

His humorous expression faded. "What do you mean?"

"I told you we had a farm in Dorset, and a factory in London. Properties that could be made to turn a profit—and quickly. I'd hoped that if you saw there was at least the prospect of wealth, you might be persuaded that you could make a life here. But now…"

"You believe me entirely motivated by money?"

"Not entirely, no. But I know it holds some attraction for you. Far more than my poor self."

"Your poor self?" A sudden laugh rumbled in his chest. "God help me if you ever come to realize the power you hold over me."

She ignored the compliment in his words. She didn't dare trust it. "Am I wrong? Now that there's no fortune to be had—"

"Your property in France is still intact. Weatherwax claims he's been leasing the land to another perfumer."

Her brows knit. "That's something, at least. The crops will have been tended, but in what state is the distillery? Neglected, I daresay. Left to rust and ruin."

"Probably," Alex acknowledged. "Which isn't to say it has no value."

She plucked at a stray thread on the counterpane. "When my father was alive, our income was derived almost exclusively from the farm in Dorset. Papa supplemented it with earnings from the flower crops in France, it's true, but the property there was always more of a fancy than a sound business decision. I've never even seen the place."

"You could."

Her gaze jerked to his. "Do you mean to suggest—"

"Why not?"

"Because…" She had ample justification for not leaving her family, but for some reason those justifications didn't roll from her tongue as easily as they usually did. She struggled for the right words. "Because I have responsibilities here. My aunt, and Teddy, and—"

"I've spoken to Teddy."

She stared at him. "*What?*"

"We've had a thorough discussion on the subject of Weatherwax and Hayes's Perfumes."

Her throat constricted. She was tempted to leap up and rush to her brother's side. "What on earth were you thinking? It's my job to—"

"Teddy's fine." Alex circled her wrist with his fingers. It was a gesture that seemed designed to both comfort and gently restrain. "He was glad to hear it first. Glad to have an opportunity to make some decisions for himself—and for the family. He wants to be the man of the house, you know. It brings him no pleasure to be coddled like a child."

"I don't coddle him!"

"You shield him from the facts you deem too upsetting. It's not much different."

She bristled at the criticism. Alex had been acquainted with her brother less than a month, and already he presumed to know what was best for him? Teddy was *her* responsibility. "Why should he have to bear the burden when I'm capable of managing—"

"You *are* capable, sweetheart. More than capable. But you don't have to bear it. That's the whole point. Your brother is nearly one and twenty. A man, not a boy. He wants the burden of it. Shouldering it would do him a world of good."

Sweetheart.

The unexpected endearment completely derailed her train of thought.

"Alex…" She exhaled a frustrated breath. "I'm never going to be one of those ladies who permit gentlemen to take charge of every little thing. I *need* to keep control. Otherwise I feel as if…as if I'm drowning."

"You *are* drowning. The responsibilities you've taken on are suffocating you. What use will you be to your family if you make yourself ill with worry over them?"

She opened her mouth to object, only to clamp it shut again. He was right, drat him. Though she couldn't admit it to him, she must at least admit it to herself.

It was a bitter tonic to swallow.

"Let your brother take the reins awhile," he said. "A month or two at the most. Just until we return. He may surprise you."

Her heartbeat quickened. "Return from where?"

"Grasse. That's where the distillery is, isn't it?"

"Yes, but…" She could think of no good excuse. Even if she could, she had the feeling he'd counter it as deftly as he'd countered all her other arguments.

"I'll take you there. And to Paris. It can be a honeymoon, of sorts."

"A real honeymoon?"

"If that's what you truly want."

She did want it, most desperately. Romance, adventure, and the thrill of falling in love. She wanted it all.

And she wanted it with him.

It felt very much like taking a step across a deep chasm. An unknown path that could either lead to somewhere wonderful, or plummet her straight down into the abyss.

She moistened her lips. "I thought that tonight…"

"I thought the same." He shot a frowning glance at the thin walls of her bedroom. The sounds of Aunt Charlotte bustling about next door were as loud as if she was in the room with them. "But this is never going to serve. Not for a proper wedding night."

"I don't understand. Aren't you going to—"

"Sleep with you, here in your childhood bedroom? With your ruffled bed hangings and porcelain dog figurines? I'd feel like some vile despoiler of innocence."

Her blush deepened.

"Not to mention the fact that your aunt can likely hear everything we say and do." He tugged absently at the ribbon trim on the sleeve of her nightgown. "I want to do this right, Laura. You deserve that much from me."

He was so solemn. So seemingly sincere. How could she not believe him? "I suppose I shall have to defer to your greater experience."

"A wise idea." His hand slid to hers. Their fingers briefly twined together. "I'm going to sleep in Teddy's old room tonight. And then—"

"Yes?" She looked at him in expectation.

"And then, if you can make yourself ready in so short a time, tomorrow we'll depart for Dover."

Chapter Twenty

Paris, France
September, 1860

Alex shepherded Laura into his suite of rooms at the Hôtel des Rois. The heavy damask curtains were open, revealing an enviable prospect of the Champs-Élysées. The fashionable Paris avenue was ablaze with gaslight. It was the same view that had attracted him so many years ago.

It attracted Laura as well.

She walked to the window as she stripped off her gloves and bonnet. He heard her catch her breath. "Good heavens."

"Do you like it?"

"I've never seen anything so beautiful."

He regarded her from across the room. She'd spent most of the rail journey from Surrey poring over the documents Weatherwax had sent to them. At Dover, however, Alex had taken charge of the papers and directed her attention to more pressing concerns. The steamer ship, and the sea, and the exciting adventure before them.

Her wide-eyed wonder as they'd crossed the channel and traveled by rail from Calais had made the sights and sounds of France new to him again. He felt as though he were seeing it for the first time. The beauty of the countryside, the dazzling lights of Paris. And most beautiful of all, his new bride. A lady he admired. That he adored beyond reason.

A lady he hadn't even properly kissed yet.

"How long have you lived here?" she asked.

"A few years, off and on." He dropped his hat and gloves on a marble-topped table near the door. "Though I wouldn't call it living."

She glanced at him over her shoulder.

"It isn't a home," he said. "It's simply a place I come to rest when I grow weary of traveling."

"You must feel some affinity for it. Why else would you keep coming back?"

"Convenience."

Her lips tilted in a smile. He recognized the expression on her face. She didn't believe him. Not entirely.

Alex couldn't blame her.

He wandered past the tufted velvet sofa to the glass oil lamp at its side. As he lit the wick, he heard Laura moving about the room behind him. The skirts of her green silk traveling dress rustled over her starched petticoats, the fragrance of her perfume a faint but stirring floral note in the stale air.

"I've never brought a woman here before." The words tumbled out, unplanned. He grimaced to hear them. "Not that you're just any woman. That is to say—you're my wife."

"I'm flattered."

He turned to look at her again, feeling oddly out of his depth. "Are you tired? I can order dinner for us here. Or we can go out. Whichever you prefer."

"I think I'd rather stay in, if you wouldn't mind."

"Not at all." He half smiled. "One of the benefits of living part time in a hotel. *And* they launder the linens."

"How long has it been since you've been back here?"

"A few months. Longer. I can't recall." It had been nearly a year, in fact. Indeed, he'd been sitting right here, in an armchair near the fire, reading the London paper, when he'd come across the notice of Justin's marriage.

> *On the 27th September at the District Registrar's Office in Abbot's Holcombe, Burlington Street, Captain Justin Thornhill, of King's Abbot, to Lady Helena Elaine Reynolds, daughter of the late Earl of Castleton, Hampshire.*

Alex wondered if Justin loved his wife. Was their marriage one of mutual respect and affection? Or had Justin wed Lady Helena solely for her wealth and pedigree? Either way, a registrar's office seemed a ramshackle place to marry. At least Alex had wed Laura in a church. They'd had a proper ceremony, with all of the trappings.

And now they were going to have a proper wedding night.

He rang for a footman. The summons was answered almost immediately by a hotel employee in impeccable livery. He took their dinner order, and departed, promising to return within a half an hour with their meal. As the door shut behind him, a knot of anxiety formed in Alex's stomach.

Never had anything been so important. He was determined to get it right.

And—for the next two hours—it seemed as if he did.

They ate a sumptuous meal of jardinière soup and sautéed filets mignon of beef, and they drank a bottle of Bordeaux. He told her about Paris. About the sights they could see, and the things they could do. Carriage rides along the Champs-Élysées. A picnic on the banks of the Seine. A visit to the music hall or the theatre.

"What about your birthday?" he asked. "Is there anything particular you'd like to do to celebrate?"

She sat across from him at the small, linen-covered table, her face aglow in the candlelight. "It's enough to be here with you."

"I'm pleased you think so. But we must do something to honor the day." He refilled her wineglass. "What did you do last year?"

"Nothing extraordinary. Aunt Charlotte helped Mrs. Crabtree to bake a fruitcake. And Teddy gave me a drawing he'd done of Magpie." Her fingers toyed with the stem of her glass. "I've never had a birthday apart from them."

"Are you going to miss them tomorrow?"

"I already miss them."

"Then I shall have to endeavor to distract you. What do you say to a champagne supper and dancing at the Salle Valentino?"

Her brows lifted. "The Salle Valentino? That sounds very grand."

"It's a fashionable dancing hall in the Rue St Honoré. It has a circular ballroom with an orchestra in the center. They play waltzes, quadrilles, any dance you can think of. And one needn't keep as much distance from their partner as at the assembly rooms in Margate."

Her mouth curved up at one corner. "Aunt Charlotte warned me about Parisian dancing."

"Yes, it's quite risqué. Good thing we're married."

A blush rose in her cheeks. She raised her glass to take a sip of wine, but there was no disguising the fact that he'd flustered her.

He felt a little flustered himself. Uncertain of how best to proceed. "There's no cause to go immediately to Grasse, is there? We can enjoy the city for another day or two. Longer if you like."

She set down her glass. "Must we decide now?"

"Not at all. We can wait and see, if you prefer." He didn't press her on the subject. Not yet. So much hinged on their wedding night. If things went well between them, no doubt Laura would wish to linger in Paris. To enjoy the city as lovers. And if not…

Well.

He'd escort her to Grasse without delay.

After dinner, they repaired to the sitting room for coffee. Laura sat down on the sofa. She unfastened the top button of her bodice. "I didn't realize how hungry I was until the footman brought in our dinner."

"I trust it met with your approval."

"To put it mildly. It was the richest food I've ever eaten—and the best. I believe they must soak everything in wine and butter and cream."

"I believe you're right." He came to sit down beside her. Her skirts bunched against the side of his leg. "Laura," he began.

"Have you enjoyed living abroad all of these years?" she asked at the same time.

They both laughed and begged the other's pardon. Two nervous newlyweds, Alex thought grimly. The tension in the air was palpable. He would have to take charge of things soon, for better or worse.

"To answer your question," he said, "it's all I've known."

She looked into his eyes. "Did you never yearn for home?"

"I've never had a home to yearn for." He took her hand gently in his. "Not until you."

Her bosom rose and fell on a breath. "Oh Alex, I wish…"

"What?"

"I wish you would tell me something of your life. Something true, even if it is unpleasant. I want to know you for who you really are."

The prospect should have alarmed him. And perhaps it did a little. But he didn't object. In truth, it seemed a small price to pay for the intimacy he was going to share with her. "What exactly would you like to hear?"

"Oh, I don't know. Anything." She hesitated. "Perhaps you could tell me about your childhood."

"In the orphanage?"

Her brows knit with concern. "Is it too upsetting?"

"No. It's…" Good God, it *was* upsetting. But it shouldn't be. Not after so many years had passed. He forced a smile, certain it must look more like a rictus of pain. "It was a long time ago."

"Had you lived somewhere else before you came there?"

He shook his head. "I was brought there as an infant. A newborn. The orphanage is all I can remember."

"Was it in London?" she asked.

"North Devon. By the sea."

Understanding softened her gaze. "That's where you rescued your friend."

Alex gave a tense nod. "We used to climb down the face of the cliffs. There was a rowboat on the beach. We'd row it to an old abbey down the coast. There were rumors of buried treasure there. Just the thing to appeal to young lads." He swallowed hard. "One day, some of the rocks on the cliff gave way. One of the boys I was with slipped and hit his head. He fell into the sea. Another of the boys dived in after him, but he couldn't find him in the water. That's when I went in."

"You saved his life."

"Barely. He was badly injured. I don't know if he survived." He moved his thumb over the curve of her palm. "I left not long after."

"For France?"

"I stayed in London for a time, but yes. In the end, I caught a steamer across the channel. I'd run away from the orphanage. I had the urge to keep running." He managed a faint smile. "I daresay I still do."

"How was it you came to live here? The truth of it—not the fiction about Monsieur Giraud."

"It's not much different from the story I told your family at dinner, though perhaps a bit less humorous." He paused before explaining, "I *did* meet a gambler on a steamer. But it wasn't while coming home from a holiday in Alexandria with my godfather. It was during the channel crossing. He was an Englishman named Henry Garrick. He'd become so recognizable in London gaming clubs that he was obliged to leave the country for a time."

"Were you really only thirteen?"

"I was. Garrick liked the idea of having an apprentice. Someone to whom he could teach his tricks. Not out of any sense of altruism, mind. Having a protégé allowed him to earn extra money without the danger of being called out as a cheat and a rogue. He'd send me out into the city to play street games and the like. It was a lucrative business for him."

She looked appalled. "He took your winnings?"

"The greater portion of them. He also saw that I had somewhere to sleep and that my belly was filled. And it's true he often told people I was his son. But I had no illusions. Had I not had an aptitude for cards, he'd have had no qualms about leaving me behind."

"How long were you with him?"

"Two years. Until I outgrew him. It wasn't as easy to take my earnings then—and I was less inclined to part with them. Garrick didn't have any use for a lad he couldn't control."

"Two years," Laura mused. "That would have made you fifteen. Still just a boy."

Alex looked into her eyes. They were as soft as blue smoke in the light from the oil lamp. Her hair was coming loose from its pins, ebony strands curling at her temples to frame her face. A face he very much wanted to kiss.

Good lord, he should be wooing her with sweet words. Coaxing her to bed, not burdening her with stories from his past.

"What did you do?" she asked.

"I traveled about, playing cards with whoever would indulge me. Luckily I won more than I lost." He brought her hand to his lips. "And one day, many years later, when I was at a faro bank in Marseilles, I met George Wright." He pressed a kiss to her palm. "And then I met you."

She drew her fingertips along his cheek. "Many, many years later."

"The only thing good to come out of any of this."

Her eyes searched his. "Do you really believe that?"

"I do." His heart thumped hard as she lifted her hand from his to cradle his face. Her thumb moved over his jaw in a slow caress. There was a tenderness in her touch. A possessiveness, too.

"I'm a little nervous," she confessed.

He set his arm about her waist, drawing her closer. "So am I," he said. And he bent his head and captured her mouth with his.

Laura's hand slid from Alex's cheek to curve around his neck. His lips were warm and firm, the evening scruff of his beard deliciously abrasive against her skin. Warmth infused her veins, just as it had when he'd kissed her beneath the yew tree. But this time...

This time, there was nothing impulsive in his touch.

He held her fast against him, so close that she could feel the heavy beat of his heart, and he kissed her slowly, deliberately. Deep, drugging kisses that turned her limbs to melted treacle.

It was impossible not to respond. Impossible not to tangle her fingers into his thick hair, and to kiss him back with soft, half-parted lips.

She inhaled a tremulous breath. He smelled of railway smoke and polished leather; of travel, and adventure, and endless, thrilling possibility. Her stomach clenched as his mouth moved on hers. Had she been standing, she was certain her knees would have buckled beneath her.

"Was that any more memorable than last time?" he asked when he finally pulled away.

She gave him a dazed look.

His forehead came to rest gently against hers. There was a smile in his voice. "Better than a buss on the cheek from an aged uncle?"

Her sharp words from the pond came back to her in a flash. She exhaled a breathless laugh. "Yes. Much better."

"Good." He pressed a kiss to her cheek, his voice a deep murmur as he nuzzled her ear. "Let's go to bed, shall we?"

She should be anxious. Lord knew she'd been half dreading this moment since they arrived in Paris. She was so worried about disappointing him—and about being disappointed herself.

But as he held her in his arms, she wasn't afraid anymore. She wasn't even the least bit skittish. All she knew was that she wanted him.

And that he wanted her.

"Yes," she said. "Please."

For the rest of her life, Laura would remember that week in Paris with Alex Archer. They spent every hour together. Mornings breakfasting in bed. Afternoons exploring the city. And evenings. Long, intimate evenings spent in each other's arms.

Her new husband was a changeable lover. As chameleon-like as in every other respect. One moment touching her with a gentleness that bordered on reverence. Another moment teasing her and making her laugh. He was frequently romantic. Always solicitous of her smallest desire. But it was in their most intimate embrace when she finally felt she knew him. He held her, and took her, and loved her.

And she dared to hope that the feelings he had professed for her in Lower Hawley were deepening to something stronger. Something more than mere caring or attraction.

Because her own feelings were certainly deepening for him.

At the end of the week they departed for Grasse. There was no more postponing it. As much as she didn't like to dwell on the matter, their future depended on what they found there. Not only hers and Teddy's future, but Alex's, too.

Despite the new intimacy between them, he'd still not committed to staying with her.

Laura owned to a certain sense of bitterness on the subject. As they settled into their first-class compartment on the train from Paris, she couldn't help but press him. "I daresay you're beginning to grow bored with me."

It was a stupid thing to say. She realized it as soon as she said it. Stupid and childish.

Alex cast her an amused look. "If I was any less bored, we'd still be at the hotel."

Heat crept into her cheeks.

Of course he wasn't bored with her. Rather the opposite. They couldn't seem to get enough of each other. Indeed, they'd lingered in bed so long this morning, they'd nearly missed their train.

At half past eight, they'd finally risen and dressed, Alex helping to lace her corset and fasten her gown, and Laura tying his cravat, the whole production punctuated with soft touches and kisses. "We're going to be late," he'd finally said, his lips at her neck.

No, he wasn't bored with her. Not yet.

She glanced out the velvet-curtained window. The French landscape passed by in a blur as the train rattled along the tracks, leaving the city far behind them. "It feels as if it's all over now that we're leaving Paris. As if we've come to the end of things."

He took her gloved hand between both of his. "It's not over."

"No," she said softly. "It's just…I suppose I don't trust it yet. It's all still so new to me."

"It's new to me, as well."

She gave a sudden laugh. "Well, that's not very comforting. You're meant to be the one with experience in this sort of thing."

Alex didn't laugh in return. "It all feels new. Because of you. Because of caring for you as I do. I'm fumbling along in the dark. It's rather unnerving. Any moment I know I shall make some irreversible mistake."

"No mistakes are irreversible."

"Some are." He toyed with her hand, his expression thoughtful. "I don't want to disappoint you."

"You haven't."

"You say that now, but…" His brow furrowed. "I don't expect you ever dreamed of marrying a man like me."

"I can't say I ever dreamed of marrying at all. Not as some girls do. Though…I do recall picturing my wedding day."

"How did you imagine it?"

Her mouth curved in a smile. "The usual trappings. The village church. Mendelssohn and orange blossoms. My friends and family all about me."

"And the groom?"

"A mystery. I never pictured him. I only knew that I'd recognize him when I saw him. That one day we'd meet, and I'd know he was the one. The gentleman I was destined to marry."

"George Wright," Alex said.

Her smile faded. "For a long while I thought it was him. But something was always missing. It never felt completely right. Not until—"

"Until when?"

She gave him a wry look. "Until I met you."

He returned her gaze, an expression in his eyes hard to read.

"That day at Talbot's Pond, I felt something for you. You felt it, too. A thread of connection. That's how you described it the day we walked to the Roman ruin."

"I did. It was devilish inconvenient." He paused for a long moment before asking, "What happened between you and George?"

She went still. It wasn't a secret. Nevertheless, it was an incident she didn't much fancy revisiting. "Does it matter?"

"Chalk it up to possessiveness. That, or husbandly curiosity. I already heard his side of the story—"

Her gaze jerked to his. "When?"

"In Margate. He didn't present himself in the best light."

A spark of anger flickered in her breast. "Nor should he."

"What happened?" Alex asked again. "Did he break your heart?"

"He never had my heart. What I felt for him was closer to schoolgirl infatuation than it was to love. After Papa died, I spent the year in mourning. George kept his distance. Out of respect, I thought at the time. The following December, when my mourning period was over, I went to Edgington

Park for their annual Christmas ball. George spirited me out to the terrace. I thought he was going to ask me to marry him."

"Instead, he asked you to be his mistress."

"I wasn't insulted. Not at first. I was too stunned. I remember staring at him, unable to formulate a single word. That was when he kissed me. If you can call it a kiss. He was very... forceful."

Alex's jaw hardened. "I should thrash him within an inch of his life."

"Oh no. A slap was more than sufficient. Indeed, in the following days there were moments when I feared I'd broken my hand. I can only imagine what his cheek must have looked like."

"You didn't see him again?"

"No. He left not long after. Gone to London, his father said. I confess I was relieved. The idea of facing him..." She grimaced. "I still had my pride, after all."

"You must have been shocked at his return last month."

"Not shocked, no. Surprised, perhaps. It was unexpected."

"I'm amazed you responded to Henrietta's summons."

"Why? It had been two years. Long enough for any hurt or embarrassment to have faded." She pressed Alex's hand. "In truth, I've actually come to be grateful for that kiss. It was decidedly lackluster. I knew in an instant that George wasn't the man for me—childish infatuation or no."

"He doesn't deserve you," Alex said. And then he laughed. "But who am I to talk?"

"You're my husband." She stretched up and kissed him, her lips clinging to his.

He drew her into a fierce embrace. "Laura... My dearest..." His breath was warm on her cheek. "You make me forget we're on a public conveyance."

"And you make me shameless," she whispered.

"It's my fault, is it?"

"Entirely." She kissed him once more before settling back in her seat. "No matter. I expect we'll arrive at our hotel soon."

He gave her a piercing look. "Not soon enough."

Chapter Twenty-One

Grasse, France
September, 1860

They finally arrived in Nice long after night had fallen. Alex ordered dinner for them in their hotel room. It was more convenient after a day of traveling. Laura could take off her corset, and unpin her hair. He was becoming accustomed to a certain level of comfort with his wife. A certain sense of responsibility, too. She was his to look after. His to have and to hold, just as he'd promised when they stood up in front of the vicar.

A month ago, he might have laughed at the very idea of feeling the way he did. But now...Laura was everything.

When the footmen departed after delivering their luggage, she slipped her hands inside his frock coat, sliding her arms around him. He buried his face in her hair, his own arms encircling her tightly.

"Coach travel on roads like these should be outlawed," she said. "My bones are aching."

Alex couldn't disagree. There was no direct rail access from Paris to the South of France. At Lyon, they had been obliged to disembark from the train and travel part of the way by coach. It hadn't been a very comfortable journey. The last carriage had jostled them mercilessly as it navigated the hills, shaking and shuddering so badly it seemed the vehicle might collapse at the seams.

"Poor darling." He moved his hand up and down over the curve of her spine. "I'll order a hot bath for you."

For the next half hour, hotel staff bustled in and out of their room, laying a table for dinner and carrying in a cast iron tub. When the last footman had gone, Alex and Laura shared the bath together—an intimacy Laura confessed she wouldn't even have been able to contemplate a week before.

"How much things have changed," she said as they ate a leisurely dinner in their dressing gowns.

"For the good, I hope."

"For the good. I don't know why I keep expecting something to go wrong. Force of habit, I suppose."

Alex didn't give voice to his own sense of foreboding.

He'd been alone for the better part of his life. Ever since he'd left North Devon. There had been other people around, naturally. Even other women. But at his core, he'd known there was no one he could trust. No one he could rely on.

But now there was Laura.

Suddenly, he was no longer alone.

The feeling was...indescribable.

That night in bed, he held her in his arms as she slept. Her slim back was nestled against his chest, her arm folded over his at her waist. He burrowed his face into her neck. The fragrance of lavender and clean linen lulled him to sleep.

He wanted to protect her from the world. To shield her from the harsh realities she'd been obliged to face for so many years on her own. But she was no hothouse flower. She was too strong-willed. Too determined. The most he could hope for was to watch over her. To stand at her side, come what may.

In the morning, when he hired a carriage to take them to Grasse, he prayed she wouldn't be disappointed by what they found there.

He'd never had much occasion to travel into the hills of southern France himself. Certainly not to Grasse. It was a quaint little medieval town, known for its perfume factories, and for its fragrant crops of flowers. Laura spent much of the journey gazing out the window.

They booked rooms at a busy hotel off of the main road. A short time later they were in another hired carriage—an open gig pulled by two sprightly bays—and on their way to the distillery.

Laura was uncommonly quiet.

"Worried?" Alex asked.

She tilted her parasol back over her shoulder. "I'm afraid we aren't going to like what we find." She flashed him a rueful glance. "I've learned to be pessimistic."

He felt an ache of sympathy—and frustration. It was completely nonsensical. He hadn't even known her at the time her father died. Nevertheless, the very idea that she'd been ill and alone, and that he hadn't been there to protect her, provoked a storm of anguish in his breast. "The last three years must have been a trial."

"Not all of it. But we've had much to contend with. I've found it's better to be realistic about things. To confront them head-on. I'd rather know the worst than be kept in the dark." She resumed looking ahead. "I hate being out of control of things."

"And yet you love the sea. A force that's completely uncontrollable."

"It's different in the water. I can't explain it." She hesitated. "I suppose I feel powerful. Unencumbered. There's only myself, and my own strength. To sink or swim alone."

"Do you still feel that way? Even after what happened at Margate?"

"I didn't at first. Even now…sometimes I think of that day—what it felt like when the sea was too strong for me— and it sends a shiver down my spine. I daresay I should go back into the water before too long. Just as one gets on a horse directly after falling off. You become scared otherwise."

"I'd rather you never went in the sea again," Alex said frankly. She gave him a look. "Do you mean that?"

"I do. But I know how much it means to you. If you want to swim again, I won't forbid it. I only ask that, in future, you never venture into the sea unless I'm there."

Her brows lifted. "You intend to go in with me?"

"Ah. As to that…no. I shall remain firmly on the shore."

"With a spyglass."

His mouth curled into a smile. "If the occasion calls for it."

She laughed. A soft, husky sound that warmed him to his heart.

"We're not far from the sea," he said. "Indeed, the clerk at the front desk informed me that we're but ten miles from

Cannes. The beaches there are quite beautiful. Perhaps, when we've finished our business in Grasse…"

She stared at him, her laughter fading. "You'd take me there? To swim in the sea?"

He shrugged. "Why not?"

"Oh, Alex." Her eyes shone soft as velvet. "I—"

"*Vous êtes arrive, monsieur,*" the coachman said. The carriage slowed to a halt in front of a modest building of cream-colored stone. It was set halfway up a hill, with an iron fence about it, and a small courtyard leading to an entryway flanked by palm trees. The same stately palm trees that lined many of the streets in town.

Laura's words were left unfinished.

Alex didn't press her. They hadn't the privacy for it.

He leapt out of the carriage to hand her down. She was wearing a dress he'd bought her in Paris. A beribboned affair of striped grenadine, with an overskirt of fine French muslin, and a silk sash at her waist. The matching leghorn hat—a dainty scrap of femininity—was pinned to her ebony hair, a white ostrich plume curving gently along its edge.

He'd have liked to have had more time with her in Paris. A chance to purchase her a whole new wardrobe. Something better than a few dresses pilfered from another lady's order—gowns Alex had had to bribe the modiste to part with.

His wife shouldn't have to wear last season's fashions. He wanted her to have the best. Not just of clothing and millinery, but of everything.

He wanted to be the best for her.

A better man, at least, than when he'd commenced this mercenary enterprise with George.

The coachman called out again in rapid French.

"What did he say?" Laura asked.

"He wants to know if he should wait for us." Alex addressed the coachman. "*Revenez dans une heure.*" He tucked Laura's arm through his. "I told him to come back in an hour."

She gazed up at the façade of the building as they walked across the courtyard. "It looks empty."

No sooner had she spoken than the front door was pushed open. An older man in a homespun linen shirt and trousers emerged. He removed his cap, mopping his brow on a beefy forearm. When he saw them, he stopped and scowled.

"*Qui êtes vous?*" he demanded. "*Que faites vous ici?*"

"*Je m'apelle Alex Archer et voici ma femme,*" Alex replied. "*Son nom de jeune fille était Laura Hayes.*"

"Hayes?" the man repeated. "Are you English?"

"We are," Laura said. "We've come to see my father's factory." She offered him her hand.

The man wiped his hand on his trousers before he shook it. "I was grieved to hear of his passing. A fever was it?" The man shook Alex's hand as well. "*Quel dommage.*"

"And you are?" Alex asked.

"Gabriel Marchand."

Alex recognized the name from Weatherwax's documents. "You're the caretaker."

"*Oui*, Monsieur. I worked for Monsieur Hayes for many years. On his death, Monsieur Weatherwax hired me to look after the property."

Laura's expression tightened. "Mr. Weatherwax is no longer involved in any aspect of my family's business. My husband and I have charge of things now. We'd like to see inside."

Marchand bowed. "It would be my pleasure to show it to you."

Laura followed along after Monsieur Marchand, taking in the vast emptiness of the building. It bore no resemblance to the distillery in Dorset. There were no stills or steam-powered machines. No great vats filled with rose petals, peppermint, or stalks of lavender. And no jars containing the precious residue produced from distillation. Only a lingering floral scent hinted at what it once had been.

"The equipment—" she began.

"Sold," Monsieur Marchand said. "On Monsieur Weatherwax's instructions."

Anger boiled in Laura's veins. She felt the reassuring weight of Alex's hand at her back. "How long ago?"

"Two years? Three? I have copies of the bills of sale, if you'd like to see them."

"We require all of the relevant documents," Alex said.

Marchand glanced at the two of them with interest. "Will you be resuming production?"

"We don't know yet," Laura answered.

"Yes, we will," Alex replied at the same time.

She looked at him, brows raised in enquiry. In response, he merely gave her one of his roguish half smiles. Her heartbeat quickened. She'd thought she couldn't feel anything stronger for him than the swell of affection she'd felt when he offered to take her to the seaside in Cannes.

She'd been wrong.

As she looked at him now, she was filled with such all-encompassing warmth. Such endless gratitude. Such…love.

Good heavens, she loved him.

She loved him.

The realization fairly took her breath away.

"Are you all right?" he asked softly.

"Perfectly all right." She slipped her hand through his arm.

Monsieur Marchand continued their tour, oblivious to Laura's roiling emotions. "You'll have to purchase new equipment and hire back some of the men. Many have left for other perfumeries."

"What of the flower crops?" Alex asked.

"You've missed the harvest," Monsieur Marchand replied. "Monsieur Beauchamps— *c'est votre locataire*... How do you say?"

"Our tenant?" Alex frowned. "The perfumer who leases the land?"

"Yes. Him. He has already taken the flowers. There'll be nothing again until next year."

"We'd still like to see the fields," Laura said.

"*Mais bien sûr.*" Monsieur Marchand motioned to the door. "I will take you there."

It wasn't far. Only a short distance by carriage, along a tree-lined road that led to a lush valley at the edge of the hills. There, the fields rolled out before them in orderly division—acres of rose and lavender bushes void of their blooms, rosemary and thyme, and Seville orange trees cut back at the branches.

Laura gazed out at them, a warm feeling of recognition settling in her breast.

The flower fields in Dorset had looked similar after the harvest. She recalled trailing down the rows of lavender behind her father as he discussed perfume production with one of his assistants. She'd often touch the plants as she walked past, sliding her gloved fingers along the stalks and leaves. It left a clinging residue of scent. Sweet, clean lavender. The fragrance she associated with the best part of her life.

Alex watched her face. "Shall we get out?"

"Oh yes," she said. "Please."

The carriage came to a halt at the edge of the lavender fields, and he assisted her down.

She inhaled a deep breath. The air was alive with the scents of fragrant leaves, woody bark, and well-irrigated soil. It was a warm day but not an uncomfortable one. Indeed, it was nothing like the English climate she was accustomed to. It was better. Perfect. The sort of place one might dream of existing, but never did except in one's imagination.

And yet, here she was. In the flower fields of Southern France, kissed by the sun and soothed with cool, hilltop breezes.

Alex stood beside her, looking out across the fields. "Do you know what all of these are?" he asked. "What you can do with them?"

"I believe so." She tucked her hand through his arm. "That's lavender, of course. And those are rose bushes. Rosa Centifolia, if I'm not mistaken. The hundred-leaved rose. Papa used to use it in his perfumes. But I'd planned to use it to make rose water."

"And those trees?"

"Bitter orange. We use the blossoms for perfume, and the fruit and the branches, too."

"What about those fields?" He directed her attention to a patch of land in the distance. There, the fields appeared empty. Nothing but clean, even soil raked into rows.

"Tuberose," Monsieur Marchand said. "The bulbs are planted in the spring, and harvested in the summer. You can still smell the fragrance. *Un doux parfum exotique.*"

They walked out among the lavender bushes. Laura touched them with her hand, just as she'd used to do as a girl.

"There's so many of them," Alex said.

"There has to be. It takes a half ton of flowers to make six pints of lavender oil."

"That much?"

"It's worse with the roses. I prefer the lavender. It's much easier, and the lavender water has always done well for us."

He gave her one of his inscrutable looks. "Perhaps it will again."

By the time they returned to their hotel room, it was early afternoon. Laura withdrew to the washroom to freshen up. It occurred to her that her new gown hadn't been the best choice for venturing out into the flower fields. Her hem was dirty, and she'd snagged the silk sash at her waist on the thorny branches of a rose bush.

She washed her face and hands, and tidied her hair, before rejoining Alex. He was sitting in a chair near the window perusing some of the documents Monsieur Marchand had given them. When he saw her, he stood.

"Everything appears to be accounted for so far," he said.

"That's something." She sat down in the chair across from him. "Did you mean what you said about reopening the distillery?"

He resumed his seat. "Do you object?"

"No. Not at all. I was merely surprised. I'd wondered if you mightn't prefer to sell the place. Getting it running again will be costly."

His eyes met hers over the top of one of the papers he was reading. "If we sell it, you'll have no property left. Bramble Cottage is let, I take it?"

"From Squire Talbot."

"Would you be content to have nothing?"

She might have asked him the same. Indeed, she was quite tempted to do so. But she didn't ask. She feared she already knew the answer.

A gentleman of three and thirty didn't spend decades of his life in pursuit of money only to give up that pursuit after a month of courtship and marriage. It was what had brought him to Lower Hawley—and what had brought him to Grasse.

"It's disappointing enough to discover Weatherwax has sold the other properties," he said. "We'd be foolish to dispose of the single one remaining."

She smoothed her skirts, watching him from beneath her lashes as he returned to reading the documents. He was clad in tan trousers, with a matching waistcoat worn over a linen shirt. His cravat was loosened, his coat disposed of over the back of the nearby settee. He looked very much like he had on the beach at Margate. Roguish. Devil may care.

The only difference was now she knew him.

She knew the strength of him. The feel of his body as it covered hers. The silky thickness of his hair. The way he looked at her. The way he kissed her.

And yet, there was still so much about him that was unknowable. A secret, vulnerable part of him that made her vulnerable in turn.

"Were you very disappointed?" she asked.

Alex glanced up again. "I was. On your behalf."

Laura supposed that was something. She held out her hand. "May I read through them?"

"Of course." He handed half the stack of documents to her.

She leafed through the pages. The majority were in French, much to her chagrin. Thanks to Papa, she could speak the language a little, but she wasn't able to read it. "I can't make head or tail of these." She gave them back to him. "I wish you would teach me proper French."

His brows lifted. "Now?"

"Not now. Someday, I meant." She rose from her chair, feeling cross and restless. "Pray don't get up. I'm only going to the desk." There was an escritoire in the corner, stocked with paper, pens, and ink. "I must write to Teddy and Aunt Charlotte."

His gray gaze followed her as she crossed the room. "Have I done something to upset you?"

"No." She sat down at the desk and opened the top drawer, withdrawing several sheets of paper.

"Then why do I have the distinct feeling that you're angry with me?"

"I'm not angry, I'm—" She broke off, muttering, "I don't know what I am."

Alex set aside his papers and came to the desk. He sank down on his haunches beside her chair. "Do you want to sell the distillery?"

She gazed down at him. He was so handsome. So exceedingly dear. She smoothed his hair from his brow, combing it back into place with her fingers. He went still. Trusting her. Allowing her to handle him as she pleased. "No. I don't want to sell it. But you know what all of this means, don't you? Another year to wait before there's any kind of profit to be had. A year of nothing but expenses."

"What would you have done if I wasn't here?"

The mere thought of it squeezed at her heart. Little more than a week of marriage, and she already couldn't imagine her life without him. "Consulted with the bank, probably. Teddy and I spoke of borrowing against the property in order to resume production. But that was the farm in Dorset."

"I don't see why we can't do the same with this property."

"We don't live here. We won't be on hand to oversee things. And after Mr. Weatherwax's misconduct…I don't want to leave it to a solicitor, or someone like Monsieur Marchand. I couldn't trust that they'd do what was right."

He regarded her steadily. "Give me some time to come up with a workable solution."

"It must be workable for all of us. Teddy and Aunt Charlotte, too."

His mouth hitched into a smile. "That goes without saying."

Laura's heart swelled.

And she wanted to tell him that she loved him. That she was *in* love with him. But she couldn't seem to work up the nerve. Not when she didn't know whether or not he felt the same.

But life was about taking risks. Wasn't that what she'd told him in Surrey? One couldn't be a spectator, watching the parade go by. She certainly wasn't. And she didn't wish to start being one now, no matter how afraid she was of the consequences.

She touched his cheek, looking deeply into his eyes as she took her courage in her hands. "I love you."

Alex flinched. For an instant, it seemed he might pull away from her touch. But he didn't move. He stared at her, his big body as still as a marble statue.

"I love you," she said again.

His throat convulsed on a swallow. "Laura—"

"You don't have to say it back. And you don't have to promise me anything. All I ask is that you be true to me. That's all I want. To know that I'm yours, and that you're mine. Just as you said on the beach at Margate."

He covered her hand with his. "I am yours. Only yours."

She managed a tremulous smile. "Well, then."

"Well, then." His eyes held hers, even as he brought her hand to his lips and kissed it. "Now that we understand each other."

"Yes."

After a long moment, he stood, drawing her to her feet along with him. "Don't think I've forgotten that we're on our honeymoon."

"I haven't forgotten either."

A glint of heat shone in his gaze. "Come here."

She moved closer to him, her pulse quickening.

He curved one large hand about her waist before bending his head and kissing her. Heat flared between them as it always did, weakening her knees and flooding her veins with warmth.

And suddenly it didn't matter that he hadn't said it back. That he might not love her as she loved him. All that mattered was that she was his wife, and that she was in his arms.

Sometime later, she rose from their bed and slipped back on her clothes. Alex was asleep on his stomach amid the crumpled sheets, the bare skin of his muscled shoulders and back rendered golden by the sunlight that filtered through the curtained window. He looked vulnerable in sleep. No longer wolfish or dangerous. His body was relaxed, his dark hair wildly disheveled.

She brushed her own hair into some semblance of order and pinned it at her nape before returning to the sitting room desk to compose a letter to her aunt and brother. It wasn't a lengthy missive. She'd already written Teddy from Paris, telling him all about the channel crossing and the railway journey through France. Now, she simply needed to inform him of what they'd discovered at the distillery.

It didn't come easily. Her every instinct told her to protect her brother. To cast events in a positive light in order to save him from distress.

But Alex was right.

Despite his infirmity, Teddy was no longer a boy. He was a man. She must begin to treat him like one. And if that meant upsetting him on occasion with the grim facts of the family finances and business, then so be it.

When she'd finished her letter, she sealed it and carefully wrote out the family's address at Bramble Cottage. It was nearly three o'clock. Still early enough to catch the post.

She ducked back into the bedroom and leaned down to whisper into Alex's ear. "I'm going down to the front desk to post a letter."

He turned his head on the pillow, his eyes opening a faction. "Wait. I'll go with you."

"There's no need." Laura pressed a quick kiss to his stubble-roughened cheek. He reached out for her, but she evaded his grasp. "I'll be back directly."

Their hotel was small but fashionable. It was run by an Englishman and his French wife, and appeared to be patronized primarily by well-to-do couples on summer holiday. There were several already waiting at the front desk when Laura entered the lobby, some to check in and others to check out.

She squeezed into an empty spot beside a bespectacled gentleman who was signing the register, and set her letter on the counter.

"Is that for the post, madame?" the clerk asked.

"It is." Laura pushed the letter to him with her fingertips. "I'm not too late, am I?"

"No, madame." He took her letter, bowing to her before moving off to help another guest.

Laura turned to leave.

The gentleman at her side cleared his throat. "I beg your pardon, ma'am."

She gave him a questioning glance. He was a respectable-looking man. Even handsome, after a fashion, with a slim build, brown hair, and light blue eyes. He regarded her solemnly from behind his silver-framed spectacles.

"Yes?" she asked.

"I couldn't help but notice your ring." His gaze dropped to her left hand, where her ruby glinted against her skin. "That's a very distinctive stone."

A lady came to stand beside him. She was tall and svelte, with magnificent auburn hair. Her blue-green eyes followed his. "Yes. Quite distinctive. And very beautiful."

Laura felt a flicker of unease. There were thieves on the continent. Alex had warned her to keep her wits about her. She took a step back. "Thank you. I certainly think so."

"Are you English?" The lady had a voice like a crisp apple. Rather like a schoolmistress. A British schoolmistress, at that.

"I am," Laura said. "As are you, I presume."

"Indeed," the gentleman replied. "We've recently come down from Paris, by way of London." He paused before introducing himself. "I'm Thomas Finchley. And this is my wife, Jenny. We're here on our honeymoon."

Laura stared at him. "Thomas Finchley? Of Finchley and Fothergill?"

Mr. Finchley didn't look at all surprised that she knew who he was. "That's correct."

"But what are you doing here?" She inwardly flinched at her own impertinence. "Forgive me. I don't mean to be over-bold. It's just… This is rather extraordinary. I had an appointment with you little more than a week ago."

His brow furrowed. "I don't seem to recall—"

"I was obliged to write and cancel it." She hesitated, somewhat abashed. "I'm Laura Hayes, of Lower Hawley in Surrey." She offered her hand. "I enquired about a matter involving my solicitor, Mr. Weatherwax."

"Ah, yes. My apologies, Miss Hayes. I was in my office for a limited number of hours in the days leading up to my wedding. It was all quite busy, as you can imagine."

"Yes of course," Laura said. "But it isn't Miss Hayes any longer. I'm lately married myself. In fact, I'm here on my honeymoon as well."

Mr. Finchley smiled. It was a pleasant smile. A kind one. But something in his face reminded Laura of Magpie when he had a bird in his sights. A flickering glimpse of a hardened predator about to pounce on its prey. "I believe, then," he said, "that I must be addressing Mrs. Alex Archer."

Chapter Twenty-Two

Alex was up and dressed by the time Laura returned to their hotel room. He was irritated as well. He'd told her to wait, and she hadn't listened. Grasse seemed safe enough, to be sure, but Laura had never been out of Lower Hawley. She shouldn't be wandering about alone. Anything could happen.

The door shut behind her with a click. She stood with her back to it, one hand still on the doorknob. She was wearing neither her hat, nor gloves.

His chest tightened with emotion at the sight of her. Good lord, he was becoming sentimental. More than sentimental. Downright mawkish. How else to describe it when the mere sight of his wife disrupted the rhythm of his heart and breath? It was a physiological phenomenon. One he'd been gradually learning to accustom himself to. But just when he'd believed he was making some progress in that regard, she'd gone and told him that she loved him.

She *loved* him.

It took all of his self-control not to react like some affection-starved madman.

He went toward her. "How long does it take to post a letter? I was just about to come looking for you."

"I'm glad you didn't."

He took in her pale face and trembling hands in one comprehensive glance. His muscles tensed. "What is it? What's happened?"

"You'll never credit it. Mr. Finchley is staying here. At this very hotel."

Alex stopped where he stood. Had she pulled out a pistol and shot him between the eyes he couldn't have been more stunned. "*Tom* Finchley?"

She nodded. "He was in the lobby with his wife. He's lately married. They've come to France on honeymoon, just as we have. Isn't that a coincidence?"

Alex didn't believe in coincidences. If Tom was here, he had a reason. "Does he know who you are?"

Laura gave another tense nod. She lifted her left hand, her thumb twisting her ruby betrothal ring on her finger. "He recognized my ring."

His breath stopped in his chest. "Did he."

"He asked if he had the pleasure of speaking to Mrs. Alex Archer. I told him that he did. I didn't think—"

"You've done nothing wrong." Alex closed the distance between them, but Laura seemed intent on preserving it. She moved away before he could reach her, walking to the hotel window, her arms folded at her waist.

"Where did this ring come from?" she asked.

He didn't follow her. If she needed space from him, she could have it—within reason. So long as she didn't leave him. "What did he tell you?"

"About the ring? Nothing. But it must be significant for him to have recognized it the way he did. I fear it has some sinister history you haven't shared with me." She twisted it again on her finger. "I suppose I should take it off."

"Don't," he said sharply. Her eyes flicked to his, startled. He made an effort to soften his voice. "Please."

She left the ring where it was. "You said Mr. Finchley was in the orphanage with you. That he was a former friend of yours."

"He was."

"And that's all? Just a friend?"

Alex briefly looked away from her. The truth of his betrayal was an ever-present weight. It seemed to double now, in light of Laura's question. To bear him down with the guilt and shame of it. "He was more than a friend," he admitted. "We were as close as brothers. Finchley, me, and two other orphan boys. Justin Thornhill and Neville Cross. They were the only family I ever knew."

"Which was the boy you saved? I assume it was one of them."

"Cross. He was the boy who fell."

"And you've never seen any of them since?"

"Nor do I wish to."

"*He* wants to see you."

Of course he did, Alex thought bitterly. Tom had nothing to fear. He hadn't hurt anyone. Betrayed anyone.

"He said to tell you that he'll be at the café on the corner at four o'clock. Alone."

Alex glanced at the small porcelain clock on the mantel. It was a quarter to four already.

"You told me in Surrey that you and Mr. Finchley hadn't parted on the best of terms. Does my ring have anything to do with it?"

He opened his mouth to reply, only to shut it again. He couldn't lie to her. "Yes," he said finally. "To a degree."

"Can you not tell me?"

"It was a long time ago, Laura."

"And as relevant today as it was then, I daresay. Else it wouldn't cause you to look like that."

He ran a hand over the side of his face. He didn't know how he looked. Probably rather like he'd seen a ghost.

"Is it stolen?" she asked.

"No," he said. And then again, more forcefully, "*No*. It was… It was part of a treasure trove. A bag of old jewelry and coins Finchley and I found buried in a wall beneath the abbey. It didn't *belong* to anyone."

She looked at him steadily, her arms still folded.

He slid his hand to rub the back of his neck. "The two of us went there after Cross had his accident. Thornhill remained behind at his sickbed. It was just Finchley and me. We didn't expect to find anything. It was so much sport. And then, suddenly, there it was. A decaying bag filled with a few pieces of old jewelry and one hundred pounds in gold coins."

Laura's face went ashen.

"It was meant to set us all free. Thornhill, Finchley, Cross, and me. To get us away from the orphanage. To make us safe.

And I took it. I beat Finchley nearly to a pulp, and I took it all for myself."

Alex could remember it like it was yesterday. The feeling of his fist connecting with Tom's nose. The crunching sound of broken bone and cartilage.

In the early days after he'd left North Devon, he'd often wondered what had got into him. What evil demon in his soul had prompted him to do that to his friend. But he could recall no legitimate reason. Tom had merely been there, trying to stop him. And Alex had been consumed with anger, too long suppressed. In that moment, it had erupted like a volcano.

He'd never forget the look on Tom's face when they'd parted. It was forever burned into his brain. That stark look of betrayal—and rage.

He will hate me for this for the rest of his life, Alex recalled thinking.

And he deserved to be hated. Deserved to have his happiness taken from him.

He forced himself to meet Laura's eyes, expecting to find an expression of disgust in them. Of disappointment. It wasn't there. Instead, she regarded him with something like compassion.

Pray God it wasn't pity.

"Why did you do it?" she asked.

He grimaced. Good lord, if she only knew. But there was no way on earth he was going to tell her about Gilbert Morley. That part of his history was too poisonous. Too depraved. He was resolved to protect her from it, whatever the cost. "I was all of twelve years old," he said. "Desperate to get away. I didn't want to wait on Thornhill's strength, or Finchley's strategy. I didn't want to be there when Neville Cross died. All I wanted was to run. And so I did."

She looked as though she wanted to say something—to ask him something more—but her eyes flicked to the clock. "It's nearly four o'clock. If you intend to meet him, you should go now."

"Laura—"

"You'll have to hurry."

Alex pushed his fingers through his hair. "I needn't meet him. You and I can leave Grasse. We can—"

"I think you should speak with him," Laura said. "No more running."

Emotion tightened his throat. "Yes," he agreed at last. "As you say." His voice was a hoarse rasp. "No more running."

He swept up his hat as he walked to the door, casting one last look at Laura before he left the room. Her mouth tilted up in a faint smile of encouragement.

The sight of it hardened his resolve.

Minutes later, he entered the small café at the end of the street. It was filled with tourists and locals enjoying afternoon cups of tea and coffee. The air was redolent with the fragrance of freshly baked pastries and bread.

He scanned the crowd, grateful for his height. It allowed him to see over the heads of the patrons at the small tables near the front of the café, and to the back corner, where a gentleman sat alone at a table.

A gentleman wearing silver spectacles.

Alex's gut clenched. He stared at the man for a moment. A man who was, undoubtedly, Tom Finchley.

Tom saw him, too. He gave him an arrested glance. And then he stood, waiting.

Alex crossed the room to meet him. When he reached the table, he stopped, not two feet from his former friend. And they looked at each other. They simply looked—studying each other's faces in taut silence.

Tom was the first to break it. "How much you resemble Justin."

A spasm of emotion nearly stole Alex's voice. "You've seen him?"

"Quite recently. We've remained close over the years."

"And Neville?" Alex asked. "Did he…?"

"He's alive," Tom said. "Thriving."

A swell of relief crashed over Alex, as powerful as a tidal wave. He sank into one of the chairs. "There were no ill effects from the fall?"

Tom resumed his seat. "He sometimes finds it difficult to form words, but there's nothing wrong with his intellect, or with his body."

"Does he still reside in Devon?"

"He does. He and Justin, both. I saw them not two weeks ago at my wedding breakfast." Tom's mouth curved slightly. "I'm lately married."

"As am I."

"Your wife is lovely."

"She is," Alex said.

"I understand she employs Harold Weatherwax as her solicitor."

"Not any longer. The man lost most of her money in some infernal canal scheme." Alex paused. "He claims you put a spy in his office."

Tom shrugged. "Needs must."

A waiter approached them, enquiring if they wanted to order. Tom lifted his brows at Alex in question. Alex shook his head. He thought he saw a flicker of disappointment in Tom's face. Perhaps he'd expected that Alex would wish to stay longer? That he'd have a desire to reminisce? But Alex felt no such urge.

"*Revenez plus tard, s'il vous plaît,*" Tom said.

"*Oui, monsieur.*" The waiter departed.

"My wife doesn't know the whole of this," Alex said.

"About the circumstances in which you left Abbot's Holcombe?"

"About the orphanage. The things that happened in North Devon. I've tried to forget."

"And yet…she wears the ring we found at Greyfriar's Abbey." Tom's features set in a puzzled frown. "Odd, that."

Alex stiffened. "Why are you here? How did you find me?"

"You assume it wasn't a coincidence."

"That you just happen to appear in Grasse? Not bloody likely. You're here for a reason, and it isn't because you're on your wedding trip."

Tom didn't deny it. "Last month I received word you were in France. Some reports said Paris, others Marseilles. My wife and I enjoy traveling. It seemed natural to come here on our honeymoon—and to search for you at the same time. I believe we've been no more than two days behind you since you left Paris."

"When did you arrive in Grasse?"

"Not a half hour before we encountered your wife. Imagine my surprise, as I signed into the hotel, to find the Greyfriar's Abbey ruby on the finger of the lady standing next to me."

"It belongs to my wife now. If you want your share of the treasure—"

"Don't be ridiculous. I don't need any money from you. And I don't want any portion of that blasted treasure."

"Then why are you here?" Alex asked. "It's been decades. Why have you come looking for me after all this time?"

"Because Justin and Neville asked me to."

"*What?*"

"Do you know, I never even told them about the treasure. All this time, they believed you'd simply vanished. That you were very likely dead. And then, earlier this year, my wife convinced me to make a clean breast of things. To tell Justin and Neville about what you'd done." Tom's expression grew somber. "That's when I learned that you visited Neville's sickbed the night you disappeared. That you told him someone was hurting you."

Alex recoiled from Tom's words.

"Neville says it was one of Crenshaw's friends. Someone at the apothecary shop."

"Good God, Tom," Alex said hoarsely. "Do you think I want to relive this?"

"What happened?" Tom asked. "Who was it?"

"It doesn't matter anymore."

"Tell me his name."

"Is that why you came here? To hear every sordid detail of why I left North Devon?" Alex muttered an oath. "I was a boy of twelve. It was decades ago."

"They're all dead, you know," Tom casually informed him. "Sir Oswald. Cheevers. The men who beat us, starved us— fathered one of us."

A derisive smile edged Alex's mouth. "Only one of us?"

Tom contemplated him from across the table. "I don't know if Sir Oswald was your father. I only ever found proof that he was Justin's. But looking at you now… My God, but you resemble the man."

It was the worst sort of praise.

To think that he looked like Sir Oswald Bannister. A gentleman renowned for being a wastrel. A lecher.

"How did he die?" Alex asked.

"He fell from the cliffs not long after Justin bought the Abbey. He'd been drinking."

"And Cheevers?" Leonard Cheevers had run the orphanage. Had beat them, and withheld their food for the smallest infractions.

A look of satisfaction came over Tom's face. "Tried and executed for theft. They hanged him in the public square."

Alex briefly rested his head in his hands. "Perhaps there is justice in the world."

"I believe that," Tom said. "Eventually, it comes to us all."

"That doesn't bode well for me."

"Have you committed so many crimes since you left North Devon?"

"Not crimes, no. Nothing like betraying my friends and leaving them to die."

Tom's light blue eyes softened behind his spectacles. "None of us died, Alex. None of us suffered any more than we already had. If that's been on your conscience these twenty or more years—"

"It has." Alex gave a huff of humorless laughter. It had ruined his life.

"You can't be doing so badly. You're newly married, traveling in high style through France. Besides, even if justice did come for you, you'd have something to weigh against your sins."

"I don't know what."

"You saved Neville's life."

Alex clenched his fist where it lay. The memories were too painful. Too raw, despite the intervening years.

"The way you went in after him," Tom said. "The sea was so rough that day, and you were under the water for so long. Justin and I despaired of you. But every time you came up, you went back down again—for longer and longer. Minutes at a time. It was miraculous. The most heroic thing I've ever seen. To this day, I still don't know how you did it."

"Do you want to know how I did it?" The words burst from Alex in a rush of whispered fury. "How I was able to swim so deep—to hold my breath for so long? It's because I didn't care whether I lived or died anymore. I was ready to drown down there. To let the sea take me. Anything to get away."

Tom went white about the mouth. "Who was it? I want a name."

"A friend of Crenshaw's from Bournemouth. A man called Morley. He used to come to the shop to buy opium. Crenshaw supplied him with that, and more. Morley sold the drugs on the street for a profit. Crenshaw would have done anything to oblige him, even given him access to his apprentice."

"Did he—?"

"No," Alex said. "But his interest was plain. He made remarks. Little gibes about my appearance. How strapping I was. How handsome. And then one day he touched me. It was naught but a squeeze of the shoulder—and a lewd whisper in my ear. But later I saw him huddled with Crenshaw. Heard them mention my name. Crenshaw was going to give me to him. To work for Morley, he said. To live with him. I may have been just a lad, but I knew what was going to happen to me. And I knew then that I had to get out of there."

"You should have told us."

"Three orphan boys? What could any of you have done?" Alex scoffed at the idea. "No. There was no one to tell. No one who would have believed me. And even if they had… who on earth would have cared?"

Tom leaned across the table. "*We* would have cared. Justin, Neville, and I. Damnation, Alex. You could have told me. You didn't have to break my blasted nose."

"I was terrified. When you said we should wait—that we should talk to Justin about what to do next—I saw red. You were holding my future in the balance. My very life, to debate at your and Justin's leisure."

"That's not what I—"

"That's how it seemed."

"You were in a frenzy."

"I was angry. I'd been angry since things had started with Morley. And when you and I were struggling over the treasure—when you wouldn't let it go—I hit you because… because I couldn't hit him." There was a burning sensation at the back of Alex's eyes. "And then I kept hitting you, because it was the only way to save myself. To burn all of my bridges behind me. To do something unforgiveable. Something there was no going back from. Because I didn't *want* to leave. You and the others…you were all I ever had."

Tom fell quiet. His face was solemn, his eyes sad. For the barest instant, he resembled the boy he'd been so long ago. Young and earnest. "I wouldn't call thrashing me unforgiveable," he said. "Not after everything you did for me over the years. You protected me from Cheevers. From the other boys. Took beatings that were meant for me more times than I can count. If it wasn't for you—"

"You're rewriting history. Turning me into some self-sacrificing hero."

"Do you imagine I don't remember what you were like? It's clear as day to me. To Justin and Neville, too. Why do you think they asked me to find you and bring you home?"

Alex bent his head. He felt a muscle spasm in his jaw. The very idea that they had been looking for him was as bitter as it was sweet. "Devon was never my home."

"And France is?"

"No. I haven't had a home. Not until now." Alex looked up at him. "I've finally found some semblance of happiness. I can't put it at risk. I can't go backward."

"You speak as though you have to choose between your past and your future. It doesn't have to be that way. You must realize that." Tom smiled. "Why else would you have given your wife that ring?"

Chapter Twenty-Three

With Alex gone, Laura had nothing to do to occupy her thoughts. She paced the hotel room, a mass of anxiety throwing sparks in her chest. She sifted through all that her husband had told her. All the things he'd done as a boy in order to save himself. He'd beaten Tom Finchley. Had robbed him of a treasure trove of money and jewelry. Had run away, and never looked back.

Or so he said.

But something in Alex's confession rang false to her. She was reminded of his history of half-truths. Of convenient fictions. The way he had of glossing over those chapters of his life that were too painful. Too difficult to face.

And this was surely one such chapter. The darkest yet, she'd wager. She'd never seen him so rattled before. So haunted.

What if he hadn't gone to meet Mr. Finchley? What if he'd left Grasse?

What if he'd left *her*?

Her hands clenched at her sides as she walked the carpeted floor. She did trust him. She trusted him to come back for her—to keep his word. But she hated her lack of control over the situation. It made her want to scream.

And she might have done, had a knock not sounded at the door.

She opened it to find Jenny Finchley standing on the threshold. She was garbed in a stylish caraco jacket with a poplin skirt, her thick auburn hair arranged in intricate plaits at the back of her head.

"Mrs. Finchley," Laura said. "I wasn't expecting—"

"Pardon the intrusion. I thought we might talk while the gentlemen are away."

"Of course." Laura welcomed her in, shutting the door behind her. "Forgive me. I'm not in the best of moods at the moment."

"Quite understandable. And do call me Jenny. We've no need to be formal, given the circumstances."

"I suppose not." Laura gestured to one of the chairs near the window. "You may call me Laura, if you like." She went to the bell pull. "Shall I ring for coffee? Or tea, if you'd prefer?"

"Tea would be splendid." Jenny sat down, fluffing her skirts, while Laura summoned a hotel footman and placed their order. "My husband said he might be gone for hours. I expect he and your husband are going to have a nice long reminisce about the past."

Laura sank into the chair opposite her guest. "You make it sound very cordial."

"My husband bears no ill will."

"Should he?" Laura asked. "I understand the two of them parted badly, but it was many years ago—"

"Mr. Archer broke my husband's nose. He still bears the scar from it."

Laura didn't know what to say.

"I don't mean it as an accusation," Jenny said. "Only to explain that the past casts a very long shadow. Especially where our husbands and their friends are concerned."

"Do you know their friends? The other boys from the orphanage?"

"Indeed. I used to be companion to Lady Helena, daughter of the Earl of Castleton. She married Captain Justin Thornhill last year. It's through him that I met my husband."

"And the other boy?"

"Neville Cross? He resides with Lady Helena and Captain Thornhill at Greyfriar's Abbey, their estate on the North Devon coast. He had a bad fall in his youth. Your husband rescued him. I don't suppose you've heard the story? It was all very heroic, or so I understand. My own husband speaks of the incident in tones of awe."

"My husband told me of it," Laura said. "It's not a pleasant memory for him, I fear."

Jenny looked at her with an expression of sympathy. "There are not many pleasant memories from that time. Not for any of them. But there is some happiness to be found in the here and now, I trust. There has been for my husband, at least."

"You said you were on your honeymoon. Were you married very recently?"

"Oh yes. Only a few weeks ago, though we've known each other much longer. We were friends first. Companions."

Jenny smiled. "It's an unconventional marriage, but it seems to work for us."

"Unconventional?" Laura was intrigued in spite of herself. "How do you mean?"

"We make our decisions together. Rather like co-regents. Though our kingdom is quite small at present. There's only the two of us, and a townhouse in Half Moon Street. Indeed, when it comes to settling down, we're still very much at sixes and sevens. I only returned from Egypt last month."

Laura's brows flew up. "You've traveled to Egypt?"

"And to India. It's been rather an adventure."

For the next hour, Laura listened as Jenny Finchley described her travels. They shared a pot of tea, and a plate of macarons— delicate little French cakes made of almonds and sugar. And they talked. They even laughed.

Jenny was a surprisingly likeable lady. There was no artifice about her. No fashionable airs or pretensions. "Lady Helena is hosting a family Christmas at the Abbey this year," she said when they'd finished their tea. "A good month of festivities, all the way through Twelfth Night. Perhaps you and your husband might consider traveling to Devon for the occasion? If you're not committed elsewhere, that is."

A pang of sadness took Laura unaware. She hadn't even begun to think of Christmas. It was less than four months away. Would she and Alex still be together? Or would he be gone from her life forever? So much depended on what happened with the perfumery. On whether she could entice him to stay despite her lack of wealth and property.

Her mouth went dry, never mind the half pot of tea she'd just drunk. "My aunt and brother will expect me back in Surrey for the holiday. I've never been away from them at Christmas."

"Oh, but you must bring them too, of course. I can speak for Lady Helena. She'd love to have you. It's her fondest wish to reunite her husband with his friends. She would count it a blessing."

Blessing or no, Laura didn't think Alex would be much inclined to return to Devon. "I shall ask my husband," she said. "But…he may need time."

Jenny nodded. "Perfectly understandable. I shouldn't like to be reunited with anyone from my childhood. A ghastly proposition. But family is family, you know. And being orphans, the four of them *were* family. We must do what we can to bring them back to each other."

Laura didn't promise anything. How could she? Today's events had made her more uncertain about her future with Alex than ever.

After bidding Jenny Finchley goodbye, she kicked off her slippers and lay down on the hotel bed with all her clothes on. Her skirts spilled all around her in a heap of expensive French fabric.

She stared up at the ceiling.

There was nothing magical about being in love with someone. It didn't cure every ill or solve every problem. It was simply a feeling. An infinitely precious feeling. Deeper than friendship. More meaningful than mere attraction. But it wasn't a panacea.

Real relationships were built on more than love. They were constructed with hard work, dedication, and patience. With honesty and mutual respect.

She was ready to do the work. Whatever Alex was facing— whatever demons from his past he must confront—she wanted to be with him. To love and support him through it. But he had to want it, too. He had to let her in. Into his thoughts, and emotions.

Into his heart.

If he didn't love her in return, how could they ever overcome anything?

It was another half hour before he came back from his meeting with Mr. Finchley. Laura's heart lurched at the sound of the door. Alex didn't call out to her. Didn't utter a single word. But she heard his footsteps as he crossed the small sitting room and entered the bedroom. Heard him remove his boots and his coat.

He climbed up on the bed and lay down beside her, turning his face into the hollow of her neck.

She rested her cheek against his head. "Are you all right?"

"I am now."

It was a long while before he spoke again. Laura began to wonder if she should press him. But he seemed so vulnerable. So tired. A warrior after a fiercely fought battle.

She smoothed his hair from his brow.

"Finchley has invited us to dine with him later this evening," he said at last. "There's a bistro opposite the café. It looked promising enough, but...we don't have to accept. Not if you don't wish to."

"Do *you* wish to?"

He was quiet again for another long moment before answering. "I'd like you to meet him. And he wants me to meet his wife, as well. I suspect he's as proud of her as I am of you."

She glanced down at him. "Are you proud of me?"

"Always."

"I don't know why."

This time, he didn't hesitate. "Because you're the best person I know. The kindest. The bravest." There was a catch in his voice. "And because you're everything to me, Laura. I don't know what I'd do if you ever left me." He gave a short laugh. His breath was warm against her throat. "I suppose I shouldn't admit to that."

"Why not? You already know that I love you. And I'm certainly not going to leave you." She threaded her fingers through his hair. "I believe I'd follow you to the ends of the earth if you asked me. A bistro round the corner will be no trouble at all."

His arm came around her waist, drawing her close.

She'd told him that he didn't have to say it back, but she waited nonetheless. Waited for him to say that he loved her, too. She certainly felt as if he did. It was in the touch of his hands, and the deep tenor of his voice. The way he held her in his arms as if he'd never let her go. She sensed it as surely as if he'd declared it from a mountaintop.

And a few moments later, it seemed as if he did declare it. Albeit, in a way that only she would understand.

"Would you like to go to the seaside tomorrow?" he asked.

Happiness was an elusive thing at the best of times. But she felt it flower within her. A bright bloom of optimism. Of hope. "To Cannes? Or to Devon?"

His chest rose and fell on a deep breath. "Let's start with Cannes. And then…we'll see."

"I remember Hayes's Lavender Water." The rims of Tom's spectacles glimmered in the light from the bistro's brass gasolier.

"I used to see it in the apothecary shop in London where I bought my shaving soap."

"Oh yes," Laura said. "It was our most popular product. For a time you could find it most anywhere."

Their table was set back near the kitchens. It was small, covered with a snow-white cloth. For the last hour, the four of the them had huddled around it, drinking red wine and eating a simple Provençal meal of lamb stew, fried artichokes, and some manner of garlic soup that seemed to contain every vegetable in the region.

Alex was quieter than usual. He was still trying to acclimate himself to the reality that Tom was here in front of him. Not only here, but in good spirits. Laughing, and drinking wine. Showing no signs of anger or bitterness.

It was the oddest thing to see Laura seated beside him. To watch the pair of them talk with each other. Smile at each other. As if Alex's past and his future had collided on a remote railway track.

But this was no gruesome collision. There was no wreckage. No injuries. Instead, he had the strange sensation that the two disparate halves of his life were interweaving before his eyes. Joining together at the seams with a strange—and altogether unexpected—sense of rightness. Of harmony.

He wondered if Tom was experiencing the same feelings.

Jenny Finchley wasn't the sort of lady Alex would have expected his old friend to have married. She wasn't shy or retiring. Quite the reverse. She was as vibrant as a flickering flame. Alive with questions and opinions. The way Tom looked at her, one would almost think he was a victim of mesmerism. He was plainly besotted.

"There are rose fields in Egypt," she said. "I'd thought perfumeries in France and England imported their flowers from there now. Or from Turkey or some such place."

Laura nodded. "In many cases, yes. Especially with roses. But some flowering plants—like lavender—are better grown at home in England. It makes for a softer scent. That's one of the reasons I was so disappointed to learn that Mr. Weatherwax had sold our farm in Dorset."

"The canal scheme," Tom said. "Was that how he lost the profits from the sale?"

Alex frowned at the grim reminder. "So he claims."

Tom's own expression grew serious. "All isn't lost. I've been investigating the matter for a client of mine, and it appears as though there was fraud on a massive scale. With luck, some of the victims of that scheme might see a percentage of their investment returned to them."

"And some of the solicitors involved might see themselves struck off," Jenny added. "You can't imagine the sort of things—"

"My dear," Tom remonstrated gently. "You know we're not to speak of the particulars."

Jenny managed to look chastened. "Was that a particular? Do forgive me, my love."

Laura glanced between the pair of them, a hopeful glimmer in her eyes. "Do you truly mean that? There might be a way to recover some of my money?"

"I expect so," Tom said. "Though it won't transpire anytime soon. Cases of this nature tend to draw out for quite a long while. Sometimes for years."

The hope in Laura's eyes dimmed.

Alex gave her a bracing look. "It doesn't matter in any event. We're well settled, whatever happens."

"Yes. We still have the farm here in Grasse." Her mouth lifted slowly in a faint smile. "It's really quite lovely here. And the soil appears to be as excellent as the weather."

"The food is quite good, too," Jenny said. "Everything is so fresh and fragrant. I shall have to ask what spices the cook used in our stew."

Tom grinned. "My wife is an expert on foreign spices. She's been attempting to teach our cook how to make a proper Indian curry."

"Poor Mrs. Jarrow. She does struggle with it so." Jenny dabbed at her mouth with her napkin. "I don't know what it is about the English palate. She won't believe it's done until all the flavor has been cooked straight out of it."

"Our cook at Bramble Cottage prefers to boil everything," Laura said. "There hasn't been spice in our food in ages. Unless you count salt."

Jenny wrinkled her nose in sympathy. "You poor thing."

"Oh no," Laura replied. "I never even noticed it until we came to France."

"Have you never been out of England?" Tom asked.

"No, indeed. Not until Alex and I married."

"We left for France the day after the wedding." Alex reached the short distance across the table to cover Laura's hand with his. "I wanted my wife all to myself."

Laura's gaze softened as her eyes met his. "Our honeymoon has been like a wonderful dream."

A wonderful dream.

The words seeped into Alex's soul.

She loved him, and she thought life with him thus far had been a wonderful dream. Despite the things he'd kept from her. Despite the appearance of Tom, and the revelations about Alex's past. She loved him, and she'd never leave him.

Jenny cast a self-satisfied glance at Tom. "A love match," she said. "Didn't I tell you?"

Tom smiled. "So you did, my dear."

Chapter Twenty-Four

Cannes, France
September, 1860

The beaches of Cannes were as unlike those at Margate as the night was from the day. Golden sands sloped gently to a sapphire sea, sparkling jewellike under the Mediterranean sun. It was warm and temperate. Perfect weather for bathing—and for swimming.

Laura spent hours in the sea, and Alex on the shore. She'd been hesitant when she'd first gone in. Alex had recognized the signs. The slight stiffening of her spine, and the setting of her shoulders. The glint of resolve in her smoke-blue eyes as she mastered her fear.

His own fears weren't as easy to manage. Every instinct told him to drag her out of the water. To keep her safe on dry land. It took all of the strength he could muster to resist those urges. To trust that his wife wouldn't come to harm.

She knew her limits now, or so she said. "I won't push myself as hard as I did at Margate," she'd promised him. "You won't be obliged to rescue me again."

Reassuring words, such that they were, but he still felt compelled to watch her like a hawk. He even employed a telescope on occasion—much to her amusement.

Had Tom been there, he'd surely have laughed at him, too. But Tom wasn't there. Alex and Laura had left the Finchleys behind in Grasse, promising to see them again on their return. They didn't plan on remaining at the seaside for long. There was too much business to sort out at the perfumery. Too many decisions to make about their future.

Cannes was merely a temporary idyll. Two glorious days of sun, sand, and Laura in his bed. But it wasn't all holiday with them. Little by little, Alex shared with his wife the details of his meeting with Tom Finchley. He told her about his childhood in the orphanage. About Sir Oswald Bannister, and Leonard Cheevers. About Crenshaw, and Morley.

"I never wanted any of this to touch you," he said one night as he held her in his arms. "All this sordid history."

Her cheek rested against his shoulder. The gaslights were turned down low in their hotel bedroom. They cast a soft shadow on the curve of her face.

"I thought I was protecting you from it. Keeping you separate and apart." He took her hand gently in his. The ruby in her ring glinted in the dim light. "And yet, I gave you this cursed thing."

"Why did you?"

"I don't know." He frowned. "I suppose a part of me wanted to marry my past with my future. To reconcile them somehow. A nonsensical impulse. At the time I'd no idea that it was possible."

"I don't believe it was nonsensical," she said. "Indeed, I have a theory."

He stroked his thumb over her knuckles. "Have you?"

"Mmm. I think this ring is a symbol of who you really are. Not the gambler. Not the man who came to Lower Hawley to woo Henrietta. The *real* Alex Archer. The boy who saved Neville Cross from drowning. The man who saved me. I think, in giving me this ring, you were pledging yourself to me. Your true self."

Alex swallowed hard.

"Have I got it right?" she asked. "Or am I being too fanciful?"

It took an effort to find his voice. "You're not being too fanciful."

The next morning, they went for a walk together on the beach. It was early hours. So early that Laura felt free to discard her hat and gloves. "It doesn't matter," she said. "No one is about."

Alex didn't have the heart to scold her. He was too enamored of her. Too indulgent by half. "If you stay in France much longer, you'll get in the habit of flaunting propriety. And then what will happen when you return to England?"

Laura came to a slow halt. "When *I* return to England?" She faced him on the sand, her shawl slipping down her arms. "You make it sound as though you're not going back."

"As to that…" Alex suppressed a grimace. He hadn't intended to tell her just yet. Not until he'd had a chance to study more on the subject. But there was no keeping it from her now. "I've had an idea. Something that will affect Hayes's perfumes—and the Hayes family, as well."

A shadow of worry crossed her face. "Go on."

Alex settled her shawl more firmly about her shoulders. "I've thought of a way we can make it all work. The distillery in Grasse, your family, and our finances. But…it would mean leaving England."

"To live here?"

He nodded. "We could find a house somewhere close to the distillery. Close enough that we could manage production ourselves."

"And sell the products…where? Hayes's Perfumes is practically unknown in France. It's England where our brand held sway."

"And that's where we'd continue to distribute it. Imagine the packaging: *Hayes's Rose Water—now made exclusively in France.* The ladies of London would snap it up, not to mention countrywomen like Henrietta Talbot. Thanks to Empress Eugénie, they all follow the latest French fashions."

"In gowns and hats, perhaps. Things the empress is actually known to wear. Rose water and lavender water aren't of that category, surely."

"They could be. It only wants a little creative advertising."

She knit her brows. "Do you truly think that would work?"

"To a certainty? I don't know. But I'd say there's a greater than average chance of success. Hayes's Perfumes is still a recognizable name."

"It would mean convincing Teddy and Aunt Charlotte to come here." Laura's face fell. "They'd never do it."

"Your brother would."

"How can you say so? Until last month, Teddy scarcely wanted to leave his room."

"Have you seen the style of his landscapes? The experimental ones he was painting at Margate? They're all light and movement. If he lived in France, he might be able to study under a painter in the same style. Someone with more experience. I can't imagine your brother would turn down the opportunity."

She paused to consider. "What about Aunt Charlotte?"

"The weather here is perfect for her health. All this sun and fresh sea air? Invalids have relocated for less."

Laura searched his face. "And what about us?"

"What about us?"

"You speak as though you'll have a hand in running the business. Does this mean you've decided to stay with me?"

He scowled. "What sort of question is that?"

"A simple one I should think." There was a sudden stark vulnerability in her face. "I just want to know that the perfumery isn't the only thing keeping you here."

"*You're* what's keeping me here."

"You say that now, but...what if the business fails? What if it all comes to nothing?"

He raised a hand to cup her face. "Do you think your only value to me lies in your wealth? I didn't even know I would gain half the perfumery when I proposed to you."

"When you proposed to me, you said you'd be content if our marriage remained nothing but a convenient fiction. That you'd be willing to leave me in a few months' time. And now—"

"I was an idiot," he said. "I thought I was being noble, when all I was being was a coward. Afraid of hurting you.

Afraid of being hurt in return. Too much of a coward to tell you that I loved you."

Laura blinked rapidly. Her lips parted, but no words came out.

"I love you," he said again. "I should have told you long ago."

"How long ago?" she asked.

"I knew it the night we danced together at Margate. But I think it must have been there even longer. This feeling within me." His gaze drifted over her face. "It's strange. When I left Marseilles for London in company with George... All the time we traveled... I thought I was coming to Surrey to meet Henrietta Talbot. But more and more, I begin to think I came there to meet you."

Her eyes glistened as she gazed up at him.

"I wonder if there is such a thing as fate. Some force that drew me to you, across continents, and across the sea. I think I knew you the moment I laid eyes on you. My love. My Laura." He brushed a tear from her cheek with the pad of his thumb. "It's not a marriage of convenience. Not for me."

"Oh Alex." She bent her head.

He tipped her face back to his. She looked as though she wanted to say something more but couldn't find the words. He could sympathize. In that moment, the right words seemed in woefully short supply.

So he did precisely what he wanted to do.

He leaned down and kissed her, right there on the beach at Cannes. In public for all to see.

Her lips yielded to his, softly, sweetly, just as they always did. Shaping to his mouth so perfectly that his heart squeezed with near-agony at the pleasure of it.

When at last they broke apart, her cheeks were flushed pink. His wife. His water nymph. The person he loved most in all the world.

She glanced down the beach at a couple who had stopped walking to watch them. "I fear we're on the verge of causing another seaside scandal."

"Let them stare." Alex tucked a flyaway lock of ebony hair behind Laura's ear. "Tell me…what do you think of my plan?"

"The plan for Hayes's perfumes?"

"And for us. You and me, here in the South of France, with a house near the sea."

"And Teddy and Aunt Charlotte, too?"

"And them, too. Your family." A lump formed in his throat. "*Our* family."

At that, Laura flung her arms around his neck, startling a laugh out of him. "Yes, then." Her shawl slid down her back. "Yes, yes."

He encircled her in an unyielding embrace, crushing her heavy skirts against his legs. "To which part?"

"To everything," she said. "I want it all. A home, a family, the perfumery, and the sea. And I want it with you, Alex. I want it *all* with you."

Alex pressed his cheek to her hair. His voice, when it came, was a husky promise. "Then you shall have it, my love."

$\mathscr{E}$pilogue

North Devon, England
December, 1860

The train platform at Abbot's Holcombe was bustling with activity. Gentlemen in heavy greatcoats and ladies in cloaks and bonnets rushed up and down, calling for porters and for hansom cabs. It was raining out and everyone seemed in a terrible hurry, shoving past each other to climb into their carriages or to take shelter in the refreshment room.

Alex didn't blame them. The wind was whistling through the station, cold as ice. His own woolen topcoat and leather gloves provided precious little protection against the chill.

He handed Laura out of their first-class compartment. She was bundled up in a dark blue coat that nipped in at her waist before flaring down over her wide skirts. Her raven hair was bound in a corded net with a velvet ribbon run through it. Alex had watched her style it earlier that morning at their hotel. Had pressed a lingering kiss to the nape of her neck as he'd helped her tie the ribbon.

She took his arm. "How are you?"

"Very well." He covered her gloved hand with his. It was the truth. On disembarking from the train, he'd had no visceral reaction. No disturbing flood of memory. "It's nothing like I remember."

"It's been two decades. I daresay it's changed a little."

"More than a little. None of this was here when I was a boy. No railway station. Not even a platform halt. Abbot's Holcombe was much humbler, then."

"Tom said that it's become a fashionable resort town. But one wouldn't think it would be so busy at this time of year." She looked about them as they made their way through the crowd. "Not in this weather."

"It always rains in Devon," he said. That was something that hadn't changed at all. The dampness. The cold. The sound of raindrops drumming on the roof. He scanned the platform. "Tom should be here. He's not the sort to be late."

The Finchleys had left Grasse at the end of September. Before they'd gone, Tom had extracted a promise from Alex. A commitment to come to Devon for Christmas. To reunite with Justin and Neville.

It was an invitation extended not only to Alex and Laura, but to Mrs. Bainbridge and Teddy, as well. The two of them would be traveling down by rail from Surrey later in the week. Teddy had a proper manservant to assist him now. A young fellow, much stronger than Yardley. Mrs. Bainbridge would be getting someone to look after her, too. Laura had placed an advertisement for a lady's companion. Someone to sit with her aunt, and to administer her tonic when needed.

As for the perfumery, until their return it would remain in the capable hands of Monsieur Marchand. When last Alex had seen the man, he'd been helping the workers to set up the new equipment. There were copper stills, vats, and mechanized devices for expression and maceration. Everything that was necessary to produce lavender, rose, and orange water in bulk.

"There," Laura said. "Isn't that Tom? Over by the ticket office?"

Alex followed her gaze. His breath stopped in his chest. It *was* Tom. But not only Tom.

A tall gentleman stood next to him, his top hat in his hand, and his frame shrouded in a dark wool greatcoat. His hair was black, and the bottom right portion of his face marked with burn scars.

Alex swallowed hard. Tom had warned him about Justin's disfigurement. Had told him how Justin had been imprisoned and tortured while serving in India during the uprising. Alex had imagined the burns would make his childhood friend unrecognizable.

They didn't.

Indeed, Justin looked much as Alex remembered. Noble. Formidable. The unofficial leader of their little band of orphans.

His eyes met Alex's across the distance. As gray as Alex's own. A spasm of emotion seemed to pass over his face. Of recognition. He moved toward them, Tom at his side.

"Is that Mr. Thornhill?" Laura asked.

"It is," Alex said, his voice gone hoarse.

Laura squeezed his arm, giving him her undivided support, just as she always did. "He looks happy to see you."

And he *did* look happy.

It was a miracle of sorts. Almost as much as it had been to see Tom, and to realize that he hadn't spent the last decades hating Alex for what he'd done. That all he'd wanted was to find his long-lost friend. To bring him home.

The crowd gave way as Justin strode through it. He came to a stop in front of them. There was a peculiar sheen in his gaze. Alex suspected it was the same moisture he felt in his own. Only the constraint of good manners—of being in public with his wife on his arm—kept him from losing his composure.

"Alex," Justin said. "Welcome back to Devon." He paused, his stern face spreading into a sudden smile. "I never imagined I'd say those words to you."

Alex's mouth hitched at the corner. "I never imagined I'd hear them."

Laura was smiling, too. Alex urged her forward, a swell of pride deepening his voice. "This is my wife. My Laura."

Justin's expression softened. "Mrs. Archer. You are very welcome." He bowed over her hand when she offered it. "My wife, Helena, is very much looking forward to meeting you. She would have accompanied me, but she's nearing her confinement, and travel is difficult at present."

Alex's heart lurched. Justin was going to be a father. The first of them to become so. The four orphan boys who'd never known any love. Any tenderness. He was going to have a child of his own now. It was as if a page had been turned on a dark chapter of their lives, offering a clean slate. A new beginning.

Laura pressed Alex's arm as she addressed Justin. She seemed to know what he was thinking. She always did. "I'd no idea you were in anticipation of such a happy event."

"Nor did I," Tom said, "until Jenny and I returned to Devon."

Alex didn't think Justin could have looked any more pleased with himself. "We expect a healthy son or daughter sometime in the new year."

"It won't be too much for Lady Helena?" Laura asked. "Hosting all of us so near to her confinement?"

"Not at all," Justin replied. "She insisted on it. She's talked of nothing else for months."

"Jenny is helping her manage the arrangements." Tom glanced out at the crowd, frowning.

"Is she with you?" Alex asked.

"Jenny? No. She's at the Abbey with Lady Helena. I'm looking for—" Tom broke off with a grin. "Ah. There he is. And he's managed to find a porter to see to your luggage. Splendid."

Alex looked across the platform. The jolt of recognition he'd felt when he saw Justin was nothing to what he felt now.

A strapping fellow with close-cropped blond hair came toward them, a porter and luggage cart at his heels. He was taller than Alex. Taller, even, than Justin, with impossibly broad shoulders, and light blue eyes with a faraway look in them.

It was Neville Cross.

Laura's hand fell away from Alex's arm as he moved toward his old friend, first slowly, and then with increasing speed. He caught Neville in a powerful embrace.

"Alex." Neville hugged him back, nearly crushing him with the strength of his arms. "I knew you'd come home."

"You knew more than I." Alex stepped back. "Let me look at you."

Neville's cheeks reddened. He thrust his hands into the pockets of his overcoat. "I look different."

"You don't. You're just as I remember you. Only bigger. My God, how did you outgrow the rest of us?"

"Working outside. I take care of the horses for Justin."

Alex's smile faded. Tom had said there was nothing wrong with Neville's mind, but his speech was another matter. He struggled with it, forming each word with visible difficulty. "Are you well?" he asked. "After the fall, I worried for you. I never stopped worrying."

"It's...difficult." Neville's brow creased. "Frustrating."

Alex nodded his understanding. "No matter. The four of us could always read each other's minds, couldn't we?"

Neville huffed a short laugh. "Yes."

The others came to join them. Laura was on Justin's arm, as naturally as if they'd known each other a lifetime.

Alex reached for her. "Come, my love. I want to introduce you to my old friend, Neville Cross. Neville? This is my wife, Laura."

Laura offered her hand. "Mr. Cross. I'm so pleased to meet you at last."

Neville's fingers briefly engulfed hers. "Mrs. Archer."

"Do call me, Laura. I feel as if I already know you." Her eyes smiled up at him. "Did you know Alex rescued me, too? I nearly drowned while swimming in the sea at Margate. He saved my life."

"It's how I persuaded her to marry me," Alex said dryly. "A shameless ploy."

Laura cast him a reproving glance. "My husband won't permit me to sing his praises."

"You can be no worse than Tom's wife," Justin replied. "Always telling us how brilliant he is."

Tom gave a rueful grimace. "I'm never going to live that down, am I?"

"Laura." Neville's blush deepened. "You're not afraid of dogs, are you?"

"I love them. And cats, too. Do you have any at the Abbey?"

"Not cats. We have two dogs. Paul and Jonesy."

"The hounds of hell," Tom said under his breath.

Justin laughed. "They only look that way if some villain is trying to creep onto the property. Speaking of which…" He cast a pointed look at the driving rain. "We'd better hurry before the road to the Abbey washes out."

Alex waited with Laura on the platform while Justin went to summon his coachman to bring the carriage round. Tom and Neville followed to see to the loading of their bags.

"No need for us all to get wet," Tom said.

Laura watched them go.

Alex slid his hand around her waist, drawing her close against him. "You were wrong, you know."

She looked up at him, startled. "Was I? About what?"

"You said I rescued you. That I saved your life."

Her brows knit. "But…you did."

"No," Alex said. "It was you who saved me."

"Oh." Her mouth trembled. "What a lovely thing to say."

"I mean it. I don't know where I'd be if I hadn't blundered into that clearing in the woods and seen you floating in Talbot's Pond."

"You said I looked like a demented Ophelia."

He remembered. He'd been wet and irritated, and smitten to his core. "You looked like a water nymph. An enchanted princess." He bent his head to hers. "Like the lady I was going to marry, and love the rest of my life."

"And you looked like a hero," she said. "*My* hero. Though I may not have recognized it at the time."

"A great lummox, you called me."

She laughed softly. "Did I?"

"Yes, minx." He held her close, shielding her from the rain and the cold. Keeping her safe in his arms. "And it wasn't the last set down you administered during my time in Lower Hawley."

"I hope I've made up for it."

"You have. Countless times." His words took on a serious edge. "Thank you for coming here with me. I know it's damp and rainy and miserable. Nothing like the South of France. But I—"

"Hush." She snuggled against him. "I don't mind it, truly. Not the rain or the sleet or the cold. As long as we're together."

"We will be," he promised. "Until I draw my last breath."

And they were.

Author's Note

Victorian seaside holidays are a favorite topic of mine in my non-fiction writing and research. I endeavored to bring the same authenticity to Alex and Laura's ill-fated trip to Margate. To that end, the descriptions of the beach, bathing machines, telescopes, and seaside fashions are accurate, as are the descriptions of the York Hotel and Margate's Public Assembly Rooms.

Laura's near drowning was based, in part, on several actual Victorian era drownings at Margate that didn't have such a happy ending. As for mouth-to-mouth resuscitation, though still a novel concept, it wasn't completely unheard of in the eighteenth and nineteenth centuries. In 1744, a treatise on the practice by Dr. John Fothergill appeared in the *Philosophical Transactions of the Royal Society of London*. In it, Fothergill explained why mouth-to-mouth was preferable to the use of the bellows when reviving a victim of drowning. One of the main reasons being—as Alex Archer discovered—that bellows weren't generally close at hand when on the beach.

I tried to be equally as accurate in depicting 1860s Paris, Grasse, and Cannes. However, I did take some authorial license when it came to French hotels. I imagined that Alex and Laura would have stayed in smaller hotels and guest houses, and it was more efficient to make those up than to base them on actual nineteenth century establishments.

If you'd like to learn more about Victorian sea bathing, seaside clothing, and fashionable perfume, please check out my non-fiction book *A Victorian Lady's Guide to Fashion and Beauty*, or visit the blog portion of my author website at:

www.MimiMatthews.com

Acknowledgments

This book wouldn't have been possible without the incredibly incisive feedback of my wonderful editor, Deb Nemeth, and my amazing beta readers and critique partners, Flora, Sarah, and Lauren. I'm also deeply indebted to the brilliant Rachel McMillan who took time away from her own busy writing schedule to read the first draft of this novel. Rachel could give a masterclass in graciousness and generosity. I'm inspired by her example, and so grateful to call her my friend.

Special thanks also go to my cover designer, James Egan; to my dear friend Charlotte Robe-Hughes for French translations; to Anne Victory and Crystalle for oops detection; to Colleen Sheehan for formatting; and—as always—to my parents, whose assistance made it possible for me to finish this book, in spite of an emergency surgery and the arrival of a new kitten.

Lastly, I'd like to thank you, my readers, for sticking with me, and with this series. Your kind messages and reviews mean more to me than I can say.

About the Author

USA Today bestselling author Mimi Matthews writes both historical non-fiction and proper historical romances set in Victorian England. Her articles on nineteenth century history have been published on various academic and history sites, including the *Victorian Web* and the *Journal of Victorian Culture,* and are also syndicated at *BUST* Magazine. In her other life, Mimi is an attorney. She resides in California with her family, which includes an Andalusian dressage horse, two Shelties, and two Siamese cats.

To learn more, please visit
www.MimiMatthews.com

OTHER TITLES BY
Mimi Matthews

NON-FICTION

The Pug Who Bit Napoleon
Animal Tales of the 18th and 19th Centuries

A Victorian Lady's Guide to Fashion and Beauty

FICTION

The Lost Letter
A Victorian Romance

The Viscount and the Vicar's Daughter
A Victorian Romance

A Holiday By Gaslight
A Victorian Christmas Novella

The Work of Art
A Regency Romance

The Matrimonial Advertisement
Parish Orphans of Devon, Book 1

A Modest Independence
Parish Orphans of Devon, Book 2

The Winter Companion
Parish Orphans of Devon, Book 4

Made in United States
North Haven, CT
14 November 2022

26734272R00212